Spellbound at Pemberley

A Pride & Prejudice Variation

Abigail Reynolds

WHITE SOUP PRESS

In memory of Deirdre, who was the first to hear the secrets of this book.
Your ideas live on inside these pages.

Contents

1.	Chapter 1	1
2.	Chapter 2	13
3.	Chapter 3	19
4.	Chapter 4	30
5.	Chapter 5	39
6.	Chapter 6	50
7.	Chapter 7	57
8.	Chapter 8	68
9.	Chapter 9	78
10.	Chapter 10	90
11.	Chapter 11	100
12.	Chapter 12	109
13.	Chapter 13	120
14.	Chapter 14	130
15.	Chapter 15	140

16. Chapter 16   152

17. Chapter 17   159

18. Chapter 18   169

19. Chapter 19   175

20. Chapter 20   185

21. Chapter 21   194

22. Chapter 22   204

23. Chapter 23   214

24. Chapter 24   223

25. Chapter 25   234

26. Chapter 26   241

27. Chapter 27   252

28. Chapter 28   263

29. Chapter 29   276

30. Chapter 30   286

31. Chapter 31   299

32. Chapter 32   308

Excerpt from The Magic of Pemberley   319

Acknowledgements   330

About the Author   331

Also by Abigail Reynolds   332

Chapter 1

DARCY RUBBED HIS HANDS over his face as he turned his thoughts inward, the open field around him fading away. He focused, inhaling strands of power from the autumnal air. Then he drew the magical forces together and flicked his wrist.

To all appearances, a herd of cattle charged across the pasture towards him.

He eyed the illusion critically, but there were no telltale flaws, at least none that he could spot. When the nearest animal was a dozen feet away, he blew out a breath to dismiss the vision. The cows vanished.

Not a bad performance. Of course, that was the easy part.

Beside him, Bingley mopped his forehead, his eyes bulging. "By Jove, Darcy, I was certain we were about to be trampled. I could see the flecks of foam flying from the bull's mouth!"

Darcy grimaced. "From that view, yes, but watch again." He gathered fresh energy, plaited it into a bundle, and cast. This time, though, the cattle ran beside them instead of at them, giving a spectator's view of the running herd.

His breath hissed between his teeth. The same problem as always. The sound of thumping hooves, the cloud of dust rising around them, the bodies of the cows bobbing as they ran, all of those were adequate. But the damned legs!

Bingley's brow furled. "Oh, dear. I see what you mean. Too many knees, or perhaps not enough?"

"And they do not move properly, either. The cows are only convincing from the front. From any other side, they will not fool even a casual observer." Worse, it would draw attention to the existence of the illusion, just when he needed people to believe in it.

"Perhaps it will be easier when you move on to horses," Bingley said brightly.

Darcy snorted. "Given that the whole point of practicing with cattle is because their legs are easier than horses, I doubt it." He bent forward, his hands on his thighs, breathing deeply. He had to find a way to do this. The price for his failure would be counted in thousands of innocent lives.

"I say, adding fire is an excellent thought!" Bingley exclaimed, pointing. "I hardly notice the legs now."

"What are you talking about?" Darcy straightened, staring. Flames billowed in the distance ahead of the illusory cows. "That is not my work!" A tenant must have ignored the message to stay away from these fields. It would not harm his casting, but someone might be frightened by the sight of cattle charging through fire, so he pursed his lips to dispel the illusion. But the cows were already veering away.

Veering away. Impossible. Illusions had no minds of their own. He had set the herd in motion, and they should have run straight ahead unless he directed them otherwise.

Had he lost control somehow? No, the connection still pulled at him, but there was something else, something pushing at his cows.

This was unheard of. Illusions might lack strength, but nothing should be able to interfere with them. Or at least nothing he knew of.

His eyes narrowed. "Bingley, I did not tell the cows to turn away, and I can sense something out there, a presence of some sort. Is there anything in your books about a power that can alter an illusion?"

"Not a thing. Illusions are immutable, except by their creator. Are you certain? Perhaps you were just distracted."

Darcy glared at him. There was no question he had been distracted of late. Distracted by a bewitching combination of fine eyes, sparkling wit, and lively intelligence, but that did not affect him now. Casting took every ounce of his concentration.

This was something different, and he had to discover what had interfered with his casting. Even if nothing could save his own life, so many others depended on his ability to create a convincing illusion. "Stay here," he told Bingley brusquely.

He released the illusion, and the cows disappeared. Cloaking himself in shadows, he strode off towards the smoke.

Elizabeth Bennet took a deep, pleasurable breath as the stirrings of life underfoot woke her Talent, sending a gratifying tingle through her half-boots. Oh, it was so good to feel the power of the earth, even if it was not as strong here at Netherfield as at home!

The fields around her were empty but for a small boy playing in a pasture. He grinned at her to show an adorable space between his front teeth, proudly holding up a ragged bouquet of wildflowers for her admiration, and she waved in return.

Her spirits rose as she continued into a field where winter wheat was starting to sprout. The seedlings tugged at her Talent, begging to borrow some of her strength, and she allowed a trickle of magic to soak into the soil, the bright flow of energy shooting through her feet and leaving peace in its wake. Her father would tell her not to waste her Talent outside Longbourn lands, but he would never know, and these seedlings would feed a hungry family next harvest. Perhaps even the child she had seen.

This was what she needed after two days sitting at Jane's bedside. Not that she minded caring for her ill sister, but it was almost painful to deny her Talent by staying indoors so long.

As she trod carefully in the center of the path to avoid trampling any of the tiny plants, the sound of distant thunder behind her made her look up in surprise. There was not a cloud in the sky.

Then she saw them. Half a dozen cows were charging across the pasture she had just passed, their heads down – directly towards the child picking flowers.

There was no time to think. She raced towards the boy, but it was clear she would not make it in time.

Her breath sobbing in her throat, she skidded to a halt and reached down to pull up a handful of weeds. If this did not work, the child would be trampled before her eyes. Biting her lip until she drew blood, she spat into the greenery.

Thank heavens she was wearing her special gloves! She peeled one off so quickly that it caught and ripped her fingernail, but she did not hesitate. Instead, she stuffed the blood-speckled weeds inside the glove and threw it towards the charging cows.

"Soar!" she cried, pouring her Talent into the flying glove. "Soar and then burn!" She could almost see it take wing, flying farther than her throw could take it, far beyond the child.

The glove exploded into a pool of fire as it struck the ground in front of the cows. "Burn, burn, burn," Elizabeth chanted. "Burn and make them turn!"

And then, through the flames, she could see the cattle veering away, back into the open field.

She collapsed back against the stone wall, hardly able to stand now that she had poured all of her energy into the magic. But she pulled herself over a stile and limped weakly toward the child, who was sobbing in fear. "All is well," Elizabeth told him. "You are safe." She looked over her shoulder to make certain the cows were keeping their distance, but they were nowhere to be seen.

How had they vanished so quickly?

She stopped short. Charging cows that came from nowhere, and then disappeared? Something was very wrong. The flames she had created were dying back now without the magic in her blood to nourish them, unable to maintain themselves in the green grass.

Beyond them, a shadowy figure wearing a gentleman's top hat strode forward through the haze of smoke. Had he been the one to startle the cows into charging? He should know to be more careful than that around livestock! Even from this distance, she could tell he was angry. And then he disappeared into the smoke.

Had he seen her using her Talent? This could be a disaster. Perhaps he was only worried about the fire, but that would burn out in a few minutes. The child leaned against her, whimpering.

She patted his head, wishing she could do more, but if she tried to pick him up after working such a feat of Talent, her legs would not hold her. She had to get him somewhere safe. "Where do you live?" she asked.

The boy did not lift his face from her skirt, but he pointed a shaking finger behind her.

"Good. Let us go there, then." And it would take her farther from the man who might have seen her. She took the boy's hand and began to walk, pretending to a strength she barely possessed. But it was enough to reach the edge of the field, and somehow she raised her feet to clamber back over the stile.

At least now they would be safe from the invisible cows. Could it all have been a figment of her imagination? No, because the boy had seen them, too.

The boy tugged her towards a small cottage with a bowl of milk set outside the door for the fae. How could she explain to his mother what had happened? She might well recognize Elizabeth and ask unwelcome questions. Better to let the boy tell the story, so that magical flames and charging cattle who disappeared into thin air could be attributed to a child's over-vivid imagination. Yes, that was the answer.

She dropped the boy's hand. "There you go. You will be safe now."

He tried to reach for her again, but she gave his shoulders an encouraging pat, urging him towards the cottage. "I will watch from here until you are inside." She had to harden her heart against his pleading look, but he was in no real danger here. She needed to escape from the man who had seen her using her Talent. Reluctantly the boy trudged into the cottage, where a muffled woman's voice greeted him.

That was one problem solved. Elizabeth hurried back down the path as quickly as her exhausted legs could manage. No, it was no use; she could not possibly outdistance the man if he truly was following her. Hiding was her only option.

The copse at the edge of the pasture would be her best bet. The man was nowhere to be seen, so she should be able to make it that far.

She took off her other glove, just in case she encountered someone who would wonder what had happened to its mate. And now she would need to make a new one. So very many hours of labor went into each of them.

A voice sounded, and nearby. Very nearby. "Wait, Miss Elizabeth!"

Startled, Elizabeth spun about, but there was no one in sight. Was she hearing things? And now the path in front of her was blurring, the air shimmering.

She must have overextended herself much more than she had thought. Usually it was only her legs that betrayed her after performing a feat of magic, but this time, even her senses were not to be trusted. She needed to get back to the house, and quickly, before someone discovered her in this condition. Gathering her strength, she strode forward.

And ran into an immovable object. A warm, breathing, immovable object, where there was nothing but an empty path before her.

Strong hands gripped her shoulders. Strong invisible hands. In desperation, she tried to push away, but to no avail. "Who are you?" she cried.

"Pardon me?" The voice sounded annoyed, and in a familiar way. "Oh. Forgive me." Suddenly the shimmering air coalesced into a solid form enclosed in a black greatcoat.

It was that odious Mr. Darcy. And she was pressed tightly against his chest.

Elizabeth gulped, sudden heat enveloping her where her body touched his. "How did you do that?"

"How did *you* interfere with my cows? I must know!"

"*Your* cows?" she exclaimed indignantly, taking a firm step backwards. "You started that charge? Your cows almost trampled a little boy."

He waved his hand, as if brushing away her objection. "It would not have harmed him."

An image of the boy's tear-stained, terrified face flashed in her mind. "Not have hurt him? Do you think a maddened cow has the sense to avoid a child?"

"It was an illusion," he snapped. "How did you block it?"

An illusion? She had heard of such things, but they were the province of mages. The few of those that existed were in royal service, not making illusory cows charge across a country field! But it made a sort of sense, how the cattle had appeared out of nowhere and disappeared as quickly, and how he had managed to hide himself only a few feet from her.

Could Mr. Darcy truly be a mage? That was a terrifying thought.

There was no acceptable answer she could give him, so she gave him the tiny bit of truth she could. "I stuffed some grass inside my glove to make a ball, and then I threw it at them, hoping it would startle them."

His eyes narrowed. "The field was afire from your glove stuffed with grass. You used magic."

"My magic, as you would call it, is only the trace of Talent that anyone in a landed family may show." If she said it with enough conviction, perhaps he would believe her.

He shook his head. "No, you must be the landed Talent, and a strong one, if I am not mistaken. That explains why I can tolerate your sister's presence so well. And you..." His eyes lit up, as if he were perceiving a miracle taking place before his eyes. "You do not repel me."

Her jaw dropped, and then she laughed in shocked disbelief. "Mr. Darcy, you amaze me! First you declare me only tolerable, and now that I do not repel you! You should be careful when you bestow such fine compliments upon a lady. She might get the wrong idea about you – but she would be unlikely to mistake you for a gentleman!"

He seemed not to even hear her. "How can this be? With the Talent you have, I should not be able to stand this close to you, much less touch you." He pulled off his glove, and, after a moment of hesitation, as if in anticipation of pain, brushed the back of his fingers lightly against her cheek. "Astonishing!"

She took another step backwards, ignoring the wave of sensation his brief touch had engendered. "You may have the physical ability to touch me, but you most certainly do not have my permission to do so!"

"What? Oh, of course," he said absently, as if his thoughts were racing far away. "But it does not matter. If your Talent can entwine with mine, and you do not repel me, then I must rethink everything."

She took a deep breath, trying to settle her jangled nerves. He was making no sense, and his behavior was outrageous. Clearly there was something very wrong with Mr. Darcy, in addition to the disaster of her Talent being discovered. "You may not find me repellant, but I am done with this conversation, sir. Pray excuse me."

"No! Do not go. I must know more of this. How did you come to have your family's Talent? Why not your elder sister?"

She had no choice but to answer that. "I have already told you I have nothing more than a trace of Talent. Jane is the heir to the family Talent."

"How could you alter my illusion? That should be impossible for any Talent, yet you did it."

"I fear you were mistaken. I did nothing more than throw my glove at your cows." It sounded so weak, but she could think of nothing better. Oh, why had she not taken greater care to disguise her magic? Not that there had been much opportunity, if she wished to save the boy from the charging cattle. The cows that did not exist.

"I do not know why you are denying it, but I was not mistaken." He moved closer to her, gazing intently into her face. "Elizabeth, this changes everything."

Heat flushed through her at the intensity of his expression. Or had it been his use of her given name, without the formal 'Miss'? The intimacy was at odds with everything she knew about him, and her own reaction disturbed her. "Mr. Darcy –"

He reached out once more, this time cupping her cheek with his bare hand.

She should pull away. He was acting like a madman, and she did not even like him. Why was she permitting this?

The rushing sound of wings cutting through the air was her only warning before a falcon split the air between them. Feathers filled her face briefly, and a strong muscled wing knocked her a step backwards.

Mr. Darcy gave a cry of pain.

The bird flew past, revealing blood dripping down the side of Mr. Darcy's face from three parallel cuts. He pressed his hand to them and then took it away, staring at his red-stained fingers. "What in God's name was that?" he demanded. He pulled out a handkerchief and dabbed at the torn flesh.

Elizabeth winced. Oh, dear! How could she explain this? The bird was still circling overhead, preparing to dive towards Darcy again. "No, Cerridwen!" she cried. "I am in no danger."

If a falcon in flight could look annoyed, this one did, but she returned to circling.

Darcy stared at her. "That is *your* bird? It is a menace!"

"She is perfectly tame." It was not true; Cerridwen always did what-ever she chose, but she would harm no one without reason. "She was merely trying to protect me. Pray permit me to look at your cuts." She stepped forward and pulled out her handkerchief, hoping to distract him from the bird.

The cuts were jagged, but fortunately not deep. She dabbed at the longest one with her handkerchief, reaching down through her feet to draw up the power of the earth. It did not come as readily as it would have at Longbourn, or perhaps it was because she had exhausted her abilities earlier, but the tiny lightning flashes of power flowed through her as she directed it to slow the blood flow. The edges of the lesion drew closer, but she stopped before they fully healed. She wanted them to look less serious, not to make them disappear in a way she could not explain.

He caught her wrist, staring at her in disbelief. "Are you using Talent on me?"

How had he known? No one had ever recognized it before when she helped a healing along, but then again, she had never tried it on someone with magic of their own before. Foolish, foolish mistake! She bit her lip. "As I said, I have a trace of Talent, and it was the least I could do when my falcon injured you."

He gingerly felt the cuts, and at his touch, the skin grew smoothly together. So he could heal, too. "I still do not understand how you could do that, but I thank you."

At least he was gracious for once! "You are most welcome. But I have a favor to ask. It is not generally known that I have these traces of Talent, and I would prefer it to remain that way."

With a slight frown, as if he found this incomprehensible, he said slowly, "It is certainly nothing to be ashamed of, but if you wish it, I will say nothing."

She breathed a sigh of relief. "I thank you."

"If I may make a similar request, I would beg you not to mention to anyone that I can cast illusions. No one must know I am anything but a landed Talent."

"I will tell no one." She would agree to almost anything to end this strange conversation. Surely she could escape now.

Or perhaps not. The falcon circled lazily down around her. With a sigh, Elizabeth held out her arm. There was no denying Cerridwen when she had her mind set on something.

"Wait!" cried Darcy. "You have no falconer's glove."

"She is specially trained, and will not hurt me." And indeed, Cerridwen alighted with nothing more than a slight squeeze of her wrist.

Darcy eyed the bird with suspicion, hardly surprising when she had cut his face. "I have never heard of such a thing. Falcons always use their talons."

"Not this one," she said lightly. "But my sister may be awake by now, so I must return to her."

He hesitated, then seemed to recall his manners enough to bow. "I hope you will find her much improved."

Cerridwen tilted her head, studying Darcy. Then, as if satisfied, she raised her foot to her beak and began to clean her talons.

Darcy slowly crossed the fields to where he had left Bingley. He had a great deal to consider, and none of it made sense.

"Well?" Bingley exclaimed. "What did you find?"

"Miss Elizabeth Bennet, if you can believe it." He could barely credit it himself. "She was frightened by the charging cows and somehow managed to make them run away. To alter my illusion."

"But that should be impossible! She might have a trace of landed Talent, I suppose, but that is only useful for crops."

"She has far more than a trace of it, based on what I saw, and that is strange enough. Still, I cannot explain how she interfered with my illusions. Even if she had a mage's ability, she would not have that power." The only other possibility was too embarrassingly far-fetched to mention. "What is more, despite her latent Talent, she does not repel me. I can touch her cheek with my bare hand with no discomfort at all." It had been the furthest thing from repulsion. A surge of desire filled him, his fingers tingling at the memory of her silken skin.

"That is beyond odd," said Bingley slowly. "Are you certain she has Talent?"

"Without a doubt. I felt her use it on me. And I think that falcon must be her familiar."

Bingley frowned. "Well, there are a few mentions in the old books of Talents who did not experience repulsion, but it is exceedingly rare. And it still does not explain what happened to your cows."

"No. Tomorrow I intend to ask her more about it."

"Good. Because if something can halt your abilities, we have to know now, before it is too late." His expression suddenly sobered. "Good God, I hate this mess!"

So did Darcy, but he could not afford to think about that. First he had to solve the mystery of Miss Elizabeth Bennet.

Chapter 2

THE NEXT MORNING ELIZABETH tiptoed out of Jane's sickroom and headed for the grand staircase. As she reached the bottom step, a voice spoke.

"Good morning, Miss Elizabeth. I was hoping to see you." Mr. Darcy rose from one of the straight-backed chairs lining the front hall and tucked a small book into his pocket.

"Good morning, sir." She strove to hide her surprise. Had he truly been sitting in an uncomfortable chair in the coldest room in the entire manor for her sake?

"May I inquire if your sister's illness is improving?" He sounded stiff, as if polite niceties did not come easily to him.

"Slowly, but yes. She ate a little breakfast and is now resting. I thought I might look in the library for a book to read."

A tentative smile flickered across his face. "I would be happy to accompany you there if you wish, but I had hoped to convince you to take a walk with me. There is something I wish to show you."

She blinked. He wanted to spend time with her? Well, she might not enjoy his company, but she needed him to keep her secret, so if he wished her to walk with him, walk she would. "I would like that. Where are we going?"

He hesitated, glancing about as if making certain no one was nearby. "Would you be interested in seeing how I created the illusion of the cows?"

Interested? She would give a great deal for such an opportunity! Mages were notoriously secretive about their art. "Very much so!" she exclaimed.

His smile widened. "Excellent."

They set forth as soon as Elizabeth had collected her bonnet and pelisse. There was more of autumn's nip in the air today, but even the tapestry of colorful leaves could not compete with her bubbling excitement. She would see magery at work!

But why was Mr. Darcy making this sudden effort? Best to be cautious until she found the answer.

Mr. Darcy said little as they walked along the gravel path beside the lake, past the folly in the shape of a Grecian temple and onto a footpath leading into the farmlands. He stopped when they reached a pasture, the same one where she had seen the cows the previous day, but from the opposite side. Today it was empty, with no evidence of humans nearby. Would the little boy avoid it after his fright there?

He opened the gate for her. "What would you like me to create? Cows again, or a different animal?"

She did not know what to do with this suddenly amiable, obliging Mr. Darcy, but she would take advantage of it. "Is there any limit?"

"A common animal, one whose ways I know, would be best. While I could make an illusory lion or elephant, they would not move convincingly, since I have never seen them in motion."

"A sheep, then?" That was common enough.

He studied the pasture, and his body became motionless. She could not have said what was different, but the air around him had somehow changed, a stillness like being in the center of an oak grove on a summer day. Then he made a quick motion with his hands.

A black-faced ewe appeared not ten feet from them, placidly grazing.

Elizabeth had seen the cow illusion only from a distance, but this sheep was convincing in every detail. Every whorl of wool, each hoof moving over the ground, even her jaw moving as she chewed grass. "Astonishing," she murmured.

"You can go closer," he urged.

She needed no second invitation. The sheep picked up her head and looked at her, for all the world as if she had heard Elizabeth's approach.

Only when Elizabeth stood next to the ewe could she see a difference, and even that was outside the illusion. The grass was not moving as the sheep grazed, instead staying upright and undamaged. Otherwise it was perfect. "May I touch it?"

"If you wish, but you will feel nothing."

She reached out to the ewe, but instead of the expected raspy fibers, her hand sank right into the sheep until it disappeared up to her wrist. It was a disturbing sight. She removed her hand – but how could she remove it when nothing was there? – and found the illusion staring at her with unblinking eyes.

"Now, if you will, Miss Elizabeth, could you attempt to interact with her? To make her move or to do something?"

She doubted it. When she chased off the cows, she had believed they were real.

Elizabeth reached down, pulled up some grass, and held it up in front of the ewe's face. "Here you are, a little treat," she coaxed.

The sheep did nothing, of course.

Firming her resolve, she let her Talent run into her from the earth. "Eat," she said, imagining the sheep taking a bite, as she had imagined the cows fleeing the fire.

The ewe sniffed the grass, then took it between her teeth. Tugging at it, she began to chew.

But the grass was still in Elizabeth's hand, and she had felt nothing when the sheep had apparently taken it. Her skin tingled. This was magic beyond anything she had ever imagined.

Mr. Darcy spoke from behind her. "Astounding. You actually altered my illusion. I have never heard of such a thing."

"What does that mean?"

"I cannot say." He pivoted, and the sheep winked out of sight as if it had never been. "Is that your falcon?" He sounded a trifle guarded.

Elizabeth looked over her shoulder. Cerridwen perched on the fence post next to the gate. "Yes. There is no cause for concern. She only attacked yesterday because she thought you were hurting me."

He studied the bird. "I have never heard of a bird familiar, either. This is a day for surprises."

Elizabeth's mouth opened in the automatic response that she had no familiar nor magic, but how could she deny it when he had seen her interact with his Talent? "She is not exactly a familiar, but she is attached to me."

"How is that different?"

She had no intention of discussing Cerridwen with him, and this might be her only opportunity to ask about illusions. By tomorrow Mr. Darcy might be too proud to speak to her again. "That is a long story. Tell me, if I can affect your illusions, does that mean I might be able to learn to create them?"

"Highly unlikely. Even the most powerful land Talents cannot cast illusions," he said dismissively. "Any family that lives on the same land for many generations and performs the rituals to bond their heir to the estate will eventually develop a landed Talent, good for making crops and animals grow. The ability to draw on the power of air to cast an illusion is much rarer, and a skill one must be born with."

"Yet you are reputed to be a landed Talent, and you can create illusions."

"I am the heir to a landed estate, but I am also descended from mages. That is why I can cast illusions. It is not something you can simply decide to learn, no matter how strong your land Talent may be."

She would not give up that easily. "You said altering an illusion is unheard of, too. Perhaps I can do this impossible thing, too."

"I suppose it would not hurt to try," he said with a touch of condescension. "To rule that out as a possible cause, if nothing else."

Elation filled her. Even if she proved incapable, this would be an experience never described in any of her reading. "How do I begin? What animal should I try to make?"

He chuckled. "Animal illusions are advanced. Let us start with something simpler. Come."

She followed him to a corner of the pasture shaded by a large oak. "This will do," he said. "We will have you try to create a little mist, right here in the corner of the stone wall."

"Mist?" she asked dubiously.

"It is the simplest illusion, and the one that we all start with."

"How do I begin?" She held her breath, hoping he would not suddenly recall that this was a closely guarded secret.

"First, picture the mist in your mind. Just a little wisp of mist, nothing elaborate. Fix that image in your mind."

Elizabeth fixed it so firmly in her mind that she might never forget it. She would never have another chance at this. "Very well."

"Now you must gather energy. Can you imagine seeing the rays of the sun reaching down to the earth, like a set of very long, very fine invisible threads?"

Could this be some sort of elaborate trick? "Threads of sunlight. Yes."

"Those are energy. Now you must gather some of those threads." He demonstrated, cupping his hands, as if tracing the outlines of a large ball from top to bottom. "Then you braid the strands together. Think of your mist, and cast the bound energy toward it." He flicked his wrist quickly, and a thick cloud of mist formed against the wall.

Astonishing!

Mr. Darcy dropped his hands, pursed his lips and blew out a breath. The mist disappeared as if it had never existed. "Now you try." He leaned back against the wall, clearly expecting nothing would happen.

Oh, how she wanted to prove him wrong! She imagined gathering and braiding the invisible threads and turning it into mist. Nothing. She tried again, forcing with all the power of her will, pulling energy from the earth, without success.

As tears of frustration filled her eyes, an image jumped into her mind, oddly distorted, as if seen through Cerridwen's eyes. It was her spinning wheel.

Cerridwen never sent to her without a reason, but why her spinning wheel?

Oh.

With new resolve, she gathered the invisible threads, but this time she could feel a sense of energy between her hands as she pictured them as strands of combed flax. Instead of weaving her fingers, she let the strands run through her pinched thumb and forefinger as if she were spinning them, her foot tapping on an imaginary treadle. With her mist image in the forefront of her mind, she sent her spun thread out into the corner.

Mist began to coalesce.

She had done it! With a triumphant smile, she glanced over at Mr. Darcy, but he was gazing off into the distance.

"Look!" she cried.

His head swiveled and his jaw dropped. "Good God."

Giddy with triumph, she kept spinning, making her mist grow and spread. It was glorious. It was dizzying. It was...

"Stop! Let it go, Elizabeth. Cut the threads!" Mr. Darcy's voice seemed to come from a long distance away.

Obediently she stopped spinning. Just as well, because now the pasture itself was spinning around her.

As her legs gave way beneath her, she felt strong arms close around her. It felt warm and safe. And then she stopped feeling anything.

Chapter 3

D ARCY'S ARMS ACHED BY the time he finally reached the folly, but that was the least of his worries. He wanted them to hurt. He deserved the pain. How could he have been such a fool?

He laid Elizabeth's unconscious body down with all possible gentleness on the marble bench. Good God, she was practically as pale as the marble! He laid his fingers against her throat to check her pulse, a difficult task when his own heart was pounding uncontrollably.

There it was, slow but steady. Thank God!

This was all his fault. He had no business letting her try to cast an illusion in the first place, and it had been beyond reckless not to warn her of the dangers before she attempted it. But he had been so certain that she lacked the ability that he had barely been paying attention. His mother would flay him alive if she ever found out.

Yes, he was a fool, and he had risked Elizabeth's life. He would never forgive himself if she did not recover.

And still she lay motionless.

Stricken, he dropped to his knees beside her, taking her hand between his and chafing it, gently, as if he could pour his strength into her. "Elizabeth, I beg you. Open your eyes. Do not give up. Stay with me." The last words resounded in his head.

What if he lost her, so soon after finding her? The consequences, both to him and to England, would be —

A flash of feathers interrupted his thoughts. Air rushed across his face as Elizabeth's falcon glided into the temple, coming to perch above Elizabeth's feet and chittering softly.

Hope stirred in Darcy's chest at the sight of the bird's gold-ringed eyes, with the black line below them looking almost like tear streaks. Could this not-quite-familiar transfer energy to Elizabeth as a true familiar might?

The kestrel spread its wings and called again, this time with a commanding "Kee-kee-kee!"

Elizabeth stirred, her hand creeping up to rub across her eyes. "What?" she asked weakly.

Relief poured through him.

Elizabeth propped herself up on one elbow, her head swimming with confusion. "How did I get here?" And why was Mr. Darcy holding her hand? She could remember nothing after creating the mist, and then Cerridwen had shouted inside her head.

Darcy's face was ashen. "I carried you here after you fainted. It was the nearest place."

"I cannot believe it. I never faint." She was sure of that much.

"Anyone would, in these circumstances." He hung his head, an unexpected gesture from such a proud man. "It was my fault. I should have warned you that casting is dangerous, that you must stop it quickly. Mages have died from draining their life force to create illusions. It is not like overusing your land Talent, which will only tire you. I am very sorry."

It troubled her to see him humbled. "It seems no harm was done." The bench was uncomfortably cold, and she felt helpless lying down, so she spent what seemed an inordinate amount of energy to sit up.

"You must promise me never to try again," Darcy insisted. "It is far too risky to be done without supervision. Next time you might not be so fortunate."

She had no intention of giving up this fabulous new Talent she had discovered. "If you had simply told me not to extend myself, I would have stopped, and nothing would have happened."

"I know! Do you think I have not been berating myself with that?" he snapped. "Had I thought there was even the slightest possibility that you were —" he stopped short, then resumed, "—able to cast illusions, I would have been far more careful."

"But you could not imagine a mere country gentleman's daughter would have such an ability, could you?"

"The last time a mage appeared outside the Three Mage-Blood Families was in the reign of Henry VIII, and even then, it was thought he was most likely an illegitimate Percy. Why should I expect that to change now?" he bit out.

"None outside the Three Families? How about you? Your name is not Percy, Fitzwilliam, or Mortimer."

This seemed to amuse him. "My mother is a Fitzwilliam, and my father's mother was a Percy. And, in fact, my given name is Fitzwilliam. Fitzwilliam Darcy, at your service." He inclined his head, as if they were meeting for the first time.

Suddenly all the odd things about him made sense. He truly was a mage. "What are you doing here, then? Why are you not in service to the Crown?"

"Perhaps the Crown wanted me to go to a benighted corner of Hertfordshire to practice casting illusions of charging cows." Laughter lurked behind his words.

It only annoyed her more. "There is nothing benighted about Meryton."

"Perhaps not, but it is far from the nearest ley line."

Did he enjoy being mysterious? Crossly, she wiggled her foot until Cerridwen flew off it with an offended squawk, lighting instead on the marble head of a Greek god. Elizabeth pushed herself to her feet.

Except her legs were not working. Before she tumbled to the ground, Darcy's hands were under her elbows, supporting her weight, his chest just inches from her, as he helped her back to the bench.

Cerridwen clucked.

"Goodness," Elizabeth said.

"You must not try to stand. Not until you have had something to eat, tea with plenty of sugar, and some rest," Darcy stated.

Now that he mentioned it, she was starving, despite the large breakfast she'd eaten only an hour ago. "If you would assist me outside, where I can sit on the ground, the land will help me." It would be improper to be so close to him, but there was no one to see.

"A good idea." Instead of offering her his arm for support, he swept her up and carried her outside.

She stiffened in shock at his forwardness. Surely it was wrong to be pressed so tightly against his body! She could feel the hardness of his chest and catch his scent of soap and spice – and a hint of the smell that comes after a thunderstorm had passed. And certainly she should not enjoy the warm pressure of his arm underneath her knees, which sent the strangest sensation spiraling through her.

Darcy carefully set her on her feet, but did not release her until she was sitting on a patch of grass.

When he took his hands away, she should have been relieved. Why was she filled with empty disappointment instead?

Likely it was just her state of exhaustion. Closing her eyes, she reached for her connection to the land, entwining her fingers in the grass, letting the steady thrum of the earth's power nourish her. It was but a thin trickle of energy here, compared to what she felt at Longbourn, but it was enough to make her breathe more easily. She sensed Cerridwen's reassuring presence on a branch overhead.

She opened her eyes, to see Darcy watching her with an oddly vulnerable look. "I thank you. This is better."

"You will still need nourishment before you try to walk." He frowned. "I dare not leave you alone yet, but I will fetch some food from the house in a little while."

"It is hardly necessary. I am certain I will be perfectly well with a little rest."

"Miss Elizabeth, you do not understand. This is a very dangerous condition, and food is absolutely necessary for recovery. Attempting to do too much without it, even walking a few feet, could kill you."

Taken aback at his intensity, she said, "I see. Then I shall rest here as long as necessary." Could it truly be so risky?

"I thank you. And once again, I must apologize for having allowed this situation to arise."

She could not help smiling. "I am not sorry. It was well worth it."

Then a motion in the trees caught her eye. It was the head of a large creature, its pointed ears topped with tufts of fur. It moved out into the open, revealing a cat-like body with a bobbed tail, easily three feet tall, with the feral face of a hunting cat.

Elizabeth froze. In a low voice, she told Darcy, "I pray you, do not move a muscle."

He obeyed, and responded quietly, "Why? What is the matter?"

"There is a wild beast at the edge of the wood." Her voice trembled. "Some sort of massive cat. Like a tiger, only spotted."

He seemed to relax, saying in a normal voice, "In that case, there is no need for fear. He will not hurt you."

Of course. He was amusing himself by frightening her, and just when she was thinking better of him. "What, another illusion? I am not entertained."

He shook his head. "Hardly. He is my familiar."

This wild beast, a familiar? "You might have warned me!"

"I did not expect you to see him. He is very private, and usually only shows himself when I am in danger. There is no need to worry, though."

"What is he?"

"A lynx."

"But they are extinct here! No one has seen one in England since the Dark Ages! Did you find him abroad?"

"No. He walked out of the forest at Pemberley one day. Apparently they are not as extinct as we believed."

"Are there more of them, then?" That was a frightening thought. She would hate to meet one of them while walking in the woods, without a nearby Talent to control it.

"I must assume so, although I have never seen another."

"Why is he here now? Did you call him?" It seemed too much of a coincidence that the lynx should appear when she was so helpless, the perfect prey.

"No. I am uncertain why he came." Darcy's eyelids drooped briefly, as if he was suddenly sleepy, and his gaze became unfocused. Then his eyebrows shot up. "He is here because he wants to meet you."

"Me? Why would he care about me?" She would have doubted him, except that he looked so shocked.

Again, the unfocused look. "He thinks it is needful." His expression turned apologetic. "He is a wild creature and does not consider why or wherefore. Just what he needs to do."

"Well, he has seen me. Can you send him on his way now?" She certainly hoped so.

"He would like to approach you, to gain your scent. Only if you are willing. He will keep his distance if I tell him to. But I promise he will not harm you."

The lynx cocked his head, watching her curiously.

He did not seem to regard her as a potential meal, and she had no wish to appear a coward or, worse, a trembling country girl. And she had to admit he was a magnificent animal. "Very well." She was pleased her voice did not shake. "But if he tears out my throat, I will never forgive you."

Darcy had the gall to smile. "He will not, though I must point out that if he did, you would be in no position to forgive anyone."

"I would haunt you." But then the lynx was padding toward her, each powerful stride a symphony of motion. Instinct made Elizabeth freeze, and she had to force herself to breathe.

The big cat stopped a few feet away, studying her. Cautiously Elizabeth extended her hand as she might to a strange dog. The lynx's warm breath tickled her skin as he sniffed it.

Then he butted her hand as he turned his head, pushing her fingers into the ruff of fur on his cheeks. It was rough and silky at the same time, and she caught a faint musky scent as he rubbed against her hand.

Could he possibly want her to scratch him under the ear, as if he were a lap cat?

Well, in for a penny, in for a pound. Daringly she turned her fingers and rubbed, first lightly, then more firmly as he pressed his head into her hand. A deep rumble merged from his throat.

She still tasted fear, but, oh, how exhilarating it was to be so close to such a powerful creature, and have it enjoy her touch!

The lynx stiffened and drew back on its haunches, his head turned towards the temple, where Cerridwen perched on the pediment, looking down at him with a supercilious expression. A powerful hiss emerged from his mouth, revealing wickedly sharp teeth.

Stupid cat. The falcon spoke in her head.

Not as clever as you, darling, Elizabeth hastened to reassure her. *But he will not hurt me.*

She tried to ruffle the lynx's fur again to distract it from Cerridwen, but he tired of her attentions quickly, giving his thanks with an utterly terrifying lick to Elizabeth's cheek. She drew in a breath. "And I thought a kitten's tongue was rough. I think your lynx took half of my skin with it."

And she glanced up to see Darcy staring at her in astonishment.

"Is something the matter?" she asked, as if it were not strange enough that this wild creature of the forest, this predator, had licked her, and was now curling up beside her.

"I do not understand what he is doing." Darcy sounded half-strangled.

It was oddly satisfying to see him knocked off his pedestal of knowing everything. Let him be the one to be overwhelmed by something altogether strange for once! With new confidence, Elizabeth reached out and ran her hand along the lynx's back, petting him as if he were a giant house cat and not a wild animal who could eat her for breakfast.

The rumbling started again, and she laughed delightedly. "I must confess that I have sometimes wished for a traditional familiar, a cat that would curl up in my lap and purr. I had not pictured this!"

"He is not a house cat."

"What is his name?"

Darcy seemed surprised by the question. "I call him Lynx. He is the only one I have ever seen, after all."

"How startlingly original." She studied the lynx, who picked up his head to watch her, something feral burning behind his dark eyes. "I think I shall call you Fire Eyes."

The lynx regarded her with no reaction beyond a slow blink. Of course that was all. True familiars could not understand the spoken word. Her experience with Cerridwen had spoiled her.

But how had Darcy bound the lynx to be his familiar in the first place? "Did you let him bite you?" she asked in disbelief. It was one thing to let a small cat or dog draw one's blood to make the bond, but to knowingly put one's arm in the way of those sharp dangerous teeth!

Darcy shrugged. "He was very gentle."

"I cannot believe you!"

He smiled. "Very well, I will confess that the first time, when he came and offered himself to me, I was terrified. I was certain I would never see my hand again."

"You did it anyway." That actually impressed her. As if his abilities were not remarkable enough already. Now she had to add courage to his list of qualities. It was becoming very difficult to maintain her dislike for him.

"It had been drilled into me since childhood that when a familiar offered itself, I should never refuse. I expected something smaller and tamer. And not seemingly extinct. I had to search the library to find a book with illustrations before I even knew what sort of animal he was."

"How old were you?"

"I was twelve."

She could picture the boy he had been, madly perusing books in search of information about the wild animal with whom he had bonded. It seemed a long way from the proud Mr. Darcy of today.

Suddenly the lynx uncoiled smoothly to his feet and took off at a run into the woods.

She stared after him, oddly disappointed. "Did I do something wrong?"

That unfocused look again. "No. Someone is coming."

And then Elizabeth heard it, too, footsteps approaching along the gravel path from the main house. She tried to gather her scattered wits, to make herself appear composed, as if there were nothing unusual or unladylike about sitting on the grass. As if there had not been an extinct wild animal licking her face a few moments earlier.

Two servants, each carrying a tray, came around the bend in the path. The first one approached Darcy and asked, "Where would you like us to put these, sir?"

Darcy looked stunned. "Next to Miss Elizabeth Bennet, if you please."

As the servant set them out, Elizabeth asked, "What have we here?" One tray held a teapot and cups, and the other a variety of foodstuffs.

The first servant bowed. "Chamomile tea, honey, fresh bread with butter, and plum cake, as Mr. Darcy requested."

She could not quite hide her amusement. "Very good. How clever of him to include exactly what I wanted." It would be interesting to see him try to explain this. Could he guess what had happened? "Would you care to join me, Mr. Darcy?"

"No, pray go ahead." He nodded to the servants, who appeared prepared to wait. "That will be all for now."

As soon as they were out of sight, Darcy paced, back and forth, back and forth, as if he could not stay still. He seemed to have forgotten her presence.

Watching him only reminded her how handsome he was, and heat seemed to grow inside her. She swallowed hard. There was no point in letting herself be attracted to a man who had been completely out of her reach even before she discovered he was a mage. To distract herself, Elizabeth poured her tea and added a generous dollop of honey. After taking a few sips, she said, "You seem disturbed."

He halted. "I must have cast a sending which told the servants to bring you food. I have never managed a sending at such a distance before, especially to someone lacking Talent. It might have been my desperation, or perhaps your presence enabled me to do it, since our Talents intertwine. I must try to recall exactly what I was thinking at the time."

"Mmm, a good idea." She tried to hide her amusement, certain there had indeed been a sending, and equally sure that Darcy had nothing to do with it. She spared a glance upward to the falcon circling overhead. Cerridwen knew her tastes.

But it would not do for Darcy to suspect that her falcon had unusual powers, so she would let him take the credit. Still, Cerridwen must get her due. Elizabeth crumbled some of the cake on the grass, and the falcon swooped down to peck at it.

Darcy frowned. "You must eat in order to recover."

"I shall, but Cerridwen is inordinately fond of plum cake. How long will it be before I can walk?"

"Once you have eaten, perhaps an hour, or a little less."

Another hour in his company? It certainly did not seem as terrible a fate as it had this morning, and perhaps she could get him to talk more about illusions. She spread butter on the bread. "And how long to recover fully?"

"After a good night's sleep. But I cannot emphasize enough that it would be dangerous for you to try this again."

So her weakness would be gone by tomorrow, and then she could ask Mr. Darcy for another lesson in illusion casting, regardless of what he said. Surely she could make a case that it would be better to try it under his supervision. In any case, it would behoove her to be pleasant to him now.

"So quickly? Good. I am learning a great deal today, between illusions and lynxes."

His expression turned serious. "Miss Elizabeth, I must ask something of you. I could find myself in rather serious difficulties if certain people discovered I had taught you to cast an illusion. Even more so if they knew how poorly I had prepared you. I would be in your debt if you agreed to keep this between us."

"If you wish it." Though it would be frustrating to keep her new accomplishment to herself when she longed to shout her ability to the world. But it was only fair. After all, he agreed to keep her secret, too.

Chapter 4

"I DO NOT KNOW why I agreed to this," Darcy muttered under his breath the following day. He had other things he ought to be doing, like discovering why he had been able to send a message to the servant all the way at Netherfield yesterday and now could not do it beyond the room he was in. Presumably his desperation had unlocked unknown skills, but it would be useful to learn to manage it without a crisis. Still, that question was far less intriguing than time spent with Elizabeth.

Elizabeth smiled so brilliantly that he could have sworn the sun had broken through the clouds. "Because I asked so nicely, and because you would rather I tried this under your supervision than go off practicing on my own."

"There is that," he acknowledged. "My sins are coming back to haunt me."

"So, how can I tell when I have done too much?"

"For now, you should stop as soon as you have created a little mist. With time, one learns the signs of being drained. A peculiar excitement, a sense of being powerful, almost like being drunk. Not that I am accusing you of ever drinking too much, Miss Elizabeth, but the idea is the same."

She said archly, "Perhaps I have never imbibed to excess, but ratafia is stronger than most gentlemen believe. It goes to my head a little. And yesterday, I did feel like that. I will be careful."

God, but she drew him like a magnet when she was in this playful mood!

"Whenever you are ready." He gestured to the corner of the stone wall.

She closed her eyes for a moment, giving him the opportunity to watch her unabashedly. It was not only her facial structure that gave her beauty, but her intelligent expression and her lively movements.

Then she did something peculiar, bringing her arms in front of her. With a subtle rhythmic motion, her forefinger and thumb pinched and her hands moved together, apart, together, and apart again. Even though she did not flick her wrist, mist grew in the corner.

He eyed it critically. It was by no means a strong illusion, but she was producing it evenly and efficiently.

Her hands dropped to her sides, and she turned to look at him. "There. Did I stop quickly enough?"

"The fact that you are still standing suggests you did."

She rocked back on one foot to admire her mist, seeming pleased with her handiwork. "How long will it remain there?"

"Until you dissipate it or until the sun goes down."

"How do I dissipate it?"

"The simplest way is to blow on it, as if you were blowing out a candle, while thinking of scattering the energy. Do you wish to try it?"

Her smile glowed again. "Not yet. I want to enjoy it a little longer."

"What were you doing with your hands as you were casting?"

She gave him a rueful look. "A trick I discovered yesterday. It did not work when I tried to braid the sunbeams, so instead I imagined spinning them into thread, the way I would with a spinning wheel. It worked for me, perhaps because I am more practiced at spinning than plaiting."

He eyed her in disbelief. "You know how to spin?" He had known Hertfordshire was primitive, but this was too much.

She gave a light tinkle of a laugh. "I have shocked you. Spinning is not a suitable pastime for a gentleman's daughter, is it? Fear not, I go to the milliner and buy my thread for most things. But my granny taught me to spin when I was a girl. She said it would prove useful someday, and it has."

He still thought it distinctly below her. Spinning was for uneducated peasants. "If you consider illusion casting to be useful."

"Oh, not just for that! Have you seen my gloves? I make them from flax grown at Longbourn. I spin it into thread, drawing the land's power into the spinning, and then I make it into gloves which store my Talent. When my sisters wear them, they can call on the land to a degree, and they strengthen me as well. That is why I could use my glove to create the flame that frightened your cows."

He had never heard of storing power in such a way. "May I see one?"

She peeled one off, revealing her elegant fingers, and held it out to him. "These are the ones I made for Jane, since I destroyed my own."

He draped the lacy glove over his palm. It was still warm from her hand and weighed almost nothing. He could see the slight unevenness in the thread, but it was heavy with power. Astonishing! "What gave you the idea to try this?"

"I read about it in a book. Not about using it for gloves, but about weaving it into fabric to be worn against the skin. It would take a very long time to spin enough thread to make cloth. Gloves are easier."

"What book is this? I should like to see it." And why had he never heard of this technique?

Her lips curved. "It is called *On Binding to the Land*. I can show it to you, but you are unlikely to find it useful, as it is in Arabic."

The light dawned. "That is why you learned Arabic," he said. She had mentioned it the previous evening when Bingley's sister asked her about her accomplishments, clearly expecting Elizabeth to deny any knowledge of foreign languages. "I thought you had only said that to shock us."

She laughed. "I will not deny that was my primary reason for telling her! Oh, her face! I could have mentioned that I speak French, too, but it would not have been as enjoyable."

Now he was thankful he had defended her choice when Miss Bingley called it a barbaric tongue. "I know there were great scholars in the ancient Arabian Empire who were a beacon of enlightenment in our Dark Ages."

"You are better educated than most, if you are even aware of the scholarship of the Arabians!"

It was a heady thing, having Elizabeth look at him with admiration. "I have an interest in history, but I never knew they wrote about the uses of Talent."

She nodded. "Apparently the subject was of particular interest to Arab philosophers after the Moors left Spain and needed to bond to their new land in Africa, so they developed techniques to speed the process. They claim to have achieved full bonding in only three generations." She sparkled with pride, as well she might about such a discovery.

It would be astounding, if true. It had taken almost two centuries after the Norman conquest for the invaders to develop rapport with their estates. Today's newly wealthy merchants would give a great deal for such knowledge, if it meant their families could become landed Talents like the old established families.

"What else does this book of yours recommend?"

She shrugged, not meeting his eyes. "Various things. Spending as much time as possible on your land. Eating only food produced there or nearby, for example."

That answered another question. "I noticed you always decline desserts and wondered if you disliked sweets, or perhaps you are an abolitionist who refuses to eat sugar produced by enslaved people. But it is something else, is it not?"

"I do believe in abolition, and I would not eat West Indian sugar because of it, but you are correct. I avoid eating anything that is not grown locally, and sugar comes from across the world." She gave him a rueful look. "It is unfortunate for me, as I am passionately fond of sweets. At least there is still honey."

The question of consuming local foods sounded like superstition, but it could be real. Talents who spent all their time in London often found their abilities fading. "Anything else?"

She looked at him with a hint of defiance, setting her chin. "Various techniques for giving blood to the land, so it recognizes and knows its tenant."

He sucked in a breath, though he should not be surprised. The Arabs were infidels, after all. "The church has forbidden blood magic." And he, better than any, knew why.

"Has that stopped any landed family from burying the heir's afterbirth so that the land will know him? What is that, if not giving his blood and flesh to the land?"

That stopped him short. "I suppose I never thought about it that way."

"And did not your lynx have to taste your blood to become your familiar?"

"That is true, as well." He was not accustomed to losing arguments. It was an uncomfortable sensation.

She seemed to sense his discomfort, for she said more gently, "I think it is like any other church doctrine. We all choose which to follow and to what degree."

He decided he would rather not know if she gave blood to the land. "These things you have done – the gloves, eating local food – do you think they have increased your Talent?" He could not deny that her Talent was unusually strong for someone living so far from the nearest ley line.

"I do. And I use my Talents frequently, rather than sparingly, as we are taught here. The book says the Talent is like any other muscle in the body, and the more we use it, the stronger it gets."

If any of this was true, it could be very important. He needed to find out what was in this book.

Once again, he had underestimated Elizabeth.

Elizabeth hugged herself as she made her way upstairs. She had not only cast an illusion again, but she had shown that know-all Darcy she knew a few things that he, in all his lordly ways, did not. It had been beyond satisfying to see the look on his face when his student suddenly turned into his teacher.

She hoped, though, that he would forget it quickly. It might have been wiser not to say anything, because if he thought too hard about why she had gone to such lengths to learn how to increase a land bond, he might come up with the right answer. He had already guessed too much, with his suspicions that she held the family Talent rather than Jane.

But there was nothing to be done for it now, so instead she entered Jane's room, where her sister was sitting up in bed speaking with Mr. Hadid. Elizabeth smiled as she went to kiss the old apothecary's cheek. Although she did not see him often these days, he had been almost a second father to her when she was a child, and she had many happy memories of her time at his house. "It is good to see you," she said in Arabic.

His face was wreathed with smiles. "And you, my little Lizzy! Have you been out walking for hours again?"

She was not about to admit she had been receiving a lesson in magery, even though Mr. Hadid was one of the few people to whom her Talent was not a secret. "Not quite that long." She switched back to English for Jane's sake. "What do you think of our patient's progress?"

"She is much improved," he said. "I believe it would be safe for her to travel back to Longbourn, as long as it is in a carriage."

"That is excellent news," she replied firmly, masking her disappointment. She had expected it, and was glad Jane was better, but leaving meant an end to her illusion lessons. That was why she had cornered Darcy and begged for another one. To think that only two days ago, she would have been excited by the opportunity to escape from his company!

Jane nodded. "I will be glad to be home. I dislike being a burden to the Bingleys."

Elizabeth laughed. "You could not be a burden to Mr. Bingley if you tried. He has been delighted to have you here. He will be a frequent caller at Longbourn, mark my words!"

"And you, my Lizzy, must call on me," said Mr. Hadid. "I found a new storybook you must see. It mentions the dragons of Arabia."

She laughed. "You know what I like! I will come as soon as I can."

It was a small thing to look forward to. But not the only thing. Even if she never saw Darcy again, Elizabeth could still practice her illusion-casting, as long as she was very careful and kept both tea and food near at hand. It was more than she had ever expected, and she should not dwell on her disappointment that she could never learn any more. She should be grateful for what she had.

The carriage containing the Bennet sisters disappeared down the lane, carrying away the delightful sparkle and excitement which had livened Darcy's spirits. It was pointless to think that way, though. Within a matter of days, Elizabeth would be by his side again, this time forever.

Though in his case, forever was not a long time.

He clapped Bingley on the shoulder. "Come, I must speak to you privately."

Bingley gave a theatrical sigh. "You cannot allow me even a few minutes to mourn the departure of my lady love?"

"Not even a second," he said with a laugh. "There is something I have been waiting two days to tell you."

When they were ensconced in the privacy of Bingley's study, Darcy related the results of his tests with Elizabeth. "Without question, she has mage blood. But even that should not give her the ability to change my illusions." He paused. "There is only one explanation. Her Talent can intertwine with mine."

"Impossible," snorted Bingley. "Do you know how rare that is?"

He had expected this. "One case in a century, if that."

"Come now, Darcy," Bingley scoffed. "You must be dreaming. Do you think you and Miss Elizabeth are another Arthur and Guinevere, practicing magic together when no one else can?"

Darcy ignored him. "This is important, Bingley. Consider the implications for my mission. If she and I are bound together in blood, and our Talent can intertwine, then I can draw on her magic when I am in France. And if she is at Pemberley...Come now, Bingley, think!"

The light dawned on Bingley's face. "Then you could draw on your land magic through her, rather than relying solely on magery! My God, Darcy, that is brilliant! It could change everything!"

"I cannot believe my luck. All of our luck." That it was Elizabeth, who had so easily bewitched him, only made it perfect.

Bingley tapped his chin. "Now you really do have to marry her. And get her with child if you can."

"That should not be a problem." Nor would consummating the marriage be a chore, as he had always expected. It seemed like a fairytale, the idea he could marry an attractive woman and make love to her without either of them feeling the cruel pain of repulsion. It was more than he had ever dreamed of.

What a pity their marriage would be so short-lived.

Bingley nodded. "And quickly, too. Time is of the essence."

"No one is more aware of that than I." As if he could forget for even a moment that his remaining life could be counted in months, rather than years. "Now that she and her sister have returned to Longbourn, I plan to ask Mr. Bennet's permission tomorrow." He grimaced at the prospect. "Will you serve as my Interlocutor?"

Bingley straightened. "I? Always happy to help, old chap, but I am not trained for it."

"It should hardly be a difficult task. You will have to send a note to him requesting the interview, but otherwise, this is merely a formality."

"True. You are the sort of match every father dreams of for his daughter."

Darcy held out the sheaf of papers he had prepared. "I made some estimates on the settlement. If I have difficulty speaking, you will need to present them."

With a long-suffering expression, Bingley took them and read the first page. His lips pursed in a silent whistle. "This is very generous."

"There is no reason not to be, and every reason to avoid giving him any excuse to delay this marriage. We have no time to waste. I must have her married and at Pemberley as quickly as possible." And that was the one part of this prospect which brought him joy. He might not have much time with Elizabeth, but he intended to take pleasure in every minute of it. Surely he deserved that much.

"I will do my best to speak for you." Bingley sounded doubtful. "If you need it, that is."

"Most likely I will not. I cannot imagine his Talent is that strong."

Chapter 5

Darcy was forced to revise that opinion as they approached Longbourn. He had never set foot there before; it would be the height of rudeness to visit another Talented landowner's property without serious business. It was always a difficult prospect.

But even though he was on horseback and this was not his land, he could feel the power flowing from the ground. The results were all around him, fields overflowing with baled hay, flourishing crops of winter wheat, plump cattle and luxuriant-fleeced sheep, well beyond what he had seen elsewhere in Meryton. Mr. Bennet apparently had more Talent than Darcy had expected.

He glanced at Bingley. He might need an Interlocutor after all. The stronger the Talent, the worse the repulsion.

The tingling in his skin began as they approached the manor house, and he braced himself for worse. Once the butler admitted them, the burning commenced.

It intensified as they were led past the parlor where Elizabeth sat with her sisters, her presence lighting up the room like a star. But wait – somehow he had known she was in there even before he could see in the door. How could that be? He had never been able to do that, even with Anne. He would have to ask his mother about it.

But he forgot his ruminations as she glanced over at them, surprise evident in her features. Would she wear that charmingly startled air when he emerged after speaking to her father and asked her to be his wife? A surge of desire coursed through him, despite his increasing discomfort.

Then the butler was announcing them to Mr. Bennet. Darcy stepped into a dim room lined with overcrowded bookshelves. Piles of books set on dark wooden side tables beside leather armchairs. It was the sort of place where Darcy would otherwise feel instantly at home, were it not for the sensation of hot coals pressing against his skin all over his body.

A typical meeting with a powerful Talent, then. Darcy bowed in Mr. Bennet's general direction. He knew better than to look directly at him. Meeting another Talent's eyes, especially on his own property, could induce a seizure or worse. It was already a struggle to breathe.

While he was still trying to collect his thoughts, Bingley said, "Mr. Bennet, may I introduce you to Mr. Darcy of Pemberley? As I told you in my note, he has asked me to serve as his Interlocutor on an important matter."

"Pray sit down, gentlemen. May I offer you some port?" Mr. Bennet rasped.

The man either had little experience with meeting another Talent or a tendency towards cruelty. Darcy had no desire to choke from an attempt to imbibe in his presence.

"I thank you, no," Darcy managed to say, though his lips felt as if they were burning to ash. "I have no desire to impose upon you, so I will come straight to the point. I wish to ask your permission to marry your daughter, Miss Elizabeth."

Mr. Bennet stared at him. "Is this a joke?"

Darcy stiffened, which only made the pain worse. "It is nothing of the sort. I most earnestly desire to marry Miss Elizabeth."

"It is the talk of the town that you said she was not handsome enough to tempt you, so you will have to forgive me for doubting you." The older man slowly crossed his arms, as if every movement was agonizing.

As Darcy tried to collect himself, Bingley rushed in. "I have observed Darcy with your daughter during this last week at Netherfield and I can assure you that he ardently admires her. He is a good man, the best of my acquaintance. He is well able to support her, with a large estate in Derbyshire and an income of over ten thousand pounds a year. He has authorized me to show you the details of the settlement he wishes to make upon Miss Elizabeth, and it is most generous." Bingley held out the papers. "If you would be so kind —"

Mr. Bennet held up a hand to stop him, wincing at the movement. "That is unnecessary. Had I been aware of your purpose, I would have saved you the journey. Mr. Darcy, if you truly feel an attachment to my daughter, then I am sorry for it. Elizabeth's ties to this estate are strong, and I will never permit her to marry any man who cannot make Longbourn his home. I am sorry to disappoint you, but this is my final word on the matter."

What? Could the man be refusing his suit? Refusing the owner of Pemberley, the man upon whom England's hopes depended? Impossible!

But apparently true. Darcy could barely think for the pain consuming him. Desperately he sucked in air, pulling every bit of power he could from it until the room seemed to stabilize. He had to convince him. Everything depended upon it. If only the burning would stop! "Mr. Bennet, this is not a passing fancy. It is inexplicable, but your daughter's Talent matches mine precisely, to the point where our Talents can intermingle. You must know how rare that is."

The older man paled. "What do you know of her Talent?" It was more of an accusation than a question, and too late Darcy recalled Elizabeth had begged him not to tell her father that he had caught her employing her art.

He raised his chin. "Perhaps it would not be perceptible to those with no Talent of their own, but it was obvious to me." He fought to keep from fleeing the room, away from this torture.

Mr. Bennet's lips tightened. "You felt it? The repulsion? And you want to *marry* her?"

"There is no repulsion, none at all. That is why I said we match. You must see why this is an opportunity I cannot walk away from."

Bingley winced.

The older man drummed his fingers on his desk, and a gasp of pain escaped his lips. "I can see why the match would benefit you, but it would cause only harm to my family. I am sorry, but my answer is no." He rose stiffly to his feet. "Good day, gentlemen."

"Wait!" cried Bingley. "There is more to it than Darcy's desire. He must marry Miss Elizabeth in order to protect us all!"

"Bingley!" Darcy snapped. "That is not to be spoken of!"

"But you need this!"

"I know," Darcy said savagely, swallowing down the bile that forced its way through his choking throat. "Mr. Bennet, Bingley has referenced a matter which should have remained private. I must ask you to forget you ever heard it." If Bennet felt half as pained as he did, he would likely agree to forget his own name if it got Darcy out of the room.

"Naturally."

By the time they reached the horses, the invisible fires burning Darcy's skin had died down to an unpleasant heat. This was always the disconcerting point, when his mind insisted his skin must be covered with angry red blisters, if not charred away completely, but he knew that if he peeled his gloves back, his hand would appear the same as always. It would take longer for his heart to stop pounding from the memory of the pain.

He made a show of checking his saddle to disguise the fact that he was leaning on the horse for support while he gathered the strength to mount. Not to mention dealing with the question of what to do next.

How could Mr. Bennet have refused the best match his daughter could ever hope to make?

Darcy called on the air to cool the heated skin of his face. An answering rumble of distant thunder shook the air.

Gritting his teeth, he mounted Hercules and urged him into motion. This was why he needed a horse with exquisite training, for those times when his body would not fully obey his commands. He probably ought to have taken the carriage.

Being with Anne had spoiled him. It had been painful to be in her presence, but not agonizing. But she had been his cousin, which had eased matters, and her Talent was weak. Now he had been overconfident in his ability to converse with Bennet as a result.

Bingley caught up to him. "Well, that was abrupt," he said hesitantly.

For a moment Darcy could not think what he meant. "The conversation? It always is. No time for polite niceties when your skin is on fire."

Bingley winced. "Sometimes I am happy to be without Talent. But I am sorry I was not more help. I did not anticipate that he would refuse."

"Nor did I." As he turned onto the road, the last of the pressure finally lifted. "We will have to find a way around him, though I cannot imagine what that might be."

"The mission is supposed to be a secret, but I think we need to tell him," Bingley said slowly. "That would be the simplest way to change his mind. No decent Englishman could refuse to help you."

"It is a secret for good reasons!" Darcy snapped.

"I know, but this marriage is important."

Darcy's head ached. "I will think about it. Right now I cannot imagine being in his presence again."

"I could do that part. I can explain it as well as you can."

He hated to admit how much of a relief that would be. "That might be best. And then Bennet will understand why he has no more choice in this matter than I do."

"Good God, Darcy. I thought you wanted to marry her."

"By sheer good fortune, I find her attractive and enjoy her company, so I will be happy to wed her. But if she were an ugly, prating hag, I would marry her anyway. Because the mission is the only thing that matters." The bitter words, the ones he had heard so often, poured out of him, but this bitterness was for a new reason. He wanted to marry Elizabeth because he admired her, not out of duty to his country. He wanted to grow old with her by his side. But the mission would make that impossible.

It was not fair. Normally he could put those feelings aside, but after being plagued by pain, his defenses were down. Was a long, loving marriage too much to ask? He urged his horse into a trot.

Bingley pulled ahead of him. "I say, Darcy, you do not look at all well. I think we had best take it at a walk."

He wanted to snap at Bingley and say he could manage his horse perfectly well, but he could not swear it was true. And he could not afford to take any chances. Not now. That, too, had been drilled into him.

Because the mission came first.

The parlor maid poked her head in the door. "Miss Lizzy, your father wants to see you in his library."

"Ooh, Lizzy's in trouble!" Lydia cried in a singsong voice.

"As always." Elizabeth made an elaborate curtsy to her annoying younger sister. "If you need me, you will no doubt find me languishing in the dungeons."

Mary frowned. "We have no dungeons here. Only the cellar."

Elizabeth laughed. "Papa will make me dig my own dungeon as part of the punishment." And with those uplifting words, she left the room.

But she felt far less cheerful than she sounded. She knew exactly why Mr. Darcy had called on her father. The only reason such a powerful man would tolerate such a meeting was to deliver a warning about Elizabeth's use of her Talent. She should have known better than to trust him to keep her secret. To think she had been starting to like him!

This would not be a pleasant interview. Still, it was not as though her father ever truly punished her for anything. No, he would simply express his disapproval, and disappointing him felt worse than any punishment.

And if a quiet voice inside her said that it was unfair, after all she had done to save Longbourn, she silenced it firmly. Her father hated to be reminded that it was her work, her blood, and her Talent that kept Longbourn flourishing.

The library door was closed, and she gave only a perfunctory knock before entering.

Her father sat in his favorite leather winged armchair, his feet up on the ottoman, his head leaning back with his eyes closed. He balanced an almost empty brandy glass between his fingers.

"Ah, Lizzy," he said without opening his eyes. "That was most unpleasant. Your friend Darcy must be a powerful Talent. It has been decades since I have felt such pain in the presence of another Talent. I am half-convinced that all my skin has been reduced to ash."

"Good heavens! Is it better now that he has left?"

"It is only the memory of it now. That, and the oh-so-pleasant reminder that another Talent can ruin my day by merely walking in the door." He opened his eyes and drained the dregs of his glass, setting it down none too gently. "But how was I to know you had made such an astonishing conquest? Who will be the next to fall at your feet?" His voice was mocking.

"What do you mean?" she asked carefully. Where was his anger over her use of magic?

"Why, Mr. Darcy, naturally. You do not know why he subjected himself to the torment of calling on me?"

"I cannot begin to guess." She tried to match his amused tone, masking her apprehension.

"To ask for your hand in marriage! The poor fellow seems not to realize that you dislike him. Or perhaps he simply did not care about that. Now, have I surprised you?"

Darcy wanted to marry her? Impossible!

Except for how he had cupped her cheek so tenderly and spoke of how miraculous her magic was. Something seemed to be melting in her chest. "How... How did you respond?"

He snorted. "I said no, of course. Under normal circumstances, he is not the sort of man I could easily refuse anything, but we need you here. And I will not allow you to be used as a magical broodmare."

"Papa!" She was almost as shocked by his unexpected crudity as by the utterly astonishing news.

He pushed himself to his feet. "That is what he wants, you must know. Do you truly believe he fell so madly in love with you in a few weeks that he simply must make you his bride?"

"Until this moment I did not know he thought of me at all, much less as a possible wife. He could easily find a woman with far more dowry and better connections." Elizabeth's cheeks burned. Darcy's opinion of her seemed to have improved since his early disdain, but to want to marry her? Or perhaps her father was right, and he did not truly care for her, only for her ability to bear mage children. After all, his behavior towards her had not changed until he discovered her Talent.

Her throat tightened. That must have been the only reason he had been kind to her. Why did she want so badly to believe it was something more?

He shook his finger at her. "But not one with your Talent. You are precisely the sort of woman they want for breeding new Talents, regardless of the cost to you." He stopped abruptly and studied her. "I was too off-balance to pay attention, but he said your Talent did not repel him. Is that true? That you can tolerate his presence without pain?"

Now it came, the part about her display of her Talent. "I feel nothing beyond a mild annoyance with his proud behavior," she said lightly. "But then, I have never had a reaction to Sir Edmund Langdon or any other landowner. Even Jane feels repulsion more than I do. Darcy's presence did not trouble me at all."

"No wonder he was so eager to snap you up." Her father rubbed his forehead. "Well, he will have to live with disappointment. But let us keep this quiet, or we will have your mother insisting that you accept him for his fortune."

"I would not want that." But her heart was still fluttering to think that he wanted to marry her.

Elizabeth's agitation and distraction had not left her by dinnertime, and the meal was clearly not destined to be a peaceful one. Her mother flew into the room waving a piece of paper. "Oh, he is gone, he is gone! And it is all your fault, Mr. Bennet!"

Mr. Bennet did not even trouble himself to look at her as he unfolded his napkin. "Have I murdered someone, my dear? I had not noticed." His expression, though, held more concern than was his wont. Was he wondering if she might be referring to Darcy?

It had been the first thing that jumped to Elizabeth's mind as well.

"Oh, do not be ridiculous! It is Mr. Bingley!" wailed his wife. "Mrs. Long writes that he has gone away to London. He called on you just this morning, Mr. Bennet. You should have forced him to offer for our Jane!"

Her father's shoulders relaxed infinitesimally. "His friend Darcy was there, and that proud fellow would never have permitted it. Jane will simply have to do without him." His good humor appeared to be restored.

"But he is the first gentleman Jane has ever been willing to consider! Whatever shall we do if she never agrees to marry?"

Jane pushed back her chair. "If I never marry, then Longbourn will go to Lizzy's eldest child, as well it should!" She ran from the room.

Stunned, Elizabeth looked at her father, but he would not meet her eyes. "Pray excuse me," she said. "I believe I will join Jane."

Picking up her skirts, she hurried to the stairs. The door to their bedroom was closed, something Jane rarely did. Her poor sister! This was so unlike her. She must be beyond disappointed.

Elizabeth let herself in quietly.

Jane was curled up on the window seat, her arms wrapped around her knees, staring out at the oak tree dressed in its autumnal russet leaves. "I am sorry I made a scene," she said flatly without turning around. "Pray tell Mama that I will be down to apologize soon."

Elizabeth pulled over a small chair. "It is very upsetting about Mr. Bingley, but I would not take Mrs. Long's word for it. I expect we will see him back very soon." Unless her father's refusal of Mr. Darcy's suit stood in the way.

"Oh, do not give me false hope! After losing James, I was resigned to never marrying. I wish I had never met Mr. Bingley. It hurts so much when hope dies."

Elizabeth gaped. "Never to marry? But why? You have your pick of gentlemen eager to court you." Men who could not believe their luck when they found that the sweetest, loveliest lady of their acquaintance was also the heir to a landed estate.

"To marry Longbourn, you mean." Jane dug her fingernails into the back of her hand. "You should be the heir, not I. And your children after you."

Elizabeth stroked her sister's arm. "You are the eldest. It is yours by right."

"It is my ball and chain," she cried. "It is why I can never trust a man to like me for myself. It is why I feel like an imposter every day of my life. Oh, how I wish Papa had said from the beginning that I have no Talent!"

"We cannot redo the past. And you are not lacking in Talent, just not well-bonded to the land. Your firstborn child will be fully bonded to Longbourn, and then it will not matter anymore."

Jane mopped her eyes with a handkerchief Elizabeth had made for her, through painstaking hours of planting flax, preparing, spinning, and weaving it, all so Jane could carry a small portion of Elizabeth's Talent with her. But it was not enough.

"But could not Mama at least wait an hour after Mr. Bingley left before she started complaining that I must marry some other man? He was perfect – a stranger here and rich enough not to be a fortune hunter. And I could tell he truly liked me. He was everything I ever wanted."

"I still think he will return. I saw how he looked at you." And it had been so refreshing not to hear the usual refrain from Jane about her suitors –

that she wanted to marry for affection, but how could she choose a man she liked, knowing she would have to lie to him about her Talent for years?

But at least it meant Mr. Darcy was out of the picture. Now perhaps Papa would go back to being his usual indolent, amusing self.

And if she regretted she would never have another lesson in casting illusions, or see his dark eyes focused on her, she pushed those sentiments away.

Chapter 6

TWO DAYS LATER, ELIZABETH awoke feeling restless, as she had ever since learning of Darcy's proposal to her father. Her mother's constant chatter about the loss of Mr. Bingley was too much for her, so she set off for a walk. Her feet led her back towards Netherfield, to the familiar pasture where she had first seen Darcy's illusions.

And where he had taught her to cast her own.

She crossed the stile and stood by the corner where she had created the mist. Darcy had acted so differently that day, answering her questions, taking the time to teach her, and introducing her to his lynx. He had seemed to enjoy her company – or had that only been a ploy to make her lower her guard? There had been moments during their lessons when she had felt close to him.

If it had not been for this unfortunate marriage business, she would have liked to see him again. Not only because he was her sole hope for learning more about illusions, but because she had begun to find pleasure in his company. Now he was gone forever, and she would never have the opportunity to expand her knowledge of magery.

Dispirited, she crossed the field. A patch of blackened grass pulled at her Talent. How could she have forgotten? This was where she had created the flames to frighten the charging cows. Or what she had thought to be cows. She should have fixed this long ago.

Pulling off her glove, she crouched down and set her palm in the middle of the dead area. Her Talent flowed into the ground, a coursing tingle running down her arm, sending growth and power to the roots of the burnt grass. She could sense them growing plumper, pulling water from the soil, gathering the energy to grow anew. A few new shoots began to form, ready to sprout into the air.

"Do not hurry," she told the grass. "It is almost winter. Sleep, and grow in the spring."

A subtle relaxation spread through her limbs. How different land magic felt than casting illusions! Feeding the land with her Talent always left her with a sense of fulfillment, and overusing it only led to weakness, not to death. It made things grow, helped feed and clothe people, and improved lives. In contrast, illusions did nothing more than trick the eye, and even that was temporary.

But, oh, how she wished she could do them!

And that there had been time for more lessons with Mr. Darcy. It was unlikely she would ever encounter another mage, so she could never progress beyond what she had already accomplished.

She stood, dusting off her hands and replacing her gloves. Better to think of what she had rather than what she had lost. There were sheep at Longbourn who could benefit from her Talent to help them put on weight for the winter, and, unlike Mr. Darcy's illusory sheep, she could feel their wool springing against her hand, the lanolin soaking into her skin. Her Talent could give them health, and that was worth far more than an illusion she could not feel.

She turned her feet towards the sheep paddock at Longbourn. When she reached it, the sheep pushed to get near her. Their fleeces were already well-thickened against the coming cold, but she poured her Talent into them anyway. Their pleasure in receiving her touch was her reward.

Returning home with a muddy hem but a quieter heart, she entered through the kitchen, hoping to avoid her younger sisters and mother. Retiring to her room for a rest sounded heavenly.

It was not to be. Jenny, the parlor maid, was wiping tears from her eyes as Cook said, "There, there. I'm certain he did not mean it."

"What is the matter?" Elizabeth asked. Usually it was her mother who upset the staff.

Cook scowled. "Your father is in a temper, Miss Lizzy. That Mr. Bingley came to call on him, and your father has not set foot outside his library since he left. Jenny knocked to ask if he'd like some tea, and he threw something at the door and told her to go away. In rather stronger language, if you don't mind my saying so, miss."

That did not sound like her father at all, but it was wonderful news that Bingley was back. She had been so certain of it! Still, what could have angered her father so? Bingley was always so amiable. "How odd. I hope he will apologize later," she said quickly before hurrying to the sitting room. Resting would have to wait until she found out what was wrong.

Her mother and all her sisters were there. Jane's expression was tight and unreadable. Mary, the closest to the door, looked up from her book. "Papa is cross."

"So I have heard." She tried to sound calm as she picked up her stitching.

"And he let Mr. Bingley escape again," Mrs. Bennet complained. "Now Jane will never marry!"

Jane's lips narrowed, but she said nothing. There was no stopping their mother when she was on one of her rants.

As usual, it went on and on, until it was finally interrupted by the appearance of her father, his face drawn. Leaning on the door frame, he said heavily, "So, Lizzy, it seems you will be marrying Mr. Darcy after all."

"Mr. Darcy?" cried Mrs. Bennet, bewildered. "But it is Mr. Bingley who is supposed to marry Jane!"

The handkerchief she was embroidering dropped from Elizabeth's hands. "What?" she cried. "Papa, no!"

"There is nothing to be done for it." And without another word, he shuffled back to his library. The sound of the door closing was loud in the sudden silence.

She could not believe it. What had changed? How could her father have agreed to it, and without even asking her?

She rose from her chair to follow him, but Jane stood in her way, offering an embrace which could not warm the coldness inside her.

"Lizzy, I know this is a shock, and that Mr. Darcy made a poor first impression on you, but this may prove to be a good thing. Mr. Bingley says he is a fine man, and he obviously loves you very much. I thought he must like you when he asked you to walk with him so often." Jane always tried to see the best in everything, but this time it was salt in an open wound.

"But I shall have to leave Longbourn!" Elizabeth cried. It was a disaster, the end of everything.

Jane did not pretend to misunderstand her. "We will manage, I am certain, though I will miss you terribly. You must write frequently."

Lydia pouted. "Why are you complaining? You will be the first of us to marry, and I, for one, would be happy to leave this place."

Mrs. Bennet, who had been stunned into silence, finally found her voice. "Oh, Lizzy, my dearest girl! Mr. Darcy! Oh, how grand you shall be! Think of it, a house in town, and ten thousand a year! What pin money you shall have! What fine carriages!"

Elizabeth could not bear it. "Pardon me, but I must speak to my father." She hurried from the room.

She did not make the same mistake the poor maid had; she dispensed with knocking altogether and strode into the library. "Why?" she demanded.

Open newspapers had been spread out over every available surface. Her father straightened from the paper he had been bent over. "That is the best part," he said, his words dripping with anger. "I cannot even answer you, because I have been sworn to secrecy. But I can tell you this much: there is no other choice. This thing is bigger than all of us."

"What thing?" she asked impatiently.

He poured himself a glass of brandy, his hand trembling. "That is precisely what I cannot say. It will be your future husband's happy task to answer your questions, and I wish him much joy of it."

"I cannot believe this! You would force me to marry against my wishes?"

He winced. "It is a position I never expected to be in, but the other choices are even worse."

"And you will not even tell me why?" Her temper started to rise. How could he do this? Longbourn depended upon her, and he was disposing of her as if she were a prize piece of livestock.

"That is unpleasantly true."

Her mind whirled. "Is there no other option?"

"None. At least we have the consolation that your Talents intertwine. Who would have thought it? That in this day and age, we should find another one of the rare exceptions to the law of repulsion. Queen Elizabeth and Sir Walter Raleigh. Harry Percy and Henry V. King Arthur and Guinevere, if the bards are to be believed. Darcy must have thought he had struck gold when he found you." The distaste was heavy in his voice.

Was that what Darcy had meant, the day of the charging cows, when he was so shocked to be able to touch her cheek and said that it changed everything? His manner towards her had been so different afterwards. Had he, at that first moment, already decided he would marry her?

His decision. And she had no choice. "You will truly force me to go through with this marriage? To leave Longbourn?"

His lips thinned. "I have no other option. And that is my last word."

She stared at her father, her indolent father who could never trouble himself to discipline his daughters, who laughed at Lydia's inappropriate behavior and never even scolded her. What had happened that this one time he would be immovable?

"But I cannot leave the land! It would be like cutting off my hand!"

He rubbed his forehead. "I am sorry for that, and God knows we can ill afford to lose you. But we will muddle through somehow, as I did before you came into your Talent."

"When Longbourn was perilously close to bankrupt! You need me here."

"We will retrench. Fewer servants, and your sisters will have to learn to do without so many ribbons. We will manage."

He was no longer even thinking about her.

Without a word, she turned on her heel and walked out. Past the sitting room where her mother was still babbling about Mr. Darcy's wealth, and out of the front door, stopping only to grab the bonnet and pelisse she had worn earlier.

Shock reverberated through her. How could her father have agreed to this? How could Mr. Darcy have done this without even a word to her? Clearly her consent mattered less than his selfish wishes. And she had been starting to care about him a little! Her first impression of him had been correct after all – a proud, uncaring, and dismissive man. And that was to be her future husband! A man who cared nothing for her opinion or desires.

How had he forced her father into this? It must have been a threat of some sort, but what power could Mr. Darcy possibly hold over him? The ache of betrayal churned in her stomach. She had always known that her father would not stand up for himself, but had never imagined she would pay such a price for it.

Without thought, she wandered through the dusk to her flax patch, now lying fallow for the winter. She had put in so many hours of labor here, following the instructions from her book, tilling the land herself, planting the seeds, tending the flax, and harvesting it, all to make certain her carefully crafted gloves held the most magic possible. Not just for herself, but so Jane could use Longbourn's power, the power that should be hers by right. Now Jane would be on her own.

She crouched down to pull a weed that had crept into the land she had worked so hard to make fertile. She sifted the soil through her hand, soil that felt like part of her own body. And now she would have to leave it behind. Someone else would plant this garden next spring. She would be far away, married to a man she despised.

It was unfair. Women should have the right to decide these things for themselves. Instead, her father had every legal right to force her to marry, and if she did not like it, her only choice was to flee and leave her family forever. Just as Granny had done.

She paused, arrested. Was that the answer? Granny would take her in. She knew what it was like to run away from an unwanted marriage. She had left her own family with nowhere to go, and still somehow made a new life for herself in Wales, a place where she knew no one. Granny would never let Mr. Bennet force Elizabeth's hand.

Her mind began to race. She could pack up a few small items and leave on the stagecoach. She could take some money from the locked coffer in the library for her ticket. It would not even be stealing. That was money she had earned by using her Talent to make Longbourn into a profitable estate once more. She deserved it.

But then her heart sank. Even if she took refuge in Wales, she would still lose her ties to this land, exactly as she would by marrying Darcy. It would save her the pain of marriage to a man whom she could never respect, but she would still pay the price for attracting his interest.

Longbourn was lost to her either way. At least if she married Darcy, she could come home for visits.

Perhaps she should at least hear Mr. Darcy out. She could not imagine what he could say that might justify his actions, but it was worth a try. She might even attempt to reason with him. If his answer was as unsatisfactory as she expected, she would make her way to Wales.

She dashed a tear from her eye. Only a week ago she had been thrilled to learn to cast illusions, never imagining it would cost her Longbourn. Now all her choices were unpalatable, and it was Mr. Darcy's fault.

Chapter 7

THE NEXT DAY, MR. Bennet, doubtless out of guilt, arranged for the carriage to take Elizabeth to Netherfield, so at least she would not arrive for this meeting with her petticoats six inches deep in mud. Not that it mattered. Clearly Darcy intended to marry her even if she had spent the day rolling in pig slops.

But Elizabeth's pride insisted that she must look her best, so she had taken extra time to arrange her hair and wore her best day dress. It was likely nothing to the ladies he saw every day in London, but it gave her a little extra confidence.

Darcy waited for her outside Netherfield. Elizabeth grudgingly gave him credit for that courtesy. She took a deep breath, reminding herself of the dangers of taking out her wrath on the man who might well be her future husband.

As Elizabeth stepped out of the carriage, a smile bloomed on Darcy's face. It softened her a bit, that he seemed genuinely glad to see her, but why should he not? He was getting what he wanted.

She allowed him to take her hand and kiss it, and an unexpected shiver ran up her arm. She had forgotten the strength of her reaction to his presence.

"Miss Elizabeth, it is a great pleasure to see you again." His deep voice seemed to resonate through her. "Would you care to come inside and warm yourself by the fire?"

"I thank you, but I would prefer to walk outside, if you are willing." Would he understand she needed to speak to him alone?

He seemed pleased by the suggestion and offered her his arm. After a moment's hesitation, she took it, and they began to stroll along the path leading to the gardens.

She had held a man's arm many times before, but it never felt this intimate. Suddenly she remembered how he had carried her in those same arms at the temple folly, and she grew hot all over.

She gathered her courage. "Mr. Darcy, I must appeal to you for assistance regarding certain questions which have arisen."

"About the wedding or about illusion casting?" He sounded amused.

How dare he act as if this were a joke? But she swallowed down her reflexive anger. "I do have questions about illusions, but at present I wish to know what Mr. Bingley told my father that led him to change his mind. He says he is sworn to secrecy, and I must ask you why neither he nor I have any choice in this matter." She struggled to keep her voice even.

His smile died. "That is indeed something which has been kept a close secret. The short answer is that I have been given a mission, a crucial one, that may end our war with France, and if you are my wife, my chances of success will be significantly higher."

The very idea was ridiculous, and how dare he try to make himself look heroic by comparing himself to the soldiers who were suffering so terribly in the war? Shocked, she dropped his arm and rubbed her hands together, as if to wash the contact off. "They would never ask a landed gentleman to take on a military mission."

He looked down at where her gloved hand had rested on his forearm, frowning. "Under normal circumstances, no, but they need someone who can cast illusions. I am not an ideal candidate, given my limited abilities, but I am the best they have."

She hated false modesty. "Is there a problem with your illusions?"

He rubbed his forehead. "My ability to draw energy from the air is weak. It requires years of study, and I was trained instead to use my landed Talent. I struggle to cast illusions when I am away from my home. That is why I was sent here, far from Pemberley, to practice the art of casting without the use of my earth magic. In France, I will be even weaker, and my skills may prove inadequate to our needs."

She scuffed her feet on the gravel path because childish behavior was safer than snapping at him. "This is interesting, but I fail to see what it has to do with me, or why your marital status matters."

"Do you know the story of Lord Howard of Effingham at the Spanish Armada, how he used his Talent to change the winds, causing the Spaniards to be driven against the shore where Drake could destroy them?"

"Every schoolchild does," Elizabeth sniffed.

"Lord Howard was a landed Talent, not a mage. His abilities should have been useless aboard a ship in the Channel, and he had never been able to control the wind. But his Talent could entwine with that of his wife, a mage who was safely on his estate. That meant he could draw on the power of his land through her, as well as her ability to control the wind. Their marriage saved England that day." He looked at her expectantly.

"You believe you could draw on your land magic through me?" It sounded ridiculously farfetched.

"There have been several cases through history where that has been the case, when a married couple could entwine their powers."

She chewed her lip. The part of her that loved learning magic was fascinated by the idea, but to have to marry him? Perhaps there was a way out. "Why marriage, though? Could I not simply travel to Pemberley and you could draw your land magic through me without that? I cannot imagine a few lines said in church make a difference to how your Talent operates."

He gazed off into the distance. "If you wish me to answer that, you will have to forgive me for discussing an inappropriate matter."

"Very well."

"It requires a blood connection. When a woman with Talent conceives a child, it creates a bond permitting the father to reach out through the baby and touch his wife's magic ability. It is rarely used, since ordinarily it would activate the repulsion between the two Talents. But you are the exception, the woman whose magic entwines with mine instead of repelling it. If you were at Pemberley and carrying my child, I would be able to draw on both your magic and my bond to Pemberley, even if I am in France. And that could be the difference between success and failure."

The idea of carrying his child burned inside her, making her cheeks hot. "Or so you believe, and you are willing to overturn my existence and bring a new life into the world, based solely on something that may have happened hundreds of years ago."

His expression turned somber. "It is very nearly our only hope."

She had no patience for dramatics. "Our only hope? This one mission? Tell me why this is so important, and why my father was deeply upset by what Mr. Bingley told him."

He winced. "You are perceptive. I can guess what they said, but I must warn you, it is very disturbing, and you may be sorry you learned it."

"I dislike being left in ignorance." And it was about time *he* learned that.

He drew in a deep breath and exhaled it slowly. "Perhaps you would like to sit on the bench while I explain this."

"I am not prone to fainting, despite what you saw the other day."

A shadow crossed his face. "It will make me more comfortable, because it will allow me to pace and tear my hair." His words were light, but the tone was heavy, and lines of tension pulled at his face. Could the great Mr. Darcy actually be alarmed by something?

She felt an odd touch of sympathy. "We cannot have that," she said with mock severity. "I will not make an enemy of your valet by permitting you to disarrange your hair."

He seemed relieved by her teasing. "I bow to your wisdom, and promise to do my best to avoid hair tearing."

"I thank you." She lowered herself onto the bench and looked at him expectantly.

"Very few people know what I am about to tell you." He took a deep breath. "The war is going badly. Disastrously, in fact. Have you heard about the ships that never returned to port?"

"Yes, the newspapers said they were lost in a giant storm."

"The truth is that they were attacked by sea serpents, and a great many more ships have disappeared than the public knows. Navy and merchant ships alike."

"Sea serpents do not attack ships, or anything else! They are peaceable creatures who help sailors in need."

"Until now, that has been true. Now they attack, but only British ships. They spare all others. But that is not the worst of it. You have heard of the massacre at Salamanca?"

"Where the French troops went berserk after winning the battle and slaughtered the English troops who had surrendered? It is shocking, appalling."

He took a deep breath. "The French did not go berserk. Indeed, they were losing badly, until they retreated and sent out three dragons who killed every living soul on the field."

How could he say such a thing about that great tragedy? "That is ridiculous!" she cried. "Dragons are extinct." She had grieved it as a child, that she would never meet any of the dragons from her beloved storybooks. Dragons who went on quests with their companions and strove for justice, not murdering soldiers in battle.

"In Britain, yes, but so are lynxes." He paused to take a breath. "We have long suspected there might still be colonies of dragons hiding in the Alps and the Carpathian Mountains. There have been a few sightings over the centuries, though no proof. But they left humans alone, so no one worried about them. And now they are apparently fighting for Napoleon and massacring Englishmen. They are impervious to all our weapons, and our armies are helpless against dragon fire and talons."

Real dragons, still alive? But then the horror of it hit her. All those soldiers, lost forever. "How could this happen?"

"No one knows. Our spies in the French court say that the beasts are under Napoleon's personal control, that they will take orders from no other. How Napoleon has managed this is beyond our knowledge."

"This is... I do not know what to say." No wonder her father had looked so devastated.

"We no longer have any chance of winning this war, or even achieving a stalemate. Our fleet is useless because of the sea serpents, and our soldiers cannot take the field for fear of dragons. Once Napoleon finishes with his campaign in Austria, we will fall under his yoke like the rest of Europe." He took a deep breath. "Being conquered will be bad enough, but it is nothing to the idea of dragons let loose to rampage through our country."

She pressed her hand to her mouth, feeling ill. "Is there no hope, then?"

"Not while Napoleon lives, since he controls the beasts. And that is where my mission comes in."

Could he possibly mean what she thought? "You are to... kill Napoleon?"

His mouth twisted. "Not I. I am to cast illusions which will allow the assassins to get close enough to do their work. He is very well guarded, and none of the others managed to get near him. This is our best chance, but too much relies on my relatively weak illusion casting. I need all the help I can get."

There was nothing she could say. Even without dragon attacks, Napoleon's depredations had destroyed so many lives. She had been only a child when the wars started, and they had hung over Britain like a storm cloud ever since. The face of James Lucas flashed before her, the childhood playmate who had become so much more to her sister Jane just before he got his long-awaited commission, and who had been the only person outside the Bennet family who knew the truth of her Talent. He had been killed only a few months later, and Jane had never fully recovered.

Now she could help stop the war, to save lives across England and the Continent. To make sure no other families would suffer that same loss that Jane and the Lucas family had. How could she put her attachment to Longbourn ahead of England's safety? "Then I suppose I must marry you," she said, her mouth tasting of ashes.

"I am very glad of it," he said gravely.

Somehow she had to lighten the moment before she burst into tears. "At least it saves me the trouble of running off."

With a look of shock, Darcy said, "Tell me you were not considering that."

"Mr. Darcy, if we are to be wed, then it is time for you to learn that I do not enjoy being told what to do or having my choices taken away." Asperity tinged her voice.

"Think of the danger you would be in!"

She shrugged. "Less than you might expect. My great-grandmother would take me in. She fled a forced marriage and faked her own death to stop pursuit."

He paused, clearly trying to maintain a degree of calm. "Your great-grandmother is still alive?"

"She is a spry ninety-three, and as near as I can tell, intends to outlive us all."

"Remarkable. I only knew one of my grandparents, and she died when I was still a child."

And apparently that was all he intended to say about the fact that she had considered running off rather than to marry him. Well, he was getting his way, so why should he care what it cost her?

So much for Darcy's hopes that Elizabeth might find some pleasure in marrying him.

He had not noticed her red-rimmed eyes when she first arrived, but he could hardly miss her glum countenance as she asked him about his mission. She had taken the ill tidings of the war well; she had not cried or railed against fate.

But there was no way to interpret her quiet, "Then I suppose I must marry you," as sounding anything but defeated.

His disappointment cut deep. True, it would make no difference in the outcome, but he wanted her to be happy about it. He had thought she liked him, at least a little.

He should have known it was too good to be true. "I will do my best to be a good husband to you," he said, hoping it might earn a warm look.

She looked up at him, startled, as if she had forgotten he was there. "Thank you." She must have seen something in his face, for she added, "It is not you. It is simply that I do not wish to leave Longbourn, and I dislike being forced into this."

That struck home. "I cannot blame you for that. I had no choice about my first marriage, and I hated that."

Her head shot up. "You were married before?"

"When I was eighteen. It was a typical mage marriage. Because of the repulsion, I barely knew her, and we could not live together. She died two years later, giving birth to a child who lived only a few days."

"I am sorry to hear it." And she sounded as if she meant it.

He did not want to think about it. He had not truly grieved for Anne. How could he, when she was essentially a stranger to him? But the loss of his son, whom he had held in his arms, still stabbed at him. And now, if he had another child with Elizabeth, he would never meet them.

"And that you were forced into such a marriage," she added.

He shrugged. "It was thought we would produce children with Talent, and there was great need for them."

"To think I once believed mages were the fortunate few," she said dryly.

"In some ways we are." That gave him an idea. "Would you like another lesson in illusion casting?"

She stilled. "Why? Will it help you with your mission?"

Did she think that was all he cared about? "No, but you seem to enjoy them, and it is something I can do for you."

She looked surprised, but not displeased. "In that case, I accept. More mist?"

"I thought we might try something new today. A stone, perhaps. Simple, but solid."

"How very exciting," she said wryly, but he could tell she was amused.

It was a relief to see her in better spirits after successfully producing a credible illusion of a river pebble. He even made her smile briefly by casting an illusory sleeping hedgehog in her hands, giving him hope they might part on somewhat better terms.

As she was about to climb into the carriage, she said, "My father tells me you are handling all the arrangements for the wedding."

"I hoped it would simplify matters."

With a dry smile, she said, "It would be easier to plan if I knew when the wedding would be."

"Your father did not tell you?" He mentally added "coward" to his list of descriptors for Mr. Bennet.

"No, he claimed not to know." Her ironic tone suggested she now understood that was not true.

He braced himself. "It is to be on Friday, and we will leave for Pemberley immediately afterwards."

"This Friday?" She sounded disbelieving.

"Yes."

"Three days from now." Her voice was ominous, like a volcano about to erupt.

"When the War Office heard, they wanted an immediate wedding that very day." He did not mention that the express they had sent had instructed him to drag her to the altar if necessary. There were some orders he was not willing to follow.

"I do not care if the High King of Faerie decreed it! I need more time."

Darcy winced. "Bingley already stood up to them, saying no lady could accept less than a week to prepare for her wedding, and they compromised on four days. One of those has passed, as your father did not tell you." He felt like a child making excuses.

"Three days. Three days to say farewell to everyone and everything I have known all my life." Her voice shook, fury dripping from every word.

"I wish it could be otherwise, but time is of the essence. My mission takes place as soon as Napoleon returns to Paris from the war in Austria, and we do not know whether that will be in two months or a year."

She glared at him, her delicate hands clenched into fists. "And I am nothing more than a weapon in your hand, to be used and discarded at will." Spinning on her heel, she stormed down the lane towards Longbourn, ignoring the waiting carriage.

Her words stung. Bitterly.

He hurried after her. "Elizabeth, I am very sorry. I wish you could have more time."

She ignored him, her shoes stirring up angry piles of dust with each outraged step.

He tried again. "Is there anything I can do to make this easier for you?"

She looked at him then, her eyes sparkling with anger. "You can leave me alone." She spat out each word. "If I only have three days of freedom from you, I want to make the most of them."

He stopped in his tracks and watched her hurry away. How he hated to let her go in this state! But he could not force his company on her against her will.

Even if it hurt.

Apparently this was to be another affectionless marriage after all.

There was no point remaining in the middle of the lane, with the coachman behind him no doubt snickering over his humiliation. Darcy lifted his foot to turn back, but encountered a surprising resistance.

He looked down to discover he was standing three inches deep in mud on the otherwise perfectly dry road.

His lips twisted in a reluctant smile. He could not help but admire Elizabeth's spirit in striking back at him in this symbolic way, using her landed Talent to draw water to the surface and make mud. It bespoke a finer control than he would have expected.

She could have tried to injure him, or thrown flames at him, as she had at the cows. Instead she had only made his boots muddy. Perhaps it was a sign she might forgive him someday.

But forgiveness took time, and that was one thing he did not have.

Chapter 8

Elizabeth dashed burning tears from her eyes as she sped down the lane. Three days! Three days until she was ripped from the land, her family, and her home. How was she to bear it?

The power of the earth rose to meet her as she approached Longbourn. Would she never know this joyous rush of connection again?

She could not face her family like this, so she detoured to her favorite oak grove. She threw herself down on the grassy slope, heedless of the stains that could ruin her dress, and dug her fingertips into the dirt.

The land's power thrummed through her, from the deep, solid roots of the trees around her and the shallow carpet of grass, from the richness of the soil and the potential for life contained in it. She felt a squirrel skittering up an oak branch and the mice nesting in the bushes nearby, preparing their home for the coming winter.

All was as it should be in the earth. It was only inside Elizabeth that everything was wrong. She sobbed, letting her tears soak into the soil, giving it life and vitality while she still could.

Then the earth told her of an approaching presence, and she stiffened. If Darcy had followed her here, she would strangle him, even if it meant all England would be ravaged by dragons. But the land soothed her, telling her this creature walked on four feet, not two, and she relaxed.

Still, the land did not recognize the animal, so Elizabeth picked up her head to look. There, between two ancient oaks, sat Darcy's lynx. At least she assumed it was his lynx, not some other one, since it sat there patiently awaiting her notice instead of attacking her.

She told him, "If your master is behind you, tell him to go away."

The big cat's only response was a slow blink of its deep-set eyes. He did not understand her words.

It did not matter. Nothing mattered. She let her head sink back onto the ground and closed her eyes. Tears began to leak out again, but slowly, rather than in great wracking sobs.

The grass rustled beneath soft footpads as the lynx drew closer. Well, if he intended to eat her, her life felt like no great loss at the moment.

Then she felt a pressure against her side. Not the pressure of sharp teeth, but a warm body leaning against her, fur covering sleek, powerful muscle. And then it began to vibrate, and a rumbling filled the air.

Could the lynx possibly be purring?

She raised her head again and found herself gazing directly into the lynx's eyes, only inches away. Slowly the cat lowered its massive head to rest on Elizabeth's arm, and the rattling of its purr traveled up her bones into her shoulder.

It was trying to comfort her. Somewhere, in the dark recesses of its animal brain, it had recognized her distress and tried to help. Why it had done so was a question beyond her ability to answer. Not on Darcy's orders, that was for certain; familiars did not take detailed instructions, or even most general ones sometimes. This astonishing behavior must have come from the lynx itself.

"Good kitty," she said dully. "It is not your fault that your horrid master is forcing me into this." It was a relief to say the words, to let its wild animal warmth sink into her body.

A small, nagging voice in her brain reminded her that it was not entirely Darcy's fault, either. He was as much adrift in this tide as she was, subject to the needs of king and country. But he had chosen to accept his part, and she had been forced into hers.

If he had come to her in the beginning, explained his position, and asked for her help, would she have consented? Would she have been willing to sacrifice her ties to Longbourn in order to save England from dragonfire? She hoped she would have.

No, as much as she would like to blame him for everything, Darcy's failings were in his manners and his approach, not an essential evil in his character. He had no desire to cause her pain. She could not blame him for placing England's safety over her happiness.

Still, he definitely needed to learn to include her in decisions.

She sat up and rubbed her hands into the lynx's fur. Somehow all her fear of the beast was gone. "Thank you," she whispered, scratching him beneath the tufted ear.

He truly was a magnificent beast. And at least she would have one friend of a sort in her new home.

She looked down at herself and chuckled. Her best dress was grass-stained and wrinkled. Traces of dirt were ground into her gloves. Her tear-stained face must be filthy, too. If she were to arrive at Longbourn with the lynx by her side, they might take her for a wild animal, too.

"Rrawrr," she said, and the lynx's inquisitive look made her laugh.

Darcy could not bear to leave matters as they were. Elizabeth might never forgive him, but he had to try.

It would be much easier if he could call on her at Longbourn. But if he did, he would be in so much pain from Mr. Bennet's proximity that he would be certain to say the wrong thing. Not to mention that Mr. Bennet would be within his rights to throw him off his land for such encroaching behavior.

Which left writing her a letter. He did his best and even humbled himself by showing his final draft to Bingley for his advice. Bingley always knew what to say to women.

Bingley whistled as he read it. "The War Office will not be happy, old chap."

"The War Office be damned. They cannot drag me to the altar. And do not dare tell me that time is of the essence, or that the mission must come first."

"I wouldn't think of it. Should I deliver this for you?"

"Thank you. She might not tear it up without reading it then. She likes you, at least." He did not at all enjoy the envy he felt over that.

"Happy to do it. Anything for another excuse to see my own Miss Bennet!"

Darcy said slowly, "Bingley, this is none of my affair, but if you have serious intentions towards Miss Bennet, you might wish to act on them quickly. Once word reaches London of Elizabeth's ability to cast illusions, the King's Mage will insist on marrying her sisters off to other Talents, including Miss Bennet. Then it would be too late for you."

Bingley's eyes widened. "I had not thought of that. Thanks for the warning, old man."

"You and Miss Bennet deserve to be happy." Someone should have a loving marriage, even if he could not.

Now all Darcy could do was wait.

Over an hour had passed by the time Elizabeth had washed her face, changed her dress, combed the stray sticks and leaves out of her hair, and asked Jane to help her put it up again in something resembling a civilized manner.

"It would be easier if I were a lynx," she told Jane. "A few licks to keep my fur in order, and no one to complain if my face is dirty." And no forced marriages, either.

"Lynxes are extinct, and I prefer you alive," Jane said. "Besides, you would not enjoy taking your meat uncooked."

"Less extinct than you might think, but I imagine you are correct about meals still on the hoof," Elizabeth replied. There were a few humans she would not mind tearing to shreds with her claws, though.

When she made her way downstairs, her mother was ready to pounce. "What did Mr. Darcy say about your wedding?" Mrs. Bennet demanded. "We need to make plans."

Elizabeth gritted her teeth. "He has matters all in hand. The wedding is to be Friday."

"Next Friday?" Mrs. Bennet squawked. "That is much too soon! We cannot possibly be ready so quickly."

"This Friday, in fact. In three days' time. And we shall be off to Derbyshire that very day." It was much more amusing to tell her mother the news than it had been to hear it herself.

"Impossible! It cannot be done! Oh, you have no compassion for my poor nerves! That is not even enough time to prepare a dress for you. We shall be humiliated, humiliated if you appear in an old dress. What if Mr. Darcy refuses to marry you?" Mrs. Bennet fanned herself frantically.

"Mr. Darcy would marry me if I appeared in my oldest shift with my hair tangled and matted," said Elizabeth. Normally she would handle her mother more delicately, but today she could not bring herself to care about anyone's nerves.

The fan went even faster. "Well, it is a fine thing for him to be so desperately in love with you, but what of the rest of us? We shall look shabby. And how is Mr. Bingley to have time to fall in love with Jane if Mr. Darcy leaves so quickly?"

Jane winced and looked away.

There was no point in trying to interrupt her mother when she was working herself into a full attack of nerves, especially when Elizabeth had provoked it herself, but she felt sorry for her sister. Still, all she could do was to sit down to work on new gloves for Jane. If she only had three days to finish them, she had a great deal of work to do.

Finally Mrs. Bennet, in typical fashion, announced she was taking to her bed. Jane followed to offer soothing compresses, leaving Elizabeth to the silence of her own thoughts.

After a time, Jane came downstairs again. "She is asleep at last."

"How much laudanum did it take this time?" asked Elizabeth.

"Lizzy, I do not understand what has come over you today. It is as if you wish to say shocking things." This was as close to a reproach as Jane would ever make, and it hurt.

Perhaps pretending to be a lynx was not the best strategy. "Forgive me, Jane. It was a shock to learn how quickly I must leave all of you, but that is no excuse."

Jane reached over to put her arm around Elizabeth's shoulder. "Oh, dearest Lizzy, I will miss you so much. I hope you will write to me very often."

"I will rely on you to do so as well, and you must visit me when you are able."

And thus it was that both sisters had tears in their eyes when Mr. Bingley arrived.

He kindly pretended not to notice anything was amiss. Elizabeth was sure her face must be blotchy and her eyes red. Jane, naturally, only looked more beautiful when she wept, tears making her eyes luminous. It was unfair to ordinary women, as Elizabeth was fond of pointing out.

After they exchanged the usual pleasantries, Bingley said, "Miss Elizabeth, Darcy entrusted me with a letter to deliver to your hand. I dearly hope you will read it rather than tearing it to shreds or burning it unread. He worked hard on it." His look was so drolly charming it was impossible to resist him.

Jane's brows drew together. "Oh, Lizzy, you did not quarrel with Mr. Darcy, did you?"

"I am afraid I did, but I will read his letter." It was only polite, after all.

With a look of profound relief, Bingley gave her the letter.

Elizabeth studied the envelope, with her name written in a close hand. Did it contain an apology or an admonishment? "Pray excuse me," she said.

It was improper to leave Bingley and Jane alone together, but once again she could not bring herself to care. After all, she would be gone in three days. Leaving the sitting room door open, she went out to her favorite alcove in the garden, where she could rest her feet on her beloved earth.

Gathering her courage, she opened the envelope. More of the same neat, even handwriting filled a sheet of letter paper. It was easier to focus on that than the actual words, but she forced herself to read.

It opened with an apology for causing her pain and for failing to break the news more gently, and continued to say that her sentiments were perfectly natural and understandable.

A sigh of relief tore through her. She had worried about losing his good opinion, but his letter was all generosity. More, perhaps, than she deserved. The second half of the letter contained a greater surprise.

> *I have reflected on your words and all that you have been asked to sacrifice for the sake of our efforts, and have concluded that I must in honor respond to your needs. I intend to inform the War Office that our nuptials will be delayed for a week. They will not be pleased, but they cannot force me to the altar, and you deserve this consideration. I remain most sincerely your servant, Fitzwilliam Darcy.*

> *Postscript - Pray tell Cerridwen that the cook at Pemberley makes delicious plum cake. FD*

She blinked back tears at the unexpectedly lighthearted closing. Had she not already shed enough of those today? She was turning into a veritable watering pot.

Another week. It was an enormous concession, that much she knew. And it sounded both wonderful and terrible. Another week on the land she loved, and another week of being torn by anger and grief over losing her connection to it. Another week of ready tears for all that she was losing, and of quarreling with those she loved because she was so distraught over leaving them.

Perhaps a clean break was better. If Darcy's mission failed, and England suffered for it, she would always wonder if that week might have made a difference.

With new resolve, she folded the letter and rose to her feet. It would be best to give her answer to Bingley verbally. She did not trust herself to put words to paper at this point.

On returning to the house, she stopped short in front of the sitting room door at the sight of Bingley on one knee in front of Jane.

Finally something good was coming out of this terrible day. With a new lightness in her heart, she tiptoed away to the dining room. There she watched as the hands of the mantle clock moved past ten minutes before returning, making as much noise as reasonably possible.

Her sister and Bingley were now standing together over the hearth, as if engaged in earnest conversation, but their faces, as they hastily turned round and moved away from each other, told it all.

"Oh, Lizzy, we are engaged! 'Tis too much, by far too much! I do not deserve it." Jane cried.

"Dearest Jane, I can think of no one who deserves happiness more than you, and I daresay Mr. Bingley agrees with me."

"I do indeed," said that gentleman, with a foolish smile.

"Oh, I must go instantly to my mother!" Jane cried. "I would not on any account allow her to hear it from anyone but myself. How shall I bear such happiness?" She hastened away, leaving Elizabeth to entertain Mr. Bingley.

Elizabeth hoped her mother's laudanum would wear off quickly. In the meantime, she assured Mr. Bingley of her delight at their engagement.

Bingley said all in a rush, "I am glad you are so happy about Jane and me. I had intended to wait, to give her more time to know me, but then I thought it might be easier for you to leave if you knew her future is secure."

"You are most generous. And indeed I do feel better, knowing that Jane will be happy," she said sincerely.

"Good," he said, smiling boyishly.

She could not avoid her business forever, though, even in the face of this good news. "Mr. Bingley, may I ask you to give a message to Mr. Darcy?"

"It would be my honor." He looked as hopeful as a puppy.

"Pray tell him I prefer to stay with the original date for the wedding."

"Oh, thank God! The War Office would have me killed otherwise."

Puzzled, she asked, "Why would they kill *you*?"

He grinned. "Because they cannot afford to kill Darcy, and I am the nearest target."

"It would not do for you to die now that you are engaged to Jane, so that is one more reason not to change the date," she teased.

"Indeed not!" Then his delighted expression suddenly turned sober. "I hope you can find some happiness with Darcy, too. He has not been himself at all since the massacre at Salamanca, but he truly is a good man." He hesitated. "Just these last few days, I have started to see something of the old Darcy again, and I know you are to thank for that."

The last of her pleasure drained away. No doubt Darcy had good qualities, but she was the one being torn from her land bonds and her family, and she had little sympathy to spare for him. But Bingley was her future brother, so she only said, "I imagine we will learn to rub along together well enough. You and Jane, meanwhile, will be the happiest couple in the world; of that I have no doubt."

"I am certainly the happiest of men!" He flushed a little, and then asked, "Is there any other message for Darcy?"

She thought for a moment. Some kind of acknowledgment might ease this tension. "I thank him for his letter. And pray tell him his lynx came to see me and was very kind. You know about his lynx, do you not?"

"Yes. It is not surprising he came to you. Darcy told me he licked you."

Puzzled, she asked, "What has that to do with it?"

"It is a way familiars mark that they have taken a family member under their protection. In the olden days, when familiars were more common, it was the equivalent of a marriage ceremony."

"Where did you learn that?" Perhaps there was another book she should read.

"Oh, my head is packed with nonsense like that. Before my father died and I inherited, I worked for two years in the King's Mage's library, cataloging and compiling records on the history of magic. That is how I met Darcy."

Elizabeth's jaw dropped. "You worked for the King's Mage?" Bingley actually knew the secretive, powerful Talent who protected King and country?

"Not for her directly. The library belongs to the Crown. I hardly ever saw her, in fact. But that is why they sent me here with Darcy, so that I could answer any questions that arose. I have all the book knowledge about illusions, and he has the ability."

"That makes sense." She paused. "Are you going to France with him, too?" She hoped not, for Jane's sake.

He laughed. "Not me. It will be too late for questions then."

A thought came to her. "Tell me, are there any books in Arabic in that library?"

"Not to my knowledge. French, German, Italian, Spanish, Greek, Latin, a smattering of Portuguese, but no Arabic. I had forgotten you know the language."

"I was merely curious." And apparently Darcy had not mentioned her books to Bingley. "About the lynx. Did Mr. Darcy know what it meant when he licked me?" She remembered his shocked look when it happened.

"He did."

"I wonder if that was why he decided to marry me."

Bingley shook his head. "No, he made up his mind the first time he saw your Talent. He was surprised that his familiar knew already, though."

Heat surged inside Elizabeth. Darcy had planned to marry her even that first day when he touched her cheek and said it did not matter if it was improper. It would not have been if they were engaged, and apparently they already had been in his mind.

Chapter 9

THIS TIME WHEN ELIZABETH arrived at Netherfield, Darcy was not waiting on the steps, but she could see him strolling through the rose garden with two ladies. He seemed to be watching for her, though, immediately turning towards her carriage as it came down the lane.

She had not expected to see him today. Indeed, she had hoped not to, but when she received a note telling her his mother had come to Netherfield especially to meet her, she felt there was little choice. At least this call could be of short duration, and there would be time on her way home to stop at the Hadids to bid them farewell. The thought left a lump in her throat.

But first she had to meet her soon-to-be mother-in-law.

Darcy approached her more slowly than his usual brisk stride, setting his pace to his companions. One was an elegant, diminutive lady who could not be past her mid-thirties, surely too young to have a son Darcy's age. The second was a veiled woman dressed in the Indian manner, heavily draped in folds of burgundy fabric embroidered with gold and silver. Without a clear view of her face, Elizabeth could not guess at her age, but her movements suggested she was older. A dusky-skinned man in an embroidered tunic followed behind her.

Surely Darcy would have mentioned it if his mother was from India. But no, she could not be; she was a Fitzwilliam by birth. Perhaps these were other acquaintances, and Lady Anne Darcy had remained inside.

Elizabeth revised her anticipation of this gathering upwards. She had seen people from India on the streets of London and even spoken to them in the shops of Cheapside, but meeting a fine Indian lady would be a novel experience. It might even make up for dealing with Darcy's mother.

Darcy's smile on greeting her seemed perfunctory, and his eyes were narrowed, but his words to her were all courtesy. Was it possible he was not best pleased by his mother's arrival?

"Thank you for sending the carriage. It was most comfortable," she said.

"It was the least I could do, since we could not call on you at Longbourn." Yes, he was definitely not happy. "Mother, may I present my betrothed, Miss Elizabeth Bennet? Elizabeth, this is Lady Anne Darcy."

That young-looking Englishwoman was his mother? She must have been practically a child when he was born. She could easily be his older sister.

Lady Anne stepped forward. "It is a great pleasure to meet my future daughter. Thank you for joining us."

"It is an honor, Lady Anne."

Lady Anne indicated the Indian woman. "This is Rana Akshaya, who has come all the way from India to learn about the Talents of England."

Rana Akshaya murmured something inaudible to her manservant, who said in a lightly accented voice, "The Great Rana asks me to express her delight in making your acquaintance, and her apologies for interrupting this family occasion. Lady Anne was kind enough to invite her to see more of the English countryside on this journey. The Great Rana is unaccustomed to being in such a large city as London, and has been longing for fresh air."

A shadow crossed over her. Elizabeth had only a moment's mental warning to brace herself before Cerridwen glided down and landed on her shoulder. Oh, dear, this was going to make an interesting impression on her future mother-in-law! But there was no arguing with Cerridwen.

Why had the falcon come? Perhaps the shiny metallic embroidery on Rana Akshaya's clothing had attracted her.

Lady Anne frowned. "A bird familiar? How...unusual."

How had she known that Cerridwen was bonded to Elizabeth?

"She is not a familiar, my lady, simply a falcon who has taken a strong liking to me."

Rana Akshaya pressed her hands together as if in prayer and bowed – not to Elizabeth, but to Cerridwen. Then she seemed to recognize that the others were staring at her. Once again, she murmured to her translator, who said, "The Great Rana says that in our country, falcons are revered. You are greatly blessed, Miss Bennet, that one has chosen you to be her particular friend."

"I feel fortunate, indeed. I am very fond of Cerridwen," said Elizabeth awkwardly.

Once again, the Indian woman spoke through her translator. "Cerridwen. That does not sound like an English name."

"It is Welsh, the name of the ancient Welsh goddess of magic and poetry. I first encountered Cerridwen in Wales, so I thought it suited her."

Darcy cleared his throat. "Would you care to come inside, Elizabeth?"

"I thank you." At least that would free her from the subject of Cerridwen.

Rana Akshaya's translator said, "If you have no objection, the Great Rana wishes to continue to explore the gardens and will leave you to your reunion."

"As you wish, my lady," Darcy said.

Cerridwen, with an air of displeasure, flapped her wings abruptly and took to the skies.

Elizabeth looked after the retreating Rana Akshaya regretfully, but followed Lady Anne into Netherfield and entered the now familiar Netherfield drawing room. It seemed so long ago that Mr. Bingley and his sisters had greeted her there when she arrived to care for Jane, and yet it had not even been a fortnight. Today the room was empty. Odd, given the presence of a titled guest.

"Is Miss Bingley here?" she asked Darcy quietly. "Since I failed to come inside last time I was here, I ought to pay my respects today."

Darcy gave her a dry look. "My mother asked the Bingleys to absent themselves for a time."

Elizabeth bit her tongue before she could blurt out anything about this scandalous behavior. What sort of guest asked their hosts to leave?

Lady Anne, apparently oblivious to this conversation, took the seat nearest to the tea tray. "How do you take your tea, Miss Bennet?"

"With milk, no sugar, I thank you."

Darcy turned to her. "The cake is sweetened with honey and currants."

"Lovely." Elizabeth tried to hide her surprise. He must have asked the cook to make it especially, and she had not expected such thoughtfulness from him.

Not that it mattered what she ate now. She was leaving Longbourn forever, and her connection to it would be a thing of the past. All because Darcy had entered her life.

She accepted the cup Lady Anne offered her, but her throat was suddenly too tight to take a sip.

Darcy said in an overly level voice, "I had assumed my mother traveled here to welcome you to the family, but it appears it is in her official capacity. Lady Anne is also the King's Mage."

The King's Mage? The anonymous Talent who lived to serve and protect the King was *Darcy's mother*? "Oh. I see." It came out more as a squeak than a statement.

At least it explained why Lady Anne could ask Miss Bingley to depart her own home.

"Fitzwilliam," his mother said reproachfully.

"I am sorry, Mother, but I will not lie to my future wife about this." He did not sound sorry at all.

Lady Anne sighed. "Well, the cat is out of the bag, and it is true that I must investigate this matter of your abilities. I understand you can alter my son's illusions?"

"Yes, your ladyship." At least here she was on solid ground. The King's Mage, standing right before her! And to be her mother-in-law!

"Can you cast illusions of your own?"

She dared not lie outright to the King's Mage, but she had promised Darcy not to tell anyone about his lessons. "I only started after observing Mr. Darcy doing so. It had never occurred to me to try before."

Darcy gave her a grateful look.

"What about sendings? Have you ever cast a sending?"

"No, your ladyship." She did not think her mental conversations with Cerridwen counted.

"Or affected the weather? Created a breeze or made it rain?"

Astonished by the very idea, she replied, "No, your ladyship."

Lady Anne raised her arm and, without warning, threw a sparking ball of energy directly at Elizabeth.

"Mother," Darcy snapped.

But Elizabeth had already caught the ball and tossed it back toward Lady Anne. "I used to play that with my Granny when I was a child, but that is landed magic."

Lady Anne frowned as she dismissed the energy. "I do not know who told you that, but it is the purest magery."

"It is? Fancy that," said Elizabeth lightly. How dare Lady Anne treat her this way?

"Her father is a landed Talent, and she has some ability in that regard, although her eldest sister is the heir," Darcy said.

Lady Anne was not to be distracted. "Is your mother from a family of Talents?"

"I have never heard of any." This was definitely more like an interrogation than a conversation.

"Your father's family, then. Who are his forebears? Where are they from? Do any have Talents beyond that of the land?"

Elizabeth blinked. "Not that I am aware of. There have been landed Talents in the Bennet family for many generations, and my grandmother also came from a family with some degree of land Talent." And apparently her great-grandmother had more than that, if throwing balls of light was magery, though she was not inclined to volunteer that information.

"Does your father have sisters and brothers?"

Despite the impertinence of these direct inquiries, Elizabeth attempted to answer with composure. "He is an only child."

Darcy said firmly, "That is enough questions, Mother. Elizabeth is a guest in this house."

Lady Anne's countenance shifted into a polite absence of emotion. She picked up her teacup and took an unhurried sip. "Pray forgive me, Miss Bennet, I have permitted my excitement over this discovery to overtake my manners. Finding magery in an unknown family is a matter for celebration."

Magery? Lady Anne thought she might be an actual mage, not just someone with a strange ability to cast illusions? A shiver ran down her back. She wanted, she needed to know more, but Darcy's lips were in a tight line. Perhaps he had a reason not to wish to discuss this.

She wavered. Lady Anne clearly wanted her to ask questions. Darcy, it seemed, did not. He might have forced her into this marriage, but he had at least tried to treat her with respect, and she had no reason to trust Lady Anne. Especially after that interrogation.

She made up her mind. "I know little of these things. If you would like to know more about my family history, I encourage you to ask my father." And since her father did not share her immunity to the repulsion between mages, Lady Anne would find it too painful to speak to him at length.

"I should like to meet him, as well as the rest of your family. For now, pray tell me a bit about yourself. What activities do you enjoy? Do you have particular interests?"

It seemed safest to continue to play the ignorant girl. She could always reveal more later if needed. "I play the pianoforte and sing, although I do not practice as much as I should. I enjoy needlework and reading. I fear I am rather dull!" Especially when she left out her needlework's magical nature.

Darcy said, "I find your singing most pleasing."

"How kind you are, sir!" she replied, fluttering her eyelashes as if delighted with his flattery.

Lady Anne frowned. "Did your parents provide you with opportunities to study? Had you a governess?"

"We had no governess, but those of us who wished to learn never wanted the means. We were always encouraged to read, and had any masters that were necessary."

"Do you speak any languages?"

"A little French," Elizabeth replied. What would Darcy think of her failure to mention Arabic, not to mention this deliberate attempt to appear ill-informed?

Darcy took over the conversation then, relating his first discovery of her ability when she turned his cows away, a story that was surprisingly devoid of fire and gloves stuffed with grass. His test of whether she could repeat her interference with his sheep illusion was told in great detail, with many questions from his mother, but the lessons in illusion-casting were missing.

Yes, it was clear Darcy did not trust his mother. Or was it the King's Mage that he did not trust?

The remainder of the call proceeded in the same manner, with Darcy answering most questions in her stead while she played the simple country girl. Though the tension did not return, Elizabeth was grateful when the prescribed half hour was over and she could depart.

Her relief in making her farewells ended when Lady Anne said, "If you have no objection, I should like to travel back with you to make your father's acquaintance."

Elizabeth drew in a breath. This was most irregular, but she supposed the King's Mage could break the rules of polite society if she chose. Still, she would rather keep her father out of this. "My lady, although my weak Talent is not enough to cause repulsion, my father is a landed Talent, and I believe Mr. Darcy found meeting with him to be quite unpleasant."

"That is no matter," Lady Anne said kindly. "One of the benefits of being the King's Mage is that I no longer experience nor cause repulsion."

What would be the best way to respond without revealing her own general lack of repulsion? "How can that be?" asked Elizabeth.

Lady Anne twisted one of her rings. "There is a magical artifact that is given to the King's Mage which blocks repulsion. Otherwise it would be impossible for me to coordinate other mages in our defense or to teach my replacement."

"I can see why that would be useful." But Elizabeth had no artifact, yet felt no repulsion.

Lady Anne continued, "That reminds me. Before we go, I would like to see if you can interact with one of my illusions."

"If you wish." Elizabeth had never considered the possibility. What would it mean if she could do it with any mage? Darcy had seemed so certain that it was unique to him.

A black cat appeared in the center of the room, although Elizabeth had not seen Lady Anne make a move, nor take on the stillness Darcy showed when he was casting.

"Can you affect it, Miss Bennet?" Lady Anne asked.

"I will try." Elizabeth bent down and rubbed her fingers together. "Here, kitty, kitty!"

The cat licked its paws and ignored her.

Elizabeth tugged on the power of the land, though it was harder through walls and doors, still without any result. She stepped towards the cat, but it did not appear to notice her, even when she stood right in front of it. Putting all of her power into it, she waved her hands and cried, "Shoo!"

Nothing happened. "My lady, it appears I cannot."

Lady Anne nodded, and the black cat disappeared. "Fitzwilliam, let me see her try with one of yours."

He raised an eyebrow but went still, his eyes unfocused. In the doorway, there was a fluffy, cream-colored tabby with a white ruff that reminded her of his lynx.

She rubbed her fingers again and pictured it coming towards her. "Here, kitty." The cat turned its head, lifted its tail into the air, and ambled over to sniff her hand.

It made her oddly happy. "Good kitty," she said, although she knew it could not hear. The cat rubbed its ruff against her hand, purring. She felt nothing, but was inordinately pleased anyway.

"Interesting," said Lady Anne.

Darcy coughed. "Elizabeth, I am afraid I must ask you to dismiss my illusion. I cannot."

She smiled warmly at the cat, who was twining around her legs. "I rather like it. Perhaps I should keep it."

His eyes widened. "Elizabeth! Dismiss it this instant! Now!"

Taken aback, and somewhat annoyed with him, she blew out a breath as he had taught her. Then it struck her. She had been feeling giddy.

Darcy rushed to her side and grasped her elbow, guiding her back to the chair, supporting her and clearly ready to catch her if she fell.

She sat down gratefully.

Lady Anne was already pouring tea and dropping multiple sugar lumps into it in a businesslike manner, unlike her slow and graceful gestures earlier.

Darcy waved the tea away and rang for a servant. "Elizabeth does not take sugar, only honey."

The footman opened the door and bowed.

"Honey, straight away, with no delay," Darcy ordered. The footman disappeared. Darcy brought her another slice of cake. "You can start with this while we are waiting."

She gazed at him. "Thank you for remembering. About the honey." She did not mean remembering, but could not think of the words for her gratitude that he took her preference so seriously.

"Of course. Now eat." His dark eyes were watching her closely.

"Has this happened before?" Lady Anne asked.

"The first time Elizabeth showed me her casting. I think she was hoping to impress me." Darcy again managed to tell the truth while leaving out the important part.

Elizabeth tried to help. "Mr. Darcy lectured me severely about it. I did not even realize I was using my Talent today."

"This is the first time you have completely taken over my illusion," Darcy said. "We know nothing of how that works."

Lady Anne studied him. "What was your experience of it, Fitzwilliam? We must understand this."

"The first two times, I was still giving energy to the illusion, even as Elizabeth made it behave differently. This time the energy flow stopped completely, as if the strands had been yanked away."

His mother frowned. "Interesting. I wonder what was different."

The honey arrived, and Lady Anne added several spoonfuls to a cup of tea. "At least two cups to restore you," she instructed Elizabeth.

Elizabeth sipped it obediently, the sweet warmth soothing.

A flicker of burgundy and gold in the doorway resolved itself into Rana Akshaya, gliding into the room in Elizabeth's direction. Her translator stood behind her.

"Forgive our disarray. Miss Bennet overextended herself with an illusion," Lady Anne said.

"So I see." Rana Akshaya, apparently able to speak English after all, moved closer and laid her hand on Elizabeth's cheek. "Look at me."

It did not occur to Elizabeth to disobey. As she gazed into the Indian woman's dark eyes through the veil that blurred them, sudden heat burst from the spot she touched, coursing through Elizabeth as if scouring her clean from the inside. A sense of dizzying light followed in its wake; light, followed by a great sense of well-being.

Rana Akshaya removed her hand and nodded.

Elizabeth squeezed her eyes shut and reopened them. Everything looked different. The colors were brighter, the edges sharper, and there was an odd distortion similar to what she experienced when she saw through Cerridwen's eyes. Then the sensation faded, and everything seemed normal again. Except that Elizabeth now felt powerful enough to climb a mountain.

"I thank you," she said, and her voice was strong and vibrant, too. "I do not know what you did, but I am grateful."

Rana Akshaya inclined her head. "Your falcon was concerned about you." In perfect English, without a trace of accent.

Neither Darcy nor Lady Anne reacted to this odd remark, and Elizabeth realized the Indian woman must have spoken inside her head rather than aloud. And how had she known Cerridwen was worried?

She filed it away with the now lengthy list of things to think about later, after she had dealt with Lady Anne.

"I feel quite well now," Elizabeth said, more for Darcy's sake than anything else.

Lady Anne eyed her speculatively. "The mages of India are more advanced in the healing arts than we are. It is something I hope to learn more about."

Rana Akshaya gestured to her translator, who said, "It is a long training which begins in childhood. An adult could not undertake it." Apparently Darcy was not the only one who did not wish to answer Lady Anne's questions.

Elizabeth stood up tentatively, but her legs held her with no difficulty. "I am very thankful to be the beneficiary of your many years of study, Rana Akshaya." She turned to Lady Anne. "I feel capable of making the journey to Longbourn now, if you would care to join me."

Lady Anne slipped back into her more distant manners. "That would be satisfactory. Shall we go now?"

The carriage waited outside the door, with Cerridwen circling overhead. To Elizabeth's surprise, Darcy leaned forward to kiss her cheek. The touch of his lips was a shock, like a spark that went straight to the core of her, startling enough that she almost missed the words he whispered. "Be careful."

Of course. He could not accompany them because of his repulsion to her father, but must be unhappy about her being alone with his mother. She gave the slightest nods, warmed by his efforts to protect her. Then she turned to thank Rana Akshaya once again for her help and made her farewell.

Rana Akshaya repeated the gesture she had made earlier to Cerridwen, the praying hands with a slight bow. "We will meet again, Elizabeth Bennet," she said, without using her translator.

Cold goosebumps rose on Elizabeth's arms. But she did not doubt for even a second that the older woman was speaking the truth. "I will look forward to it."

Chapter 10

THE CARRIAGE RIDE TO Longbourn had not gone badly. When Lady Anne returned to asking questions about Elizabeth's family, this time with more subtlety, Elizabeth had taken the bull by the horns and told her all about her sisters. In detail. Including the embarrassing parts about Lydia's and Kitty's behavior. After all, Lady Anne could find out the same information by asking anyone who knew them.

There was a certain irony in bringing Lady Anne to Longbourn. Under normal circumstances, Elizabeth would be nervous about introducing an aristocratic lady to her mother and younger sisters, whose manners left a great deal to be desired. Today it would serve her well to have her family on their worst behavior. If she wanted Lady Anne to underestimate her cleverness and resourcefulness, her foolish mother and sisters could be her best allies.

Elizabeth had high hopes for extreme silliness as she made the introduction to her mother, but while Mrs. Bennet babbled a little, she seemed too much in awe of her titled visitor to speak at length.

"I pray you, Mrs. Bennet, to introduce me to these lovely young ladies, who must be your daughters," Lady Anne said regally.

"Yes, your ladyship. This is my eldest, Jane, and Mary and Kitty are over there. My youngest, Lydia, is in Meryton visiting her aunt."

"Five daughters! What an excellent family you have."

Mrs. Bennet beamed. "Your ladyship is too kind."

"How old are you?" Lady Anne's voice had an odd resonance.

It took a moment for Elizabeth to recognize Lady Anne was not speaking aloud, so her mother could not hear the blunt question. Elizabeth had no intention of answering this impertinence.

Mary looked up. "I am nineteen, your ladyship." So she must have heard it, as well.

Kitty said, "I am seventeen, and Lydia is but fifteen."

Jane frowned at her sisters, but pursed her lips and said nothing.

"Excellent," said Lady Anne, and it sounded as if she truly meant it. "I am so glad you will be part of my family once Miss Elizabeth marries my son. I look forward to knowing all of you much better."

Mrs. Bennet fanned herself vigorously. "You honor us, your ladyship!"

Suddenly it was all too clear what Lady Anne had done. She had tested Elizabeth's sisters for latent Talent by employing some sort of sending, and Kitty and Mary had passed her test. Now they would be in her cross-hairs, too.

"Her ladyship especially requested to be introduced to my father," Elizabeth announced. "Pray excuse us so I may take her to him."

Lady Anne gave her a sharp glance, but said only, "I hope we will meet again at the wedding."

Mrs. Bennet made a curtsy so deep she almost stumbled. "Your ladyship is most kind, most kind indeed!"

Elizabeth indicated the door. "This way, Lady Anne." Would her father be in his usual playful mood or still angry? She was not at all certain which would be better. If Lady Anne had a sense of humor, she had yet to show evidence of it.

She knocked before entering the library. Her father rose to his feet, peering over his spectacles at the lady beside her. "Lizzy, to what do I owe this pleasure?"

She took a breath. "Your ladyship, may I be permitted to present my father to your acquaintance? Papa, we are honored to be in the presence of Lady Anne Darcy, who is the King's Mage as well as Mr. Darcy's mother."

Her father's eyebrows rose, and then the corners of his lips turned down. "Well, that explains a few things. You are welcome to Longbourn, your ladyship." But his voice was chilly.

Lady Anne inclined her head. "I thank you. My duties require me to return to London tonight, so I hope you will forgive me if I come straight down to business."

Mr. Bennet pressed his fingertips against his desktop. "Naturally, but I have a question of my own first. I understood the King's Mage was still a Fitzwilliam."

"I was born Lady Anne Fitzwilliam. My brother is the Earl of Matlock," she said coolly, as if she thought it none of his business.

Her father straightened into an uncharacteristically stiff stance. "Then this is a very interesting meeting indeed, my lady," he said. "Or should I say, Cousin?"

"I beg your pardon?" said Lady Anne.

Elizabeth's mouth fell open in shock.

Mr. Bennet continued, "We are cousins, of a sort. Or rather, your father and my mother were cousins."

Lady Anne's expression of confusion cleared. "Oh, on the Carlisle side of the family, then?"

Mr. Bennet's lips twisted. "No, on the Fitzwilliam side."

"That cannot be. I know of every Fitzwilliam descendant in the last four generations."

He shrugged. "Apparently you missed one branch. My grandmother was Amelia Fitzwilliam. Lady Amelia, although she never used the title after she left the family."

Elizabeth's eyes grew wide. Could this be true? Why had he kept it a secret?

Lady Anne's brows drew together. "Amelia – no, I recall it now. She died young."

Her father now looked to be almost enjoying himself. "Is that what they told you? In fact, she ran off to avoid the future they had planned for her and led them on a merry chase. She faked her own death by making it appear she had jumped off a cliff." He crossed his arms.

"It cannot be. They would never believe her dead unless they saw her body." Her voice trailed off, and she sank uninvited into an armchair, as if her legs would no longer support her. "But I suppose that would explain your daughter's abilities."

"The abilities we hoped you would never learn about. I would never have revealed our heritage, had your son not come along and made that unfortunate discovery."

Elizabeth's heart pounded. Why had he never told her any of this? But the news was no excuse to forget her manners, so she said, "My lady, this has been a shock to you. May I offer you something for your relief? A glass of wine, perhaps?"

"I thank you. That would be welcome." She was still pale, and her breathing was too rapid.

Elizabeth went to the shelf where her father stored his wine and poured a glass. She handed it to the King's Mage, feeling as if she had entered some strange, unknown world. Impossibility on impossibility - that she was engaged to proud Mr. Darcy, that he was the son of the mystery-shrouded King's Mage, who had now proved to be a distant relation of her own? That Papa had known this and never said a word? Oh, it was too much, simply too much!

Perhaps she needed a glass of wine, too, but she did not dare. If it loosened her tongue, she might say altogether too much.

"Thank you, my dear." Lady Anne's color began to return as she sipped the wine. "This is indeed a surprise, but by no means an unwelcome one. A new branch of the family is cause to celebrate."

"I am glad *you* think so," said Mr. Bennet, without enthusiasm.

"I would very much like to know what became of Lady Amelia after her disappearance," she said cordially.

Mr. Bennet seemed unsurprised. "She made a life for herself in Wales, where she married and raised her daughter. And she spent a great deal of time preparing defenses in case her family should ever come after her."

Lady Anne gamely ignored his last point and asked, "How many children did she have apart from your mother?"

"None." He seemed to wish to say no more than he must.

Elizabeth stared at him. Why was her father telling a flat-out lie? She had over a dozen cousins in Wales, from Granny's three other children. And he made it sound as if Granny had died.

"A pity." Lady Anne sounded truly disappointed. "I should have been delighted to meet even more new relatives. I am looking forward to a closer acquaintance with your other daughters, too. We can find opportunities for them in society once their Fitzwilliam connections are known."

Mr. Bennet folded his hands. "My daughters have no need of your connections or the *ton*."

She eyed him inquisitively. "I can offer them a great deal, not least a Season in London. Surely you would not wish to deprive them of such an opportunity?"

"Your ladyship, it is a generous offer, but my grandmother made it clear she wished us to steer clear of the Fitzwilliams. Since I have no choice but to permit Elizabeth to marry your son, I can no longer do so completely. But that does not mean I will encourage or endorse any other connection."

Lady Anne's air of well-bred surprise did her credit. "I am sorry you feel that way, Mr. Bennet, and I can only hope that closer acquaintance may improve your opinion of me. The stories of my great-grandfather, Lady Amelia's father, are indeed rather frightening, but he died long before I was born. I am not answerable for whatever occurred between him and your grandmother, whom I also never met. Perhaps you and I can forge a different path."

Her father steepled his fingers. "Nicely said, my lady, but do recall that my first encounter with your family was to receive a demand that my daughter marry your son, whether I liked it or not. And I do not like it."

"That was none of my doing. You must blame my son for that."

Mr. Bennet pounced. "Will you ask him to release her from the engagement? Since we are family?"

Elizabeth held her breath, her heart pounding.

Lady Anne shook her head slowly, as if regretfully. "These are matters beyond any of our reach. I regret it is distasteful to you, but I am as powerless as you in this affair."

Mr. Bennet's jaw stiffened as he made a new realization. "Good God. Is he to be King's Mage after you?" It was an accusation more than a question.

A spasm crossed Lady Anne's face. If she did not know better, Elizabeth might have thought it to be grief.

"No," said Lady Anne in a hollow voice. "His mission is different from mine. I am training my niece to follow me."

"Another Fitzwilliam, then?"

"I wish I had another choice. The Percy family has no girls with Talent in this generation, and the Mortimer line has ended. Fitzwilliams are our only choice. I am sorry Miss Elizabeth will be forced into a marriage not of her choice. I can, however, tell you that my son will be a good husband. He is not always the most tactful soul, but his heart is true and he is a generous man. I have never seen him ill-treat anyone, not the lowest servant or beggar, even though he has had a difficult time of it these last few years."

A difficult time? Elizabeth stored away that tidbit for further consideration. In the meantime, it would hardly be diplomatic to tell her future mother-in-law how infuriating she found her son. "I am sure he is a good man, but I have always wished to stay at Longbourn. This place is my life, as Pemberley is his, and I think it unfair that I am to be dragged from it without my consent."

For a moment, Lady Anne's face seemed to show her true years, lines of fatigue dragging at her eyes. "Unfair? Yes, it is, but when has life ever been fair for women, especially those with Talent? It is the way of the world, although I am sorry for your loss." She sounded as if she meant it, too. "I must take some time to consider this matter of our family connection. May I call on you again tomorrow, Mr. Bennet?"

He pushed up his spectacles. "I thought you were returning to London tonight."

"I had planned to do so, but this must take precedence. My niece can take over my duties for a day or two.".

Her father's mouth twisted. "Then we will meet again."

It was not a flat refusal, but hardly an invitation. But Lady Anne seemed to take it as such, rising to her feet. "Mr. Bennet, I will look forward to it. Miss Elizabeth, will you be so kind as to see me to the door?"

At least Lady Anne did not attempt to make conversation, bidding her a simple adieu as she climbed into her carriage.

Elizabeth did not stay to see her off, but hurried to rejoin her father, ignoring her mother's call. As soon as she closed the library door, she burst out, "Why did you never tell us, Papa? Surely it was our right to know that we could be mages."

He rubbed the bridge of his nose. "If we had lived in the wilds of the Welsh mountains, where you could practice your Talent without fear of discovery, I would have. My mother's misfortune was to fall in love with my father, who lived but twenty miles from London. Granny warned her she would have to hide her Talent, but she was in love and did not care. Then I was born, and my gifts were almost all magery. A trace of landed Talent, but barely enough to make a difference."

"*You* are a mage?"

He lifted a finger, and suddenly a waterfall seemed to spring from the top of the bookcases, falling over a wall of rocks, the water dancing and spraying in sunlight that did not exist. Ferns grew out of the stony soil and bobbled in an invisible wind.

She gasped. Now she could see why Darcy claimed his illusions were weak. This world her father had created so easily made Darcy's cows look like child's play.

The illusion vanished, and an icy breeze ruffled Elizabeth's dress. Snowflakes began to fall, right there inside the library. Even knowing they were illusory, she could not help reaching out to catch one.

It was cold, melting into a droplet of water. Wet water. Not an illusion, then. True weather magic.

The breeze and snow stopped, though a few stray flakes still decorated the carpet and Mr. Bennet's desk.

"That is truly astonishing." Her voice shook. How could her father, her retiring father who so rarely took an interest in anything outside his library, possess such marvelous abilities? "I do not understand why you have kept it to yourself."

"Because I am tied to Longbourn, and I refuse to be dragged into the service of the King's Mage." He snorted. "And therein lies the jest. I only agreed to your marriage to Darcy when Bingley said that he would arrange for the King's Mage to explain to me why it was needful. And I was so desperate to avoid her interest that I sacrificed you rather than have her discover all of us. And it turns out she is Darcy's mother."

Elizabeth's throat grew tight. "I thought it was because of the threat of the dragons."

"Well, that, too, though I am more concerned about the sea serpents. I find it hard to believe in dragons attacking people, but if the serpents are sinking all our ships, it comes down to the same thing. Still, I hoped to avoid her notice."

"So that you would not have to become one of the government's mages." It tasted bitter, though hardly surprising, that he would choose himself over her.

"Not just that. There is the matter of your sisters. I knew if she discovered my abilities, all of you would have been disposed of as she saw fit. I kept this secret so you could have normal lives." He shook his head sadly. "And it almost worked. If only that damned Darcy had not come along."

Darcy's arrival had created this situation. She did not want to have to leave Longbourn, nor to have her sisters forced into marriages of their own. But she could not regret learning to cast illusions, and she was determined to play a part in stopping Napoleon.

What if her father had taught her these things years ago, as he had instructed her in using her land Talents? Would she be creating wonderful illusions like his, instead of patches of mist and river pebbles? She might have known to stay far away from Mr. Darcy. Instead her father had kept her ignorant.

"Who trained you to do that?" she asked.

"My mother and Granny, mostly. Many of the family in Wales are mages."

She had not been to Granny's house in Wales since she was eight. Her child's memory was that it was an enchanted place, with towering mountains, wild rivers, and strange happenings. Every year Granny had reminded her never to speak to anyone outside the family of the unusual things she saw there. To keep her secrets from the rest of the world.

And Granny had taught her to spin, because it might be useful someday. "Did Granny want to train me?"

"If she had, you would never have been satisfied with your life here. I have seen how hungry you are for magic. You would have had to live in Wales, and I would have sadly missed your company."

He had not answered her question. Perhaps it was an answer in itself. "Why did you tell Lady Anne that Granny had no other children?"

He sighed, setting down his spectacles. "Because if she knew about the family in Wales, she would have them all taken away to serve the government, just as she is already trying to bribe me for your sisters. She would strip the valley of all its magic and use it for her own purposes. She must never suspect their existence."

She would never let anyone harm her beloved Welsh village. "But what if Mr. Darcy sees the letters I receive from Granny or my cousins?"

"Tell him they are your friends. Their surnames will mean nothing to him, in any case. Or better yet, do not write to them, and stay far away from Wales."

Give up her connection to Granny on top of losing Longbourn? Never. "I will be careful. But I want to know more about their magic."

He rubbed the bridge of his nose. "You always want to know more." It was not a compliment.

"I deserve to know, if my life is to be turned upside down on account of it!"

"I wish I could tell you, but..." He paused, taking a deep breath. "I cannot break my promises. There are secrets they do not wish the world to know. Keep Cerridwen away from Darcy, too, and never let him suspect there is anything unusual about her." There was an unusual pleading note in his voice.

Oh, no. She had already told Darcy that Cerridwen was not a typical familiar. He had not seemed particularly interested, though, so perhaps that would not matter. "I will do what I can. But what of my sisters? We must warn them they have mage blood."

He sighed. "What good would that do?"

"If we do not tell them, Lady Anne will. She has already tested them to see if they can hear her sendings."

He grimaced. "I suppose we must. But Jane and Mary only. Lydia would announce it to the entire world, and Kitty will not keep a secret from Lydia."

He had a point, and telling Jane and Mary was better than nothing. "Only them, then."

"You may do the honors, since you wish it." Her father picked up his book and opened it, a clear dismissal.

Naturally he would put the burden on her. He hated difficult discussions.

Chapter 11

ELIZABETH COLLAPSED ON JANE's bed. "I told Mary." Informing Jane about her heritage of magery had not been difficult, as her elder sister was accustomed to the idea of having a Talent, weak as it might be. Convincing Mary had been a challenge.

"How did it go?" Jane asked.

"Well enough. At first she thought I was teasing, but once she took me seriously, she asked if there were books she could read to teach her how to use it."

Jane smiled as she ran the brush through her golden hair. "She has taught herself everything else. Why not this?"

"Because it is different from land Talent. Magery can be deadly dangerous. It is not something to experiment with. Mr. Darcy has already had to rescue me twice," she said ruefully.

"I imagine you did not like that!"

"No, I certainly did not! But it was still worth it." It had been so exciting, discovering her new ability. "It is my one consolation about this cursed marriage, that I will be able to learn new magic. I never thought it would be possible."

Jane's hand stopped in midstroke, and she turned to Elizabeth in dismay. "Pray do not say that! There are many good things about marrying Mr. Darcy."

Elizabeth grimaced. Trust Jane to always see the best. "Money, I suppose. But giving up my land connection – I cannot bear it. Here, I have a purpose. I am able to help our family and our tenants in a way no one else can. Once I leave, I will be useless."

Jane gave a soft laugh. "Only you could call it useless! Mr. Bingley says you will be in a unique position to help end the war, and that it is terribly urgent. And all those hundreds of thousands who have died, of all the people who cared about them." Her eyes filled with tears, and Elizabeth knew she was thinking of poor James Lucas, her first love, but she went on bravely. "Or Mr. Robinson, without his legs, when he was such a fine rider and loved to dance? Stopping that bloodshed is far more important than making one estate's crops grow."

Her cheeks burned. "I suppose you are correct, but it does not feel as if I am doing anything, merely being there for Mr. Darcy to draw upon. Perhaps it is foolish pride, but I want to accomplish something myself."

Jane took her hands. "And you shall! I know it. You will find new ways to use your Talent to help, as you did here. And you will have the chance to travel. Aunt Gardiner always goes on about the beauties of the Peak, and just think, you will be living there! I cannot wait to visit you."

"I hope you will, and frequently," Elizabeth said firmly. How could Jane, who had never experienced a deep connection to the land, understand what she was giving up? But dwelling on that loss would not change anything. By nature, she could never have Jane's happy contentment, but she could try to focus more on the positives of her situation.

And she could work to defeat Napoleon.

Mary burst into the room then, without even bothering to knock, more excited that Elizabeth had ever seen her. "Lizzy, if I have mage blood, does that mean I can get a familiar?"

Elizabeth laughed. Mary had spent her entire life begging for a pet cat, and there had been a couple of barn cats who had shown a particular interest in her. "Perhaps so, if one of them offers themself to you. I imagine Mr. Darcy could tell you about it."

Finally the last of the stream of callers departed, leaving Elizabeth exhausted from the effort of keeping a smile pasted on her face as she received congratulations from one neighbor after another on her brilliant match. But as she stood up and stretched, thinking she was finally free, Hill came in, a frown on her face.

"You have another one, Miss Lizzy." The housekeeper's brow crinkled. "At least, I think she is a caller."

Not one more! Calling hours were over. "Surely she either is or is not."

"She says she is a servant, but I have never seen a servant like that. Dresses funny, talks funny. And she came to the front door, not the back."

Elizabeth's shoulders sagged. "I suppose the fastest way to get rid of her is for me to see her."

A few minutes later, Hill showed in a young woman dressed in the Indian fashion with draped fabrics. Not rich ones, like Rana Akshaya had worn, but still beautifully patterned. A messenger from the Indian mage, perhaps? After all, she had promised they would meet again.

"Good afternoon," said Elizabeth cautiously. "How may I be of assistance to you?"

The woman curtsied. "The great Rana Akshaya has instructed me to put myself at your service."

"I beg your pardon?" Elizabeth asked, confused.

"The great Rana learned your household must prepare for your wedding in a hurry, and she wished to offer me as an extra set of hands to lighten the load. I am trained in all household tasks, from cleaning to serving as a lady's maid."

Was this a custom from India? "That is very kind, but I believe our staff has matters in hand." Her mother would not agree, but it would be altogether too strange to borrow a servant from a high-born Indian mage. Especially one who was a friend of Darcy's mother.

A shadow passed across the newcomer's face. "I am willing to help in any way. Surely there must be some task where I could be useful. I can scrub floors or do laundry."

She was dressed too well for either of those tasks, but there was a certain desperation in her air. Would Rana Akshaya punish her if Elizabeth sent her back? She did not wish to create any difficulties.

Or perhaps it was a different sort of trouble. Would Rana Akshaya take offense if Elizabeth refused her gift?

Oh, this was a tangle, and Elizabeth was too tired to deal with it, but the poor woman looked so worried. "Is this something Rana Akshaya has done before, sending you to help someone she has just met?

"No, never. But you are the chosen companion of a falcon, so she wishes to do every honor."

That was as clear as mud. Not to mention disconcerting. Darcy and Lady Anne thought her odd for having a bird as her familiar, and Rana Akshaya believed it was a signal honor.

Well, she did feel honored that Cerridwen had bonded with her, so perhaps she should act that way. "Then I thank you and Rana Akshaya for your generous offer. Do you sew?"

"Indeed, I do."

"That is a task with which I would appreciate help. It would be lovely to add some ribbon to the dress I will wear at the wedding, since there is no time to make a new one."

"I would be happy to assist you with that."

That was settled, then. She could give her the dress and the ribbon, and then she could finally have a little time alone.

It lacked but an hour until dinner time of her last day as a single woman, and Elizabeth was still putting the final touches on her packing. She had spent the day walking the fields of Longbourn, pouring her energy into the tenants' crops one last time before she left. Darcy would be displeased if she was tired tomorrow, so perhaps it would be better not to mention it to him. She certainly would not tell him she had long since instructed the local farmers to give their plots a few drops of blood every spring.

The bedroom she shared with Jane had already been stripped of her identity, with only those few things she would need in the morning still out. Soon there would be no trace of her left at Longbourn.

Jane appeared in the doorway, looking concerned. "Lizzy, Lady Anne has just arrived. Will you come downstairs?"

"Now?" Elizabeth grimaced. "Only she would think it acceptable to call at this time of day, and on the eve of the wedding."

Jane shrugged helplessly. "She told Mama she had something important to discuss."

"In that case, I am definitely coming down." She hurried towards the sitting room, where her other sisters were gathered with their guest.

Her mother was speaking as Elizabeth walked in and curtsied to Lady Anne. Mrs. Bennet stopped mid-sentence to announce, "And here is our Lizzy!"

"Miss Elizabeth, I am so happy you can join us," Lady Anne said. "I feared you might be too busy with your preparations." Had the older woman hoped that might be the case?

"I could never miss an opportunity to see your ladyship," she said demurely. At least she was setting a good example for her younger sisters.

"How charming you are!" She turned to Elizabeth's mother. "Mrs. Bennet, I must confess this is not simply a social call. I would like to speak to you about the future of your younger daughters, if you will permit me to do so."

Mrs. Bennet fingered her handkerchief. "I would be honored to hear anything your ladyship condescends to say."

Lady Anne smiled graciously. "I thank you. You may be aware that your daughters possess a latent Talent for magery. I would like to give them the opportunity to develop those Talents. Specifically, if you are willing, I would like to take Miss Mary and Miss Kitty back to London for training, and to stay for the Season."

Elizabeth's jaw dropped. Was this not the same offer her father had already refused? How dare she?

"A Season in London?" Mrs. Bennet's face flushed. "Your ladyship is most generous, most generous. I am quite undone!"

"It would be my pleasure. I have heard a great deal about Miss Mary's studious nature. Should she apply herself to developing her Talent with the same devotion, I believe she has the makings of a fine mage. Miss Kitty also has potential, and if she dislikes her studies, at least she can enjoy the pleasures of the Season before returning home." She turned to the girls. "Would you like that?"

Kitty, wide-eyed, cried, "Oh, yes, my lady! I should adore to have a Season." Then her face fell. "But I have no Talent, I fear."

"Then allow me to be the first to tell you that you do, indeed, have Talent." Lady Anne did not seem surprised at Kitty's ignorance of this, or at least she hid it well.

Mary looked as if Lady Anne was an angel who had stepped down from heaven and addressed her personally. "I would be honored. I do not care about the Season, but I will study very, very hard, and never disappoint your ladyship."

"Excellent," said Lady Anne. "How delightful it will be to have two young ladies to introduce to London."

"What about me?" blurted out Lydia. "I wouldn't mind being a mage, if it meant I had a Season!"

Kitty tried to hush her sister, perhaps fearing this incredible generosity might disappear in the face of Lydia's antics.

Lady Anne turned her cool gaze on Lydia. "You have a degree of Talent, it is true, but self-discipline is a necessary prerequisite for studying magery. Based on all I have heard, that is something you lack. Perhaps you may develop it with time." Her chilly tone held out little hope for such an outcome.

Lydia's hands clenched. "I still want a Season. It is not fair that Kitty gets one and I do not!"

Lady Anne's expression turned frigid. "That is an excellent example of why you are unsuited for this. A Season is out of the question. You are far too young to be out in society."

"I have been out for an entire year!" cried Lydia.

"I cannot understand why. No fifteen-year-old should be out." She spoke with absolute certainty before turning back to Mrs. Bennet. "It will take me a fortnight to make arrangements in London, and then I will send for Miss Mary and Miss Kitty. If that suits you, Mrs. Bennet."

Mrs. Bennet glanced worriedly at Lydia, and then apparently decided that two daughters with Seasons in hand were worth one in the bush. "Oh, that is perfect! Just think of it! A Season in Town! Girls, you must behave very well for her ladyship and do everything she tells you."

Lydia ran out sobbing. Kitty simply stared in awed silence at Lady Anne.

Elizabeth felt this ridiculousness had gone on long enough. "Should we not seek my father's approval for this arrangement?" It was simpler than saying that he had already refused the plan.

"Oh!" cried Mrs. Bennet. "Hill! Send for Mr. Bennet at once! Now, girls, you must thank Lady Anne."

Mr. Bennet appeared promptly. His eyes narrowed at the sight of Lady Anne. "How may I be of service?"

Mrs. Bennet jumped up and laid her hand on his arm. "Oh, Mr. Bennet, it is the finest thing! Her ladyship is taking Mary and Kitty to London for the Season!"

"To study magic," added Mary.

"Oh, Papa, may we go? May we?" begged Kitty.

Mr. Bennet's lips tightened. "If the girls wish to go, I will not stand in their way." He left the room without the courtesy of a farewell, leaving a cloud of angry disapproval in his wake.

After Lady Anne departed, Elizabeth sought her father. "Why did you agree to it when you refused the same offer not two days ago?"

He turned weary eyes to her. "Because I will never have a moment's peace until they go. And if I had refused, Lady Anne would simply find a way to get around me, just as she did with you. I will not waste my energy so pointlessly."

"Oh, Papa!"

"At least she has a good sense not to take Lydia. Can you imagine Lydia with magical abilities? I shudder to think of it."

She frowned. "Will you tell Granny what has happened?"

He rubbed his hand over his forehead. "I must write to her, I suppose. Those silly girls will tell that woman everything about her, so we must warn her."

He was clearly set on letting them go, and there was nothing she could do about it. She said, "We can only hope for the best." And she would pray that Darcy's mother had more kindness and goodness in her heart than she had shown so far. "I will see you at dinner."

"Wait, Lizzy. I have a gift for you."

Crossing to the bookcase behind his desk, he lifted a wooden box from the bottom shelf. He unlocked it with a key from his desk and carefully removed a cloth-wrapped bundle.

Curious, Elizabeth leaned forward as he folded back the cloth to reveal three small volumes. She gasped. The familiar elaborately tooled covers were a match to her two Arabic books of magic.

"I kept these from you, lest they tempt you to experiment with magery," he said ruefully. "Now that you have discovered it on your own, you may as well have them. Especially as there is no time for me to teach you what I know."

Reverently Elizabeth lifted the top book, carefully opening it at the back to the title page. *On Harnessing the Arts of the Air*. She drew in her breath sharply. What treasures would she find inside it? More secrets lost for generations? She reached for the second book. *On the Arts of Seeming and Perception*. Illusions, perhaps? And the third was titled *On the Gifts of Dragons*.

She looked up at her father. "Mr. Hadid never mentioned there were more books."

"I asked him not to. I hoped you would never discover this part of your Talent. It is an unsafe thing, as you have seen."

She would not argue that point. "I thank you for the books."

"Promise me you will not stay up all night reading them. We cannot have you falling asleep at the altar tomorrow."

She smiled. "I will save them until after I leave. And I should write to Granny tonight." Her father was always slow to compose letters, and this one was important.

"Good. That will give her time to prepare defenses, in case Lady Anne decides to investigate. She may not have taken my word that there were no other Fitzwilliam descendants there."

Elizabeth nodded. Then she went upstairs to spend her last night at Longbourn penning a missive with all the recent events, plus a great number of questions. She shed a tear or two as she wrote the final words, "Pray send any reply to me at Pemberley."

She put it in the pile of outgoing post and went to sleep in her own bed for the last time.

Chapter 12

THE NEXT MORNING, JANE poked her head around the door. "Oh, there you are! I was wondering if something had happened to you." Then, as Elizabeth turned to face her, she gasped. "Good heavens! How did you do that? You look beautiful!"

Elizabeth held out her arms and turned in a slow circle. "Astonishing, is it not? That Indian servant did it. She took my dress back to Netherfield yesterday to finish sewing on the new ribbons, and she brought it back this morning looking like this!"

It was barely recognizable as her simple day dress. Now it was adorned by a wide band of embroidered trim at the hem and a new gauze over-skirt that sparkled with metallic threads, with a matching layer over the sleeves. Fine lace lined the entire bodice.

"And look at this shawl! I feel like Empress Josephine!" She had never owned a garment so rich.

"How on earth did she do that so quickly? And where did she get the fabric? That is not from the milliner in Meryton."

"Staying up all night, no doubt. Unless Rana Akshaya routinely travels with all manner of trims and fabric, she must have taken apart another dress to do this. Why she would do something so radical is beyond me, but it seemed churlish to refuse it."

"Indeed you could not! And I am sure Rana... Rana..."

"Rana Akshaya," supplied Elizabeth.

"No doubt she hopes to please Lady Anne with this gift."

Lady Anne Darcy. Her wedding. Leaving Longbourn. The weight fell back on her shoulders after her brief distraction over the remade gown. "At least I will have one dress I will not need to blush for when I reach Pemberley," she said with an attempt at lightness. "If half of what Miss Bingley says is true, I will be woefully underdressed."

"Nonsense," said Jane stoutly. "And it would not matter if you wore rags. Mr. Darcy must love you violently to insist on such a quick wedding."

How very like Jane, to make this odd arranged marriage into a love match. But if it gave her comfort, Elizabeth would not argue. There might be little enough pleasure in her future, but she did not want her sister to grieve for her.

Or to think too hard about it herself, not when she had only an hour left as Elizabeth Bennet of Longbourn.

"Well, Lizzy, I doubt I shall be able to be coherent soon, so I will make my farewells now," Mr. Bennet said as they reached the church door. "I hope Darcy turns out to be a decent fellow. I like him better for knowing he distrusts that mother of his."

Elizabeth was not inclined to quarrel, not today. Her goal was to make it through this ceremony without crying. "I believe he is a good man under all that pride. Perhaps some teasing will puncture his shield of superiority," she said lightly.

"If anyone can, you will." It was an unusual vote of confidence, and she appreciated it. He held the church door open for her. "Well, let us get this done."

It did not seem real as she started down the aisle on her father's arm. Surely this was just playacting.

Her father stiffened as they approached the altar where Darcy stood. He, too, froze in place. Poor man, having to be tortured by repulsion at his own wedding!

The rector began the familiar service, but instead of letting the words wash over her, Elizabeth mentally urged him to hurry, to speak faster, so that her father could say his one line and retire to the pew, a few feet farther from Darcy. But she noticed when her bridegroom, who was making visible effort to keep his fists unclenched, still managed to promise to love, comfort, and honor her.

Now it was her turn to say, "I will," and she did it in a steady voice, feeling more concern for the two agonized men beside her than for herself.

Finally the rector asked, "Who giveth this woman to be married to this man?" Her father stepped forward, unable to suppress a soft groan of pain before he forced out, "I do," in a strangled voice.

Thank God this part was nearly over!

Mr. Bennet gave her hand to the rector and stepped back. This was truly it. She was tied to Darcy now, not her father.

Then, as she felt the warmth of Darcy's hand when the rector joined hers to his, twin gasps came, one from behind her and the other from her side. Darcy staggered slightly, and then a broad smile crossed his face as he repeated his vows in a firmer voice. If she did not know better, she would think he truly meant to love and cherish her until death.

She tugged her hand from Darcy's when the rector instructed them to do so. He turned white and instantly grasped for her left hand with his own.

What in the world was he doing? It must look very odd! But she took his right hand in hers, making their hands cross, and repeated her vows.

Somehow Darcy managed not to lose her hand even as he placed the ring, first on the Bible and then on her finger, though the rector was glaring at him.

Then they knelt for the blessing, Darcy still clutching her hand tightly, and she finally had a moment to think.

Somehow it must transmit her immunity to repulsion to him. It had not done so when she touched her father. Was this another instance of their magic entwining?

Perhaps there was something to his insistence that they must work together after all.

They stood again to be pronounced man and wife. Darcy's lips pressed against hers softly, tenderly, and something seemed to melt inside her. It was over almost before it had begun, and far too soon.

She was married to him.

Darcy kept a firm hold of Elizabeth's hand until the carriage had traveled halfway through the village. That ought to be a safe distance. Indeed, he felt no pain upon releasing her. "I thank you," he said.

She held her hand out in front of her, studying it. "Did it help the repulsion, then?"

"It vanished completely as soon as you touched me, like a miracle. I had underestimated how difficult it would be to stand so near your father." He had been close to running screaming from the church.

"But you had spoken to him before." At least she sounded only curious, rather than upset.

"From across the room, not a few feet away. The repulsion grows stronger the closer he is."

"You must have stood even nearer to your wife at your first wedding."

He did not want to think of that today, but Elizabeth deserved an answer. "She was my cousin, which reduced the repulsion to a degree, and we were both dosed with laudanum and calendula, which made it more tolerable."

She frowned. "Calendula? What does that do?"

"It temporarily blocks the ability to use one's Talent, which eases the repulsion. Unfortunately, it also blocks the ability to think clearly. The curate had to have us say our vows one phrase at a time, since we could not concentrate long enough to remember even a sentence."

Her lips twitched. "It sounds difficult, but amusing to imagine."

And suddenly he could see the humorous side of it, too; he and Anne stumbling through the vows they could barely understand as the witnesses held their arms to keep them from wandering. "Holding your hand is far better than taking calendula. My mother will be interested in the effect."

All humor fled her face. "Yes, your mother," she said coldly. "She has to have her fingers in everything. Did she tell you she is taking two of my sisters away?"

Confused, he said, "Yes. Are you not pleased they would receive training and have a Season? She said they were very excited about the prospect."

"Training, a Season, and the chance to be drugged to tolerate the presence of the man they will have to marry. How charming." Her words dripped ice.

"No one is forced into such a marriage," he said uncomfortably. He did not care to think of how often he had been told that Britain's future depended on his marrying Anne.

"Is that not how we came to be wed? And I do not believe that my great-grandmother ran away from home and faked her own death to avoid a marriage when she could have simply said no."

"Many of us see it as our duty—"

"Did your mother mention that my father had expressly refused to let her offer a Season to my sisters, and that she went behind his back to do so, getting them so excited with her promises that he had no choice but to agree?" Her eyes sparkled with fury.

A heavy weight seemed to settle on him. "No. I was unaware of that."

"Do you think it was acceptable for her to ignore my father's objections merely so she could have her way?" She threw the challenge in his face.

Stung, he said, "Of course not. She must have seen it as her duty to recruit potential mages, but she should not have ignored your father's wishes."

"You did the same thing."

That was enough. His fingernails bit into his trousers. "I had Bingley explain to your father why it was necessary. I never went behind his back, nor did I try to convince you when he had refused his permission."

She seemed to deflate at that, slumping back on the seat and crossing her arms. "I will grant you that much," she said grudgingly.

"I thank you for that." For what little it meant.

"In part, though, because it is clear you do not trust your mother, either."

He wanted an end to this quarrel, to say that it was nonsense, or to simply ignore her, as he would have done for anyone else making such an impertinent statement. But he had only just promised to love, comfort, and honor her. And, for whatever reason, he still wanted her good opinion.

He rubbed his forehead. "My mother was kind to me when I was a child. She changed later. Now her duty comes ahead of everything, and sometimes she can be overly single-minded about her tasks."

She nodded, as if somewhat appeased by his answer. "Did she push you to marry your cousin?"

At least this was a simple answer. "Not at all. At the time we believed my mother to be long dead, so she is acquitted of any responsibility for that." He felt obligated to add, "That is not to say no one encouraged the marriage. There was definitely pressure, but not from my mother."

She stared at him. "You thought she was dead?"

"Yes. She disappeared when I was twelve." Even now, his throat ached at the memory of losing her, of the months he had spent in a daze of grief.

"Disappeared?"

"Without a word. At first, we all hoped she would return. We searched and waited for her. Eventually we accepted she must be dead. With her gone, there was no good candidate for King's Mage. My cousin, Anne de Bourgh, was chosen to succeed her, though she was sickly and ill-suited to the task. I did what I could to help." Up to, and including, marrying her.

Better not to think of that now, nor of Anne's mad, dangerous mother. He continued, "When she died, we hoped to wait until my sister grew into her abilities and could assume the position. Georgiana was the daughter of two of the strongest Talents in the kingdom, who had been brought together precisely to produce her. But to everyone's shock, she has not a trace of Talent."

She bit her lip. "I had not realized you have a sister. We have had little time to become acquainted, have we?"

"No." And the less she knew about Georgiana at this stage, the better.

She seemed to wait for him to say more, but when he remained silent, she asked, "What did you do?"

"Tried to get by. The pressure was terrible, since the King's Mage is our final defense, and Napoleon's power was growing." As it still was.

"But your mother is clearly alive."

He forced himself back to the present. "Yes. Twelve years after she disappeared, she returned, looking not a day older, and wearing the same clothes."

Elizabeth's eyes were wide. "She was in Faerie?" she whispered.

"Yes. On her return, she became the King's Mage again. But what had been one day to her had been twelve long, difficult years for me, and we were strangers to each other. I have never felt the same about her."

Elizabeth frowned. "But if she was taken by Faerie, it was hardly her fault."

"She was not taken. She traveled there deliberately, believing her Talent would allow her to return on her own terms." His voice felt rough.

Her face grew pale. "I see. Is that why you do not trust her?"

"Part of it. I rarely see her now because of her insistence that I marry again and breed more mages, which I refused to do. At least, until I met you. She was beyond delighted by the news of our engagement." Irony weighed down his words.

She grimaced. "I am not surprised."

Something she had said earlier about her great-grandmother had been niggling at him, and finally the pieces fell into place. "The day you agreed to marry me, you told me that your great-grandmother would take you in. Were you speaking of Lady Amelia Fitzwilliam?"

She looked away. "I had forgotten I said that. Yes, I suppose so, although I never knew what family she was from."

"Is she still alive, then?"

The color faded from Elizabeth's cheeks. "We had hoped to disguise that. Truly, it would be far better if your mother never discovers she is still alive. My great-grandmother despised her family. There would be no happy ending if your mother seeks her out."

"Surely that is all past, though. She has never even met my mother, and it is not as if anyone can try to marry her off now!" The Fitzwilliams might be autocratic, but they were not evil.

She shrugged. "I cannot say. I was a child the last time I saw her. But I beg you not to tell your mother that she is alive."

"If that is your wish." It was not as if anyone was likely to get much sense out of a woman of that age, anyway, and his mother had caused too much trouble for Elizabeth as it was.

It was barely midday, and Elizabeth was already exhausted. Perhaps brides who were pleased about their marriages would not find their wedding day so trying, but every time she tried to rally her spirits, something would remind her of all she had left behind. Even the shock of hearing Lady Anne's history could only distract her briefly from her worries. Nor did she like having to beg her husband to keep Granny's existence a secret. If only she had never mentioned running away to Wales!

And tonight would be her wedding night, with a husband she barely knew, en route to a place completely unknown to her.

When they reached Hatfield, they turned onto the Great North Road. On the rare occasions she had traveled this way, her family had always gone south towards London or west to Wales. Now she was truly on new territory. As the carriage picked up speed, she asked, "How long is the journey to Pemberley?"

"We will spend two nights on the road. In the summer, when the days are longer, it can be done in two days, but not now."

Three days stuck in this coach with him! She did not even want to think about the nights.

She could not avoid it forever, though, so she gathered her courage. "Where do you think we will stop tonight?"

"Stilton, if we make good time, or Alconbury, if we do not. Both have excellent coaching inns." He paused, seeming to weigh something. "You will have your own room at the inn. It is crucial that our child be conceived at Pemberley. Pray forgive my impropriety in speaking of this. I thought you might wish to know."

"I thank you for informing me of your plans," she murmured. A reprieve, if very brief. A room of her own where she could be alone and not have to keep up this false front.

He said little after that. She watched the countryside pass outside the window, but her mind kept traveling back to her last connection to the land at Longbourn, shifting her Talent into the soil and feeding the roots of the apple trees in the orchard by the church, enriching the slumbering buds which would burst forth in the spring into blossoms she would never see. Just as she would never have that deep connection to the land again. All sacrificed, along with her life with her family and all the Longbourn tenants whom she had helped, the friends she had said goodbye to, and all the ones there had been no time to see.

It did not help to dwell on it, though, so she took out the book she had brought to distract herself, an old, beloved volume of dragon stories, a gift from Granny many years ago. Tales of innocence, now, of an ancient time before Napoleon's dragons slaughtered soldiers. Still, it was comforting to read the familiar legends of dragons who rescued people from floods and landslides, who journeyed together with their human companions to make discoveries and explore the unknown, who were renowned for being fair and just. She had always mourned the absence of dragons from this modern world. She could never have imagined what their return would cost her.

For now, she would live in the past with the heroic dragons, because it was better than spending this long journey crying over all she had lost.

She kept her nose buried in the book until they stopped to change horses, though even the adventures of Ethelreda the Wise and her dragon Blackthorn could not make her forget what she had left behind, much less that she was now married to the near-stranger sitting across from her.

It would only be a brief stop, but there was something she wanted to do, a sore spot she could not resist poking at. She stepped out of the carriage, heading to the side of the stable yard where a clump of grass had forced its way between the cobblestones, now turning brown with the winter chill. Pulling off her glove, she reached down to touch it, but all she could feel was the individual blades brushing against her fingers. No tingling to show it was alive, no sense of the roots burrowing under the stones. Nothing.

It was gone. She was too far from Longbourn and the soil that had nourished her. She had expected it, but it still hurt, like a sense that had been amputated, leaving her only half-present in the world.

You still have me. It was Cerridwen, hovering far overhead.

It was something. *Yes, dearest, I still have you, and I am grateful for that.* Otherwise she would have been truly desperate.

But there was nothing to be done for the loss of her land sense. Slowly she made her way back to the carriage, emptiness echoing inside her.

Darcy watched his new wife crossing the yard with a worried frown. Despite the chill in the air, she had not wished to come inside, instead choosing to wander this unremarkable area instead.

He had hoped this journey would give her time to get to know him better, but apparently she had no interest in that, especially after his mother's interference with her sisters. Not that it had surprised him that his mother would play such a trick, but Elizabeth clearly blamed him for it as well. As if he had any control over what his mother did.

His jaw stiffened. It was hardly the first time he had been left with the repercussions of his mother's decisions, but this was personal. He wanted Elizabeth to care about him. Or at least to think he was more interesting than her well-worn book.

But it must have been a difficult few days for her, and perhaps she simply needed time to adjust to being married. He would do what he could to make her comfortable on this long journey.

Finally she returned to the carriage, and he followed behind her. A servant from the inn was waiting outside holding a large, steaming mug. Good; the innkeeper had lived up to his reputation for speedy service.

"I asked them to bring tea for you," Darcy told Elizabeth. "And they have put new hot bricks by your feet."

"I thank you," she murmured, but she did not meet his eyes, nor did she take the tea, not until he handed it directly to her. At least she took a sip of it then.

No, there would not be any softening. He might as well accept he would be nothing but a stranger to her.

Chapter 13

ELIZABETH CHOKED DOWN THE tea Darcy had provided for her. At least it warmed her body a little, even if nothing could raise her spirits. Her only goal was to keep her composure, or at least not burst into tears. That would not help.

But he kept asking her questions, rearranging the blankets over her skirts to keep her warmer, as if that could make a difference. She responded in as few words as possible, trying to hold back the sobs that wanted to emerge every time she spoke.

Finally he asked, with a certain exasperation, "What can I do to make this easier for you?"

She gulped down a breath. "Your concern is kind. I cannot help being..." No, heartbroken would not be a good word to use. "Sad about what I have left behind." Could he not see that she needed to be alone?

But apparently his sympathy was limited, as evidenced by the anger heavy in his voice. "Elizabeth, I am sorry you had to marry me against your will. I am sorry you will miss Longbourn. But I fail to see why this is such a tragic fate for you. You will be a very wealthy woman with a fine home."

Rage rose in her chest. How dare he? "I do not care about wealth! Longbourn is part of me, and leaving it feels like my heart has been ripped out. I will be nothing at Pemberley, unable to use my Talent, living among complete strangers. And you offer me wealth." She spat out the word.

"Then return to Longbourn, if it is so important to you! All I ask is that you remain at Pemberley until our child is born – if there is one – and then you will be free to do whatever you like, including returning to Longbourn," he snapped.

She caught her breath. "You would let me do that?"

He barked a harsh laugh. "How would I stop you?"

"Very easily! All you need to say is, 'Wife, you may not leave.'" What was wrong with him?

He eyed her for so long that she began to feel nervous. Finally he spoke in a changed, distant tone. "Elizabeth, do you understand what my mission is?"

She studied her gloved hands, because it was safer than telling him his offer made no sense. "You are to accompany assassins who will kill Napoleon."

"What do you think will happen to me if we succeed? Do you think Napoleon's officers will say, 'Fair enough, go home now?' No. They will kill us." Still in that same distant tone.

Her mouth went dry.

"And if we fail? Napoleon will not say, 'Better luck next time.' He will have us executed, if he does not cut us down where we stand."

Her breath caught in her throat. It could not be true. "But you would be a prisoner of war. Will they not trade you?"

His lip curled. "That is only for military officers, not spies and assassins. None of us will return from this mission. We have accepted that price. You, on the other hand, will be a rich widow who can go wherever you want. You can live at Longbourn. You can marry again and have a family. I will not be there to object." With those last, heavy words, he turned away from her.

No. It was impossible. "But you can make yourself invisible! All you need to do is to walk away!"

"I can be unseen for a few minutes, not long enough to escape from a palace full of soldiers. And then only if I have a sufficient reserve of energy, which I will not after making an illusion powerful enough to fool hundreds of men. That will take everything I have."

Everything I have. The words seemed to echo through the carriage. What had he told her that day in the folly, that mages had died by overextending their power while making illusions?

Her eyes widened. "You mean it to take everything, do you not? You are planning to deliberately exhaust your life force in making the illusion," she accused.

He frowned. "If I will not survive, I would rather die doing my utmost to help the mission succeed rather than face execution at the hands of Napoleon's men, who will have no mercy. This, at least, will be painless."

"To let yourself die? But why did you agree to this mission? Certainly you have a duty to our country, to do what you can to stop this, but to die for it? What of your duty to your estate and your family?" She desperately wanted Napoleon gone, was willing to give up her freedom for it, but not this!

His lips tightened. "I am not doing my duty to my estate if I allow Napoleon to send dragons to attack England."

"It is a horrifying prospect, but has there been any evidence that he is using them against anyone but soldiers?"

He turned haunted eyes on her. "Soldiers are people, too."

"They are, naturally, but–"

"My brother was killed at Salamanca." He had never interrupted her before, and the odd flatness of his tone stopped her anger in its tracks even before his words sank in.

"Your brother? Oh, no. I am sorry." How little she knew of this man she had married!

His mouth twisted bitterly. "That Corsican bastard had him murdered, slaughtered like an animal, unable to defend himself. Yes, I will give my life to stop him before I will let him do the same to anyone else." A savage anger filled his voice.

He had lost his brother, only a few months ago. That explained why he had seemed so grim and humorless when she first met him. If only she could offer him some comfort, but what could help when faced with such a loss? "What was his name?"

"What does that matter?" he snapped, and then his shoulders slumped and his gaze dropped. "My apologies. It is difficult for me to speak of him. His name is...was John. We called him Jack." He pulled out his watch, but did not open it, instead rubbing the fob chain between his fingers.

"I am the one who should apologize. I had no idea." Her voice shook. The poor man! Bingley had told her that Darcy had changed after Salamanca.

He seemed to hear that, for he raised his eyes to her again. "I bought him his commission. He had always wanted to join the Army, and he promised to be careful."

But no one could be careful in the face of a dragon attack. "I am sure he tried."

He lifted his hand, pointing to a misshapen signet ring attached to the watch fob. "That was Jack's. One side of it was melted by dragon fire."

It made it all so vivid, seeing that lump of metal, that someone Darcy loved had died in flames. And now he had a chance to avenge him.

No wonder he was willing to die for the cause. To die, and to leave her a widow.

Tears filled her eyes, but she turned her face away and blinked them back. He truly was going to do it, to leave her in two months or a year and walk straight into his own death. She would never see him again, just as he would never see his brother. Their child, if she had one, would grow up fatherless.

It was unbearable. She might not have wished to marry him, but she had not wanted him dead.

Even if she had thought of strangling him more than once.

"No!" she burst out. "I will not have it!"

A look of surprise spread over his face, quickly replaced by confusion. "The mission is already arranged. I cannot withdraw from it."

"I know, but there must be a way to get you out alive!" Even saying that tore at her, as an image of his lifeless body passed before her eyes.

"The best military minds in the country have looked at every possible option."

Could he possibly be so indifferent to his own death? "You have not considered *me*," she said fiercely. "I have done things everyone believed to be impossible, and I can do it again. I will find a way to bring you home."

He breathed heavily, as if he had been exerting himself, but he spoke with gentleness. "Elizabeth, do you not see? This will set you free. You can return to Longbourn. There is no need to rail against it, when it will give you everything you want."

"There is every reason! I may be angry at you, but I do not want you to die!" And then she did burst into tears.

She buried her face in her hands. It was pointless to stem the sobs bursting up from deep inside her, or even to understand them. Had she not hated him?

Except when he had been patiently teaching her to cast illusions, even though he admitted it was only for her pleasure. Except when he tried to protect her from his own mother. Except when he seemed to understand the pain of a forced marriage.

Except when she remembered he had been a boy terrified of a wild creature, and still let it bond to him, because it was his duty. Except that he had held her hand like she was the only thing standing between him and insanity.

Except that, despite having every advantage in the world, he was giving up his life to save others.

An arm came around her shoulders, warm and protective. He had moved from the facing bench to sit with her, his body pressed against her side. "Elizabeth. Pray do not cry." He sounded pained.

It only made her sob harder. She turned her face into his shoulder.

He stroked her hair. "Hush, Elizabeth. I am right here. Nothing has happened to me."

"Yet," she hiccoughed.

"Yet," he agreed, sounding amused. "And I am still the man you detest."

"Oh, stop that!" But his teasing helped her regain control, enough for an instinctive reaction that she should not be allowing a gentleman to touch her in this way. But there was no impropriety in her husband holding her in the privacy of a carriage. The ridiculousness of it made her gurgle with laughter, even as tears still ran down her face.

Lowering her hands, she raised her head. "Forgive me. I am not usually a watering pot." Though one would not know it from her behavior this week.

"I am the one who should apologize. I thought you understood the consequences of my mission. I would not have told you in that manner otherwise. Certainly I was wrong to do so in anger." He pulled out a handkerchief and dabbed gently at her eyes.

She could not remember anyone ever drying her tears for her.

"I should have thought," she murmured, her voice still trembling. But she had been too caught up in what it would cost her, and having to leave Longbourn, to think about what might be in store for him.

"I forget how new this all is to you." He cupped her cheek with his hand. "I cannot make up for what you have lost, but is there nothing I can do to make it more bearable for you? I have always admired you, and the last thing I want is to cause you unhappiness."

Surely he could not think her such a fool as to believe that! "You admired me so much at our first meeting that you said I was tolerable, but not handsome enough to tempt you!" There was a snap in her voice.

He winced. "I was in poor spirits that night, and my skin ached from the presence of too many people from landed families. And you seemed happy when I thought I might never smile again. It angered me, for no good reason. But soon enough, I wanted more of your smiles."

"You are only saying this to make me feel better."

He laced his hand in hers, which felt all too intimate, his fingers pressing on the tender webbing between hers, making her feel hot and cold at the same time. "You bewitched me. Enough that I tried to keep my distance from you, because I knew I could bring you nothing but sorrow."

Now she did believe him. Why did it hurt to know he had found her attractive? "I did not know."

"I thought I was so obvious! Always watching you, trying to get your attention."

"I believed you only looked at me to criticize." It was almost amusing how badly she had misread him.

"Far from it. But my point is this: I am pleased to have this time with you. It is selfish when I know you would rather be at Longbourn, but I am a selfish creature." His face was only inches from hers.

He desired her. It was far from a protestation of love, not that she would have believed one when he had known her barely a month, but she had always thought him handsome, and had felt drawn to him during those days at Netherfield. And they were married, whether she liked it or not. Was there anything wrong with acting on their attraction, in finding some comfort in each other during the little time they had?

And then she stopped thinking at all because his soft, warm lips were caressing her own, tempting and tantalizing her. It was only a slight, gentle pressure, yet a flush of heat shot through her at the captivating sensation. Her mouth tingled, craving more, and as if he could sense her reaction, his teeth nibbled her lower lip, and suddenly her legs and belly filled with a heavy longing.

Oh, heavens, the fluttering hunger she felt, the desire to impel herself towards him, to feel his body against hers, to embrace the essence of him! How could a mere kiss create such a burning ache, a yearning that ran so deep it might never be filled?

And that it should be Darcy who brought her this exquisite pleasure! He smelled of spice and soap, and the air around him held the calm that came right after a thunderstorm. But the storm was in her, and she would never be the same again.

Then he brushed his mouth against hers once more, and pulled away, his eyes darker than ever. "Yes," he whispered.

Breathe. She needed to remember to breathe. Surely she could keep her composure, no matter how much she craved more.

She had to focus. What had they been speaking of? Oh, yes, his mission – and that was enough to shake her out of the sensual haze evoked by his kiss. "That is all well and good, but I am not accepting your fate. I am going to find another answer," she said fiercely. "We will defeat Napoleon *and* bring you home safely."

"There is no reason we cannot try, if you wish it, but all the resources of the King's Mage and the War Office have found nothing of use."

She narrowed her eyes. "I have done the impossible before, and you said yourself that I had techniques for land magic you have never heard of."

"If you can find something in your Arabic books, I will be most grateful." But he was simply being polite. The aristocratic son of the King's Mage clearly did not expect to learn anything new.

"You do not know how wonderfully stubborn I can be." And she would consult Granny, whose abilities were far beyond the norm.

But his intent gaze fixed once more on her lips, and it made her pulses race.

It did not take long for her thoughts to go from how to get Darcy out of France alive to why he was going in the first place. She turned to him and asked, "How did you come to be selected for this mission?"

He shrugged. "There was no other choice. Napoleon's spies keep track of all our mages, specifically for fear of illusionists. None of them could get near him. My abilities with illusion have always been a secret, so Napoleon, along with the rest of the world, thinks me only a landed Talent, and therefore no threat to him."

"Why is it a secret? Surely you did not foresee a day when it would be necessary."

"No, simply to avoid the common assumption that anyone trained in both land Talent and magery will be weaker at both. I only had a year of mage training as a boy, against my father's wishes, I might add. It was between the time when my mother decided she might never have the daughter she hoped for and when Georgiana, my younger sister, was born. After that, she saw no point in teaching me further. I had plenty of other studies to take up my time, so I rarely practiced. I did not start again until a few months ago, when this mission arose. That is why my abilities are weak. Illusion-casting requires years of practice."

"You simply gave it up?" she said in disbelief. She would have done anything for those lessons!

"Except for making myself invisible. It was a useful skill for an eleven-year-old boy, so I practiced that. As for the rest—" he gestured helplessly, "—it did not seem important to me. Every woman in my family could cast illusions. Why should I bother?"

"And you thought of it as women's work," she guessed.

He grinned. "I was a boy. What else would I think? Most of the great mages have been women."

"Perhaps that is only because men choose to focus on their land Talents, which are more practical. Who else is going on this mission?"

He hesitated. "If I tell you, it must remain a complete secret. Their lives depend on it."

"My word on it," she said.

He peered out the windows, first the one on the left and then the right, as if there might be French spies racing down the turnpike beside them. Then he said in a low voice, "Two French nobles who have grown disenchanted with his reign. It must be someone Napoleon knows, you see. No one else would be allowed near him."

Her chest tightened. "Frenchmen? Who are they? How do you know it is not a trap, designed to capture an English mage?"

"For reasons of safety, I do not know their names, but I assure you, the War Office has investigated them thoroughly. They have good reason to despise the Emperor."

She shivered. Somehow that detail made it all more real. She leaned her head against his shoulder. It was so much warmer to be snuggled next to him, with his arm around her. She could almost imagine she wanted to be here.

Chapter 14

THE COACHING INN WHERE they stopped for the night was larger than the ones Elizabeth vaguely remembered from her childhood journeys to Wales, when she had shared a room with all her sisters and their nursemaid. It certainly catered to a finer clientele. They ate a hearty dinner at a long table shared with other travelers. Under normal circumstances, she would have found it exciting to meet so many new people, but all the stresses of the day weighed her down with bone-deep fatigue. It was a good thing this was not her wedding night.

Darcy was solicitous of her comfort, but he too seemed tired and disinclined to talk, although he was perfectly courteous to an older Scotsman traveling to London who asked him about the road ahead. He made no objection when she announced her desire to retire immediately after finishing her food, and escorted her up to her bedroom door.

When she turned to bid him goodnight, he took advantage of the empty corridor for a light kiss, only a brief touch, only long enough for his tongue to quickly trace the line between her lips. She gasped as heat melted through her.

Darcy straightened, a slight smile hinting at his satisfaction. "Sleep well, Elizabeth." His voice was husky, her name a caress in his mouth. "I will see you in the morning." Then he turned and disappeared down the passageway.

Elizabeth sagged against the wall as soon as Darcy turned the corner. Who could have known that such a fleeting kiss could leave her with a hot flame inside her and her legs weak? Clearly there were some benefits to this marriage that she had not considered.

They still had two more days of travel before they reached Pemberley, and she had a puzzle to solve. She intended to learn as much as she could from her new Arabic books in the meantime, no matter how tired she was. Determinedly she opened the door to her room.

And froze at the sight of the Indian maidservant who had altered her wedding dress, now laying out her nightdress on the bed. At this coaching inn miles from Meryton.

"Good evening, Mrs. Darcy." She was no longer dressed in the Indian style, but rather in the fashion of a lady's maid.

Elizabeth found her voice. "May I ask how you come to be here?"

"I rode in the luggage carrier with Mr. Darcy's valet. Did he not tell you he had brought a maid for you?"

"No, he failed to mention that." Perhaps he simply took it for granted that he must provide a servant. "I thought you served Rana Akshaya."

"I do, but when none of the maids at Netherfield agreed to make the journey, the great Rana said I might offer my services if I wished."

It made no sense. "You wished to take a long, cold, uncomfortable journey simply to serve as maid, which you could do at home?"

The woman smiled warmly. "I traveled halfway around the world to reach London. It is a fine city, but if you were to travel to India, would you be content to spend all your time in a single place, or would you seize the opportunity to see more of the land?" She gestured around the room. "I have never been in an English coaching inn before, nor a town like this. Everything is new to me."

The familiar kee-kee-kee interrupted them, and Elizabeth turned abruptly towards the hearth, where Cerridwen sat on an improvised perch made from a chair covered with towels. "How did you get in?" she asked the bird.

I have no nest here, and it is cold out, the bird said in her mind.

The Indian woman said, "I hope I did not overstep in admitting your falcon when she tapped at the window." She sounded unsurprised, though, as if it were a completely normal thing for a bird to come into an inn room, not to mention knowing to tap at a particular window.

Amused, Elizabeth said, "No, you did well. When my grandmother was still alive, Cerridwen always slept in her room during the winter." After her death, Elizabeth's mother would never allow the falcon inside the house, though, saying she must live in the stables with all the other animals. But the stable master had insisted on using a jess to bind the kestrel, and Cerridwen would have nothing to do with that. Eleven-year-old Elizabeth had spent several long days single-handedly cleaning out the old ruined dovecote for Cerridwen's use. It took weeks to get the smell out of her clothing.

Perhaps that might be one small benefit of this marriage. At Pemberley, she would be mistress of the household, and no one could stop her from creating a perch for Cerridwen indoors.

"I hope you will give me direction how I may serve you best," said the woman.

"I think you will find me easy to deal with," said Elizabeth. "I am accustomed to sharing one maid with my four sisters, and for this journey, I packed only dresses I can put on by myself." But if she had to have a maid, this one was at least interesting and not put off by Cerridwen's presence in her life. That was something. "What is your name?"

"You may call me Chandrika," she said gravely, and then she smiled.

The next morning, Darcy hesitated before knocking at Elizabeth's room at the inn. It felt improper, even though there was nothing wrong with a man going to his wife's bedroom. But she did not truly feel like his wife yet, and if he thought too hard about that fact, he might give up on the idea of both breakfast and waiting to consummate their marriage at Pemberley.

No. Do not think about consummating anything, he admonished himself. Think about anything else. Think about the door.

He rapped firmly on it.

"You may enter." Elizabeth's low, musical voice made all his senses come alive.

He opened the door and stepped inside, instructing his disobedient hand not to close it again. It listened, but barely. "Good morning, Elizabeth."

She was sitting at the small vanity inserting a last hairpin in her hair, a bewitching look of concentration on her face. "Oh! It is you." Color rose in her cheeks. "Good morning. I am almost ready."

Her Indian maidservant set down the clothing she was folding, curtsied to Darcy silently, and left the room, shutting the door which he had worked so hard to keep open. Leaving him alone with Elizabeth.

No, do not think about the closed door! And certainly do not think about removing all her hairpins and letting those dark curls fall loose over her shoulders. "I trust you slept well?" And do not, under any circumstances, look at the bed where she had slept. No, no, no.

The covers were still turned down. He groaned inwardly and tore his eyes away. Unfortunately, they landed on the exposed back of her neck, where a few stray curls escaped from confinement. The sight of it drew him like a magnet.

"Tolerably well, once I actually slept," she said cheerfully. "I stayed up too late reading. It is a bad habit of mine."

He could not help himself. He bent down and brushed his lips against the tender skin of the nape of her neck, her scent of lavender wafting over him.

She shivered as she looked up at him, her fine eyes wide. "Oh, my."

Think of anything, anything except her lips. "I have arranged for breakfast to be served in the private parlor."

She pushed back her stool and stood, only a foot away from him, close enough that he might have taken her in his arms, if it had not been such a bad, bad, bad idea. "I thank you. Shall we go down, then, Mr. Darcy?"

He could tolerate not kissing her, almost, but not the formality. "Call me William, I pray you."

Her cheeks grew rosy. "I thought your name was Fitzwilliam."

"My sister calls me William, and it would make me happy if you did as well." It was an excuse; Georgiana had called him that as a child because she struggled to pronounce Fitzwilliam, but he was almost certain that his full name had negative implications for Elizabeth. Better to use the shorter version that did not remind her of the family her great-grandmother hated.

"Very well, then, William." Her voice was breathy. "I imagine you are eager to get on the road again."

She could not know how anxious he was to reach Pemberley, where he could make her his wife in truth. He had thought separate chambers on the road would suffice to keep him from her. Perhaps separate inns might have been a better idea.

At breakfast it was easier, with servants walking in and out, but he still struggled for a safe topic of conversation, one which would neither lead to inappropriate thoughts nor bring back their earlier quarreling. He did not want to lose this precious new alliance. "Was the book that kept you up late a good one?"

"A challenging one, rather," she said ruefully. "It is in Arabic, but it is about illusion making. I had not planned to work on it until we reached Pemberley, but given the urgency of the situation, I intend to waste no time."

He doubted she would find anything useful, but her eagerness to help him warmed his heart. "Have you read it before?"

"No. My father only gave it to me before we left. He had hidden it lest I discover my own abilities, and I am still cross with him about that."

"I cannot blame you." But he did not want her to be cross, not now, so he asked, "Where did your father find these books?"

"In an old bookshop in Cambridge. They were inexpensive because no one could read them, but he could feel the magic in them. He thought Mr. Hadid, the apothecary in Meryton, could translate them for him. When he discovered their true nature, he decided I must learn Arabic to read them."

"Their true nature?"

"No one without Talent can read them. The writing turns into nonsense for anyone else."

Now she had his full attention. "Are you certain?"

"Yes, we checked it with several people. It affects copies, too. If I copy a word or two, Mr. Hadid can read it without difficulty, but for a sentence or more, he cannot make it out. And if I try to write a translation in English, the ink fades away before I reach the end of the page. It is the strangest thing."

"An Artifact," he breathed. "Do you know how rare that is?" Perhaps there truly was some useful information in those books of hers.

She smiled impishly. "Rare enough for my father to make me learn Arabic, which is more complicated than it sounds."

That smile sent a rush of desire through him. "Because it is a difficult language?"

"Not in itself. I learned it as a child does, living with the Hadids for weeks at a time, playing with their children, always speaking Arabic, or at least the version of it spoken in Tunisia. But the books are in classical Arabic, which is quite different. Have you ever read *The Canterbury Tales* as Chaucer wrote it?"

"In Middle English? Yes."

"Classical Arabic is at least that different from spoken Arabic. Mr. Hadid could teach me the basics of it, but he knew nothing of the terminology about Talent, so I must figure that out from context or guesswork. It would be wrong to say I read these books; rather I decipher them with great effort."

"Books? There are more than one?"

"Five in all. Though they are not all by the same person; the handwriting is different in two of them."

Five Artifacts? He knew of only half a dozen objects which carried their own magic in the entirety of England. And these had been sitting in Mr. Bennet's library gathering dust? "I would like to see these books."

"I was planning to bring this one to read on the road. The others are in my trunk. Is something the matter?"

That she had a king's ransom casually slung on the back of the luggage carriage? Perhaps he ought to hire more outriders as protection against highwaymen. "Nothing at all. Your efforts are impressive, and I am eager to learn what is in the books." He was fortunate that she would share it with him.

Light broke over her countenance. "Truly? I thought you found my books foolish."

"Not at all. I am fascinated."

"I wonder if we might experiment with how our talents intertwine, too. Since we are doing nothing else as we travel. Perhaps we might learn something."

"An excellent idea." And perhaps it would keep his mind off all the other ways he would like to entwine with Elizabeth.

They crossed the stable yard to the carriage, Elizabeth casually carrying a netted bag with something the shape of a book in it, and Darcy struggling not to demand that she be more careful with it, or better yet, give it to him to protect. The turnpike was considered safe, but the roads were fairly empty at this time of year, and it could put them in danger of being robbed if anyone realized they had something of value.

She gave him a warm smile as he handed her into the carriage. Something only a day ago he had despaired of ever seeing.

As they set off, Elizabeth removed the book from her bag and held it out to him. "This is the one I am reading now, or rather, attempting to read."

He took it from her carefully. It was a small volume, not overly thick, bound with leather tooled in a Moorish gilded design. Not particularly prepossessing in appearance, although clearly antique. Opening it revealed incomprehensible flowing script. It seemed in excellent condition for its age, but had nothing to mark it as a priceless Artifact.

Setting it on his lap, he removed his gloves and picked it up in his bare hands. Good God, the thing was heavy with magic! His fingertips tingled wherever he touched it.

"It feels strange, does it not?" Elizabeth asked. "I am always careful not to use my Talent when reading it, since otherwise it burns my hands. Not real burns, though it feels like it."

"Like repulsion, then. I have never heard of such a thing in a magical item." But why would the book want her not to use her Talent? And how could a book want anything?

"Perhaps you can help me with a question from my reading last night," Elizabeth said. "The book says there are two kinds of illusions, one which can be seen and heard but not touched, and one that can be touched but not seen or heard. The first must be like your animal illusions, but can you tell me about the other?"

"I have never heard of an illusion that can be touched." If such a thing even existed, which he doubted.

"It says they are rarely used." She took the book, opened it from the back, and flipped through a few pages. "Here it is. 'Illusions of touch are often not worth the effort, except for those of... unusual ability, although simple ones may be helpful in battle when one wishes an opponent to trip over – something, something – or to drop his sword or – something, maybe a dagger? – because it seems to be burning hot.' I wondered if that would work for pistols, too."

An illusion that would make someone drop a pistol would be useful indeed. "Does it give instructions?"

"Not in the few pages I have read. It mentions an illusion of coldness on a hot summer's day, too. I wondered if your mother might know something of it."

"She would have trained me in it if she did."

She looked up at him. "Perhaps it is worth experimenting with it. Not everything in the books works, or perhaps I should say that I could not make everything work, but we could try."

"I pray you, no. Your stamina for magery is still low, and I fear what might happen if you attempt untested magic. Especially when we are far from assistance."

A shadow crossed her face. "Then you try it," she suggested.

It was better than allowing her to make the attempt, even if he doubted it would work. "A fine idea. If only we had a sword to practice on."

She pulled out a sheath from her pocket and removed a tiny knife from it. "How about this? Think of it as a very small sword." She made a teasing movement as if to stab him with it.

He laughed. "Doubtless you have had moments of wishing to use that on me, so I suppose I should learn to defend myself." He gathered energy, and the knife began to glow.

She looked at it doubtfully. "It looks hot, but it feels no different."

He tried again, and this time flames danced over the blade between her fingers.

"Perhaps cold would be easier," she suggested.

He tried to imagine it being icy cold, and a layer of frost appeared on it.

"It seems as if you are making it *look* hot or cold, which makes sense, since you are accustomed to using a visual image. Perhaps tactile illusions use a different method."

Or they did not exist. But she wanted him to try. How could he do it without an image? Perhaps putting his energy inside the knife, imagining it growing hotter. Imagining her fingers burning when she touched it —

"Ouch!" Elizabeth dropped the knife, which skittered across the carriage floor. "My goodness! That felt real."

He scooped up the knife, and his fingers burned. He forced himself to hold it for a minute before releasing it. His fingertips were not even red, though they felt as if they were blistering. He blew on the knife to dispel the illusion, and abruptly the knife was cool again. But the pain in his fingers lingered another minute before it faded.

"It worked!" cried Elizabeth with delight. "Oh, well done!"

He was more pleased by her praise and excitement than by the discovery of a new form of illusion that had apparently been lost for hundreds of years and might someday save his life. But that could wait, and right now he wanted to enjoy the sparkle in Elizabeth's eyes, which warmed his heart more effectively than his Talent had heated the knife. "I thank you for teaching me this. It could prove very useful."

"Do you think so?"

"Indeed. Mages have so few ways to defend themselves. A technique like this will be valuable."

Her smile faded a bit. "Will you tell your mother about it?"

There was only one answer. "I must. Her safety might depend upon it someday."

"I suppose so." She bit her lip. "Could you leave out the part about the book, though? I would not wish her to take it away, and it would do her no good without an Arabic-speaking Talent, anyway."

If his mother knew the book was an Artifact, that alone would attract her interest. "Perhaps I could tell her you discovered this while experimenting with your new abilities."

She brightened. "Against your advice. She will believe that of me, that I would try it even if you told me it was impossible." She appeared delighted with the idea.

Because he could not resist her mischievous expression, he took her hand and raised it to his lips. He turned it over and brushed a kiss against the tender skin inside her wrist.

She gasped, so he redoubled his efforts, tracing the tip of his tongue along her blue veins, drinking in her newly rapid breathing. Good God, but she was enticing! Desire ripped through him.

Enough was enough. He gathered her in his arms, and this time she deliberately slid closer and allowed him to pull her onto his lap. He claimed her tempting lips, because a new use of his Talent was nothing to the magic of Elizabeth's kiss.

Chapter 15

THE UNREMARKABLE INN THEY stayed in that night was outside of Retford, nestled between the forest and a rushing stream. The following morning, the sky was growing brighter outside Darcy's room when his valet said, "Sir, it appears Mrs. Darcy is already outside."

"What?" Darcy dropped the ends of his partially tied cravat and hurried to the window. Yes, there she was, standing on the grass in the first morning light, her head cocked as if listening to something. But there was no one with her except her maid, who stood some distance away. The sky was empty, too – not even a sign of that damned bird of hers.

"Tie this quickly," he told the valet. "Any knot you like, as long as it is fast."

Usually he preferred to do his own cravat, but when time was of the essence, Wilkins could do it in half the time. He tipped his chin back to let the man work.

"There you are, sir. Hat and gloves?"

He grabbed them and hurried out, not even pausing for his greatcoat. What was Elizabeth doing?

She had not moved by the time he reached her, seeming oblivious to his approach. At least the maid curtsied to acknowledge him, but Elizabeth seemed lost in a different world. Did she not even see him?

"Good morning, Elizabeth," he said.

She jumped. "Oh! Good morning."

"I had not expected to see you outside. Were you displeased with the inn?"

"Not at all. I simply wanted to..." She gestured around the green. "To listen to the land."

He raised an eyebrow. "Listen to the land?"

"I noticed it last night when we arrived. I can hear it a little. Not to interact with it, more like eavesdropping on a distant conversation. Yesterday when we stopped for the night, there was nothing at all, just silence." A shadow fluttered across her face. "I expected it would be the same here, since we are even farther from Longbourn. I do not understand it."

Nor did he. "Surprising, but not impossible. The power of the land grows stronger the closer we get to the Peak. Natural philosophers claim the ley lines there make it easier to reach the power. It is much more of a challenge in the South of England."

She cocked her head. "Is that why you were training there?"

"Yes, so it would mimic the conditions in France. I could not feel the land in Hertfordshire." Here it was already tugging at him, even half a day's travel from Pemberley. But that did not explain why she felt it, unless it was through his Talent.

She chewed her lip. "How will you practice at Pemberley, then? Will you not end up using your land Talent when you make illusions there?"

It worried him, too, trading the infinitesimally slow improvement from practice time for the possibility of a blood tie to Pemberley. "I will make less progress, but the benefits from our marriage will outweigh that." Still, it was a gamble.

"I know!" she exclaimed. "You could stand on iron when you are casting!" Her excitement lit her face, even though her words made no sense.

"I beg your pardon?"

"My book advises landed Talents to wear shoes with no nails in them, since iron interferes with drawing power from the land. It is true – I tried it myself. My Talent is stronger when I wear boots made only of leather. My footwear does not last as long, but it helps. If you stood on a piece of iron, it might block you from using your land Talent while you are practicing your illusions!" She looked so pleased with herself that he smiled, too.

"It is worth a try," he said. After all, if it did not work, he would have lost nothing. "But come, shall we not break our fast and be on the road?"

Elizabeth regretfully set aside her book when they turned off the main road onto a narrow lane running beside a wide stream. Wooded hills rose steeply on both sides, and the frequent curves and bumps were not conducive to reading. It would not do to arrive at Pemberley queasy from trying to read in a rocking carriage.

At least the scenery was striking, so different from the broad fields and gentle hills of Hertfordshire. Would she be able to feel this land, too? When they had stopped to change horses last, she had perceived nothing, but there had been no plants in the stable yard, and she had not wished to ask Darcy – William – if she could walk off into a field. He was in a hurry to reach Pemberley, and after all it did not matter whether she could sense the earth at some small coaching inn.

She glanced up at him. Once again, he had chosen to sit beside her rather than on the facing bench, an informality she would not have expected of him. He truly was handsome, she could not deny that, with those sculpted features and strong shoulders. And his kisses! They were a revelation.

Heat filled her belly as she recalled the exhilarating heat of his tongue against her lips. She had never truly credited why women could be foolish enough to let their passions outweigh their reason. Common sense and practicality had to come first, and they had not allowed their desires to get out of hand, tempting as it had been. But she understood better now how someone's cravings could lead them astray.

Yes, she was eager to reach Pemberley, too. If the marriage bed was even half as pleasant as kissing him, she was eager to experience it. An odd, pleasurable ache grew deep inside her and her cheeks grew hot. Oh, dear, best to think of something else!

Like her unexpected ability to sense the land outside the inn this morning, and what it meant for her plans.

Originally she had thought to make the best of a bad situation and do her best to bond to Pemberley, knowing her connection to it could never be as deep as what she had at Longbourn, the land where she had been born, where her afterbirth was buried, where she had grown from infancy on the bounty of the soil. Then, when her new husband had confessed that he might not return from France, the hope of going back to Longbourn flared in her. She would rather he survived and would work for that, but if that failed, would it not be better if she kept her bond to Longbourn, and with it, the option to return home?

Unless there was a child, who would have to be raised at Pemberley in order to keep a bond to the land they would inherit. How could she go home, if it meant leaving her baby behind? Perhaps William's mother had found that idea reasonable, but she did not.

And would Longbourn's land still answer to her if she returned? Most likely, but her connection would be weaker once Jane had a child of her own that bonded to it. Then Elizabeth's presence might even interfere with the child's Talent.

No, there was no going back. A sigh escaped her as she let the brief dream go, imagining it taking wing and flying out of the carriage. Pemberley was her future, whether she liked it or not, and she should be grateful she could sense the nearby land at all.

Darcy studied Elizabeth's expression. She had been quiet ever since they left the main road, biting her lip, her expression troubled. Was she worried about what lay ahead?

He had guessed wrongly so often about her. Perhaps it would be wiser simply to ask. "Is something the matter?"

Straightening, she said, "Nothing at all. I was admiring the river. It is lovely."

"It runs by Pemberley House, where it widens into a small lake. Beyond that, it becomes an excellent trout stream."

She stared out the window, seemingly fascinated by the view, but looking no happier. "Could we stop for a few minutes? I would like to go down by the water."

"Could it wait? We are but a mile or two from Pemberley."

She turned to face him, but avoided his eyes. "I would rather do it now." It was as if the words came out reluctantly.

He was beginning to recognize that evasive look. "Is this for something from your Arabic books?"

"It will help Pemberley to know me if I wash my hands in its waters before I arrive."

It sounded like rank superstition to him, but it would be harmless enough and clearly meant something to Elizabeth. "Very well." He banged his cane on the roof of the carriage to signal the coachman.

"I thank you." She did not look pleased, though, as she removed her gloves and set them on the seat beside her.

It would only be polite to match her informality, so he stripped off his own. It was a good excuse to feel her touch as he helped her out of the carriage, a pleasurable bonus. Very pleasurable.

As he stepped out onto the roadside, her hand still in his, the shock of his land Talent came rushing up to meet him, staggering him with the intensity of it. The tide of welcoming warmth, powering through his veins, the sudden, overwhelming knowledge of the complex world below the surface, and the peace of being in his proper place, where he was rooted as firmly as giant wych elms on the riverbank.

"Oh, my." Elizabeth sounded awed.

He shook himself free of the pull of the land. "What is it?"

"This land." She raised their joined hands. "I can feel how glad it is to see you." Her voice was wistful.

How could she be intertwining with his land magic already, before she even carried his child? "I have rarely been away from Pemberley for so long before."

"I had not realized your Talent was so powerful."

Her praise embarrassed him. "We are practically on top of a ley line here. It runs along that ridge in the Dark Peak, or so the philosophers say. It makes it much easier to use Talent."

She took the last step down from the carriage and her expression grew thoughtful. "I can sense the land here a little, even with no connection to it. Or perhaps that is because I am touching you."

"Perhaps, but most Talents sense the land better near a ley line." Still, he let her drop his hand, even though he missed the warmth and connection.

He kept a few steps behind her as she picked her way down the bank to the water and knelt on a rock next to the stream.

His Talent luxuriated in the vast underground web of tree roots, the interlacing fibers connecting the mushrooms, the dead leaves on the surface beginning to decay and sink into the earth, all of it distracting him from Elizabeth. Then, just as his consciousness was sinking into the ground like the leaves, he felt a disturbance in the land, a small distortion right in front of him. Right where Elizabeth was kneeling.

He snatched his attention back to the human world. Elizabeth's left arm was extended over the water. Drops of blood fell from it, making ripples in the clear water.

Part of him shrieked that this was dangerous blood magic, but another, stronger part said this was his wife who deserved his support. Acting on the instinct that seemed to rise from the ground beneath him, he stepped forward and placed his hand on her shoulder.

She stiffened, but kept her arm out. Now he could see her lips were moving as she murmured something so softly that her words were drowned out by the stream.

And suddenly he was all of those things – the water flowing past, the blood dripping into it, the trees and the roots in the leaves. He could feel the stones digging into his knees, even though he stood on both feet. It was Elizabeth's knees he was feeling, as the power of the land ran in circles through him, through Elizabeth, through the trees and water and sky.

Elizabeth bowed her head and drew in her arm, turning it over as she rose to her feet. With her other hand, she ran a finger over the top of the cut, but it continued to bleed.

"Oh, bother!" she exclaimed. "I forgot."

Of course. She could not heal the cut, with no land Talent to draw on here.

He did it for her, sliding his finger along the soft skin of her inner arm, feeling the tingling of her flesh knitting beneath his touch.

His wife's flesh. And tonight they would be one flesh.

She seemed to tremble all over. Then she stilled and said, "I thank you. Especially as I know you disapprove of blood magic." She bent down to pick up her small knife, the same one he had put an illusion of heat on. Was this why she carried it?

After the intimacy of the shared power, it was disconcerting to feel a distance between them again. Picking his words with care, he said, "I have been taught to do so, but I cannot deny it seemed to have an effect."

"How is your land to know me if I do not give it something of myself?" It was obviously a rhetorical question. "The location of this stream is a stroke of good fortune. It will spread that knowledge widely." But her voice was brittle, as if she might fracture at any moment.

"Does it still hurt?" He gestured to where the cut had been. He would have sworn the healing was complete.

"No." She stepped carefully up the bank towards the carriage, but her eyes were shiny and she blinked rapidly.

He hated seeing her pain. "Elizabeth, what is wrong?"

Her shoulders slumped, and she turned to face him. "A Talent can only belong to one land."

"What of it?"

"I gave my blood to Pemberley." She said it as if speaking to a particularly slow child. "My bond to Longbourn is broken. It was my choice, and I did it deliberately, but that does not mean I do not feel it."

It made no sense. "But it is your sister who is bonded to Longbourn, not you. You told me so."

She seemed to collapse in on herself, wrapping her arms around her body and closing her eyes. "I thought you knew the truth," she whispered. "You said you could tell I was a landed Talent. Which I was, until just now."

He gazed at her in horror. "I thought that at first, but I could not imagine why you would lie about such a thing, so I assumed what I had seen was the results of your tricks from your book." But he ought to have known it was no such thing. "And it is not uncommon for a second child to share some sensitivity to the land."

No wonder she had been desperate to stay at Longbourn and furious with him for dragging her away. He could no more imagine giving up his bond to Pemberley than giving up breathing.

Now her shoulders were shaking and tears leaked from her closed eyes, and the only thing to do was to take her in his arms and allow her to weep on his shoulders while he stroked her back, unable to ease the pain he had caused. "I am so very sorry, my love." The words slipped out before he could catch them.

She quieted, but did not pull away. "As I said, it was my choice." Her words were muffled.

"Perhaps it is not so final. If a few drops of blood on another estate could break the land bond, why, every Talent in London would live in fear of cutting their finger."

She sniffled, raising her head. "It is not just the blood, but the intention. I told the land I was giving it my blood to nourish it, as I hoped it would nourish me. That it would be my home, and part of me. And something happened. I do not know what, but the land was not indifferent to my offering."

"Yes, something happened. I felt it too." He paused to listen to the land. It seemed satisfied. "And it reacts to the two of us together."

She stepped back, leaving his arms empty. Was it the land that was disappointed, or only him?

"Good. If I can bond to the land, even if only slightly, then I will be able to give you that much more power when you need it."

Then it struck him, a bolt of lightning from the blue. She had done this for him, had broken her bond to Longbourn in a quixotic effort to offer him a tiny chance at survival. There were no words to give justice to the emotions welling up inside him. "I am humbled by your generosity."

"Let us hope it works." She walked towards the carriage.

He followed her and was about to hand her in when the ground tugged at him, as though his boots were stuck to it. He sent a question, but there was no clear answer, only more tugging at his boots.

He could only guess at what it meant. "Elizabeth, are your shoes suitable for walking?"

She glanced down at her footwear and gave him a puzzled look. "They are sturdy enough."

"I think the land wants us to walk the rest of the way, or at least onto the estate. It does not wish us to go back into the carriage." He must sound like an idiot, claiming that the land had opinions. He had never thought this way before.

But she nodded, as if it made perfect sense to her. Perhaps it did; perhaps she had always spoken to the land at Longbourn, or it might have been something she read in her books. "Then let us walk." And she held her hand out to him.

He instructed the coachman to go ahead, and they set off once the dust from its passage had settled. The tugging lessened, the ground beneath them apparently satisfied. Darcy tried not to consider what the staff would think when he and Elizabeth arrived on foot and ungloved, and decided holding Elizabeth's hand was well worth the price.

As they rounded the curve, Elizabeth caught her breath as a clearing revealed a striking view of the distant manor house. Her feet slowed to a halt at the sight of the elegant, modern structure, perfectly situated by a lake which reflected its lines in harmony with the landscape surrounding it. A line of hills rose behind the large, handsome stone building.

"My goodness," she breathed. Now she understood why her new husband would expect most women to jump at the chance of living there. "It is lovely. I assumed Miss Bingley was exaggerating in her praise of Pemberley, but I see it was nothing more than the truth."

"Why would she have exaggerated?" He sounded offended.

She tilted her head to look at him. "Because women often flatter the gentlemen they are interested in, hoping to catch their eye. Men do the same thing, I suppose."

The corners of his mouth twitched. "I daresay you never flattered any gentlemen."

She laughed. "I always thought it would be asking for trouble. If I flattered a man into wanting to marry me, I would either have to continue to flatter him for the rest of my life or deal with his disappointment over why I had changed. Far easier not to begin! But I grant you Pemberley has the finest setting I have ever seen, and that is no flattery."

He gazed out over the prospect, his countenance suddenly serious. "I thought I might never see it again. Coming home is another thing I have to thank you for."

A lump formed in her throat, and she swallowed hard. "I shall force you to show me every nook and cranny in return."

"I should be delighted to do so."

"Your staff, on the other hand, will be less than delighted with me, I fear. They must be expecting a fine lady with excellent connections, not a country gentleman's daughter without even any wedding clothes. They may mistake me for the governess," she teased. But it was a joke of ill comfort; she did not like to think of the odd looks she would get when the locals learned how hurried her wedding had been. They would assume she had either entrapped him or been so badly compromised that there was no other choice.

"My staff is too well trained to be surprised, and they will be thrilled that I have married at last."

That was easy for him to say. "Tell me, what would you think when a wealthy man marries a girl he had only just met in a rushed ceremony?"

Color stained his cheeks. "This is different, and everyone at Pemberley will understand that. But I will have to consider how to present it to outsiders."

She gazed down at the beautiful house that seemed to have grown from the surrounding land. "It does not matter. Even if your staff do not understand, it is done, and they will learn to live with it." But it would not be pleasant for her. She was accustomed to servants who respected the hard work she did on the estate, but that would not help now, when she had only a tiny trace of connection to the land.

He looked puzzled. "Elizabeth, I do not think you understand. For the last century, ever since George I became the first king without Talent of his own, every heir of Pemberley has married a woman of strong Talent, in order to help secure the kingdom. The staff have seen the cost of that, as each Mrs. Darcy had to live separately, with children going back and forth between father and mother. They have seen the pain of repulsion between husband and wife. Once they realize you have Talent yet no repulsion to me, they will understand. You are a great prize, even if you do not seem to realize it. And that is not counting our ability to entwine our magic."

She blinked at him, unable to imagine so many generations in these odd non-marriages. "Are all Darcys that bound by duty, to give up so much for it?" No wonder he had readily agreed to a hopeless mission.

His lips twisted. "We are not as unselfish as that. The crown, mindful of its need for mages, supplies extremely generous dowries in these cases, as well as preferment for the rest of the family. That house was built with the first royal dowry. My great-great-grandfather was well pleased with his bargain."

Did her father know about this? "Then my sisters…"

"They will be well dowered, if they marry a man of Talent."

An unpleasant suspicion entered her mind. "And you? Will you get that dowry for marrying me?"

He shook his head with a smile. "I would have, but I already signed it over to your father. It did not seem right for me to profit from a marriage you did not want."

So there was no reason to worry about Longbourn going bankrupt. It was a relief, and it spoke well of William. "What about my eldest sister, if she is marrying Mr. Bingley?"

"It is only for marrying another Talent. I believe Bingley has already explained this to your sister." He cleared his throat. "I also advised him to marry as quickly as possible, before it occurs to anyone to interfere."

No doubt anyone, in this case, meant his mother, but Elizabeth did not wish to provoke a quarrel, not now, when they were so close to Pemberley. After all, his mother's behavior was not his fault.

Chapter 16

P EMBERLEY HOUSE WAS BEAUTIFUL beyond measure, but Elizabeth also found it overwhelming, from the astonishingly long double line of servants waiting inside the door to greet them to the spacious rooms, each more elegant than the last. The dining room could fit half of Longbourn in it. The parlour was suitable for entertaining royalty. Even the grand staircase, splitting into two halfway up, would have looked at home in a palace. It was the sort of place that travelers would come to gawk at.

And she lived here now.

Darcy's pride in his home seemed to radiate from him, and for his sake, Elizabeth expressed her admiration readily. It was easy to do; there was little not to admire.

Especially the library. She had expected a fine library from Miss Bingley's descriptions, but had not imagined such a vast, high-ceilinged room, replete with the smell of fine leather bindings and the vanilla scent of old paper. Circular iron stairs led to a balcony that ringed the room with even more bookshelves lining it. Her father's library was considered the best in Meryton, but this one dwarfed it. "I had best only admire it from the door," she said. "If I go in and look around, I may not emerge until next week."

His expression warmed. "I hoped it would please you."

"How could anyone not be pleased?"

He took her through the public rooms, including a brief walk through the portrait gallery. "I will be happy to tell you about my ancestors when you are not tired from the journey," he said, keeping his eyes averted from one particular painting, more recent that most of the others, of two young boys, perhaps six and eight. Even as a child, Darcy's expression had been serious.

Then he took her upstairs. "Your bedroom is here," he said, sounding apologetic. "I asked the staff to prepare it, but they had little time. It has never actually been used by the lady of the house, since repulsion kept my mother and grandmother from living here. I hope you will redecorate it to your tastes." He threw open the door to an airy space filled with sunlight from three large windows.

The furnishings were exquisite, from the canopied bed with an elaborately carved headboard to the inlaid cabinet and vanity which balanced on delicate curved legs. But it was the walls which dominated the room, papered in chinoiserie showing delicate paintings of flowering trees filled with colorful exotic birds. A heron stood in one corner, and an elaborately detailed dragon with tigers crouched at its feet covered much of the opposite side. Good heavens, she could spend hours exploring her walls!

"It is beautiful," she whispered.

He beamed. "Your dressing room is through here." He opened another door.

Inside it Chandrika was already unpacking her trunks. The Indian woman made a silent curtsy before returning to her work.

Darcy continued, "And this door leads to my bedroom." He gestured at the painted dragon.

Door? What door? But then he put his hand on a tiny latch hidden in the dragon's tail. Now she could see the outlines of the frame, disguised in the branches of a tree by an expert craftsman.

"Astonishing!" Then she forgot the beauty of the furnishings as heat rose within her. That was the door he would come through tonight to share her bed, to make her his wife in truth. She peeped through it, getting the impression of heavy furniture carved from dark wood and heavy draperies, then drew back, suddenly shy. She had never been this close to a man's bedroom, apart from her father's.

"Shall I leave you here to refresh yourself after our travels?" he asked, looking concerned. What had he seen in her face?

"That would be welcome," she said. A few minutes with no one watching her reactions would be a relief. None of this seemed real – except the broodingly attractive man whose eyes were traveling warmly down her form.

There was no reason that taking her first bath at Pemberley should differ from doing so at home. The embossed bathtub the servants had carried in was a little larger, and hot water to fill it arrived faster with more staff available to carry it up from the kitchen, but a bath was a bath, was it not?

Except now, when Chandrika helped her undress and step into the tub, it was for her final bathing before the consummation of her wedding. And she was completely uncovered in front of the adjoining door to William's bedroom, the door through which he could theoretically walk at any moment, even though he had said he would leave her alone to wash. As she sank into the blessedly hot water, the image of him standing in that doorway filled her thoughts – and her body. It was not the bath which kindled a flame deep inside her, making her skin burn with the anticipation of his touch. She struggled to swallow, imagining his expression if he walked in to see her wearing nothing at all.

Good heavens, what a ninny she was being! This was an arranged marriage which would be consummated tonight as part of a decision by the government on furthering its aims, not a love match. And it was not as if she was ignorant of what the wedding night involved. It was impossible to be bonded with the land without being well aware of how lambs and calves came to exist. Not to mention that she often helped the midwife delivering babies and had heard many secrets shared in the intimacy of a birthing room.

But still her body ached for something that she could not identify, and Darcy's kisses burned in her mind.

At another time, she would have lingered in the tub, letting the last soreness from the road drain away, but she could not shake the thought of her husband appearing through that door hidden in the wallpaper dragon, a smoldering look in his eyes. Instead she hurried through her ablutions and climbed out while the water was still warm.

Chandrika already had one of her favorite gowns pressed, and Elizabeth let her style her hair. There was no need for cosmetics, though. Her mirror showed her flushed cheeks and reddened lips. Did simply thinking about being kissed cause such a change?

When a knock finally came, she jumped to her feet. But it was from the door into the rest of the house, not the adjoining room. Most likely a servant, but her voice still shook a little as she bade them to enter.

She truly was a ninny, to be acting so foolishly!

It was Darcy, though. He had changed for dinner, and looked darkly handsome. "I hope you are finding everything to your satisfaction," he said.

She lifted her chin, determined not to show her discomposure. "Very much so. It is a pleasing room."

A smile lit his face. "I have taken the liberty of requesting dinner to be served in our private sitting room. After our days of travel, I thought you might prefer a less formal meal, but if you would rather eat in the dining room, it would be no trouble to change it."

"A quiet meal sounds perfect." It would certainly be easier not to feel as if all the staff were watching her tonight. A drawn-out supper of several removes, surrounded by footmen standing at attention, had little appeal. And she appreciated him for thinking of that.

Darcy had planned this dinner carefully. No matter how impatient he was to take Elizabeth to bed, it was even more important for her to be comfortable. Her response to his kisses had shown the passion simmering beneath her surface, and he was determined that nothing should happen tonight that might inhibit that. If there had been a finer moment in his life than watching Elizabeth's eyes darken with desire for him, he could not recall it.

"I hope you do not mind a simple dinner tonight," he told her. "My French chef wanted to provide a feast to impress you, but I sent word it should wait until tomorrow."

She looked at the table laden with elaborate dishes. "This is his idea of a simple meal? It is far more than we have at a family dinner at Longbourn, and that is for our entire family, not just the two of us. Now, have I shocked you?" she teased.

"I could not stop him from making something of an exhibition," Darcy admitted. "But I hope you will enjoy it."

"I am certain I will! Though it is novel enough to dine with you alone, since I am accustomed to a much fuller house."

"Whereas I am used to quiet meals. It will be a pleasant change to dine with you every day, as often I used to do so alone when there are no guests."

"Then your sister does not live here?" She seemed to be studying him.

Not his favorite topic, but he could not avoid discussing Georgiana forever. "She has her own household in London."

"Does she prefer to be in Town, then?"

Definitely not a question he wanted to discuss, especially not on his wedding night. "Yes, but I have asked her to join us here so that she can make your acquaintance."

"I hope she will not mind the trip," she said, but with a slight frown. "I do not wish to cause her any difficulties."

"She always enjoys visiting Pemberley." That was an easier answer.

"Do you know when she will arrive?"

"She has not said yet, but I thought we should have a little time to ourselves first." And hopefully much of it would be spent in her bedroom. "Or mostly to ourselves. My French tutors will be here in two days. I cannot escape that duty, as understanding French conversation is vital to my mission, and my abilities are sadly deficient. I learned the basics long ago, but I never troubled myself to work hard at it since I expected to spend my life at Pemberley." But he did not want to think of his mission, not tonight, when he would finally be completely alone with Elizabeth. He wanted to focus on her. "You speak some French, do you not?"

"Yes, although I am told that my accent is atrocious. I learned it along with Arabic from the Hadids. They lived in France before the Revolution, so my French is that of a Marseilles tradesman with an Arabic accent," she said with a laugh. "But it suffices."

What was it about her laughter that made him ache to kiss her? Not much longer, now; a quiet dinner to put her at her ease, and then, finally, they would be husband and wife. "I am beginning to think you were most fortunate in your acquaintance with the Hadids. Or perhaps I am the lucky one, since I am benefitting from your years of learning from them, as well as in many other ways."

A becoming flush rose in her cheeks. Was she, too, thinking of the wedding night to come?

He dearly hoped so.

The image of her dark curls spread across a pillow, her lips swollen with his kisses, felt so vivid that he had to force himself to remember that he must be patient. Instead of telling her all of his hopes for tonight, he offered her a dish of fine ragout. "If there is anything else you would like, pray do not hesitate to ask. Either for dinner, or if there is something about your rooms which could make you more comfortable."

She lowered her eyes. "It is all delicious, and I have no complaints. I am quite enamored of the wallpaper in my room. Has it been there long?"

Finally, a safe topic of conversation which would not inflame his desire any more than it was. He could talk about Pemberley for hours. And then it would finally, finally be time.

Chapter 17

A SURGE OF PLEASURE rushed through Darcy as the maid showed a pink-cheeked Elizabeth into the breakfast parlor the next morning. Less than an hour since he had left her bed, and already he missed her.

Her eyes darted around the room before finally turning to him with a rueful smile, her color even higher.

So often Darcy's ability to guess what Elizabeth was thinking had failed him, but it did not take any great insight to guess why a gently bred young lady would be embarrassed to see her husband for the first time after their wedding night. And what a wedding night! She had lived up to every promise of passion he had perceived in her and more. But if he thought too hard about that, he would end up trying to coax her back to bed rather than eating breakfast.

And he was proud of the breakfast. He wanted her to appreciate it.

Still, he was not a saint, so he took her hand and pressed a lingering kiss to it. "My dearest Elizabeth, I hope you know that you have truly made me the happiest of men."

Her cheeks were almost scarlet. "I am glad to hear it," she said in a strangled voice.

If he was disappointed not to hear a similar expression of pleasure, he was not surprised. Her enjoyment last night had been evidence enough.

"May I make up a plate for you? I can recommend both the ham and the bacon, which are from the estate, as are the eggs. The bread is made with flour milled not ten miles from here. There is honey from our own beekeeper. The wild plum jam and blackberry preserves are from the local hedgerow fruit, though they contain sugar, I fear. We have coffee and tea, but also the housekeeper's special blend of chamomile and rosehips." He eyed her hopefully.

This time there was no disappointment. "How kind of you!" she exclaimed. "This is most welcome. I had been dreading trying to explain my food preferences to your housekeeper, so I thank you for taking that on. I would like some of everything, if I may."

And to his delight, she pressed a kiss on his cheek.

"You give me too much credit," he said as he loaded her plate with food. "I only asked for local food for today and told her you would give her further instructions."

"Still, you have broken the ice. Will she understand if I explain to her about the effect on my Talent?"

"Mrs. Reynolds? Absolutely. She has been with the family since before I was born, and I trust her implicitly. She will make certain that our meals follow your requirements."

Her eyes brightened. "That will be delightful. At home I could not eat much of what was served, and often ended up in the kitchen later because I was still hungry. There is no reason they cannot serve other dishes which you like, but it will be a pleasure for me to eat freely."

How could Mrs. Bennet have allowed her daughter to go hungry? "I am sorry your mother did not make arrangements for you. You are the mistress here, and everything will be in accordance with your wishes."

Elizabeth took her plate eagerly. "It was not her fault. I never explained it, as she does not know about my Talent."

Had he heard correctly? "Your own mother?"

"She cannot keep from gossiping, so it was better for her to believe that Jane had the Talent, not I."

"I take it your eldest sister has no Talent?" It was unusual, but not unheard of.

"A little, but it is not strong. She was born early, on a visit to London, and my mother did not know to save the afterbirth to bury at Longbourn. So when I came along, my father took all the precautions to make certain I could connect to the land if Jane did not."

"But why keep it a secret?"

Her cheeks flushed. "Jane's birth was only a few months after my parents married. My father was afraid of what people would think if she also had no Talent."

"Still, how could you hide it when your power came in? Surely it must have been obvious that something odd was happening."

"By sheer good fortune, I was in Wales when it happened, without my mother."

"I thought you had not been there since you were a child."

"Yes, I was eight."

His sip of coffee went down the wrong way, leaving him coughing. "Your powers came in when you were eight?" His mother had been able to draw out his magery to a degree when he was ten, but he could not access it fully until several years later, when the usual illness that presaged the use of land Talent had beset him.

"Some of them," she said easily, as if there were nothing remarkable in it. "My ability to connect to the land grew stronger when I was thirteen."

When she was eight. There was something significant about it. "Was that not when you bonded to Cerridwen?"

She stopped to think. "It was the same summer, I think." But then she looked away, as if uncomfortable with the topic.

But he wanted her to enjoy his company, not to feel uncomfortable, so he changed the subject. "Have you any plans for the day?" he asked.

Her expression turned cautious. "I thought to meet with the house-keeper, and I must decide what to do about Chandrika, the maid. She has offered to stay here for a time until I can choose a lady's maid of my liking, but I do not know if Mrs. Reynolds already has someone in mind."

"Would that be able to wait? I would be glad of the opportunity to show you around Pemberley. The grounds are particularly fine." Was that tactful enough, or would she feel as if he were was giving her orders?

Her expression brightened. "I would enjoy that. You must know the best places to see."

He should not be so pleased that she was willing to accept his company. "If you wish, there is an attractive circuit around the lake with many pleasing views. Or we could go around the whole estate, but that is some ten miles, and might be best done in a phaeton."

She tilted her head. "Perhaps we could start with the walk around the lake."

The weather had shifted, bringing a brisk chilly wind down from the Dark Peak, so Elizabeth bundled herself up in her pelisse before setting out with Darcy. Her husband, whom she had lain with last night. The very idea made heat rise within her, despite the cold.

The sun was shining, adding a golden glow to the natural beauty of Pemberley. It was easy to remark with enjoyment at the vistas they passed, the many charming aspects of the valley, the opposite hills, and parts of the stream.

"I am glad you are pleased with Pemberley," Darcy said, a touch of pride in his voice.

"I have never seen more beautiful grounds." And she meant it.

But for all that her eyes were delighted by Pemberley, a nagging grief over the absence of her land Talent dragged at her. Yes, she could feel the slightest sense of the soil under her, but not the rich life beneath the surface, nor could she pour the energy of her Talent into it. It had been her favorite thing in the world, connecting her power with all the organisms that made up Longbourn.

Now it was like overhearing a few sounds from a distant conversation. All sentences were muddled together without meaning, where once she would have caught each individual word and all the interchanges.

How she ached for it, that sense of being part of the land, of feeling her Talent flow! Was this what it was like to suddenly lose the ability to see or hear, this sense of being cut off from the world? It was agonizing to have known the full glory of connecting to the land and then to lose it.

Closing her eyes, she took a deep breath, pushing the pain away. Darcy had gone out of his way to be kind to her, even though it gained him nothing. Last night he had been both gentle and attentive to her pleasure. She could not have asked for more in that regard.

And perhaps not all of her Talent was lost. "Do you think I could still learn magecraft here, even without a true bond to the land?"

"There is no reason why you could not. Most mages never develop their land Talent." He seemed to study her for a moment. "I would be happy to teach you what I know, if it would please you."

Anything to allow her the use of her Talent again! "I would like that very much, if you can spare the time."

Can you hear me? Darcy's voice inside her head made her gasp.

Yes, I can. She spoke inwardly to him as she would to Cerridwen. Would that work?

He stopped short and stared at her. "You are a very quick study, but do not try to send too much. I have no honeyed tea for you here."

Once again she had surprised him! "This is easy. I do it all the time, and it has never weakened me."

He frowned. "You have been sending? To whom?"

"Cerridwen, of course."

Shaking his head, he said, "Touching the mind of your familiar is not the same as true sending."

She tensed at this sign of the old Darcy, the one who was so certain he knew everything. "Perhaps not for you, but I speak to Cerridwen the same way I just sent to you."

"In words?" The pitch of his voice raised in disbelief.

"Often, yes. Sometimes in images."

"What is the point? She cannot understand your words."

"She certainly –" And then her throat closed off as she was bombarded by an image from the distant past. In her memory, Granny loomed over her, taller than the child Elizabeth, saying, 'Tell no one about this. Not your parents, not your sisters, not your friends. No one must know.'

What was wrong with her? She had almost told him Granny's secrets, and that was dangerous. Granny and the family in Wales were depending on her to protect them. Suddenly she could breathe again. "Sometimes it feels like she can, but it may be my imagination," she hedged.

His smile was indulgent. "It is easy to believe our familiars comprehend us more than they do. But in this case, at least it gave you practice at sending. I am impressed at how quickly you managed that. You are full of delightful surprises, my dearest Elizabeth." He reached up to touch her cheek.

The gentle caress sent a shiver of desire through her. Her lips began to tingle, longing for the pressure of his, to forget all this confusion in the pleasure of his touch.

But she could not afford to let him close. He was her sole connection in this new world of Pemberley, and his lovemaking had shifted something deep in her. But he was still a stranger, and a danger to her family in Wales. She had come within an inch of exposing them, all because he was playing at romance.

All Darcy wanted from her was her Talent and a baby. They might be allies in the war on Napoleon, but he was not in love with her, or even a close friend. He considered her untrained and looked down on her blood magic. This game of seduction would cost him nothing, since he intended to die in a few months. She would be the one left bereft and heartbroken.

His brows furrowed. "What is the matter? Pray tell me what I did to upset you."

She did not dare to look at him, lest she weaken again. "I have agreed to help you with your mission. I will share your bed at night. I hope we may be friends of a sort, but pray do not dress it up with romance and sweet words."

His face stiffened. "I do not understand."

Her chest ached. It went against her nature to be unkind, but she had no choice, not with the safety of her Welsh relations at stake. "You only married me because of my Talent. I do not need to be bought with romantic phrases that you do not mean."

"I regret the circumstances of our marriage, but my sentiments are genuine. I am grateful to be wed to you, and would be if your Talent vanished tomorrow." His voice was cool, though. Clearly he did not like her honesty.

"Tell me, would you have married me if you had not discovered that my Talent can engage with yours?"

His answer came slowly. "I imagine not."

"Even though it would have been to your advantage to marry any woman to breed an heir before you vanished?"

"So my mother said many times, but I thought it would be unkind."

"Unkind?" Her voice rose. How dare he say that to her, after forcing her to leave Longbourn?

"I spend nearly all my time training. Such a wife would have had the bare scraps of my time and then be left a widow with a fatherless child. And since no woman would agree to such a marriage for anything but mercenary reasons, I would leave my unborn child to be raised by a mother who cared only about money. No, I thank you."

"Yet you married me," she said bitterly. "Was that not unkind?"

He looked away. "I thought it might be a little better, that I might spend more time with you, and I could trust you with my child. Still, I cannot deny your usefulness to the mission was the deciding factor."

Why did it hurt, when she had already known it? She straightened her shoulders. "Now that we are clear on that, is that a waterfall I hear?"

There was a brief pause, then he replied in a calmer tone, "Yes, and you will see it just beyond the next bend."

Admiring the beauties of Pemberley was much safer than admitting to the feelings that threatened to swamp her.

When they reached the house, Elizabeth asked for the housekeeper to join her, because it was better than being alone with her thoughts.

The older woman appeared promptly, her face unreadable. She must be nervous about this first meeting. "How may I be of service, Mrs. Darcy?"

"Thank you for coming, Mrs. Reynolds. Pray close the door and join me. No, I insist. I have a great deal to discuss with you, and we might as well both be comfortable."

"Should I bring the account books first, or would you rather discuss the general management of the household?"

Definitely nervous. "Neither, actually. Pray sit down."

"As you wish, Madam." The housekeeper perched on the very edge of the chair, touching her mob cap as if to make certain it was still straight.

Elizabeth took a deep breath. "You have doubtless guessed that there is more to my sudden marriage than meets the eye."

The older woman raised her chin. "I take no part in gossip, madam. Mr. Darcy saw fit to marry you, and that is the only thing that matters."

"I am happy to hear it. My husband told me you could be trusted implicitly. I raise the issue simply to acknowledge that there are matters I cannot explain which will affect how I interact with the household, and I will require your assistance."

"I will do my best, madam."

"First, pray permit me to thank you for arranging the breakfast of local foods. It was perfect for my needs, which are to develop a connection to the land here. Mr. Darcy married me for my Talent, and he needs me to develop an affinity to Pemberley as quickly as possible. In normal circumstances, that would happen naturally over many years. But I do not have years. Fortunately, there are techniques that can speed this process, and one of those is eating foods that are produced on the land."

The housekeeper's lips tightened. "We can certainly try, but the local produce is mostly not of the quality you would expect to be served in a fine household."

Elizabeth tried to see herself with the housekeeper's eyes, an unknown country girl with no connections, hurriedly married, without even proper clothing, who had appeared at the door of this elegant mansion on foot and dusty. And she could hardly explain that the fate of England might rest on her abilities! "Let me be clear. Increasing my connection to the land here is crucial, and therefore I would rather be served coarse brown bread from local wheat than the finest white flour from elsewhere. Honey from Pemberley bees, not sugar from the Indies. Trout from the stream, not lobsters from the sea. Small beer brewed at Pemberley is better than wine from Spain. There is no food that is too low for me to eat if it comes from Pemberley."

She pursed her lips. "Madam, we have an excellent French cook who takes pride in the quality of our table here."

"Perhaps you could present it to him as a challenge," Elizabeth suggested. This was not going well, but she could not afford to back down, not when Darcy's life might depend upon her connection to Pemberley. "This is not something I pursue for my pleasure. I miss eating many of my favorite foods. Sometimes I actually dream of marzipan! But I must do what will strengthen my Talent so I may best serve my husband." That last argument was designed to stop all hesitation.

Apparently it was not enough. "Lady Anne Darcy never mentioned such an approach."

This was perilously close to insubordination. She said firmly, "Lady Anne had no desire to form a bond to the land, and I do. This is what I expect for meals."

Mrs. Reynolds stiffened. "Yes, madam."

Inwardly, Elizabeth sighed. Perhaps the housekeeper would like this part better. "The next matter is one of the household. I must compliment you upon your management of it. For now, at least for the first few months, I would ask you to continue to handle it. My studies will not permit me the time to do so properly."

"As you wish." Was that a hint of satisfaction in her voice? Since Lady Anne had never lived at Pemberley, Mrs. Reynolds must never have had a mistress overseeing her work. "In order to make certain I have adequate staff, may I inquire about your plans for entertaining?"

That was easy. "We will not be entertaining at all. My focus will be on bonding to the land." And then Darcy would be gone, and there would certainly be no parties then.

"Shall I pass the word to neighboring estates you are newlyweds and wish to seclude yourselves for now? Otherwise they are likely to call."

"That would be perfect. I appreciate your willingness to rise to these challenges. I know they are not what you expected from a new mistress."

Apparently that was the right thing to say, for once, for the housekeeper said, "I will do my best. I will speak to the cook about your preferences, but I cannot promise he will take it well. It would be easier if I could give him a reason. Would it be appropriate to tell him it is for the sake of the child you may have, to strengthen their bond to Pemberley?"

Elizabeth nodded. "That even has the benefit of being true. Have you ever wondered why Talents were much stronger in the olden days, when even wealthy landowners ate the produce of their land? Now we dine on imported delicacies instead of the fruit of our own estates, and weaken our Talents while pleasing our tongues."

"I never knew that," the housekeeper said. Elizabeth could practically see her turning over these new ideas in her head. Perhaps it might thaw her disapproval a little.

"Pray tell the cook I will not be making any menu requests. Whatever he feels he can do best with the material at hand will be perfect."

"That will make it easier. At least meat will not be an issue. We have plenty of grouse and partridges here, and all manner of livestock and deer."

"Perfect." She could live with the housekeeper's barely hidden disapproval as long as she met her requests. But her stomach felt heavy with disappointment. She would have liked an ally.

Chapter 18

Elizabeth looked up from her book as a footman entered the room, carrying a silver salver.

"Your post, Mrs. Darcy," he intoned.

At last! Her incipient headache from squinting at the faded Arabic text forgotten, she reached out eagerly for the letters. Jane's handwriting was on one, and Aunt Gardiner's on the other. Disappointment pricked at her.

Not that she was unhappy to hear from either of her loved ones. Letters from home were a rare pleasure, but she was desperate for replies from Granny and her father. She had filled pages to them begging for advice on illusions. She could say nothing of Darcy's mission, of course, but she had implied his safety depended upon their answers.

Perhaps her father might have added something to Jane's letter. Elizabeth broke the seal and began to scan through it, jumping to the end, reserving her sister's words to read through and savor later. There was a different hand at the end, but it was Mary's spiky writing, telling of her packing for London and her excitement over learning to use her newly-discovered Talent.

Even that small bit of news brought back poignant memories of Longbourn. Oh, how she missed her family, not to mention the useful employment that had filled her hours there!

She shook her head briskly. She would not give in to low spirits. Hundreds of thousands of men had given their lives to defeat Napoleon. If losing her home and her landed Talent was the price she had to pay, so be it. She would find a way to make the best of her new life.

"Do you mind if I join you?" It was Darcy's voice, coming from the doorway.

She turned to him in pleased surprise. "I would be glad of it. I thought you would still be practicing your illusions." That was how he spent his days, in a clearing halfway up the ridge where no one could see his efforts and wonder why a landed Talent was practicing magery.

"I have a letter to write," he said. "To London."

To the War Office, then. Darcy was always careful with his words when a servant might overhear. Fear twisted in her stomach. "I hope you have not received ill news."

He studied her with a frown, but then his face relaxed. "Nothing that would have any immediate impact on me, but the news is rarely good these days."

The knot inside her loosened. He was not called to his mission yet, then. And she could ask him more questions that night, when he came to her bedroom, their only real time alone.

Her cheeks grew warm. He might be nothing more than a friend who shared her bed, and one with whom she must be cautious at that, but those times were the highlight of her days. Not only for the exquisite love-making, but because of the conversations they shared afterwards, lying together in bed, about his training and what she was learning in her books.

He must have seen something in her expression, for he came closer and bent down to press a lingering kiss on her lips, tracing the line between them with his tongue until she opened her mouth to his explorations. Heat kindled deep inside her, and her hands moved of their own accord to cup his face.

All too quickly it was over, but it was satisfying to see his eyes grown dark with desire and the reluctance with which he pulled away.

"Later," he murmured.

She gave him an arch look. "I shall look forward to it."

Darcy's French tutors joined them for dinner. It was the usual pattern, to use the mealtime to improve Darcy's understanding of French conversation, making the most of every minute for his training. Elizabeth might have appreciated the chance to practice her own facility in that language, but the subjects were dull, always focused on teaching Darcy about the notables in Napoleon's court.

And she would rather have been alone with Darcy.

The butler hurried in just after the first remove. "Sir, if you will forgive the interruption, there is a child missing in the village."

Darcy rose immediately. "Pray excuse me. I must go, in case my Talent can help."

"May I accompany you?" She never heard of such a use of Talent, and she did not want him to disappear into the night. And watching M. and Mme. de Cardevac wince at her accent for another hour had little appeal.

He looked surprised. "If you do not mind the cold night. This may take some time."

A few minutes later, they started down the lane, bundled up against the winter wind, with two footmen carrying lanterns to light their way.

A dozen villagers awaited them. A woman with reddened eyes ran to Darcy. "Thank heaven you are here! Our Mary has been gone all day. We thought she would be home by dark, but we cannot find her anywhere, sir."

Darcy nodded. "You have something of hers? Clothes she has worn, or a toy she is fond of?"

"Right here, sir." She turned to the man behind her, who held out a doll and a child's nightshirt. Apparently they had known what he would need.

"What does she look like? What is special about her?"

The man held his hand out flat by his hip. "About this tall. Light brown hair, blue eyes, loves to sing and dance. She sings lullabies to her doll."

Out of the dark, the lynx appeared and padded to Darcy's side. No one seemed surprised by this event, although some took a step backwards.

Darcy turned over the nightshirt and doll in his hands, inspecting them by the lantern light. He held them out while the lynx sniffed them. Then he stood perfectly still, his eyes closed.

Even with her limited connection to the earth, the sense of his presence moving through the land washed over Elizabeth, raising goosebumps on her skin. How could he do that, reach out from his body like that? At Longbourn, she could usually feel nearby animals and people if she tried, but she had never attempted to go beyond what she could ordinarily see.

He stayed there for long minutes, the girl's family silently watching their magical landlord at work, the mother wringing her hands, the lynx standing erect, his tail lashing back and forth.

Could this work? The tenants certainly seemed to believe in him.

Darcy's shoulders suddenly slumped, as if relieved of an enormous weight. His voice seemed to come from a great distance. "She is alive, in a sinkhole just to the north of the old Tor." He pointed up the hill. "Be careful – the ground is not stable there. The lynx will lead you."

Her mother fell to her knees, tears pouring down her cheeks. "Bless you, Mr. Darcy! Thank you!"

He did not seem to see her. "Bring bandages. Her leg is bleeding."

Elizabeth stared at him in awe. This was Talent beyond her understanding. Was this what she might have been able to do if she had been trained by an expert instead of struggling to teach herself from her Arabic books?

Now she had just a trace of connection to Pemberley and a few lessons in simple magery, but she could still play the role of his wife and the lady of Pemberley. She helped the girl's mother to her feet. "All is well. She will be back before you know it."

"Thanks to Mr. Darcy." The woman dashed away her tears. "Bandages – I must find bandages! Oh, my poor lamb." She hurried back to the cottage.

The men had gathered together, looking nervously at the lynx. Elizabeth could hardly blame them. They were doing much better than she had at first with the creature, and she did not have to follow the big cat into the forest on a dark night.

She held her hand out to the lynx. "Hello, Fire Eyes," she said. It turned its face into her palm, and she scratched it beneath the ears. Hopefully this display of tameness might reassure the men.

Darcy had not moved since he had begun.

When the girl's mother reappeared with the bandages, Elizabeth nudged Darcy. "I believe it is time to send the lynx to lead them."

He looked at her as if she were a stranger, and then nodded. His eyes unfocused again. A moment later the lynx trotted over to the head of a footpath, and the rescue party followed him.

As soon as the crackling twigs and crunching leaves of their passage had faded, Elizabeth stripped off her gloves and touched her husband's face, the only exposed skin on his body. "William, are you there?"

There was a sudden tug on her Talent, like that of young plants seeking nourishment, but this was stronger, a deep thirst for her magic, like an empty well. Concerned, she let her Talent flow into him. It was a strange intimacy, like being inside his mind, so different from their usual interaction. But this time she felt only the land.

A sigh escaped him. "It is hard," he said haltingly, "to return when I have gone so deep."

"Come back," she urged. "Come back to me."

But his face remained frozen. "I am trying."

Should she worry? Clearly he had done this before, likely many times, without her presence. But it troubled her to sense his emptiness and be unable to help.

What could bring him back to himself? There was one thing that always worked when she wanted his attention. And so, regardless of the footmen and the villagers nearby, she stood up on her tiptoes and kissed him.

At first he did not respond. His lips were still soft and warm, but as unmoving as a statue. And he still smelled of soap and spice, but now that scent of a just-passed thunderstorm was stronger than ever.

She nibbled on his lower lip, first gently, and then more aggressively until a quiver went through him. Thank heavens! She traced the line of his lips with the tip of her tongue, in the way he often did to her. For a moment it did not seem to work, but then a groan slipped out of him.

He hauled her tightly against him, deepening the kiss with sudden demand, as if the connection between their mouths was the only thing keeping him alive. Hot desire sprang to life inside her at the raw intimacy of his hard body pressed against hers.

But it was altogether too shocking to take place in a public setting, and he must have sensed her withdrawal, for he ended the kiss and buried his face in her neck. "Ah," he said, and it sounded like his voice again. "That is one way to bring me back to myself."

Chapter 19

DARCY GRUNTED WITH FRUSTRATION as he released the illusion. His stampeding cattle were fairly convincing now, even from a close view, but casting an illusion of even one galloping horse still exhausted his energy – and would not even fool a child. Horses in motion had so many details. He could make either the mane or the tail flow realistically, but not both, and then there were the damned legs. How was he ever to manage a herd of them?

And that was even with his ability to draw on Pemberley's power, since the iron plate he usually stood on to block his land magic was covered with ice.

As he rubbed his hands together for warmth, he spotted Elizabeth hovering at the edge of the clearing, wrapped in a pelisse and muff. A lovely distraction, just when he needed it. He hurried to her side. "This is a pleasant surprise."

"An improvement on creating the same illusion over and over on a freezing day? I am honored," she teased.

"I am losing hope in my ability to cast horses." A few months ago, he would never have admitted to such doubts.

"You have improved noticeably," she said. "And in the meantime, I am very impressed with your cows, since I cannot even cast a sleeping hedgehog."

"You will." And because he wanted her to smile, he used the reserves of his energy to cast a hedgehog waddling across the grass to sniff at her boots.

She scooped it up in her hands and laughed delightedly, a small victory. "Now that is a much more pleasing illusion! Perhaps I will learn it someday. Which brings me to the purpose of this visit. I have received a letter from your mother."

That was not a promising sign. "Dare I ask what she had to say?"

"She was very cordial, expressing her hope that I was pleased with Pemberley. And she is sending someone here to instruct me in magery, with the request that I have the Dower House made ready for her use." She held out a folded paper to him. "You may read it if you like."

He took it. "I do not suppose she troubled herself to ask your opinion of this plan."

"Of course not," she said with a laugh. "Apparently she believes the King's Mage has a right to decide these things."

"She can give orders about the Dower House, I suppose. It is hers to use for her lifetime, though she has not been there since her jaunt to Faerie. She stayed there even when my father was alive, since they could not be in the same house."

An expression of unease flickered across her face. "At least we do not have to resort to that."

And he was glad of it. "If you do not wish to study with this mage she is sending, I will support you. It is your choice, not hers." At least he learned that much in the weeks of his marriage. Elizabeth did not like to be told what to do.

"I admit I resented her high-handedness when I first read it, but I am eager to learn more about magic. I will try studying with her mage, and if I do not find it useful, I will stop."

"That seems more than fair." He skimmed through the letter, a brief missive written in his mother's clear, flowing hand, and his eyebrows shot up. "Why is she sending Frederica, of all people?"

"Yes, who is this Lady Frederica Fitzwilliam?"

"My cousin – and my mother's apprentice." He frowned at the letter.

Elizabeth's eyes widened. "Then I can depend upon her being a spy, I suppose."

"Most likely, though I was fond of her when we were children, before she began training and the repulsion started."

"Do you know anything about what she is like today?"

"Only that my mother was not completely happy about taking her on as an apprentice. 'The best of a bad lot' was how she put it."

"Interesting." Her voice turned cautious. "I do not think I will tell her pet mage anything about my books."

"That is wise, if you do not wish to face more questions about them."

"And I am grateful that she will stay at the Dower House rather than here."

So was Darcy. He was already having to share his brief times with Elizabeth with too many people.

The Dower House was a red brick building in the Jacobean style, surrounded by an orchard, the trees now stripped of leaves. Elizabeth stuffed back the thought that if Darcy did not return and there was no child, this would become her home. Despite all her practice over the last weeks at avoiding such ideas, they kept breaking through.

Determinedly she mounted the steps. She would have to introduce herself, even if that was improper, and that made her feel at a disadvantage. As if being completely untrained was not a big enough shortcoming, compared to someone who had been prepared since childhood for her position.

The butler announced her at the doorway to the drawing room. It was smaller than Pemberley's, but well furnished. The young woman sitting on the sofa, perhaps a few years older than Elizabeth, looked the picture of elegance, with flaxen hair piled on top of her head.

The newcomer rose and offered a friendly smile. "I hope you will forgive me for introducing myself. I am Frederica Fitzwilliam, and you must be Darcy's new wife."

Interesting, that she had dropped her title. "I am indeed Elizabeth Darcy, your new student." Might as well get that right out there.

Lady Frederica waved her hand. "If you wish it. I will be happy to teach you what I know, but do not feel obliged to accept my instruction just because Lady Anne has decreed it. I think she sent me here more out of a desire to rid herself of me than from a concern for your education. Pray, sit down, and I will order some tea to warm you. I had forgotten how much colder the North is than London."

"The weather was fine until the last two days," Elizabeth said, taken aback by this unexpected barrage of words.

"I will become accustomed to it soon enough. I grew up in Matlock, not far from here. It is good to be back among the hills and moors. This countryside must be a change for you, though."

"Yes, but I like it." And it was true, to her surprise. She had expected to dislike any place that was not Longbourn, but the wild landscape here called to her somehow. "I am rather fascinated by the Dark Peak. I long to go exploring there someday."

"Oh, yes! I have gone past it, but never through it. My father said it was no place for a lady." Her voice made a mockery of the last words. "Perhaps you and I could go there when summer comes."

The familiar pain twisted her stomach. When summer came, Darcy would be gone. She could not afford to think of that now, so she blurted out the first thought that came to her head. "Why would Lady Anne wish to send you away?" Good Lord, now she had been incredibly rude.

Lady Frederica seemed to see nothing wrong either in the blunt question or the abrupt change of subject. "Oh, I am a very unsatisfactory apprentice, and I daresay she hopes one of your sisters will prove better. She cannot train them while I am there since my Talent would repel them, so I had to leave for a while. But from what I have seen of your sister Mary, I doubt

Lady Anne will want me back." She sounded not the least disturbed by this possibility.

"You think Mary's Talent is that strong?" She would never have guessed it.

"Strong enough, but more importantly, she has the right temperament. A good apprentice must be both Talented and biddable. I meet the first criteria, but anyone will tell you I am not the least bit biddable." She paused, her finger tapping her chin thoughtfully. "No, that is not true either. I am willing to obey when there is a good reason, but I have a mind of my own."

So that was what Lady Anne had meant by describing her apprentice as the best of a bad lot. "Perhaps we will get along, then. I am not biddable, either."

Lady Frederica's eyes widened. "Never tell me that you disobey Darcy! Everyone always seems to take his word as law. Well, except Lady Anne, but she is a law unto herself."

Elizabeth smiled. "Darcy is learning to accept disagreement from me. I will not claim it is easy to convince him, but I have been able to prove my case several times. He does not always like giving in to an ignorant country girl, but he is improving."

Lady Frederica's laugh was a pleasant tinkling sound. "How delightful! I imagine it is good for him. Oh, look, here is the tea!"

A maid carried a tray laden with biscuits and cake. "Mrs. Darcy, I am to tell you that Mrs. Reynolds sent the food from Pemberley."

"Perfect," said Elizabeth. "I will have to thank her." The housekeeper might not approve of her, but she followed her instructions to the letter.

"Is the cook here so bad?" Lady Frederica looked worried.

"Not as far as I know. Mrs. Reynolds simply knows I follow a very particular diet."

Lady Frederica's brows drew together, no doubt wondering what odd sort of diet included buttery cakes and biscuits. "That is kind of her. Do you take milk and sugar?"

"Milk and honey, if you please." She would not refuse the honey when such an effort had gone to providing it. "I prefer to eat food grown here, you see. I believe it strengthens the land bond."

"Interesting. I have never heard that before." But she said it as if it were an idea worthy of consideration. "A slice of cake? Plum cake, if I am not mistaken."

Elizabeth laughed. "I am certain you are not mistaken. Mrs. Reynolds has noticed that I always take plum cake, although I do not believe she has worked out that it is for my familiar, who is passionately fond of it."

Lady Frederica's eyes lit up. "Oh, yes, I was so envious when Lady Anne said you had a bird familiar! I always wanted one. Sometimes I think that is why no familiar ever approached me, because they somehow knew anything but a bird would disappoint me. I used to be fascinated with Great-aunt Amelia's portrait. Not really her, but the bird on her shoulder. Its eyes seemed so wise and trustworthy. I used to tell that bird my secrets. What kind do you have?"

Elizabeth could not help smiling at her enthusiasm. "A kestrel, although I think she would say that she has me, not vice versa."

"Not that one?" Lady Frederica pointed to the tall window beyond Elizabeth.

Elizabeth twisted in her chair. Cerridwen perched on a branch outside the window watching them. "Yes," she said. "Somehow she must have known there was plum cake in the offing."

Since Lady Frederica was clearly not a stickler for propriety, Elizabeth did what she would have at home. She cranked the window open and crumbled a bit of plum cake onto the windowsill. Cerridwen promptly glided down and pecked at it.

In an almost inaudible voice, Lady Frederica asked, "Would it frighten her if I come closer?"

"It depends on whether you bring more plum cake, I imagine."

Lady Frederica crept up behind her carrying an entire slice of cake. "What should I do with it?"

"First, only give her a few crumbs, so she does not make herself sick. She will allow you to place them on the windowsill."

Cerridwen plaintively warbled, "Kiyu-kiyu-kiyu."

Elizabeth laughed. "And hurry. That is how a kestrel says, 'I am faint with hunger,' but she is not. She simply wants your plum cake."

Gingerly Lady Frederica placed a generous amount of crumbs on the sill. Surprisingly, Cerridwen did not dive into them immediately, instead cocking her head and seeming to study Lady Frederica.

"What a beauty you are!" crooned Lady Frederica. "Those yellow rings around your eyes are so distinguished. Just look at those feathers! My father kept falcons for a time, but I never went close to them because I could not bear to see them leashed. One time I even tried to sneak out to the mews to free them, but they caught me."

The kestrel, seeming to come to some conclusion, pecked at the plum cake. When the last crumb vanished into her beak, she spread her wings and returned to the tree.

"I hope you will come back to see me," Lady Frederica called after her. "I will ask for more plum cake." Then, seeming to remember herself, she said, "How foolish I must sound, talking to a bird! But it almost felt as if she understood. You are so fortunate in your familiar!"

"I am, but she is going to become dreadfully vain and spoiled between your admiration and Chandrika always curtsying to her as if she were the mistress of Pemberley."

"Who is Chandrika?"

"At the moment she seems to think she is my lady's maid, but she is a servant of Rana Akshaya – you know who she is? – who has attached herself to me. Out of respect for Cerridwen, apparently."

"Do not tell me she is one of the silent servants who never speak to anyone except to say yes, no, or I must ask the great Rana?"

"She is certainly not silent with me, although I will grant you she barely says a word to anyone else. She says Rana Akshaya gave her permission to speak to me because I was trustworthy. Why she thought that when she had exchanged only half a dozen sentences with me, I cannot tell you."

"Astonishing. I spent weeks trying to get one of them to converse with me. I must not be trustworthy," she said with an amused smile.

"Along with being unbiddable?"

She laughed. "You can see why I am an altogether unsuitable apprentice!"

Elizabeth hesitated before taking the risk of speaking her mind. "You seem untroubled by the prospect of my sister replacing you as Lady Anne's apprentice."

"Oh, I am! I never cared much for the position, having no desire to risk my life for Prinny or the mad King. She is welcome to it."

"I pray you will forgive my inquisitiveness, but then why did you accept the apprenticeship in the first place?"

She wrinkled her nose, as if smelling something distasteful. "It seemed a simple way to avoid the constant pressure to marry. It meant I could plead my duties every time my father came up with a new suitor, if you can call them that when all they wanted was to breed with my Talent."

"That seems to be one of the most unpleasant things about being a lady mage. I hope the offers do not start again."

Lady Frederica waved her hand airily. "They will, but I am older now and in a better place to refuse. Also, having four new Talented marriageable ladies from your family will lower the pressure somewhat."

"Three marriageable ladies," Elizabeth said sharply. "My eldest sister is to be married tomorrow." And Elizabeth would miss the ceremony, instead of standing up with Jane as she had always imagined.

Color rose in the other woman's face. "Forgive me; I miscounted. Think nothing of it." But she said it too quickly.

Elizabeth narrowed her eyes. Something was wrong about this. What was this otherwise astonishingly frank woman hiding from her? Was Lady Anne planning to interfere with Jane's wedding? Could she do that, when the banns had already been called?

Then it hit her. Lady Anne was looking towards the future.

She should say nothing, but she could not let it go, not with her anguish so close to the surface. "No, that is what Lady Anne says, is it? Since she sees me as soon to be widowed, and therefore available?"

The other woman's stricken look was all the answer she needed.

But Elizabeth was not done. "I refuse to accept that my husband is doomed to die. But even if he does, I will never marry to please the woman who sacrificed her own son!"

Lady Frederica's face paled. "Darcy told you she did that?"

"He did not need to. His mother was the only one who knew of his training in illusions. Who else could have told the government that he was an unknown mage?" Elizabeth's hands clenched into fists.

The flaxen-haired woman shook her head slowly. "No. Or yes, she told them, but she did not know what the mission would be. She was devastated when she found out, after he had already agreed to do it. She cannot bear losing him, too."

Elizabeth had not considered that possibility. "Then why is she not training him herself to give him the best possible chance of survival?"

"She does not think it possible. She even volunteered to go herself, but Napoleon knows of her powers, and the War Office refused even to consider risking the King's Mage."

Some of Elizabeth's anger leached away, leaving a bitter taste in its wake. "Well, I have not accepted that it is hopeless. If you are willing to teach me, I would like to learn everything you know about illusions, and any other magery that I can use to help my husband."

"Brava, Mrs. Darcy! I am glad you are not giving up on him. I will be happy to teach you what I can, although unfortunately illusions are not a strong point of mine. Lady Anne would tell you I have very few strong points." She made a face.

"I am certain that is not true, since she agreed to take you on as an apprentice in the first place."

She wrinkled her nose. "My Talent is uneven. I do not even have a familiar to anchor my power and add to my strength. The one thing I am actually good at is creating wind, and that is only useful for naval battles and bringing ships into port, neither of which I will ever be allowed to do. It was, however, helpful in keeping my pesky brothers from teasing their only sister. Nothing like knocking them down with a gust of wind!" She looked so delighted with the memory that the last of Elizabeth's anger fled.

"Clearly practice makes perfect, then. The only illusion Darcy can do easily is making himself invisible, and that is only because it was useful to him as a mischievous young boy." And for her, the most important thing had been learning how to increase Jane's bond to the land, so she had intensified her own. Now she sympathized with Jane's frustration. It was miserably frustrating, trying to build a connection with the land one drop of blood at a time.

But she was determined to do it, no matter how difficult it was. Just as she would take any help she could get from Frederica's lessons.

The other woman grimaced. "Perhaps that is my problem. I do not have the patience for much practice."

"Fortunately, I do, and I am looking forward to learning anything you can teach me."

Chapter 20

A s Elizabeth entered the drawing room at the Dower House the next day, holding Darcy's bare hand in her own, Lady Frederica's eyebrows rose. "So it is true! This is astonishing. No repulsion at all! Well, hello, Darcy. How many years has it been?"

"More than a decade. Since you started using your Talent, I suppose."

"I remember feeling put out when I realized it would exclude me from summers at Pemberley. Not that you would have had any time for me then, but I missed my brothers when they came to visit you without me."

"They are not Talented?" Elizabeth asked.

"They have the potential, but no desire to use it. Richard was always destined for the Army, and the risk of repulsion would be too high there. He would not have wished to employ his Talent anyway, not if it meant skipping all those social gatherings he loves. Being able to cast an illusion is small compensation for giving up society."

It had never occurred to Elizabeth that anyone would not wish to use their Talents. "I suppose it has that cost."

"My eldest brother cannot escape his landed Talent, but he refuses to develop it until he inherits, and perhaps not even then. He says the increase in harvest is not worth everything he would have to give up, and he will never be one of those old-fashioned landowners who sacrifices everything for their estate."

Darcy said, "It made more sense in the past, when there was little social interaction between landholders other than attending the king's court, and when a poor harvest could mean starvation for everyone on the estate. Or when landed Talents could repel invading barons. In this modern age, when we do not attack each other and can buy food from another area or even another country, it seems less important."

Lady Frederica said, "That is why so many frivolous young people choose the parties over their Talents."

"Yet both of you chose to develop your Talents," Elizabeth said.

"I started very young, as a way of having an upper hand over my brothers, who seemed to have every other privilege. By the time I realized it would limit which balls I could attend, it was already too late."

Elizabeth turned to Darcy. "What of you?"

He shrugged. "I never thought I had a choice. Both my parents were powerful Talents, and I was told often enough that it was the reason for my existence. But it has not troubled me much, since I am not fond of balls or large parties. I do still go sometimes, but hostesses know not to ask me if other Talents will be attending."

Lady Frederica teased, "And your position is such that they often arrange their invitation list on your behalf, hoping one of their daughters might catch your interest! How disappointed they must all be now."

Elizabeth was feeling very provincial. How little of this she had known! "No wonder you were so surprised when I did not want to marry you. They taught you to think very well of yourself indeed!" But she squeezed his hand to take any sting from the words.

Lady Frederica covered her mouth with her hand. "You refused him? That must have been a shock."

"It was," said Darcy ruefully. "After all those years of trying to avoid entrapment, I had not considered whether I needed to try to please her."

Elizabeth smiled up at him. "And you did not realize how angry I would be over being told I had no choice. But we have moved past all that."

"For which I am eternally grateful," he said softly, and she could feel the heat of his gaze on her.

Elizabeth glanced over her shoulder to make certain she was alone on the wilderness path. No one in sight. Darcy was off practicing his casting in the clearing on the opposite side of the estate, and she had just left a lesson with Frederica.

She knelt down and dug a small hole in the soil under an elderflower bush. With her small knife, she pricked her finger and let a few drops of blood slip into the hole. Then she covered it, walked a short distance, and hunkered down to do it again, trying not to think of how Darcy would disapprove.

But it needed to be done, no matter how much her husband disliked blood magic. Yesterday he had received a letter from the War Office laden with bad news. The sea serpents were intensifying their campaign of ship sinking to the point where merchants were reluctant to send out their vessels and warships were forced to stay in port. While there had been no more dragon attacks, the Army dared not put soldiers into battle, and had lost much of the ground they had gained. If Napoleon had not been preoccupied with his desire to conquer Austria, their situation would have been dire indeed. And the Austrian campaign would not last forever.

Darcy had clearly tried to hide his worry from her, but his grim countenance had told her the truth.

Building a connection to the land was the only tool she had, her only way to fight Napoleon and to try to save her husband. She had been at Pemberley for nearly two months, and despite all her other efforts, she could still only feel the faintest of pressure from the earth. Given ten years, it might grow into a good, solid tug.

She did not have ten years. Or even ten months.

It was too early for any sign of a child, but she could not think about that or she would collapse into despair. If only she could create more of a bond to the land, she might still send him some power through their joined Talent.

She dashed a stray tear away, then immediately regretted it. She should have given that tear to the earth to help her connection. A foolish waste.

No. This kind of thinking would get her nowhere. It was not her fault that binding to the land was such a slow process.

But the idea of being a widow this time next year, of never seeing Darcy again, was intolerable.

She sank to her knees, digging her fingertips into the cold dirt, begging it to respond. For Darcy's sake, not for hers. To protect the man who had been born to this rocky soil, who was an integral part of it. But the land remained silent.

Cerridwen glided over to land on a branch in front of her. *Help? To bond the land?*

Was it possible? How could the falcon aid her? But she would take any chance. *Yes. Anything.*

The kestrel cocked her head to one side. *It will hurt.*

I do not care.

You may be ill for a day or two.

Elizabeth hesitated. *Will it keep me from conceiving?* That was even more vital.

The bird seemed to consider. *No.*

Then yes. Help me, I beg you.

The kestrel sent her an image of herself, holding out her arm, palm upwards, with the skin of her forearm exposed.

Elizabeth hurriedly doffed her pelisse, tossing it over a large mossy stone, and rolled up the sleeve of her winter dress to the elbow. Could this actually help? Cerridwen's mind did not work in the same way as a human's, but the falcon had never misled Elizabeth. And she was desperate.

Cerridwen's weight landed on her wrist, her talons carefully sheathed. The kestrel cocked her head, as if studying Elizabeth's arm. Then, with great care, she lowered her razor-sharp beak and delicately broke the skin, just as she had in their initial bonding, all those years ago.

It stung, but no more than that. Blood welled on the surface of her arm. Elizabeth sent a wordless query to the bird.

In a lightning-fast movement, Cerridwen raised her own leg and bit it, then held it out over Elizabeth's arm until three drops of crimson blood had fallen to join Elizabeth's.

Oh, heavens. This truly was going to hurt. She still had nightmares of the only other time their blood had joined.

And there it was, the prickings of lightning beginning at the cut and moving up her arm. She could almost hear Granny's voice telling her not to move, no matter how bad the pain became.

But this time was different. Cerridwen hopped off her hand, and an image filled her mind of turning her arm so that their combined blood would fall to the ground.

Somehow Elizabeth did so, giving her intention to the land with it, even though the lightning was up to her shoulder now. She swallowed a scream of agony.

Cerridwen hopped around the spilled blood, digging it into the dirt with her talons, but Elizabeth could no longer think. The lightning was ricocheting around her body, scouring her until every inch of her was a fount of pain.

Her only remaining thought was a silent prayer that this would work. Granny always said that the most powerful magic had the highest price.

And then she could do nothing but rock back and forth, curling herself into a ball and whimpering.

Finally it was over. It might have been minutes or an hour, she could not tell. But the pain was gone, leaving only lassitude in its wake, as if she had walked for fifty miles.

Tentatively, almost timidly, she reached out and laid her palm on a patch of moss, sending her Talent out.

And found roots and rhizomes, earthworms and mice sleeping in their nests. Her sense of it was not strong, but it was there. Like being able to hear again after months of utter silence. Like being alive again. Gratitude and relief flooded her.

"Cerridwen?" she asked weakly.

"Kee-kee-kee." The kestrel fluttered to a nearby branch.

Elizabeth could not muster the strength for sending, so she said, "You are magnificent. Thank you."

She could feel the bird's satisfaction.

She wanted to stay there and luxuriate in the earth's power forever, but she knew her strength would ebb rapidly. Even now, she had to use her hands to push herself to her feet. At least she remembered to roll down her sleeve over the cut Cerridwen had made. Darcy would be un-happy when he saw it, but she would have good news to counterbalance it.

Her feet dragged as she walked. The kestrel circled overhead, clearly watching over her. At least it was not far to the house. Even if it felt as if she would never reach it.

After a few minutes, Darcy appeared, running towards her. He looked desperately worried.

"What is the matter? Are you ill?" he demanded as he approached.

Taken aback by his earnestness, she said, "It is nothing. I am only a bit fatigued."

He frowned. "But your sending – you said you needed me. And I felt a shift in the land. What did you do?"

She turned her gaze upward at the falcon circling overhead. Her mind was turning sluggish. How could she explain the unnatural tear in her skin without exposing Cerridwen's nature to him? "Cerridwen accidentally broke my skin, and I used the blood to try a binding. I think it worked. I can feel the land now." She would have to let him believe the sending had been hers, even though the kestrel must have done it.

He looked shocked, though whether at her success or her use of blood binding was unclear. "I beg you to be more careful," he said. "Are you badly hurt? Shall I carry you?"

"I can walk, I assure you." Did he even believe her about her new bond?

"If you are certain. Where is your pelisse? You must be freezing."

Oh, dear. She must have left it draped over the boulder, but cold was the last thing she felt. "I think I left it behind, but I am truly quite warm." Too warm, in fact. "But I would be glad to have the support of your arm."

He offered it instantly, and they began to walk again. It was a comfort to have him beside her, more than she cared to admit.

Darcy could hardly miss Elizabeth's slight pause as they reached the steps of the portico, nor how slowly she climbed them. As soon as they were indoors, he dispensed with that nonsense by sweeping her up in his arms and carrying her upstairs.

She protested weakly, but with what might have been relief, so he only said, "Perhaps it might be unnecessary, but I would rather give you too much assistance than too little."

She simply leaned her head against his shoulder. Dearest Elizabeth! What had she done to put herself in this condition, and more crucially, was it dangerous? This did not look like the usual over-drawing of energies, although he intended to make her drink honeyed tea as soon as possible, even if he had to pour it down her throat.

Inside her room, the maid Chandrika was already turning down the bed, and towels lay ready on the bedside table. How had she known to be prepared? Most likely that damned bird again.

He gently placed Elizabeth on the bed and kissed her lightly. Good God, she was burning hot! And her eyes, before they drifted closed, were unnaturally dark, the pupils so wide he could barely see the circle of rich brown around them.

On the other side of the bed, Chandrika dipped a towel in a basin of water. "Mrs. Darcy, I am going to put a cool cloth on your forehead to bring down your fever. There is tea coming, and you must stay awake to drink it."

The Indian woman rolled up Elizabeth's left sleeve to reveal a jagged cut several inches long. Darcy drew in a sharp breath. That damned blood magic of hers! Had it caused this illness?

Chandrika laid two fingers above the cut. "You are greatly blessed," she said reverently.

Elizabeth opened her eyes. "Yes, I am, although I did not much care for that part."

The maid smiled. "No one does, though it is the price of great magic. I will clean around it, but you must leave it open to the air to heal."

The tea arrived then, and Darcy helped Elizabeth to sit up to drink it. "I am going to send for a doctor."

Elizabeth looked as if she wished to disagree, but she merely shook her head as she sipped her tea, clearly too fatigued to argue.

"I have seen this before, and a doctor can do nothing, for it is magical in nature," Chandrika said. "It happens when a human takes part in magic with a powerful companion. It is too strong for our weak bodies."

It was more words than the Indian woman had spoken to him in the entirety of their acquaintance, and she said it with such quiet assurance that he could not help believing her. And he wanted to believe her.

"Are you certain? Have you treated this before?"

"A few times. It is not uncommon in my homeland. We call it naga-pani." She smiled suddenly. "Knowing her situation, I likely would have recognized this, but since her falcon told me they had done magic together and it would give her nagapani, I am absolutely certain. Come, Mrs. Darcy, you must drink the rest of this tea before you sleep." She held the cup to Elizabeth's lips.

The rush of relief was so great that he did not even care that he was taking the word of the bird and a servant. If it meant Elizabeth would recover, he would be happy to humble himself. "Does Cerridwen speak to you often?" He had not believed it before when Elizabeth said that Cerridwen could use words in her sendings. One more mistake he had made.

For the first time, the maid looked surprised. "Never before. I am most deeply honored."

Not an assessment Darcy shared. He wanted to wring the bird's neck for hurting Elizabeth. He took her hand between his, shocked at the heat of it. "It is not worth endangering yourself. I could not bear it if something happened to you."

A wistful smile drifted onto her face. "You are hardly in a position to criticize me for taking risks. And I knew it was not dangerous, just unpleasant. The same thing happened when we first bonded."

Chandrika said sharply, "Unpleasant? Everyone says the pain is excruciating."

Elizabeth waved her way. "That is over. I can feel the land, and it was worth it. But I want to sleep for a while."

The maid said, "Yes, Mrs. Darcy." She began closing the curtains against the weak winter sunlight.

"You can go back to your practice," Elizabeth told him sleepily.

As if he would allow her out of his sight while she was ill from blood magic! Not when he knew all too well how dangerous it was. He leaned forward and kissed her cheek. "This is where I want to be."

Chapter 21

B Y EVENING, ELIZABETH'S FEVER was raging, and Darcy cursed himself for not trying harder to convince her of the dangers of blood magic. If only he had not been too proud to tell her about his own disastrous experience with it! Now all he could do was to worry as she shivered and demanded more blankets. Her maid kept quietly replacing the cool cloths on her forehead and sponging her down, while other servants fetched a constant stream of ice chips from the icehouse.

Should he have insisted on calling a doctor after all? His parents had always taught him that blood-letting was dangerous for mages, and it was highly unlikely any doctor outside London would know anything about a magical malady.

Chandrika requested a poultice of ginger and turmeric from the kitchen, claiming it was used in her native land in such cases. Whether it helped or not, Elizabeth had taken deeper breaths when it was applied, apparently calmed by the pungent scent. She had fallen into a sounder sleep afterwards, and by the next morning she seemed to rally a bit.

It did not last, though. Her fever returned by afternoon, and her mind began to wander. She fretfully called for her Granny and her sister Jane, and then asked questions in a strange language which sounded like Welsh. What if her words were of import, something that might help her, and he could not understand it? Frantic, Darcy sent off a servant to find a Welsh speaker. It proved fruitless; no one nearby knew any Welshmen.

At one point, she drowsily told him that a dragon had visited her during the night, putting their head on her arm and giving her strength. Fear tightened Darcy's throat. Was she losing her grip on reality?

But Chandrika only patted her arm, shaking her head at Darcy. "Fever dreams are often strange. The dragon painted on the wallpaper may have inspired this one."

By evening, Elizabeth did not recognize him, though she did not seem to mind when he held her hand. But no one could deny that she was getting worse, or that her very life might be at risk.

It was his fault. If he had left her alone in Hertfordshire, she would never have tried that dangerous bonding. But no, his mission and his desires came first, and now he might lose it all. Why had he kept his secrets so close? If only she had known he had nearly died from blood magic once, perhaps she would have taken more care. Foolish, foolish mistake, and now he was paying dearly for it.

He would have taken on her suffering in a second, anything to bring her back to herself. The danger she faced was exactly calculated to make him understand his own wishes, how little anything mattered to him beyond the opportunity to share his life with her. Now, when all such hopes must be in vain, he would trade his mission in an instant for the chance to see her healthy again, teasing him in her enchanting way, touching him with her affection and light.

He bowed his head until his forehead touched the back of her hand. *Elizabeth.*

"Are you ill? Perhaps some tea with honey would help." Her voice was cracked and dry, but full of concern.

For the first time in years, he had to fight to hold back tears. "Thank you. I will try that," he whispered.

"Good." And she closed her eyes.

There was no way he could leave her, his stomach drowning in a dread that nothing could soothe. His own bed be damned. He must have drowsed in the chair by her bedside, though, because when he opened his eyes, the first light of dawn showed through the curtains. Was she still alive?

He dropped to his knees beside her bed and took her hand in his, his heart pounding until she opened her eyes and gazed at him. Was there the slightest bit of curve to her lips? And then her eyelids drifted down again.

He looked up at Chandrika, who looked as fatigued as he felt. She shook her head silently.

After that, Elizabeth simply lay still, not responding to anything, not a cold towel on her forehead, not a touch to her hand, not even Chandrika's attempt to sit her up to take a sip of tea. She was like a lifeless doll, apart from her breathing and the heat that still rose from her skin.

She was dying. It was obvious even to him, and he could not bear it. He stayed on his knees, the growing pain of the hard floor beneath them a punishment he welcomed. He would do anything, if only she would live. He would give up any claim to her, take her back to Longbourn to live with her family again, give her everything in his possession, if only she would live.

All he wanted was to look into her eyes, for her to continue to be part of this world, even if he never saw her again. A world without Elizabeth was inconceivable.

Why had it taken him so long to realize that he loved her? That it was more than simple desire and affection, more than a romantic attraction. She was part of him. He loved her, and now she was near death because of him.

He pressed her limp hand against his cheek, willing her to live, ignoring the servants carrying fresh washcloths and ice. The breakfast brought for him sat untouched.

But it did no good, no matter how much he pleaded with God. He was losing her.

"Mr. Darcy, I must speak to you." It was Mrs. Reynolds. How had she come to be by his side?

"Not now," Darcy grated. Perhaps not ever. How could he go on if Elizabeth died?

"I must insist, sir," said the housekeeper firmly. "Or rather, your lynx is insistent."

Her words penetrated slowly. "My lynx?"

"He has brought a woman here, a local midwife, and he is growling at everyone who stands in the way of bringing her to you." She glanced back over her shoulder nervously.

A midwife. A bitter reminder of all he was losing. "We have no need of a midwife."

Mrs. Reynolds hesitated. "Mrs. Sanford also has a Talent for healing. And if you will not allow her in, I must ask you to explain it to your lynx before someone is injured."

"You know this woman?"

"Yes. Many local folk seek her out."

An unholy yowl echoed, making his hair stand on end. "He is *inside* the house?" That had never happened before.

"He pushed his way through, and we are in no position to stop him."

Darcy looked back at Elizabeth's still, silent form. Her chest still rose and fell ever so slightly. She was dying, and it was his fault.

This healer his lynx had found could do no worse. "Let them come," he said huskily.

Mrs. Reynolds' skirts rustled as she departed, and a minute later were replaced by another set of footsteps. Darcy dragged himself to his feet and turned to the newcomer.

Not the crone he was expecting, but a woman near his own age, dark-eyed and dark-haired, with a vaguely familiar visage. Perhaps he had seen her among the tenants. His lynx wound about her legs, herding her into the room as if he did not expect her to go of her own accord.

Darcy sent a questioning thought towards his lynx.

Can help. The image of Elizabeth accompanied the sending.

Goosebumps rose on his arms. *When did you learn to use words?* It was his lynx in his mind, no question about it; he knew that presence as well as his own, but the big cat's thoughts had always been non-verbal and vague.

A lynx-eye view of Cerridwen filled his mind. *She shows me how.*

Rage rose in him. *That damned bird is why Elizabeth is hurt!*

Help. An image of the midwife.

Mrs. Sanford said in a soft voice, "Forgive me for disturbing you. Your lynx left me little choice."

Her presence made his skin prickle, but he was willing to grasp at straws. Gesturing towards Elizabeth, he said, "Can you help her?"

She stepped to Elizabeth's bedside. "I can try. What happened to her?"

Once, he would have hesitated to admit it to anyone. "She performed blood magic with her familiar, trying to bond to Pemberley. She was weak immediately afterwards and soon became feverish and confused. Now we cannot rouse her."

She wrapped her hand around Elizabeth's wrist and became still, her gaze fixed on Elizabeth's face. Was this merely a show or was she actually doing something? Perhaps it was just his desperation speaking, but Mrs. Reynolds had said the woman had some Talent, and her presence itched against his skin. Not the full burn of repulsion, only an unpleasant tingle. And Talent sprang up in odd places among the common folk.

She stood there in silence for so long that he returned to his previous occupation of watching Elizabeth breathe. Finally she said in a hushed voice, "Her thread of life is very weak. It is only the bond to her familiar keeping her alive."

As if he could not tell that she was dying! "Is there anything you can do?"

The woman's brow furrowed. "You said she was bonding to the land. Did she succeed?"

"Yes, or so she claimed. She thought it might help me." Despair filled him. If only he could go back in time and stop her!

She cast a nervous glance at him, then looked away. "Then we should bring her to the land and see if she can gain sustenance from it."

He grabbed onto the thread of hope, as weak as it was. After all, touching the land at Netherfield had helped her when she was depleted. But was it safe to move her?

The lynx bumped against his leg none too gently. *Go. Do it.*

Chandrika was already folding down the counterpane and wrapping a blanket around Elizabeth's still body. "Is there a litter we can use?" she asked.

"I will carry her." Darcy stepped in and scooped her up in his arms, as he had that day at Netherfield when she cast her first illusion. This time she was hot in his arms, fever still raging through her. His heart turned over at holding her precious form against him.

Down the stairs and out the front door, ignoring the footman who held out his hat. He paused on the portico before heading to the lake and setting her down gently on the grassy bank. Somehow that seemed like the right place.

She looked so forlorn there, lying unconscious on the ground. He tenderly tucked the blanket around her feverish form. Did she even know he was there?

The midwife knelt on Elizabeth's other side. Taking her hand, she spread Elizabeth's fingers and moved them into the grass, letting the individual blades come between them, and pushing her fingertips into the earth.

Clumsily he followed suit on his side. Even touching Elizabeth's delicate hand made his heart clench in his chest. The fine lines of her fingers, the elegant curves and pale crescent moons of her fingernails. With the utmost care, he pressed each beloved finger into the grass. *Elizabeth. Live, I beg you.*

She sighed, just a tiny sigh, and her head turned as if to face him. But her eyes remained closed. Was there more movement in the muscles of her face, as though she were dreaming instead of that awful preternatural stillness? Yes, he was sure of it!

The lynx padded to stand beside him and curled up against Elizabeth's legs, purring fiercely.

"Mr. Darcy," said the healer, sounding reluctant. "Your Talent gives strength to the sheep and livestock. It is a sort of healing. Could you use that now?"

He would try anything. Placing his hand over hers, he drew up the land's energy until it trembled through him, and then poured it into Elizabeth. Poured and poured, letting the earth feed her directly, while the slight pressure of another presence pushed power into her through the ground. The midwife? He did not care, as long as it helped Elizabeth.

Elizabeth's eyebrows twitched, and her fingertips pressed into the soil under her own power. It was helping! He redoubled his efforts.

But it was not enough. Her body was moving again, if slightly, but her eyes did not open. Darcy tasted despair.

Then Cerridwen flew down from the trees, landing on Elizabeth's chest, her wingtips brushing against his chest. The lynx picked up his head to examine the kestrel, then lowered it again in an un-feline manner.

Darcy did not even spare the energy for his usual surge of rage at the falcon for causing this. He had to keep his focus deep in the earth.

His hand caught the echoes of a thrumming of power in Elizabeth's hand. Not her own Talent; he knew what that felt like, nor the midwife's energy he had sensed in the land. This was something different than he had encountered before, powerful and foreign, more like his lynx than anything else, with the taste of fire and metal. That damned bird.

Cerridwen cawed, "Kee-kee-kee."

This time, Elizabeth's eyes opened. She looked around her wonderingly. "What... Where am I?" Her voice, her beloved voice, sounded rusty, but he had never heard anything so sweet.

Relief, almost painful in its intensity, swept through him. "Thank God," he whispered.

The midwife said sharply, "Do not stop, Mr. Darcy. She is still badly depleted."

He could hardly comprehend her words at first. Oh, yes, in his surprise, he had stopped giving Elizabeth power. He had to do better. No matter how much he wanted to speak to Elizabeth, he had a different task.

As he sent his focus down into the land again, Chandrika stepped forward from a circle of servants who had somehow formed around them. "You have been very ill, Mrs. Darcy. They are replenishing you from the land."

"The land," Elizabeth said faintly. "Yes, I can feel it. Cerridwen, I do not need feathers in my face, thank you." She lifted her head to see the lynx. "Oh, hello, Fire Eyes."

"Pray rest, Mrs. Darcy," Chandrika said firmly. "Allow them to do their work."

A ghost of a smile curved Elizabeth's enchanting lips. "Oh, very well. But I would not mind a pillow. The ground is hard."

Chandrika flicked her hand, and a servant raced off towards the house.

But Darcy focused only on the steady power of the land traveling through his hands to Elizabeth in strange harmony with that of Cerridwen, the midwife, and the lynx. She needed him, and he would give her all his strength.

Elizabeth pushed away the cup of honeyed tea Chandrika held in front of her. "I already had three cups outside," she said fitfully.

Chandrika's gaze did not waver. "And now you will have a fourth. You were near death a few hours ago, Mrs. Darcy. Your falcon was the only thing keeping you alive."

That was a frightening thought, so she sipped the cloyingly sweet tea. "Where is Cerridwen, anyway?" Not that her maid could have any idea, but Darcy had been so firm that Elizabeth should not use her Talent at all right now, not even for the smallest sending.

A week ago she would have ignored him, but now she had almost died doing the very kind of blood magic he had warned her against time and again. Not that she could regret it, since it had bonded her to Pemberley, but she had not truly considered the risks. She was too much in the habit of experimenting with her Talent. Perhaps it was time to start listening to the conventional wisdom, too.

It was not an idea she liked.

Chandrika seem to pick her words with care. "While you were ill, your husband ordered the falcon to leave. He blamed her for your illness."

The tea caught in her throat, and Elizabeth coughed. "That is ridiculous. I asked her to do it. Perhaps if you open the window, she will know it is safe to return." This would be difficult. Darcy had never liked Cerridwen.

"Yes." Chandrika turned the latch and pushed the window sash up.

Impatiently Darcy settled the various concerns of the staff, and then finally he could go to Elizabeth. He took the stairs two at a time, ignoring the barely suppressed smile of the footman. He did not care. The entire staff could laugh at him if they chose, as long as Elizabeth was well.

He stopped with his hand poised to knock at her bedroom door. What if she was asleep? He did not wish to disturb her, so he strode through his own room and opened the adjoining door a crack to peek through.

And there she was, sitting up in bed, with her maid combing her luxuriant hair. Awake. Alive. His Elizabeth.

Her visage lit up when she spotted him, flooding him with heat and joy. Her face seemed a little thinner, hardly surprising after her illness, but her color was better, without the flush of fever. Thank God!

How different it felt to come to her bedside now, without the fear of losing her! He raised her hand to his lips, caressing it gently. "I am happy you are so much improved."

"Likely because Chandrika has been forcing me to drink tea! But I had not expected to see you again today. I thought you would be off practicing."

Practicing? The thought could not have been further from his mind. "I have used enough of my Talent today already, and besides, I want to be with you."

Her lips curved in an arch smile. "I am told you saved my life."

"It is praise I do not deserve. It was the midwife's idea, and my lynx was the one who brought her. I merely provided some of the energy, as did Cerridwen." Left to himself, she would still be lying motionless in the bed. That guilt was something he would never forget.

She bit her lip. "The midwife. I wanted to thank her, but she left so abruptly, without a word."

"Likely she had other demands on her time." He tried to sound as if this had not been troubling him. No one would answer his questions about her, not Mrs. Reynolds nor his steward, beyond saying that she was very private. That did not explain her reluctance to speak to him, nor why he had a tenant he had somehow never heard of. Particularly one with Talent.

Not that it was unusual for a tenant family who had lived on the land for generations to develop a trace of Talent, enough to make their plots more productive, but she had been able to call upon the land and use it. Yet he had felt only the barest hint of repulsion. It all added up to an answer which he did not wish to consider. She had saved Elizabeth's life, though, and that he could never repay.

Better to keep Elizabeth from thinking too hard about it, still, so he deliberately changed the subject. "Did you know your bird is teaching my lynx to use words in his sendings?"

Elizabeth lifted her head. "No, truly? Familiars can speak to each other?"

"Apparently so, although I have never heard of such a thing. Or that familiars can understand words at all. He only ever sent me feelings and images before." Nor had the lynx ever taken such initiative in the past. How had the wild cat known about the midwife, or that she could help Elizabeth? What had inspired him to seek her out?

It seemed there was still more to learn about his familiar.

Chapter 22

To Darcy's very great relief, Elizabeth's health improved steadily over the next two days, until she declared herself ready to resume her usual activities. Or rather, she finally convinced Darcy that she could do so, though he would rather she rested for a little longer to be safe. But she announced she had listened to him the previous day when he had said the same thing, and that was enough. So he had given in with all the grace he could muster.

Still, when the maid told Darcy that Elizabeth was almost dressed, he returned to her room to walk her down to breakfast.

"I am perfectly capable of making my way downstairs," she teased him.

"Would you deprive me of the pleasure of a few extra minutes in your company?"

"I would be flattered if I believed that was your only reason. I assure you I am quite well now. In fact, I intend to go out for a walk after breakfast. A short one, I promise you." She gave him a playful look.

"May I accompany you?"

She studied him. "I am impressed at your restraint! I am certain your first instinct was to forbid me to do so, but there is no need. I can take a servant with me, if that will reassure you."

Once he might have agreed, but that was before her illness had brought home to him how dear she had become to him. "I want to go with you, truly."

"Do you not need to be practicing?" she asked.

"An hour or two will make no difference in my abilities. May a man not wish to spend a little time with his wife?"

"Then I would be happy to have your company," she said.

An hour later, they stood on the portico outside the front door. "Where would you like to go?" Darcy asked.

She tipped her head. "Someplace that is a special to you."

"To me?"

"Yes. I have wandered all over the estate, but I do not know which places have particular memories for you. Show me one, I pray you."

He considered this. "Many of my favorite places are on top of our high hills, where the view extends for miles, but that is too much for today. Would you like to see where I spent most of my time when I was younger? It is not far."

"Perfect," she said, taking his arm as they walked down the steps.

The sun was out, with only a few clouds floating across a blue sky. There was a slight breeze, and two hawks circled overhead.

Her reaction when she stepped onto the land was visible, a deep breath and a straightening, matching his own sensations as the power of Pemberley flowed into him. Her whole countenance brightened, taking on new liveliness.

"You are feeling it?" he asked.

"Yes. It is different from Longbourn, and my sense of it is not as deep. Still, to feel anything is glorious. Like coming to life again."

"Good." He wanted her to be happy here. "Though I never wish to go through this sort of thing again. Will you permit me to order you a hawking glove, so Cerridwen cannot injure you?"

She lowered her head, walking a little faster. Finally she said, "If I tell you something, will you hold it in strict confidence, most especially from your mother?" She sounded worried.

"Of course. I have told no one about your Arabic books."

"I know." She paused, scuffing her half-boots along the gravel. "It was not an accident. Cerridwen was deliberately trying to help me bond to the land."

"What? Impossible!"

"She is not just a familiar. You have already discovered she can use words, but it is more than that. She has her own Talent, and she used it to create the bond."

"And almost killed you!" He tried to force down his anger. Elizabeth was finally confiding in him, and he did not wish her to stop.

A smile flickered across her face. "I do not believe she intended that part, and she is as distressed over it as you are."

He doubted that. "Did you ask her to do it?"

"Not at all. I did not know she had that ability, or I would have begged her to use it sooner." She turned her face up to the sun. "She saw I was distressed and offered to help."

He took a deep breath. Elizabeth was alive and well, and walking beside him. "Why did you keep this a secret so long?"

She wrinkled her nose. "I almost told you, more than once. But I was afraid of your mother finding out about Cerridwen's abilities."

"What could she do? Familiars choose mages, not the other way around."

"Would that stop your mother from trying to learn more? The Indian mage, Rana Akshaya, recognized what Cerridwen is, and she hid it from Lady Anne. Cerridwen is my beloved friend, and I will not endanger her."

He still could not see why it would make a difference, but he would keep her secret. "Thank you for telling me." Later, he would ask her more about the kestrel's abilities, but this was not the time to press her.

A smile broke out on her face. "I feel better for it. Now that I can feel the land, I can sense how much it trusts you, and I thought it was time for me to do the same." Her step became lighter, as if she had been relieved of a heavy burden.

They reached the edge of the garden and entered a wooded path. It was still wide enough for them to walk abreast, but narrow enough to give him the excuse to move closer to her, so that her side brushed against him with each step. How could her mere nearness give him such intense pleasure, and how had he lived his entire life without it?

Thank heavens for her new connection to the land! Even this short walk was tiring, but strength flowed into Elizabeth from the soil each time she set her foot down. Even the breeze caressing her cheeks felt full of energy. There was something different about how Pemberley affected her, as if its magic might run deeper than Longbourn's. She would have to explore it when she was feeling stronger.

And she had Darcy by her side, which gave her more happiness than she cared to admit. Especially now that there was one less secret between them.

The footpath forked, and Darcy gestured to the left. "This way. It is not far now."

Elizabeth peered down the path. "Is this not the way to someone's home? I came here once, but I did not want to intrude."

"Someone's home?" A slow smile came across his face. "Mine, in fact. To me, this is the heart of Pemberley."

"I suppose all the houses at Pemberley are yours," she said as they entered the small glade surrounded by towering oak trees, a tiny cottage at the center, only large enough for a single room.

"This one more than the others. This is where the original keep once stood, the one raised by Guillaume D'Arcy who came over with William the Conqueror. It was abandoned in the fourteenth century in favor of the new manor, which is now the Dower House. This cottage was built out of the stones of the old keep."

Elizabeth could sense the centuries in the land underfoot. The power of Pemberley was even stronger here than at the house, tingling through her body. She drew in a deep breath of still winter air, and a memory struck her. "This place. When you do magic, it reminds me of the stillness of the center of an oak grove, and I smell moss and dried leaves. Just like here."

He looked down at her. "Does it? I never knew. This is where I first learned to use my Talent."

Surprised, she asked, "Why here?"

His face stiffened. "It is a long story, but when my Talent was emerging, I stayed in that house."

"I like long stories," she said stubbornly. After all, it might be her only chance to hear it.

He tapped his foot, as if he wanted to refuse, but then his face softened. "If you wish, but let us go inside and get warm first."

Go inside? Surely they could not simply walk into this cottage. "Do you mean we should go back to the house?"

He stepped up to the cottage door and fished for the latch string with a practiced hand. "No. In here." The door swung easily with no telltale squeaks of rusty hinges, and he held it open for her.

Curious, she walked into a room with rustic whitewashed walls and a flagstone floor. The furnishings, while simple, were of a higher quality than she would have expected, the well-worn rug on the floor still showing an intricate design. A faded quilt covered the narrow bed, and wood was neatly stacked by the fireplace. There was none of the dust she would have expected. "Someone has been caring for this place."

"I imagine Mrs. Reynolds makes certain of that, at least when I am in residence." He knelt by the hearth and arranged the tinder and logs in it, looking far more efficient than any man of property should when going about such a menial task. There was something appealing about it, and a wave of affection filled her. How little she had understood the complexity of his character when they first met!

He leaned back on his heels, seeming to study his handiwork, and became still. A moment later flames rose from the tinder, licking at the wood above it.

Elizabeth came forward, holding her hands out to warm them at the welcome heat. "How fortunate that your Talent has practical uses as well."

"I learned this one early, as I was never particularly adept with flint and steel."

The fire leapt up, perhaps in response to his Talent. She perched on the small chair by the hearth, while Darcy brought over a stool.

"I can see this will be very cozy," she said lightly. "How did you come to find it?" Perhaps that would be a simple place to begin the story he seemed reluctant to tell.

He settled himself on the stool. "As a boy, I loved to explore the ruins of the old keep, pretending to be Guillaume D'Arcy or one of his fearless knights. I was always aware of this place. It had been abandoned for decades, and the other children said it was haunted. Once, on a dare, I came inside. I found many cobwebs, mouse droppings, and an incredible, peaceful silence." He smiled slightly at the memory.

"Silence?" she prompted.

"Pemberley was always full of sounds, the noise of servants coming and going, conversations, and activities. Even outdoors was not quiet, between bird songs, animals, tenant farmers, and all. Except here. These thick walls kept all the noise out."

"You liked the quiet?"

"I was a fussy child. Everything seemed to agitate me – scratchy stockings, tight shoes, unexpected noises, even something as simple as two conversations going on at the same time. I spent half my childhood with my hands over my ears."

She would never have imagined it of this self-possessed man. "No wonder you dislike balls and parties, then."

"Exactly. It is much better now, though noise can still grate on me. Then I simply loved this place that was silent and still. I asked the housekeeper for a broom to sweep it out, which was a much bigger endeavor than my six-year-old self could imagine. Fortunately, the next time I came back, it was all clean. I took that as a sign that this was a miraculous place, having little understanding of how servants work. Later, the desk and chair appeared, and gradually the other things I might want. It became my haven. My nurse, noticing I was calmer after spending time here, encouraged me."

"So this was your playhouse?"

His eyes seemed to fix on the fire. "Until my land Talent appeared. Then it became more. You have been spared the discomfort of repulsion. While generally there is no significant repulsion between parent and child, or sisters and brothers, there can be a trace of it. In my case, it made my skin itch. Most people can overlook that, but I was a child who could not even bear the touch of wool against my skin, and that itching sensation kept me from sleeping or even thinking clearly."

It was easy to see where this was going. "So you stayed here."

He gave her a rueful smile. "My tutor suggested I live at the Dower House, but my father would not have it. He was horrified that his heir could not tolerate a slight discomfort and did not want anyone to know. Somehow, between my tutor and the housekeeper, the plan was hatched to allow me to spend most nights here, which I did for several years. Once I could reliably draw on my land Talent, I was more able to control my reaction, and started sleeping at Pemberley again. I still came here when I craved quiet, though." He glanced up at her. "You must think me a rather poor sort of fellow."

"Not at all. My sister Mary has similar challenges. That is why I shared a bedroom with Jane, so Mary could have one to herself. And there is a reason my father has always closeted himself in his library. He hates noise, too." But she could imagine it must have been even harder for Darcy, since the expectations for him had been so high.

He looked at her as if she had said something miraculous, and then reached over and ran his finger along her leg. "Have I ever told you how incredibly fortunate I was to find you?"

Her throat tightened. How could she bear this? Words she longed to hear, yet could not allow herself to listen to. She turned her head away, even the sight of him making her heart ache.

She should say something polite, something to distract him from this agonizing closeness. It would be safer, but the lump in her throat would not let any words past.

"My apologies," he said stiffly. "I should not trouble you with sentiments I know you do not share. Perhaps we should return to the house."

Somehow her hands had found their way into fists, her fingernails cutting into her palms, and she banged them on her lap. "Stop it! It is not that I do not share them, but that I cannot afford to! If this were a true marriage, one with a future, I could feel fortunate, but how can I when I am about to lose you, and will have to live the rest of my days without you?"

He looked taken aback. "I did not mean—"

"You did not mean to make me care about you? How would you feel if I were the one going off on a mission to my death, knowing that you have only this short time with me, and then you will spend decades knowing what you have lost? You can afford to fall in love because you will never have to face losing me. But I have to go on living when you will have taken the easy way out and died!"

He shook his head once, twice, and then again. "I have no choice. You know that."

"You must go on your mission, yes, but you are not even making an effort to survive it! You have been humoring me when I attempt to find a way out for you, but it is only that. It is so much easier to let your life force unravel. I am the one who will be left alone. If you truly cared about me, you would be fighting to find a way back!" She glared at him, breathing heavily. "Do you know what it is like for me, knowing you are going to die?" A sob choked her throat.

He buried his face in his hands. After a long moment, he said in a muffled voice, "Three days ago, I was terrified that you were dying."

"Because that would have ruined your mission," she said bitterly.

His hands dropped away, revealing an agonized expression. "No, because I was afraid of losing you!" He inhaled raggedly, clearly attempting to calm himself. When he spoke again, his voice was distant. "Which, I suppose, only proves your point. I would never wish you to suffer that same pain over my death. I have been selfish in wanting to be close to you. I will keep more distance in the future, if that is what you wish."

Elizabeth brought her fists down on her thighs in frustration. "No, that is *not* what I wish! I want you to try to survive. Yes, you have a duty to England, but you also have a duty to me!"

He shook his head slowly. "If only it were that simple."

"Why must you see it as black and white? Perhaps you will reach Napoleon's presence and discover that your task is impossible. Will you still make the attempt and die for it, or will you walk away and come back to me? Suppose you cast your illusion, and it seems to be succeeding – could you not stop while you still have enough energy to turn yourself invisible and try to escape? If you do not care about living for yourself, can you not do it for my sake?"

He swallowed visibly, and then suddenly he was on his knees before her, his hands tangling with hers. "I want to live. Even more, I want to live *with you*, so badly that I can hardly bear to think of it. It might be possible, I admit, but I cannot let myself hope, for fear that my courage will fail me. But I beg you to believe me. I want to come back to you."

Tears filled her eyes. "Foolish, foolish man, to even worry that you will not do your duty! I saw you risk yourself for a lost tenant girl. I know you will do your best for your mission – but you can afford to plan an escape. And if you do not consider your options, you will not be in a position to seize an opportunity if it arises."

He laid his head in her lap, as if the weight of it was too much for him. "Dearest Elizabeth, I will try. I promise you. And not only for your sake, but because I want to come back to you so badly. While you were ill, I realized how much. These last weeks with you have been the best of my life."

She bent down and pressed her lips against his forehead. "That is all I ask. I can work with you to find a way. Now that I have bonded to the land, I can spin and weave Pemberley's power into cloth for you to carry. You could practice remaining invisible for longer periods of time. There are things we can do – together."

Hope and grief combined in his expression. "But I beg of you not to take any risks. When I thought I had lost you..."

She cradled his face in her hands. "I will be careful. For you."

Then he was pulling her to her feet, into his arms, and seizing her mouth with his own, his kisses wild and demanding. And something in her responded with the same abandon, as if by the force of her passion she could keep him safe, as if only his kiss and his touch could fill the raw need rising in her. Her body ached for him, for the fulfillment he could bring her. And she never, ever wanted to let him go.

But it was beyond her own desire and his. A powerful rush of Pemberley's magic raced through her, and she could feel the tingling in his lips as well, as if the land's own force was bringing them together. And suddenly awareness filled her, of how his ardor for her overpowered his senses, of how her every touch intoxicated him.

When he drew in a sudden, sharp breath, she knew he could feel it too, that they were one in their need. As his fingers skimmed down her spine, sending unquenchable heat deep inside her, he gently propelled her backwards towards the bed. "Dearest, loveliest Elizabeth, I cannot wait," he groaned.

She yanked at the knot of his cravat, eager to nibble at his skin. "Nor can I."

Chapter 23

I T WAS A TURNING point for Elizabeth, their coming together in the cottage. Unable to forget the intense power of their connection, she redoubled her efforts with her books and in her lessons with Lady Frederica. There had to be a way to help Darcy escape his fate.

A week later, the butler appeared in the drawing room where Elizabeth was practicing illusion casting with Lady Frederica. A look of slight distaste hovered over his usually stoic expression. "Madam, there is a... gentleman asking to see you." His emphasis made it abundantly clear that he did not, in fact, consider the caller a gentleman.

"Who is it?" Elizabeth asked.

After a stately pause, Hobbes said, as if it pained him, "He does not have a calling card. He appears to be of Welsh extraction and claims to have a letter from your great-grandmother."

She smiled. Poor Hobbes! Too many impossibilities all at once. "I thank you for your concern, Hobbes. As unlikely as it may seem, my great-grandmother is alive and living in Wales, and I am expecting a letter from her. Pray show the gentleman in." Finally, an answer to her letters pleading for advice!

Hobbes bowed. "As madam wishes."

Cerridwen, who had been drowsing on her perch near the fire, picked up her head.

The butler returned. "Mr. Ruttickry," he pronounced, his nose in the air.

The dark-haired Welshman was tall, thin, and dressed in a country style, with a simply knotted cravat and a coat which, while well-made, was several years out of fashion.

Would he make the obvious mistake? Lady Frederica's appearance was more in keeping with what would be expected of the lady of Pemberley, while Elizabeth herself was still wearing her old clothes from Longbourn.

But his eyes passed immediately over the golden-haired woman and he made his bow to Elizabeth. "Mrs. Darcy."

"Mr. Roderick, you are welcome to Pemberley."

His mouth quirked at her correction of the butler's mispronunciation. "I see you recall your days in Wales."

His musical accent made her homesick for her adventurous girlhood days visiting Granny, and a memory snapped into place. "Or is it Roderick ap Rhodri?" she ventured.

He inclined his head. "You remember, then. I was not sure you would. It has been many years. It is simpler if I remain Mr. Roderick in England."

"Indeed." She had admired the wiry boy, a few years older than her, who had seemed so adult to an eight-year-old. He had been a frequent visitor at Granny's house and had been kind to her, although far too dignified to play with the Bennet children. "Lady Frederica, may I present Mr. Roderick? Lady Frederica Fitzwilliam is Mrs. Morgan's great-grandniece."

"It is a pleasure," said Lady Frederica, examining the Welshman with obvious interest.

With a guarded look, he said, "I am honored, your ladyship."

Elizabeth said, "Pray sit down. You must be half-frozen, traveling in this weather."

He took the seat by the fire she had indicated, rubbing his hands together. "It is much like the mountains at home, but I will be glad to see spring."

"May I inquire as to my great-grandmother's health?" He was not wearing black, so presumably it was not the worst news.

He hesitated, casting a mistrustful glance at Lady Frederica. "She has had a difficult winter. I would be happy to give you more details in private."

Well, that was much more direct than an English gentleman would be! "If you prefer it, but I can assure you that Lady Frederica and Granny would find a great deal to agree upon, if they were ever to meet."

"Perhaps so, but Mrs. Morgan was clear that she wished me to avoid dealing with any of her former family."

Cerridwen spoke inside Elizabeth's head, and she turned to stare at the bird doubtfully. Well, people in Wales might be more understanding about her falcon's abilities, so perhaps this would not go as badly amiss as it might with another person.

With a shrug, she said, "Mr. Roderick, my falcon wishes me to tell you she has tested Lady Frederica and found her worthy. I hope that will mean more to you than it does to me." Later she would have to ask Cerridwen what this test had involved.

He turned to Cerridwen. "You did?" He sounded astonished. And apparently expected the bird to understand English, unlike Darcy or Frederica.

Cerridwen flapped her wings before settling on the perch again.

"She says, *I have said so,*" Elizabeth translated.

The Welshman turned his palms up. "In that case, Lady Frederica, pray forgive me."

Lady Frederica's eyes were wide, and Elizabeth could almost see her struggle to keep a hundred questions inside.

One did escape, though. "You would not accept Elizabeth's endorsement of my character, but you believe her bird?" she asked disbelievingly.

He shifted in his chair. "When a stranger comes to my door, I trust my dog's assessment of him. Animals are sometimes more insightful than humans."

Cerridwen gave an annoyed squawk and flew across the room to perch on Elizabeth's shoulder, her talons digging in more than usual. Elizabeth managed to hide a wince, reaching up to stroke the bird's literally ruffled feathers. "I am happy we are all in agreement now," she said, with a cautionary glance at Lady Frederica.

The Welshman drew out a folded paper from his pocket and presented it to Elizabeth. "Mrs. Morgan asked me to give you this letter. She dictated it to me, so I am aware of its contents."

Elizabeth examined the letter without opening it. "How unwell is she? She has always written to me herself." Even if her notes had grown briefer and briefer over the years.

"She is well at present, although age has made her fragile, and we fear what will happen when next she is ill. Her mind is as formidable as ever, but her fingers cannot bend easily to hold a pen, nor can her eyes make out clearly the words on a page. She will deny those things if you ask, because she has no patience for weakness, but it is obvious to everyone around her."

Poor Granny! "She must hate that."

"She does. She still insists on perusing personal letters by seeing them through her bird's eyes, rather than asking one of us to read them to her."

"I can imagine she would prefer that."

Lady Frederica burst out, "Wait! Does that mean you can see through Cerridwen's eyes?"

Oh, dear. "When she allows me to, yes," Elizabeth said apologetically. "Which is not often."

"And she talks to you, too?" Lady Frederica threw her hands up. "I hated you before, and now I totally detest you," she said plaintively.

Elizabeth laughed, both at her words and at Roderick's shocked expression. "Lady Frederica has never forgiven me for bonding to a falcon. It was her childhood dream, since first seeing the portrait of Lady Amelia Fitzwilliam with her falcon, painted shortly before her supposed death. I hope it does not shock you."

To her astonishment, he said, "I would call it perfectly natural. Who would not envy those fortunate people chosen for that privilege? I certainly do." And he sounded utterly sincere.

"Thank you," said Lady Frederica firmly.

He added, "It is good to know there are those among the English who can appreciate that honor."

Elizabeth ran her finger under the seal of the letter and scanned the lines, paying no attention to the other two. There was no question these were Granny's words, even in a man's hand; her sharp wit and acerbity came through clearly. Including her familiar insistence Elizabeth must come to see her in Wales as soon as humanly possible. If only her father had not prevented her from attending to Granny's earlier requests!

She raised her eyebrows at the next part. "Mr. Roderick, this says you can help my husband improve his illusion casting."

He dipped his head. "Since she cannot travel, she sent me in her stead."

She glanced at Lady Frederica, who was showing no signs of discomfort. Was he like Mr. Bingley, knowledgeable in the theory but without Talent of his own? "She must feel you have something to offer, then."

He clearly heard the doubt in her voice, for his mouth twisted. "You doubt me? Perhaps I should demonstrate. Do you remember Mrs. Morgan's home?"

And then an image of a familiar stone edifice rippled into place, complete with the babbling brook in front of it, crossed by the narrow arched bridge that Granny claimed dated from Roman times. A gray rabbit hopped across the grassy slope, and the scent of mountain pine seemed to fill the room.

Elizabeth caught her breath as homesickness captured her once again. Then a curtain in an illusory window was drawn aside, and a shadowed face peered out, distorted by the glass, yet still with the familiar features of her great-grandmother.

Tears filled her eyes, and she gasped in disappointment as the illusion faded into nothingness.

Lady Frederica said sharply, "Well, that was quite the exhibition."

He raised an eyebrow. "I thank you."

"Do not thank me. I cannot decide whether I am more cross with you for being able to cast moving water or for being another one of those annoying people who are immune to repulsion."

"Mrs. Morgan can cast a waterfall," he said with a trace of smugness.

"No," Lady Frederica said disbelievingly.

"I assure you it is true." His voice carried laughter.

"Why, even Lady – the King's Mage cannot cast moving water! She counts herself proud of her ability to cast sunlight reflecting on still water."

Elizabeth stared. Her father had cast a waterfall, and she had not known there was anything unusual about it.

"If it helps, I am not immune to repulsion. I am simply wearing dragon silver." He held up his right hand to display a simple ring circling his middle finger. "Were I to remove it, you may be assured I would be in pain."

Lady Frederica's mouth dropped open. "You have an Artifact, too?"

With a guarded look, he said, "Mrs. Morgan loaned me this so I could teach Mr. Darcy. Who else has one?"

"The King's Mage," she said in a matter-of-fact manner. "Have you any idea how much that is worth?"

His expression went from guarded to completely closed. "It is worth more than my life, should I fail to return it. These rings are only to be used in matters of great necessity, not to be hoarded by an individual."

Lady Frederica studied him. "You do not approve of the King's Mage having one?"

"It is not for me either to approve or to disapprove. Mrs. Darcy, is it possible for me to meet Mr. Darcy? I will need to depart soon for the inn."

"My husband is practicing his illusions out on the ridge and should be back soon, but I simply cannot hear of your going to an inn. You have traveled halfway across the country in the dead of winter to offer your assistance; you must stay here with us," said Elizabeth warmly.

His gaze swept over the room, from end to exquisitely decorated end. "You are everything that is gracious, Mrs. Darcy, but I believe I might fit in better at an inn," he drawled. "I am certain your butler would agree."

"I decide who to invite to Pemberley, not my butler. And false modesty does not become you, Roderick ap Rhodri. I recall who your forebears are," Elizabeth replied.

"And you need not worry about having to deal with me." Lady Frederica tossed her head. "I am staying at the Dower House, since neither Darcy nor I are fortunate enough to avoid repulsion. Unless he is holding Elizabeth's hand."

"How lucky for him that he has that option," said the Welshman, seeming not at all surprised by this concept.

Perhaps she could ask him later what else he knew about people who lacked repulsion.

Elizabeth came into Darcy's arms like a dream as soon as he walked through the adjoining door to her bedroom the following week. She seemed to melt as she pressed herself against him, murmuring, "Finally."

He leaned in to kiss her, a slow lingering caress that stoked a fire inside him. Her cheeks were flushed and her breathing rapid as he finally pulled away.

It had been another long day of illusion practice with Roderick, and he was about to make it longer with news Elizabeth would not like. "We must make the most of our time together. Tomorrow I must leave for a few days."

She stiffened. "What has happened?"

"Nothing to be concerned about. The War Office wants a meeting to go over plans. Apparently there have been some minor changes, but they can only tell me about them in person."

"Can they not come here?"

"Not without drawing the wrong sort of attention. French spies are everywhere. As it is, everyone must believe I am going to Nottingham to visit an ill friend, but I wanted you to know the truth." Or some of it, anyway. He would actually be traveling by mail coach to London under an assumed name, while his own carriage proceeded to Nottingham carrying his valet, who would stay at an inn as Mr. Darcy. He hated lying to Elizabeth, but the War Office had insisted on absolute secrecy.

She stepped back to look at him. "How long will you be gone?"

"Five days." Keeping it that short would mean sleepless nights on the mail coach and spending only a day in Town, but it would be worth it to be return quickly. "I want to be back with you as soon as I can. And it will be a good opportunity to test whether I can draw any power through you at a distance."

She bit her lip. "If you will be away in any case, could I not take this time to make a quick journey to Wales to see my great-grandmother? I do not care if it has to be very brief, but Roderick says she is fragile and her next illness is likely to carry her off. I wish to see her before she dies."

He studied her. It was a terrible idea. "I wish it were possible. It is a much longer trip, and over hard roads. It would take at least a fortnight, even if you only stayed a few days, and we do not have that much time." He hated to disappoint her, but chances were good the old lady would outlive him, and then Elizabeth could go to see her anytime.

"Even if I could only stay there overnight and return here the following day, it would be worth it to me." Tears glistened in her eyes. "I left my home and my family for your mission. I have not complained about missing Jane's wedding. But I want to see my great-grandmother one last time." Her voice broke. "She has been begging me to visit for years, but my father could not spare me. This may be my last chance."

It was a reasonable enough request, and under any other circumstances, he would not hesitate to agree. And he certainly did not want to be like her father! "I can ask the War Office if they have any better idea of when I will be needed. If it is more than a few months away, then we will find a way for you to go to Wales." And perhaps after he returned, she might feel less distressed and understand the need to remain.

She swallowed visibly. "Thank you."

It broke his heart to watch her attempt to be brave.

Taking her hands, he raised her to her feet and drew her into his arms. "I wish I could bundle you into a carriage this minute and take you to her," he murmured in her ear.

"I know." Her voice shook, though. "It is so unfair."

"That it is." It was all unfair, every bit of it, that he should find such a reason to live just when he had agreed to die for his country.

Chapter 24

THE ELDERLY SOLICITOR RUBBED his hands together. "Now, Mr. Darcy, it is always a pleasure to see you, but I assume this must be a matter of some urgency to bring you all the way to Town, and I do not wish to waste your time."

"Indeed. I wish to change my will." He only had an hour before his meeting with Cattermole, but he had to take advantage of his brief time in London to do this. It was not something he could explain in a letter.

Haskins cocked his head. "Again?"

"Yes, again." He had completely rewritten it as soon as he learned of his mission. "You received word of my marriage."

This seemed to reassure the old gentleman. "Ah, yes, naturally. Very happy news it was indeed! I received a copy of the very generous settlement you made on her."

"Since my situation has changed, I now wish to add a codicil to my will, if I should die without issue."

"Yes?" Haskins dipped his quill in his inkwell, prepared to take notes.

"Should I die childless, I wish Pemberley to be held in trust for my wife for her life, and left to any future children she may bear. Should she die without offspring, however, it will revert to the Darcy line as spelled out in my current will."

The solicitor's quill frozen in midair. "You wish to leave Pemberley to the children your wife may have with another man?" His tone was carefully neutral, but it could not disguise his disbelief. Just as Darcy had expected.

"This has nothing to do with my wishes, but the best interests of Pemberley. The estate has thrived far beyond its neighbors since the Darcy Talent has grown more powerful. Our crops, our animals, all are unusually productive. Our tenants are healthy and thriving." It was impossible to truly explain it, but he had to try. "My wife has an unusual Talent that permitted her to bond to Pemberley. Any child of hers, whether or not I am the father, will inherit that bond. Anyone else would take generations to develop such a connection, by which time Pemberley will be good for little more than grazing land."

Haskins set down his quill. "It is more important for you to have a landed Talent at Pemberley than a Darcy?"

"Yes. Especially since Francis Darcy has no hint of Talent nor any financial sense." He had never been happy about the choice of his cousin as heir. "If his elder brother Henry had lived, it might have been different."

"Indeed." At least Haskins knew better than to bring up the possibility of naming Georgiana as his heir. He was the only person outside the family who knew the truth about her. "Do you intend to inform Lady Anne of your plan?"

That was the problem of dealing with an old family retainer. "I do not expect she will object. Mrs. Darcy is of Fitzwilliam blood, so there is that connection."

An eyebrow went up. "That would explain her unusual Talent. You mentioned holding Pemberley in trust for your wife, should the worst occur. Do you have a trustee in mind?"

"My cousin, Colonel Richard Fitzwilliam." It gave him a pang to say it. Richard was by far the best choice to be Pemberley's trustee, but he would also be a likely candidate for a new husband for Elizabeth. As much as Darcy might rationally wish for her to remarry and have children for Pemberley, he could only bear to imagine her future husband as a faceless stranger.

He forced those thoughts away before he could change his mind. It was his duty to do what was best for Pemberley. And for Elizabeth. How would she feel, bonded to Pemberley as she was, if she had to watch Talentless, dissolute Francis Darcy ruin the estate? No, this was better for her, too.

Even if the very thought of her remarrying made his throat ache.

Foreboding filled Darcy as he shook Cattermole's hand. This meeting might tell him his idyll with Elizabeth was over. The last time he had met his War Office contact in person, Darcy had still been in shock over Jack's death and had accepted dying for his country with a certain dull equanimity. Leaving Elizabeth was a different matter. He had so much more to lose now.

"What news?" he asked abruptly after the bare minimum of polite niceties.

Cattermole settled back in his chair. "Nothing good, I fear. The Austrians are barely holding their own, but if all else were normal, we would predict they would keep Boney busy for another six months, if not a year. But our source tells us that Corsican bastard is working on a plan that will bring him back to Paris by summer with a surrender in hand."

Darcy's chest constricted. As soon as Napoleon returned from Austria, his mission would begin. "Do you think there will be another dragon attack?"

Cattermole's face seemed to age ten years before his eyes. "We have been expecting one for months. It is a mystery why he has held back so long, spilling his army's blood in the field rather than sending in the dragons. Still, it could happen, or he may have some other damn trick up his sleeve. In either case, we would depend upon you more than ever. Once Austria falls, England is next. With the Navy paralyzed, we have no hope." He drained his port and poured another glass from a decanter, his hand trembling slightly.

Dread pricked at his skin. How easy it had been to forget the grimness of the situation, even as he had spent his days preparing for the mission! "I will do my best."

"How is your training going? Any sign of a pregnancy that could help you? I tell you, Darcy, if I can pass along even the slightest hope, it would be a great gift. Spirits here are very low. Hardened soldiers talking of keeping a loaded gun at hand in case of the worst. Talk of fleeing to Canada, if they could only be sure of getting past those damned sea serpents. I have never seen the like."

And he had been snug in the oasis of Pemberley. "It is too early to know about a child," he said slowly.

"Bad luck, that. Is there still time? How does it work? Does the blood tie start as soon as she has one in the basket, or not until the babe quickens?"

Darcy winced internally at the coarseness, but it was a good question, one he had somehow failed to consider. "All we know is that Lord Howard of Effingham was able to draw on his land magic through his wife when she was increasing, but I do not know how far along she was. Still, if he was aware of the child, it must have already quickened." There were months between conception and quickening, were there not? He would have to ask Elizabeth.

"Well, we will have to hope, though luck has not run our way so far," Cattermole said heavily.

He hunted for shreds of encouragement. "There is some progress, though. My wife has established her own bond to Pemberley, and we can connect through that."

A spark of hope lit the other man's face. "Does that make a difference?"

"It helps, to a degree. My illusions are more stable. I will need to experiment with it, though. Right now it is like trying to write with my left hand – possible, but clumsy and inefficient." But practice would mean more time away from Elizabeth, a price he hated to pay.

"I pray it will work. Now, we have had a change in plans as to how you will travel to France when the time comes." Cattermole brought out a map and set it on the table.

Darcy leaned forward. He wanted to know every detail of this, in hopes of finding a way he could also return from France.

His last task in Town should have been the easiest, but the moment he walked in the door to the house he had taken for Georgiana, it was clear something was wrong. His sister stood unsmiling, and she curtsied rather than racing into his arms as she usually did.

Darcy hardly needed the wide-eyed warning glance from her tall, dark-haired companion, Miss Lowrie, to know something was wrong. Miss Lowrie might only be a few years older than Georgiana, but she was an eminently sensible young woman. And Georgiana trusted her, which was an exceedingly rare thing.

He stepped forward to kiss his sister's cheek. When she still showed little response, he took a seat and said, "What did she do to you this time?"

Georgiana bit her lip. "Who do you mean?"

"Mother, of course. You have barely answered my letters since I returned to Pemberley and you have ignored my invitations to join me there. Obviously she must have done something to upset you."

Now she met his gaze, but her expression was opaque. "I have had no contact from Lady Anne. I saw her once, across the theatre at a concert, but I do not believe she noticed me."

Damn. He had been so certain that must be the problem, but Georgiana never lied. She might evade a question, but whatever she said was the truth. "What is it, then?"

She squeezed her eyes shut and shook her head.

Stymied, Darcy glanced at Miss Lowrie, raising an eyebrow. She understood Georgiana better than he did.

The young woman said gently, "Your sudden marriage was a shock. When your new wife made no effort to meet Georgiana, I believe your sister feared the worst."

Georgiana paled and said in a rush, "I thought you had changed your mind about me."

Good God. Not this again. "I will never change my mind about you. How many times must I tell you? Elizabeth would have liked to meet you, but she had only three days between learning we would marry and the wedding."

Georgiana's brows drew together. "So quickly? Which was it, then? Did she entrap you, or was this Lady Anne's idea?"

Darcy rubbed his hands over his face. Had Georgiana truly been thinking this all this time? And how could he answer her without giving away secrets? "Neither. The War Office wanted it, because her Talent can help mine. Admittedly, Mother was delighted, but only because she wanted me to marry any woman of mage blood. Elizabeth – well, in fact, she rather desperately wanted to avoid marrying me."

His sister's chin jutted out in indignation. "Why? How could any woman not want to marry you?"

Her sudden change of mood almost made him laugh, but Georgiana would not take that well. "She did not wish to leave her home and family. But she and I have become good friends." And much more, but that was not for the ears of his much younger sister.

"Does she know about...me?"

Finally an easy answer. "Only that you are my beloved sister. She dearly wishes to meet you, but it is best for her to stay at Pemberley for now."

A bit of color returned to Georgiana's cheeks. "Then I will come to meet her. When do you plan to return there?"

He grimaced. "Tonight, by mail coach." He had barely slept on the way to London.

"Then Belinda and I will follow you there in a few days." At least she sounded more like herself again.

Miss Lowrie smiled. "Excellent. I will be glad of the chance to see my family."

Georgiana poked her companion with an elbow. "Your family, or a certain young man?" she teased.

Roses bloomed in Miss Lowrie's cheeks. "Can it not be both?"

It was good to see his sister joking with her friend, like an ordinary girl.

"I have never been driven by a woman before," Elizabeth admitted to Frederica as she gazed at the high hills around them. "Much less in a curricle. How did you learn how to do it?"

Frederica laughed. "Sheer stubbornness and a desire to keep up with my brothers. My father offered as a compromise that I could drive the phaeton, but as soon as I mastered that, I pestered my brother Richard to let me drive the curricle. He was always game for a prank, so he did."

"I am grateful for it, because it is good to get out today." Pemberley simply felt too empty with Darcy away. How strange it was that after only a day apart, it felt so very long! And it was too easy to fall into fretting over what the War Office might have in mind. Yesterday Roderick had kept her distracted with dragon stories and lessons in illusion-casting, but today he had letters to write, so she had leapt at Frederica's suggestion that they take a drive into the Dark Peak.

"We could have found someone to drive us, but this is better."

"Much. I am glad to be away from all the servants. I am not accustomed to having so many around." Not that they were free of them even now; three grooms followed them on horseback, too far to overhear their conversation. "No doubt you are used to them always being present, but I come from a much smaller household." Not to mention one where the staff liked her.

"They have been there all my life," said Frederica. "At least your housekeeper is pleasant. The one at Matlock is a martinet. I was always terrified of her."

Elizabeth looked away. "Mrs. Reynolds tries hard not to show her disapproval of me." It was a relief to say it, even though she could not imagine why she had allowed the words to escape her mouth. Usually she tried to avoid complaining about things she could not change.

Frederica glanced at her. "Mrs. Reynolds? Why would she disapprove of you?"

"What is there to approve of?" Elizabeth ticked off her sins on her fingers. "A hurried wedding, from a family no one has ever heard of, improper behavior like spending hours wandering the estate doing heaven knows what, and requiring very particular foods. I am too odd to be the lady of Pemberley. I hear the servants whispering."

Lady Frederica set her eyes back on the road, her brow furrowed. "Does the housekeeper know why you are doing all these things? Not that she has any right to, I suppose, but sometimes it helps."

Elizabeth turned her hands up. "Darcy's mission is supposed to be secret, so I told her it was to improve my bond to the land. And she does her job; I have no complaints about that. Liking me is not a requirement for her position." But, oh, how much more comfortable she would be at Pemberley if the staff were a little more welcoming instead of merely doing their duty!

"Is that why you still have Chandrika as your lady's maid?

She shrugged, though it was true enough. "I suppose so. She offered to stay on in the position, and I saw no reason to refuse. I expect she reports back to Rana Akshaya, and likely to Lady Anne as well, but as I do little worth reporting, I do not care. And at least Chandrika does not disapprove of my clothes. Which is yet another reason the servants and housekeeper dislike me, because I dress like the daughter of a country gentleman of modest means – which is exactly what I am." Bitterness crept into her voice.

Frederica raised her eyebrows. "I understand you had no time for wedding clothes, but do you not wish to have new ones made now?"

Elizabeth scowled. "Darcy says I should get them in London, and when I point out I cannot leave Pemberley, he tells me to write to his mother and ask her to make the arrangements for a modiste to help me. I would rather wear rags."

"Good for you!" exclaimed Frederica. "Anyway, Darcy knows nothing about how to obtain lady's clothing. There are perfectly fine modistes outside of London. Leave it to me – there is an excellent one in Derby who would be delighted to come to Pemberley to gain your custom. I will write to her tonight."

"Would you? That would be a great relief. Especially since eventually the neighbors will insist upon calling on me, and I do not wish to embarrass anyone by dressing below my station." What was wrong with her? It was not like her to be so cross and full of complaints.

"That is easily fixed. And look – that must be Winnat's Pass! Now we shall see how the horses manage it."

And indeed, the road ahead seemed to disappear into the wall of mountains. Surely there could be no path through them?

But there it was, a narrow roadway winding through a deep cleft with steep slopes on each side, as if a giant had taken a knife and carved it out. The mountains towered over her in imposing glory as the road twisted back and forth, climbing higher, ever higher. Had a river once flowed through here? There was no sign of one now.

The horses slowed as the incline increased sharply. It was breathtakingly beautiful. Elizabeth's ears popped, and then a shiver overtook her.

Suddenly the hills seemed to close in on her. The jagged rock outcroppings loomed like strange wind-carved monsters. What if the horses grew tired and could no longer pull the curricle up this endless chasm? What if she could never escape?

Her breath caught in her throat, pressing on her heart. Her chest tightened painfully, her skin burning.

She did not belong here, in this wild, nightmarish mountain pass. She was a creature of the fertile green fields of Hertfordshire, not this barren moorland. The Dark Peak, which had seemed so untamed and beautiful at a distance, now felt outright malevolent.

What was wrong with her? She had never reacted this way before. She clung to that thought through the overwhelming sense of panic, even as her body ached to scream and run away. But she would not allow herself to be intimidated by a strange landscape!

She clasped her hand to her pounding heart, but even that small motion burned inside her joints and made the world spin around her. With a whimper, she lowered her head onto her arms until she was almost bent double.

"Elizabeth, is something wrong?" Frederica's voice seemed to come from far away.

"Dizzy," she managed to squeak out.

"Oh, dear. And there is no space to turn out here. Wait, I think we are almost in the clear. Hold on."

Somehow Elizabeth grasped the bar in front of her as the curricle speeded up. Time passed, what felt like hours, but might have been just a few agonizing minutes, and then the carriage slowed and bumped to a halt. Her stomach knotted with each movement.

"What is it?" asked Frederica. "Was my driving too rough? Richard always says I have too heavy a hand on the ribbons."

"Not that. I am ill. Perhaps it is the altitude." Elizabeth uncovered her face. The land was mostly flat again, but the open space spun around her, like the hawks circling dizzyingly overhead.

Frederica frowned. "I suppose we climbed a good bit in the pass," she said doubtfully.

"Are we in the Dark Peak now?" How she longed to be here, and now all she wanted was to leave! This very instant, if possible.

"I am uncertain where the Dark Peak begins, but we are certainly in the mountains. Look, there is Mam Tor." She pointed to the right.

And there it was, the familiar shape rising high a few fields away. Its mysterious fascination still tugged at her, drawing her like a magnet, even though her innards lurched. "It is so big."

"Are you well enough to keep going? According to the directions, the road to Mam Tor turns off soon."

Elizabeth felt a bit better now that they had stopped, and it would be pity to give up when it was so close. "Yes, let us carry on."

But as soon as the curricle moved again, Elizabeth's skin burned anew, her chest aching. She gritted her teeth. Whatever strange affliction this was, she could tolerate it long enough to reach the peak, or however close they could get in the curricle. Whether her feet could carry her farther was a different question.

Then Frederica turned the horses into a lane that was signposted to Mam Tor, and suddenly it was no longer tolerable. An invisible arrow seemed to have split her head wide open. She pressed her hands to her temples as if they could hold her skull together, a whimper escaping her lips. Oh, it hurt, it hurt, it hurt!

"Elizabeth?" Frederica sounded worried.

Blinding flashes of light filled her mind. She forced out the words, "Take me home."

Chapter 25

FREDERICA SET DOWN HER book when the knock came at the door to Elizabeth's sickroom. At least Elizabeth was finally asleep, although her face still showed lines of pain.

She held her finger to her lips as Elizabeth's maid entered. Not that Chandrika ever made much noise, but the tiny action made Frederica feel marginally less useless.

The maid gestured to her to follow, something no English servant would have done, but Frederica rose and followed her out of the room.

Only to find Mr. Roderick standing there, clearly disapproving of her again.

He bowed. "Forgive me for troubling you. One of the servants said you would be returning to the Dower House soon, and I wished to beg the honor of escorting you there."

He wanted to spend time with her? Perhaps he thought it was his duty, or more likely, he hoped to get some information from her. Well, he could try! "If you wish. I might as well go now, since Elizabeth is sleeping. Chandrika, would you be so kind as to send word if you think Mrs. Darcy might appreciate my company?" Elizabeth would never make the request herself, but her maid seemed independent-minded enough to act on her own.

"Yes, Lady Frederica," Chandrika murmured.

Frederica hated being so helpless, especially when Elizabeth's illness might be her fault.

As they set forth, Mr. Roderick asked, "How is Mrs. Darcy? Any improvement?"

"She is still dizzy and short of breath, but her head does not pain her as much." Or so Elizabeth claimed, but Frederica was less sure of it.

"Did the doctor come to see her?"

She huffed. "For what little that was worth."

"He could not help her?"

It would be better to say nothing, but she could not stop herself. Imitating the doctor's nasal tones, she said, "Delicate young ladies who have not been married long often have these difficulties." Reverting to her own voice, she added fiercely, "He would not even listen to me when I told him how suddenly it had come upon her or what pain she was in. He had made up his mind before he ever saw her."

"How frustrating. I wish Darcy were here."

"So do I, although perhaps it is better that he is not. He would be frantic. Elizabeth was seriously ill a month ago, and it gave all of us a fright. She nearly died."

His brows furrowed. "Is this a recurrence, then?"

"No. That was more of an injury. A magical injury. But she recovered from it."

"A magical injury?" He seemed suddenly alert, as if her next words were of grave importance.

She hesitated. Was there truly any reason not to tell him? Elizabeth seemed to trust him, and perhaps he might have some knowledge that could help her. "She had done blood magic with her bird, helping her bond to Pemberley. Apparently blood magic with a bird familiar always makes people ill. She knew it would happen."

His jaw dropped. "Mrs. Darcy and Cerridwen made a blood bond to the land?"

With a sidelong glance, she said, "Yes. Elizabeth says the land is alive to her now."

He rubbed his gloved hand over his mouth. "How...resourceful."

"But this illness is nothing like that. Actually, it seemed more like repulsion at first – her skin burned, her head felt like it was splitting, and she had a hard time breathing. I thought she must be reacting to me, even though she never had before, and I was sad because it has been so lovely to have a friend with Talent. But I tried getting out of the carriage and walking away from her, and it made no difference. There was no one else up there with us except the grooms, so it could not have been repulsion."

"Up there? Where were you?"

"The Dark Peak. And she was absolutely fine yesterday morning when we set out." She had wracked her brain trying to think if she had missed something, but Elizabeth had seemed so pleased with the idea of the excursion.

He stopped in the middle of a step. "You went to the Dark Peak?"

"Did I not just say so?"

His concerned expression smoothed over into an unreadable look that would have made a butler proud. "Did Mrs. Darcy become ill on the way back to Pemberley?" He seemed to choose his words with care.

His attitude annoyed her. "No, it started when we were almost at the Dark Peak."

"Of course it did," he breathed.

"Do you have any idea how aggravating it is to converse with men who will never tell you what they are truly thinking?" The words slipped out without any intention on her part. How mortifying! She braced herself for the inevitable mockery.

He eyed her thoughtfully. "My apologies. You are correct that I am not telling you everything I know, but I mean no disrespect. I am not your enemy, only someone who has secrets that must be kept."

He had not laughed at her.

But she would not let herself soften to a man who looked down on her, so she narrowed her eyes. "What of Mrs. Darcy? Are you her enemy?"

The corner of his mouth quirked up. "I am her friend."

Elizabeth's friend, but not her own. "And Darcy?"

He considered. "Neither friend nor enemy, I suppose."

What an odd conversation!

They reached the narrow footbridge, and she dropped his arm to walk across the rushing stream. At least it gave her a minute of freedom from his closeness, this not-enemy of hers. She tensed when he caught up with her on the opposite side.

He offered her his arm again. "Mrs. Darcy's great-grandmother is a truth-caster, too. I suppose I should not be surprised."

"A truth-caster? What is that?"

He stilled. "You do not know?"

"I am not in the habit of asking questions whose answers I know," she snapped. "Now tell me."

He pursed his lips. "A truth-caster is a mage who can compel a person to answer truthfully."

"She can force someone to tell their secrets? Could she make French spies tell us Napoleon's plans?" It could change everything if the War Office had someone with that ability. Even if it was a decrepit old lady.

He shook his head. "She cannot compel anyone to speak, only to tell only the truth if they choose to say something. As I did just now, telling you I had secrets I could not share, which was the truth. You could not make me reveal those secrets, though."

"Except that I am not – what you call it? – a truth-caster. If such a thing even exists," she grumbled.

He laughed. "I cannot believe the skill has been forgotten here! And yes, you have the ability. Perhaps no one here can recognize it, but I have been on the receiving end of truth-casting often enough to know it when I feel it."

Annoyed, she pulled her hand from where it rested on his arm. "You are trying to play a trick on me."

"As if I *could* tell you a lie when you are in this mood! Tell me, do you not find that people are surprisingly frank with you, that they confide in you and then are startled at their own words – and that this happens especially when you are irritated, which is when truth-casting occurs most easily?"

She chewed her lip. Yes, people confided in her, but they just as often insulted her to her face. Or was that truth telling, too – losing the ability to hide what they thought behind pretty words? "It is only that I am overly frank myself, as anyone in the entire *ton* will tell you. Perhaps it encourages others to speak the truth."

"It may seem that way to you, but it is truth-casting. I am quite familiar with the sensation, like all the children who grew up in Mrs. Morgan's village. Our mothers dragged us to her whenever they thought we were fibbing." He smiled as if in recollection. "She is a mischievous soul, and sometimes she would not truth-cast at those times to allow us our childish lies, so we learned early to tell the difference."

"She does not do it all the time?"

"No." He paused. "But I fear I cannot explain to you how or when it works, as I have never asked Mrs. Morgan."

She glared at him. "I think you had better tell me everything you know about truth-casting!"

"I will do my best." His lips twitched. "At least you need not worry I will be lying!"

Elizabeth closed her eyes. Watching Frederica's energetic pacing was making her dizziness worse, even while lying in bed.

"And you believe him?" Elizabeth asked.

"I spent all evening making the servants try to tell me lies." Frederica grinned. "They thought I was out of my mind. But they could not do it, not as long as I was paying attention to their answers."

"So you have to focus to make it work?"

"And I have to care about whatever they are saying. Go on, tell me a lie about something that does not matter to me."

Something unimportant. That would be hard, since Frederica seemed so interested in everything. And Elizabeth's head already throbbed. "At

Longbourn, there is a portrait of my grandfather Bennet. He is wearing a blue coat with golden buttons." It was not at all difficult to say.

"And that is a lie?"

"Yes, it is green with silver buttons."

"Now something that I care about," Frederica demanded.

Elizabeth was about to plead an inability to think, when the pain in her head suddenly ebbed, along with the pressure on her chest. She took an experimental breath – yes, it was easier now. Doubtless it would not last long, but it was a wonderful relief, and she could try to think of a lie for Frederica. "My great-grandmother's falcon will land on my hand." She blinked. "Oh, dear, that was not what I meant to say. That one is true." What an odd sensation! She had often found herself telling Frederica more than she meant to. Was this why?

"See? It works! I must know more. I came here full of questions for Mr. Roderick, but your butler says that he is gone away. Frustrating man, to tell me such things and then leave! Where did he go?" At least her rapid pacing had stopped.

Still no dizziness. "He did not say. He told one of the footmen it was an errand for my great-grandmother, and he might not return for a day or two. He left at first light."

Frederica gazed out the window, her fingers tapping against her hip. "I wonder where he went."

"I cannot say. I have not seen him since I took ill."

"And here I am chattering at you when you should be resting. I have not even asked how you are!"

"Better." Elizabeth pushed herself up to a sitting position. "In fact, I think I may get up and have something to eat."

Frederica narrowed her eyes. "Are you certain? This seems very sudden."

She swung her legs over the side of the bed. Still no dizziness! "Remarkably sudden, but I am not complaining. Perhaps the news of your astonishing new Talent has cured me," she teased.

"It is exciting, is it not? But you should not rush things. Darcy will kill me if I let you relapse."

"Nonsense. I am tired of resting, not to mention starving." And it was true. Her old energy was back, the illness vanishing as suddenly as it had come on.

Chapter 26

DRIVEN BY HER HUNGER, Elizabeth dressed quickly and hurried downstairs to the drawing room, where the tea tray was already awaiting her. A piece of cake and a roll was hardly enough, though, and she asked for a plate of cheese and fruit as well.

"I never realized lying in bed could give me such an appetite!" she said to Frederica, who had only eaten a few bites.

"You do seem startlingly recovered," Frederica agreed.

"It is inexplicable, I admit." In fact, now that her hunger was appeased, restlessness danced through her legs, as if it took enormous work to simply sit still.

Elizabeth's skin tingled as the spacious room seemed to shrink around her. Suddenly she ached to get out, to fill her lungs with fresh air, to feel the power of the land beneath her feet, the wind against her cheeks.

It would be rude, though, to leave Frederica. While she could invite her to come on a walk, this abrupt urge of hers to be out of doors also demanded that she be alone, able to tear off her bonnet and gloves and run.

It would have to wait. With barely concealed resignation, Elizabeth folded her hands. She could not focus, her feet tapping impatiently like an unruly child's. The air in the room was so thick, almost too thick to breathe. Perhaps opening the window would help.

It did not. And now that she was on her feet, she could not bring herself to sit down again.

The words burst out of her. "Forgive me, Frederica. This is terribly uncivil of me, when you have been so good as to keep me company, but I am suddenly seized with the need to go out walking. Would you mind terribly if I abandoned you?"

Frederica tilted her head. "Not at all, but I should go with you. Only an hour ago you were too ill to sit up."

She was perfectly right, of course, but it would not do. "I just need to be alone. Truly, I am quite well, as if my illness never happened."

"Which is a little disturbing in itself." Frederica rose to her feet. "I understand wanting to be away from everyone, but you must tell me where you plan to go, so that if you fail to return, we will at least know where to look for you."

It was a reasonable request, even if she did not like it. "The clearing on the ridge, the one where my husband practices his illusions."

"At least that is not too far," Frederica said. "Pray be careful."

After bidding her caller a quick adieu, Elizabeth fumbled with the ties of her bonnet as she hurried out the door. The beauty of the vista held no appeal for her today, even with fields of snowdrops blooming. She set off at a brisk pace past the gardens, as if her feet could not move fast enough onto the wooded ridge.

She rarely went this way, since the clearing was not particularly scenic apart from two enormous boulders that stood like sentinels, but she craved that particular place today. It was very private, hidden by the surrounding trees, and no one ever went that way except an occasional gamekeeper.

Inexplicably eager to reach her goal, she did not slow her pace even when her breathing became rapid. Finally, as she pushed past a low-hanging pine branch, light broke through where the towering oaks opened into the clearing. She stepped into the open grassy area.

And froze in place, her hand clutching at her throat in shock. It was impossible. Utterly, completely, and totally impossible.

Two dragons blocked her view of the standing stones, like an ancient illustration come to vivid and colorful life. They stood nearly twice her height, each one longer than a horse, their forms were elegant, with wings folded neatly against their sides. Their chests rose and fell with each terrifying breath.

Could it be her illness returning, this time making her see visions? But she felt perfectly well, with no dizziness or headache, nothing except the racing heart which came from unexpectedly encountering *dragons*, when there had been none in England for hundreds of years.

It had to be an illusion. Had Darcy somehow returned early from his journey and prepared it to surprise her? But this was far beyond his ability. These dragons were utterly perfect, from the sun glinting on each scale to the dark shadows cast when the sea-green one stretched its enormous, scalloped wings.

Shadows. Illusions made no shadows.

She took a shaky breath, locking her knees to keep them from giving way. These dragons were real. And they were looking straight at her.

The hair rose on her arms from the thick swell of magic in the air. The dragon closest to her was covered in red scales that reminded her of ripe currants in sunlight, with a shimmering clarity as if they were both translucent and opaque at the same time, with a spiked crest on his head that marked him as a male, if the old books were to be believed. His massive, gold-circled eyes studied her. The other dragon, with no crest, gleamed in shades of blue and green, like a painting of the ocean.

It was as if she had stepped into one of her beloved stories from ancient times. Ethelreda the Wise's dragon companion had been called Blackthorn the Sea-Green. Was this what he had looked like? A terrified laugh caught in her throat at the ridiculous thought.

"Blackthorn is one of my forebears." The voice fluted from the second dragon, the one who bore those colors.

Her mouth fell open. "You – you can hear my thoughts?"

The dragon tossed her head. "Only when you push one out with such force directly at me."

Her pulse pounded in her ears. Even her thoughts might not be her own.

"Greetings, Companion Elizabeth." These words came from the red dragon, in a low-pitched, reverberating voice. He took a step towards her, and an oddly familiar scent of hot metal and cinnamon filled the air. "We mean you no harm."

The dragon knew her name.

Then it struck her why she had suddenly felt propelled to leave the house and come to this particular place. A shiver ran up her spine. "You called me here," she said slowly.

"We did," the red dragon said, with a certain apology in his voice. "There are questions we must ask you, and we required privacy. Come forward."

Her skin prickled into goosebumps. If they wished to hurt her, running away would do no good, not when three Spanish dragons had easily destroyed an entire army with all its cannon and weapons.

This could be an opportunity, if only she could master her terror. Perhaps she could learn something that might help to understand the mysterious dragon attacks in Spain. If the War Office knew about this encounter, they would be begging her on bended knee to talk to these dragons, to make them her allies, to gain any insight she could.

She would do her duty, and she would not let these astonishing creatures intimidate her. Sinking her Talent deep into the land, she pulled the power of Pemberley around her like a shield. It might be little defense against the might of dragons, but it was a reminder that she was not without resources of her own.

Raising her chin, she walked forward, stopping just far enough from the red dragon that she would not need to crane her neck to look up at his head. "You know my name. May I have the honor of yours?"

Somehow she could tell he approved of her question. Was this the famed dragon aura that the old tales told of, which let humans sense dragon emotions?

"I am Rowan of the Dark Peak," he said, tilting his head briefly.

The sea-green dragon spoke. "You may call me Quickthorn. Where is your companion?" It felt like a demand.

She blinked. "My husband? He is away, but we hope he will return tonight." What did they want with Darcy?

"Not your mate, your companion." A sense of annoyance drifted from Quickthorn.

She tried again. "If you mean Lady Frederica Fitzwilliam, the apprentice to the King's Mage, she is back at the house."

"Do not attempt to mislead us! *Where is your companion?*" Quickthorn snapped, the scales on her neck rising, making her seem even larger.

A human figure stepped out from Rowan's shadow. "She means Cerridwen," said Roderick.

It was one shock too many. Roderick was here? Among the dragons, and he had never said a word about it?

And why would the dragons want her kestrel? She reached out to Cerridwen, sensing freedom of flight, of cold air under her wings. *Dearest, you may find this difficult to credit*, she sent, along with an image of the dragons in front of her. *They are asking about you.*

A sense of surprise, quickly overlaid by outrage and intense purpose. Then the connection stopped abruptly, as if cut off.

That had never happened before, and she did not like it. "If you mean my familiar, she is flying near the border of the estate."

"You call her your familiar." Quickthorn sounded disapproving.

She hesitated. The stories spoke of the dangers of lying to dragons. "She is not exactly a familiar, but I am unsure how else to name her."

The dragon tossed its head. "What do you believe she is?"

"A kestrel, one with some sort of magical abilities, but I do not know the details of them."

"How can you not know such a thing?" A sense of outrage flowed from Quickthorn.

Elizabeth mustered her courage. "Because I have not asked her. She dislikes being questioned about her origins, and I have respected that."

Quickthorn sat back on her haunches, swiveling her head to Roderick. "You are correct. This one is ignorant."

"As I told you," Roderick said.

"A barbaric custom." It was almost a sneer.

What was she to make of this, these fantastical dragons who had pulled her from her home and now called her ignorant and barbaric? But this was far too important an opportunity to miss because of injured pride. "I am indeed ignorant of what has displeased you, but I would be happy to attempt to resolve this matter, if only you would explain it to me."

"You may tell me this, then. Did your companion instruct you to make this place your home?"

She could not restrain a disbelieving laugh. "Cerridwen? Of course not. She did not even know my destination when she followed me, just that we were going to my husband's land."

The dragon shifted its weight. "Then it appears neither of you is at fault, although I cannot say the same for your Nest. Since you did not deliberately trespass on our territory, we will hold no animus towards you, but you may not remain here. We cannot have a bonded companion of another Nest living so close to our own."

Nests? Trespassing? Surely this must be a misunderstanding. "You want me to leave Pemberley?"

"If you wish to remain bonded to your companion, yes. If you are willing to break the bond, you may stay with our blessing."

Breaking her bond to Cerridwen would be like cutting off her own arm, and leaving Pemberley was impossible. She stuffed that thought back, though, lest the dragons catch a glimpse of it. She would do better to gain more information rather than make a flat refusal. "I have no idea what Nest you mean."

Suddenly her mind was filled with an image of snow-lined mountains. The jagged peaks were familiar, an old memory. Wales. Those were the mountains near Granny's house.

"That is your Nest," the dragon rumbled.

"If I may speak, honored Quickthorn?" Roderick asked.

"There is no time," interrupted Rowan. "Her companion is approaching, and we must not meet her. Companion Elizabeth, I do sympathize with your situation, which is not of your making. It is not my place to remove the strictures set by another Nest, yet something must be done. You seem an intelligent woman, so I will give you a hint that may help your understanding."

Rowan seemed to blur around the edges and then suddenly vanished. No, not vanished, just collapsed in on himself, leaving a bird in his place. A peregrine falcon, a little larger than Cerridwen. Quickthorn followed suit, and the newly-formed birds spread their wings and took flight, circling the clearing before soaring off into the dark clouds. As they went, Rowan's voice spoke in her head. *We will speak more anon.*

She stared after them in shock. Dragons. In the form of birds.

Of course. The dragons in the old stories could take the shape of other creatures, but she had thought it an exaggeration, perhaps some sort of illusion. And certainly she had never expected to see it with her own eyes.

As hints went, it was an unmistakable one.

Many Talents had familiars, but none were ever called companions. That term was reserved for the more powerful bond between human and dragon. And that aroma of hot metal and cinnamon? She knew it. That scent had clung to Granny's clothes after she had been out all day. Granny, who lived near a Nest, and had helped her bond to Cerridwen.

There was only one possible answer, and it defied belief.

It dizzied her, her head reeling. How could it be true, after all these years of her bond to Cerridwen? Why had she kept it a secret?

Then, with a wild cry, the kestrel herself flew into the clearing. She circled once above Elizabeth, sending an image of perching on her arm.

Elizabeth held out her hand, just as she had so many times over the years, but this time she trembled. It felt impossible, and at the same time, so perfectly natural and wondrous.

The bird's talons closed around Elizabeth's forearm, her head pivoting to face her. *They are gone already?* Her sending was sharp-edged with disappointment. *Show me what happened. I must know.*

Elizabeth ran through her memory of the brief interaction with the dragons. Suddenly, with fresh eyes, it was so utterly clear. How could she ever have thought Cerridwen was nothing more than a magical bird?

She gazed into the kestrel's gold rimmed eyes. "Cerridwen, is there something you have not been telling me?

Many things. Many, many things. The kestrel bounced on her wrist.

"Those dragons. They said you were my companion and that you had a Nest. Then they turned into falcons."

Yes. Cerridwen sounded excited and pleased.

Saying it sounded almost too ridiculous, even though the truth of it resonated through her body, echoing down into the earth beneath her. "I feel silly asking you this, but are you... are you a dragon?"

Yes! It was a silent shout of triumph.

Releasing her wrist, Cerridwen spread her wings, and glided to the ground. The air around her seemed to thicken, as if she were surrounded by mist.

And then a dragon stood where the kestrel had been.

Not an enormous one like those who had questioned Elizabeth, though. This was an elegant creature only a little larger than a stag, her folded wings gleaming in blue and bronze, a living sculpture, from her iridescent scales to her multi-jointed talons.

She was beautiful. And she had Cerridwen's eyes.

Elizabeth sank to her knees beside the dragon. "Is that truly you?" she whispered.

"Who else?" the dragon said in a high, melodious tone.

"I have never heard your voice before," Elizabeth said shakily.

"That is because I sound foolish when I speak through a bird's beak." Cerridwen stretched, reaching out her forelegs to grasp the ground and pull herself forward. "Ah, it will be good to be in my true form more often!"

What would it be like, being a dragon trapped in that tiny body? "Why did you never tell me?" Elizabeth blurted out.

The dragon rose to sit on her haunches again. "I had to wait until you asked directly. That is the rule of companions."

"I am sorry I did not guess sooner." She should have, especially with Roderick telling her stories every day with dragons transforming into other animals. Though who could have believed the truth?

Cerridwen's eyes blurred as a membrane came down over them, like a sleepy cat. "Would you have preferred a true kestrel?" The words had none of the usual confidence of her sendings.

"Nothing could be better than this!" Elizabeth reached out to stroke the dragon's shoulder. The scales were warm to her touch. "When I was young, my sister Jane wanted nothing more than for everyone to like her. Mary wanted to be the most accomplished girl in Meryton. And I wished I could be a dragon companion, even though I knew it was impossible." She could not let her dearest Cerridwen live with any doubt.

"And all this time you were one." Cerridwen bumped her scaly shoulder against Elizabeth's arm.

It was incredible. What did it mean, though, to be a dragon companion in this modern age of factories and big cities where no one even believed dragons existed? In the stories, human companions accompanied the dragons as they rescued people in danger, hunted for lost treasures, or sought to right injustices. What could she do? And why had Cerridwen limited herself to accompanying her all these years? Surely any dragon would want more than to follow their companion in falcon form.

But there would be plenty of time for these questions. Now there was only her beautiful Cerridwen, her scales warm and sleek under Elizabeth's fingers. And, oh, so full of power! She had always sensed the barely restrained magic in Cerridwen on those occasions when the kestrel had perched on her arm, but now it rolled off her in waves, in harmony with the thrumming energy of the land beneath her.

And the beauty of her! Elizabeth's eyes could not stop greedily devouring every detail of her, from the overlapping lustrous scales that edged her gold-ringed eyes to the dusky talons emerging from the ends of her agile feet. Larger scales made an elevated crest on her spine, almost like the keel of a ship. Elizabeth longed to ask Cerridwen to spread her wings so she could see those as well, but instead she just said, "Dearest Cerridwen, I always thought the illustrations of dragons were lovely, but you are so much more. I do not know how you came to choose me, but I am very glad you did."

The dragon preened. "You were the most interesting of those presented by Companion Amelia."

Amelia was her great-grandmother's name. Granny must be a dragon companion, too. And there was another Nest of dragons here, somewhere in the Dark Peak.

Then it struck her. She tore her eyes away from Cerridwen and turned to face Roderick, who still stood by the great boulders, silently watching them. "You knew," she said slowly, anger beginning to rise in her. "All this time, you knew, and you said nothing."

He grimaced. "I could not tell you."

It was too much. "Certainly you could have. I might not have believed you at first, but I am not a fool," she snapped.

He shook his head. "You do not understand. I am under a binding that prevents me from telling anyone about the present-day dragons. Including you. I literally could not say it, any more than Cerridwen could."

"Nonsense. The art of bindings has been lost for centuries!" But even as it slipped out of her mouth, she knew what his response would be.

"Not among dragons. It is how they have managed to remain hidden all this time." His expression lightened a bit. "But I did tell you every single story I know about a dragon who changed into a bird, and even made up one or two."

She glared at him. "Would I ever have been told the truth, if these dragons had not come?"

"As soon as you returned to Wales," he said promptly. "That is why we have tried so hard to get you there." Then he glanced upwards, to where the dark clouds were rolling in overhead. "We should return to the house while we still can."

He was right, but she did not want to be parted from Cerridwen for even as long as it took to walk there. Her very own dragon companion!

But just then a large raindrop plopped onto Elizabeth's sleeve, followed by several more. Cerridwen hated getting wet. "Perhaps we should seek shelter," she said. Before she could act on it, though, the clouds opened fully, and it began to pour cold rain.

Cerridwen squawked in dismay. The air blurred around her, and then her familiar kestrel form took wing, speeding off into the clouds.

The brim of Elizabeth's bonnet kept the worst of the water from her face, but it was rapidly soaking through her sleeves, chilling her arms. She raised her voice to be heard over the pounding rain. "Back to the house – and then we must talk." It was time for Roderick to give her some answers.

Chapter 27

I T WAS A BIT of a shock, still, finding a dragon curled up in front of the drawing room hearth at Pemberley, but Elizabeth could not have been happier about it. Her Cerridwen, a dragon! Was this why her father had warned her to keep Cerridwen's abilities secret?

Before she could even sit down, though, Roderick strode in, his cravat slightly askew. He must have hurried through changing out of his wet clothes from their hasty return.

A fine thing, as the first of Elizabeth's questions burst out without even a greeting. "What is this nonsense about wanting me to leave Pemberley?"

Roderick raised an eyebrow. "Dragons are territorial. They will not tolerate a companion from another Nest living on their land, much less an unknown dragon."

The scales on Cerridwen's neck rose. "Not that they have even tried speaking to me," the dragon said, her anger and hurt filling the room.

"You know they cannot," Roderick told her gently. "Not while you are under the Silence. First we must get that removed."

"What is this Silence, and how do we remove it?" Elizabeth demanded.

Roderick threw an apologetic glance at her. "When you did not return to Wales to take your final vows, the Nest ordered Cerridwen to break her bond and return to them. She refused, and they placed her under Silence, which means that no dragon will acknowledge her or speak to her."

Elizabeth caught her breath. Cerridwen had been punished for staying with her? "How cruel!"

"It is how they enforce their rules, which exist for good reasons. The lack of final vows has stunted Cerridwen's growth, and would eventually cause her to grow ill. But there is an easy remedy. Once you go to Wales and take your final vows, they will lift the Silence."

Poor Cerridwen! "I suppose I must, then." And it would allow her to see Granny, too. Darcy would simply have to accept it, regardless of his mission. She would not allow Cerridwen to suffer any longer. "How long will it take?"

The Welshman drummed his fingers on the chair arm. "For the vows, only a matter of days. But returning here will not be simple. There will have to be negotiations with the Dark Peak Nest as to whether they will permit you to live at Pemberley."

A twinge of fear turned into anger. "They can hardly stop me. This land has been in the Darcy family for centuries!"

Roderick winced. "They have ways of making it impossible for you to stay. They caused your recent illness in an attempt to keep you away from their Nest. They only stopped when I explained to them that you had not meant to trespass on their territory, but if you remain here without their permission, they could do it again."

"Those dragons made me ill? How dare they?"

"They were protecting their Nest from an incursion by an unknown companion to a renegade dragon who had not approached them in the proper manner. It is not something they enjoy doing, but it is sometimes the safest choice available to them."

Was that why her symptoms had started and stopped so abruptly? It was a terrifying idea, that the dragons could force her to leave. "But I must remain at Pemberley."

"Darcy can accompany you to Wales if he wishes, and with luck, it will only be a matter of months, or perhaps a year, until the Nests can negotiate a solution." He said it easily, as if the fate of Europe did not rely on her presence at Pemberley. Which to him, it did not; he knew Darcy had a mysterious mission, but nothing of Elizabeth's role in it. That had to remain a secret.

Her chest tightened. "I cannot be away that long. I am unable to explain it to you, but it is impossible."

He cocked his head. "Do you think Darcy will not permit it? He seems a reasonable sort to me."

She held up her hands. "It is not about his permission, and that is all I can say. But it is a very serious matter."

Distress flooded from Cerridwen. "You would rather lose me than leave Pemberley?"

Hurriedly Elizabeth knelt on the floor and wrapped her arms around the dragon's neck. How odd it felt, those scales against her skin, and yet so right! "Never, dearest Cerridwen. I will not allow anything to come between us. We simply must find a different solution."

Roderick pursed his lips. "We can but try. The Nests are not known for making quick decisions."

Elizabeth asked, "Could I meet with Rowan and Quickthorn again, now that I understand the situation?" Or at least had the vaguest sense of what was at stake, but she would not simply be a passive participant in this decision.

He paused to consider this. "I can ask them. Whether they will agree or not, I cannot say."

Darcy reined in his horse in front of Pemberley. Home, at last. To Elizabeth. An entire day sooner than expected. Would her eyes light up when she saw him, after racing through his business and hurrying home?

How had she grown so necessary to him that every day apart was painful, like a toothache that could not be assuaged?

Never mind; he was here now. He swung off the horse, tossed the reins to a groom, and hurried up the portico steps.

The butler was too well trained to show any surprise at his early arrival. "Welcome back, sir."

"Thank you." Darcy handed him his hat. "Where is Mrs. Darcy?"

"I believe she is in the drawing room with Mr. Roderick, sir."

He ought to change into fresh clothes first and wash away the road dust and the stink of the crowded mail coach, but any delay felt intolerable, when Elizabeth was only a few feet away.

The drawing room doors were closed, but he thought nothing of that oddity as he threw open the last barrier between him and Elizabeth.

Roderick, sitting near the doors, jumped to his feet, smoothly converting the movement to a bow. But where was Elizabeth? Ah, there in the shadows at the far end of the room, next to an illusion that made him start.

Darcy's chest tightened, as it always did with any reminder of dragons, but he pushed away the familiar nightmare of Jack screaming as dragon fire burned away his skin. It was just an illusion, no doubt cast by Roderick to amuse Elizabeth.

She hurried towards him, a broad smile lighting her face. "William!"

He caught her in his arms, heedless of Roderick's presence. It had been too long since he had held her soft form against him. Her scent of lavender enveloped him, along with something else – could it be cinnamon? He buried his face in her hair to hide his rushing joy.

And he had only been away four days. How would he tolerate weeks of separation during his mission?

She leaned back to gaze up at him, her fine eyes now wide with concern. "Did your trip go well? Is there any news? Did something happen to bring you back early?"

"No news, just routine matters, and I could handle them more quickly than I expected," he said, pressing a kiss to her forehead.

"Oh, good. For a moment you worried me! But I am glad you are here, for the most astonishing thing has happened. You always said Cerridwen's abilities were impossible for a bird, and you were right. She is not a bird at all, but a *dragon*. Is that not wonderful?"

Her words made no sense, but that did not matter, not when she was back in his arms. "What do you mean?" he asked.

"She can shift forms, and her chosen one was a kestrel, until she could reveal herself." Elizabeth lowered her arms and stepped back, gesturing towards the illusion. "There she is, in all her true glory. And I am her companion!"

Finally it sank in. What foolery with this? He spared a glare at Roderick, who must have some role in this trickery, before he forced himself to look straight at the so-called dragon.

It was small and graceful, nothing like the giant monsters in Spain, but his chest still ached over Jack dying in agony. He would never see his brother again, never laugh with him over the foolishness of society or fight with him about his risky choices. Never.

This apparition was out of a child's story book, not a battlefield. And it was not real, of course. He forced himself to speak gently. "That is an illusion, Elizabeth. A very fine one, I grant you."

She laughed. "That is exactly what I thought when—" She stopped abruptly, and then took a deep breath. "I thought so at first, too, but she is real. Come closer, and you will see." She grabbed his hand and tugged him forward.

Had he suddenly stumbled into Bedlam? "There are no dragons in Britain."

"So they said, but there is one right here in our own drawing room!" she said gaily.

The thing was only a few feet away now. It picked up its head to gaze at him with gold-ringed eyes beneath a ridge of iridescent scales. The detail was incredible; he would give Roderick credit for that, right after he thrashed him for tricking Elizabeth so cruelly. The smell of cinnamon strengthened, cinnamon and something acrid.

The dragon's mouth opened, revealing sharp teeth. And then it spoke. "You see, I am more than just a 'damned bird.'"

The last words came out in Darcy's own intonation, as he had thought them so often in his head, and muttered aloud more than once.

Perhaps he was the one who belonged in Bedlam. He had to be imagining this.

"You still do not believe." The dragon held out her foreleg, sharp talons curving at the end, talons capable of ripping flesh. "Touch me, then, and know that I am real."

Horror curdled his stomach, because even without touch, he knew. No one could make an illusion of a voice like that.

And no matter how small it was or how civilized it might look in his drawing room, those talons were like the ones that had ripped into British soldiers, disemboweling and tearing long, jagged wounds. The conscript he had met who had lost his eye and half his face. The burned flesh.

Icy fear surged through him. "Elizabeth, I want you to step away very slowly and carefully."

Her brow puckered. "There is nothing to fear. Cerridwen would never harm me."

"I must insist!" he snapped. "It could hurt you even without meaning to do so."

She shook her head. "She could have injured me anytime as a kestrel. Have you not seen how she lands on my arm without even a hawking glove? Look at her eyes. She is the same creature."

"Dragons are dangerous!" His voice tipped into hoarseness. "Do you not recall why you agreed to marry me? They killed my brother. They are already costing me my life and my future. I will not let one hurt you, too."

Do not be silly. It was Cerridwen, sending directly to him. *I have never harmed a human and I never will. No sane dragon would.*

He recoiled at the presence in his mind. A dragon, touching his thoughts? "No dragon would? Tens of thousands of British troops were massacred in Spain, torn apart by dragon talons and scorched by dragon fire. Including my brother, who was so badly burned that they could only identify his body from his signet ring." He fished out his watch fob and held the ruined ring out as if it were a weapon.

"Ridiculous!" cried Roderick. "Who has been telling you this rot? Dragons are peace-loving creatures who would never hurt anyone. They would sooner die than deliberately kill."

Devil take it. He should not have revealed that secret, but, dammit, there was a dragon sitting not a dozen feet from him! "I have heard it from many eyewitnesses," he said savagely. "I did not believe it either when the War Office first told me. Not until I met some survivors."

"There must be some mistake," insisted Roderick. "Napoleon's mages must have cast illusions of dragons and caused a panic."

"Then why did the surgeons who never set foot on the battlefield report treating men who had been torn apart and burned, with nary a bullet or shell fragment to be found? I have seen the scars where talons raked them. Perhaps some dragons may be peaceful, but those were engines of war." The memories left him breathing heavily.

"No!" It was a cry of despair, on a long, descending note. And it came from the dragon.

Roderick crossed to her quickly. "Cerridwen, it cannot be true. Do not let it distress you."

The dragon raised her head. "But it is true. I saw it."

"What do you mean?" The Welshman asked gently. "You have been in England all this time."

"I *saw* it. Just once. Three dragons I did not know, attacking an army, and one of them going up in flames at the end. But I did not know it had already come to pass." The dragon keened softly, her head sagging down to the ground.

"You *saw* it?" Roderick looked from the dragon and then to Darcy, an expression of horror suffusing his face. "This happened in Spain?" His voice shook.

"Yes. Near Salamanca, with a second, smaller dragon attack at Granada. Since then, our army has not dared to take the field at all." And now he was staring at one of the monsters in his own drawing room. "I can show you the reports if you do not care to believe me."

The Welshman wiped his hand across his mouth. "Dear God. The Silent Nests." Despair weighed down his words.

The dragon was keening again. Despite already knowing about the attacks, despite lying to Elizabeth for years about her very nature and nearly killing her with that damned blood binding.

Elizabeth was stroking the monster's head. "The Silent Nests? What is that?"

"Months ago, two Nests in Spain went silent, refusing to allow messages to be delivered to them and sending none. We knew something was wrong, but not what. They must have gone mad." Roderick buried his face in his hands.

"Or they simply sold out to Napoleon," said Darcy bitterly. "Apparently they answer directly to him."

"No man could make dragons behave so against their nature," argued Roderick. "Dragons have on occasion lost their minds and become violent, but not on command."

Darcy shook his head firmly. "Napoleon is controlling them. Our spies are clear on that. And the sea serpents as well. Our ships are hiding in harbors because the sea serpents have sunk so many of them – but only ones bearing the British flag. They ignore all others. Somehow Napoleon has won their allegiance, too."

Roderick's eyes were almost wild. "He must be forcing them. They would rather die than kill!"

Darcy snorted at this ridiculous idea. "If this is true, what would make them fight now?"

Roderick swallowed hard. "I cannot imagine. I know dragons, but I am not deep in their councils."

"*You know dragons?*" The words tore out of him. "There are dragons here in Britain? Apart from this one?"

The dragon said, "Do not answer that."

He glared at the creature, even if she could tear him to pieces without the slightest effort. This was his home. What gave her the right to give orders here?

Dragons in England, devil take it! And a spy in his own home, bonded to his beloved Elizabeth. What if Cerridwen revealed his mission to the other dragons? He had never hesitated to speak about it in front of the kestrel, for what harm could a bird do? Now his entire effort was jeopardized. They would arrest him the minute he went near Napoleon.

And then England would fall.

Damn all dragons! He turned on his heel without a word and left the room.

Oh, dear. That had not gone well. Elizabeth stared after her disappearing husband's back.

She had not expected him until tomorrow, and had been so caught up in the shock of discovering Cerridwen's true nature that she had not thought how he might react to the news, beyond that she would be able to give him useful information about dragons.

Could it be that it was only the shock that angered him so? Darcy never liked it when he was confronted with something new to him. Elizabeth rubbed her hands over her face. No, it was not just that. His brother had been killed by dragons.

How could she make him understand that those dragons in Spain did not represent all of dragonkind? And most especially not her beloved Cerridwen, her most trusted ally for years.

But she could respond to Darcy's anger later. Cerridwen was still keening in distress, and Elizabeth had to deal with that first. "We will find a way to fix this," she told the dragon. "However they were forced to fight, we will discover it and put a stop to it." She did not know how, but somehow they must manage.

"You never told me," Cerridwen said in her fluting voice.

Elizabeth turned her palms up. "I did not think it would matter to a kestrel, and you always hated hearing about the war. I told you something very bad had happened, that Napoleon had terrible new allies, and that was why I had to marry Mr. Darcy. I am so sorry, dearest!"

"It cannot be mended, but it must be ended." Despair filled the dragon's words.

Elizabeth put her arms around the dragon's neck. What an odd sensation, those warm, metallic scales tingling with magic. She was hugging a dragon! *Her* dragon.

But if she wanted to keep the bond to Cerridwen, she had other duties as well. Turning to Roderick, she said, "I must speak to the other dragons as soon as possible. Tomorrow morning, if may be."

His face was still ashen. "Very well, but we need to be cautious. It had not occurred to me that Darcy might view dragons as a danger. The Nests must be protected."

"I would never harm them!"

"But can you say the same for him? I beg you to say nothing to him of the Nest."

How could she keep secrets from Darcy? "I must consider this."

"And then there is Cerridwen's vision. A far-seer in my time!" He shook his head in disbelief. "This is far beyond my remit. I must return home immediately to consult with Mrs. Morgan and the dragons there."

A wave of panic rolled over her. She needed his help to understand what was happening with the dragons here. What if she became ill again? "Perhaps you could send her an express with the news. That would arrive faster than you could ride, and still allow us to go the Nest tomorrow to discuss my problem."

He considered this. "A good thought. They will wish to know about this horror in Spain, too. What more can you tell me about it?"

She told him what she knew, and then added, "If you read the newspapers, you will see how few ships are arriving and the lack of news from Spain. Lady Frederica may know more. As apprentice to the King's Mage, she has been privy to more details than I have."

He rose to his feet, slowly, like an old man. "I will call on her immediately, if you will excuse me."

"Of course."

She did not watch after him as he left, closing the door behind him. Too much was happening. Cerridwen a dragon, Darcy's anger and distrust, the Dark Peak Nest. The fear of losing her bond to Cerridwen.

A knock sounded. Elizabeth scurried away from Cerridwen. Should she ask the dragon to shift back into a more acceptable falcon?

But the door opened before she could do so, revealing Mrs. Reynolds. The housekeeper opened her mouth to speak and stood dumbfounded at the sight of Cerridwen.

Elizabeth said firmly, "We have been practicing illusions. It is nothing to be concerned about."

The housekeeper wiped her hands on her apron. "An illusion. I should have realized that." Her voice trembled a bit.

"Is there something I can help you with?" It would be best to get her out of the room before Cerridwen did something that could not be justified as an illusion.

The older woman's brow creased. "No, simply a question. Mr. Darcy's valet tells me he has been ordered to pack for an immediate journey to London." She hesitated. "Should I have your trunk readied, too?"

Elizabeth's hand flew to her chest. Could it be the start of his mission? Had he received word it was time to travel to France? Her heart pounded. Oh, she could not bear it!

But then her sense reasserted itself. He would have told her if that was the case. No, there was another reason he would suddenly decide to go to London merely an hour after his arrival, and it was sitting on the floor behind her. He would want the War Office to know about the dragons immediately.

Which was better than leaving for France, but it raised a slew of other problems.

And she had a dragon to protect.

She straightened. "Thank you, Mrs. Reynolds. I will not be traveling, but you were quite right to tell me."

Chapter 28

DARCY SORTED THROUGH THE papers on his desk. This pile to go to the steward for immediate attention. That pile for someone else to deal with eventually. Someone who was not him. More things left undone.

Then Elizabeth walked in, her steps quick and her color high. "Were you even planning to tell me you are leaving?"

Her words struck him like a blow. "Naturally," he said numbly. "When I was ready to go. I did not want word getting to the dragons first."

"How thoughtful of you. It will be a final goodbye, you know. The War Office will never permit you to return here, and even if they did, I would be long gone." Every phrase was like a lash.

He stiffened. "You would choose that dragon over me?" It should not hurt, but it did.

"When you are planning to betray me to the War Office? What other choice do I have? When they learn I am a dragon companion, they will take me prisoner, if not kill me outright. And then they will go after my family in Wales. None of them will be safe. My great-grandmother, all my cousins and their friends and neighbors, who have lived in peace with dragons for centuries, Roderick, who traveled across the country to offer you his help – all of them will be hunted down."

Swallowing hard, he said, "They would never touch my wife." Surely that much was true. But he had not thought this through, how the War Office would react.

"Why not? They are desperate for any advantage in this war. They are willing to let you die in their cause. And you *will* die now, since I will be unable to feed land magic to you once I have left Pemberley. Who do you think will protect me from the War Office then?"

"Elizabeth, you must calm yourself. They are not your enemy. They will want to learn about the dragons, to talk to them, to make allies of them."

Her upper lip curled. "Just like you did." Each word was slow, dropping like a stone. "Just like you tried to talk to Cerridwen, to learn about her, to ally yourself with her. No, you decided instantly she was your enemy and planned to run off to get an army behind you. And you expect me to believe that the War Office will simply want to talk to them?"

"The safety of England is at stake! I have only Roderick's word that the dragons here are not in league with Napoleon. Cerridwen may already have told them all about the attacks and my mission."

Elizabeth's eyes flashed. "She has not. Cerridwen cannot even speak to another dragon."

"How can you be certain of that?"

"As it happens, she is under a something called Silence imposed by her Nest. No dragon will acknowledge her, much less listen to her. Even a dragon serving Napoleon."

"The dragons rejected her? What did she do?" If Cerridwen was anathema even to other dragons, what might she do to Elizabeth?

"The fault was mine, in fact. She refused to leave me when I did not return to Wales, and the Nest placed her under Silence until she obeys or I go back to take my vows."

Darcy blinked. "Cerridwen chose you over her own family and the company of dragons?"

"Yes! Whereas you have chosen the War Office over me," she said bitterly. "Do you think I *want* to leave Pemberley, when I have finally bonded to the land here? Now it is just another thing I will lose."

He covered his face with his hands. How had everything gone so wrong so quickly? He had to move past his own panic.

The problem was that he and Elizabeth were both right. The War Office needed to know that there were dragons in Britain, but that might endanger Elizabeth, not to mention the possibility of angering the currently peaceable dragons. "I will not tell them about you or your family, but there is too much at stake to leave the government in ignorance. This is much larger than you and Cerridwen and the Welsh Nest. And it is too convenient – discovering dragons here at the same time they are attacking our army in Spain. I cannot trust it."

"How can you protect me when Cerridwen and I are your only evidence that dragons exist? They will lock you in Bedlam if you claim there are dragons here with no proof, and then you will have to tell them the truth, regardless of what it means for me." She shook her head, and her voice trembled as she said hopelessly, "There is no help for it, is there? You feel you must tell the government, and I cannot stay here if you do."

In her mind, she was already leaving him. He could see it in her distant look and the stiffness of her body.

He stepped forward and caught her wrist. "Elizabeth, I beg you. Surely we can find a solution," he said urgently. He could not bear to lose her.

She looked down at his hand, clearly debating whether to pull away from him, but she did not move. Her chest moved up and down with each breath, as if she had been running. "Must you tell them immediately? Could you not give me a fortnight to send word to Granny and find out if the Welsh Nest knows anything about the Spanish dragons? Then you would actually have some useful information to give the government." It was her voice of careful reason, but with an edge of pleading.

When she put it that way, it made some sense. Darcy said slowly, "As long as I am not called for duty, I suppose a brief delay would make little difference. But this is not something that can remain a secret for long."

She straightened, her chin going up. "I suppose that is the best I can hope for. Will you promise me this much – that you will not tell anyone about the dragons without informing me first?"

His mouth went dry. She wanted a warning so she could leave him. "You have my word."

Her shoulders sagged. "Then we are in agreement." Though she did not look any happier about it than he was. This was an armed truce, not a peace treaty.

Damn all dragons! Just when Elizabeth had finally admitted she cared for him, this had to happen.

But he had agreed to it, and he would keep his promise, and hope he learned more about the dragons than they did about him. "Can Cerridwen read my thoughts?"

She shook her head. "She cannot even see mine unless I offer to share them with her."

It was something, he supposed - if it was true. But Elizabeth might repeat anything he said to Cerridwen. Devil take it, why could the creature not have remained a kestrel? Now Darcy would have to watch his tongue with his own wife. "Will you agree not to tell Cerridwen anything further about my mission?"

"If you wish. Cerridwen hates hearing about violence of any kind, so that will not be hard." She hesitated. "I am trying to meet you half-way."

That, unfortunately, did not help Darcy's conscience. He was not delaying for the sake of the dragons, but because riding for London – doing his duty – would cost him Elizabeth. For her, he would grasp at straws, hoping something might miraculously change in the next two weeks.

Elizabeth took Roderick's offered hand as she clambered up a slope covered in loose scree. The dragons had certainly not chosen an accessible meeting place, although this might not be the easiest route. Roderick had apologetically asked her to wear a blindfold on the earlier part of the journey, the section which could be traversed in the carriage, because he did not have the dragons' permission to reveal their location.

She did not like all this secrecy. Including that she had hidden this outing from her husband, merely leaving him a note at his desk where he would not see it for some hours, rather than telling him directly where she was going. But what choice did she have? Darcy would have stopped her, and this could not wait.

And she could not bear a resumption of their quarrel.

It did not help that Darcy was keeping his own secrets, too. When he had come to her last night, he had been different – not unkind, but distant. And when she had asked him about his trip, he had said that it was better not to discuss his preparations.

After four days apart, their first separation since their marriage, it had been heartbreaking. Clearly he did not trust her anymore.

Even worse, she was not sure she could trust him, either. She had woken during the night wondering what to take with her if she had to flee Pemberley, even while Darcy lay asleep beside her, his arm thrown over her body.

"Almost there," the Welshman said. "Past that outcropping."

At least the uneven ground distracted her from fretting over this meeting, too. If only Roderick had been willing to tell her more! Instead, she was like an actor about to set foot on stage without ever reading her script.

They rounded the ledge and suddenly the rough terrain gave way to a small grassy valley, almost like an amphitheater, with a cairn in the middle. It stood some three feet tall, with a small fire ring on the ground in front of it with a few sticks beside it.

Roderick strode to it. He pulled out a compass and studied it, pivoting slowly in place. Finally he stopped, picked up a loose stone, carried it a few feet, and set it down carefully. He repeated the action in the opposite direction, and then across, consulting his compass each time.

"North, south, east, and west?" she asked. A signal?

He spared her a smile. "This will let them know we are not strangers to dragons. A calling card, if you will. Had you done this when you came near, they would not have chased you away by making you ill." He crouched down by the fire ring and began to shave a twig into tinder.

"Should I look for more wood?" she asked. The bare moorland did not sport any trees, though, only gorse and heather.

"No need. We do not require an actual fire, only a little smoke to draw their attention." He piled up the tinder and struck the flint.

Elizabeth took the time to study the surrounding mountains. Were there any landmarks that might tell her where she was? The lines of hills looked different from here, but that prominent ridge must be Mam Tor. The sun and the angle of the shadows told her which direction was west, and that meant the first stone Roderick had set was to the north.

She let her Talent sink into the ground and almost jumped at the power beneath her. She was far enough from Pemberley that the connection was weak, but she had never felt such potent magic in the land, rising and ebbing like waves in the ocean, thrumming with intensity. And – oh, yes! – she could feel Pemberley tugging at her in the distance, reminding her of its presence, off to the southeast.

It was a small success. She might struggle to pinpoint this particular valley on a map, but she could make a good guess as to its approximate location. If she needed to flee Pemberley, she might well be able to find this place again. She hoped she would never have to, but before yesterday, it had never occurred to her that she might be in danger there.

With a lump in her throat, she sent a tendril of Talent into the roots of the grass and heather, which received it gratefully. Perhaps that might create a connection, too.

Roderick stood and dusted off his gloves. "There. Now we wait. It may be some time, though, depending on whether anyone is watching."

Who would be looking for the smoke? That hawk circling in the far distance? An ancient dragon peering in some mysterious magical mirror? There was so much she did not know! "The land here has powerful magic."

"Hardly surprising. It is stronger near dragon Nests."

Was that why Pemberley's power ran so much deeper than Longbourn's? Dragons nested on high ground, and Hertfordshire was a long way from any mountains. Darcy had said it had to do with the presence of ley lines, but was that just a modern scientific theory to explain the strength of magic near Nests?

She bit her lip. "What will happen now? Or is that one more thing you cannot tell me?"

"Hard to say, since I do not know this Nest." He hesitated. "I intend to ask them to read me – to go into my mind and see what I have learned. It is not necessary, but our news will definitely strain their credulity. This way they may be certain that I am not deceiving them. You need not do that, though."

Let a strange dragon into her mind? It was one thing with Cerridwen – beloved, trusted Cerridwen – but with an unknown dragon? And she was certain what Darcy would say about letting a dragon rifle through her thoughts. "When you do that, let them read you, can they see everything?" She had agreed to keep his mission hidden, and she meant to stand by it.

He grinned. "Never fear, your embarrassing secrets are safe. It is like reading a book – they only see the thoughts that I present to them. They cannot tell what I ate for breakfast unless I choose to put that before them."

"That is reassuring, I suppose." But it was still frightening.

"They have no desire to hurt you," he said, almost absently. "One thing, though. Dragons do not use family names with the people they interact with. It will confuse them if you call me Mr. Roderick, and I must refer to you as Companion Elizabeth. I hope that will not trouble you.

"Not at all. We used those names perfectly well as children."

"So we did," he said with a smile. "Those were good days."

"Life was simpler, certainly." On an impulse she did not care to examine too closely, she said, "As an old friend, may I ask you something that has nothing to do with dragons?"

He shifted to face her. "Of course."

She fixed her gaze on the line where Mam Tor's jagged top met the sky. "If there ever comes a time when I have to leave Pemberley, do you know of a safe place where I could go?

His indrawn breath was audible. "Has something happened?" he asked in a low voice.

"Not at present. But it might." Somehow she kept her voice even. "I hope never to need it, but I want an option in case things go badly."

"I...see." He paused. "I have a cousin in Wrexham, just over the Welsh border, but close enough to the Gwynedd Nest that Cerridwen could fly there with a message. She would take you in. I can give you her direction when we return to the house."

Tears welled up behind her eyelids. How had this happened, that overnight she had gone from longing for Darcy's return to relief that she had a place to go if she needed to flee from him? She took a deep breath to calm herself. "I thank you. I would feel better for having it." There, she sounded perfectly steady.

He considered this, then said slowly, "If I may ask, what is it you fear? I cannot believe Darcy would deliberately harm you."

She shook her head. "No, but he wants to inform the War Office about Cerridwen. If he does, I cannot let them find me."

"Ah, but you need not worry about that. Cerridwen has already bound him, so he cannot tell them or anyone else." He smiled. "That, at least, is one worry I can spare you."

Her shoulders sagged. A reprieve, that she could stay at Pemberley, but Darcy would be even angrier when he found out Cerridwen had interfered in his ability to speak. And there was still the question of whether the Nest would permit her to remain. "That will help, but what about you and Granny? If he tells them there are unknown mages in Gwynedd, they will come after you."

The lines of his face grew stark. "We will not permit them to find us. But your point is a good one. We can ask Cerridwen if she is willing to bind him about that as well."

"Good." How she hated this, forcing Darcy's hand, but she could not let him endanger Granny!

"If any other difficulties arise, pray remember you may depend on me."

A motion out of the corner of her eye made her tip her head back. "Look there! Are they true hawks or dragons, do you think?" The pair made lazy circles overhead.

He gazed upwards. "No telling. Another hawk would know the difference, but my eyes are not good enough — wait. It appears they have noticed us."

And, in fact, one dove down towards them, while the other winged away to the north.

"That was quick," the Welshman said. "They must have been expecting me."

Was that good or bad? But there was no time to ask; the falcon was already gliding into the valley. And then it shimmered, growing so quickly that Elizabeth had to fight the urge to duck as it came to land in front of the cairn, not six feet from them. Roderick did not move, apart from grasping his hat to keep it from flying away in the wind of the magnificent creature's wings.

It was Rowan, the red dragon whom she had met the previous day. At least he had seemed more well-disposed towards her than the irritable Quickthorn.

The dragon tilted its head towards her. "You are prompt, Companion Elizabeth, Friend Roderick."

She curtsied, more from habit than anything else. "Your hint was most helpful."

"I commend you on your quick understanding of your companion's nature."

"Roderick, er, Friend Roderick, was very helpful. And I had long since realized that Cerridwen was far more than she appeared, even if my initial guesses were incorrect."

"What had you guessed?" A sense of amiable curiosity pushed at her.

Her cheeks warmed, but she had already admitted to being mistaken, so how much more embarrassing could it be to admit her actual error? "I thought she must be fae."

The amiable curiosity shifted to puzzlement. "Why do you say you were incorrect, then?"

Baffled, she cast a look at Roderick.

He opened his mouth, paused, and then coughed loudly.

The dragon swung his head back to him. "You are not ill, I hope, Friend Roderick?"

The Welshman laughed. "Not ill." He tapped his forefinger on his lips.

"Oh! Yes." The dragon took a step towards him, placed a taloned foreleg on his shoulder, and gazed into his eyes. "There; now you will be able to speak. Only to Companion Elizabeth, though."

Roderick staggered, and the dragon quickly leaned down to support him beneath his elbow. His other foreleg suddenly proffered an intricately worked metal flask. Where had that come from? He had not been carrying anything, she was sure of it.

The Welshman uncorked it and took a careful sip. His eyes closed, a shiver rippling through him.

Elizabeth could sense the shifting magic. What was in that flask?

Roderick's eyes opened. "Ah, that is better." His voice sounded stronger, more resonant. "Companion Elizabeth, my binding against speaking of dragons has been loosened, so now I may explain that all dragons are fae. Your premise was not incorrect, only incomplete."

"We rejected the land of Faerie and chose to live in exile among the mortals, but that does not change our nature," the dragon added.

Dragons were fae? Then there was a flicker in her mind, and something settling into place, like a displaced log in a fire after the poker had been applied. "Dragons are fae. I knew that once," she said slowly.

The dragon's gold circled eyes regarded her with approval. "You will likely remember more early teachings now."

"That will be a relief," said Roderick. "Companion Elizabeth has something she wishes to tell you."

She dragged her mind back from wonder at the depths of the dragon's magic. "Rowan of the Dark Peak, I seek assistance in resolving the difficulty of my presence in your territory. I give you my personal assurances that I did not know of your Nest, or even that dragons still lived in this country, when I came to live here. It was a fault of ignorance, not of deliberate incursion."

"That is well said, Companion Elizabeth. It is clear you acted without intention to cause harm, and we bear you no malice. But we still face a dilemma. We cannot have an unaffiliated dragon on our lands, especially one whose own Nest has placed her under Silence. She must leave."

Elizabeth's heart sank. "That is another difficulty. By human laws, I must live on my husband's lands, which are in your territory. If you force Cerridwen to leave, it would mean ending our bond, which she has given up so much to maintain."

The dragon eyed her with a sympathetic air. "I regret your situation. It would not be the first time that a conflict between human law and dragon law has caused the rupture of a companionship, but it is always a matter for sorrow. Were your companion not under Silence, we could consider other possibilities, but that is not the case."

Elizabeth swallowed hard. "Might I inquire what those possibilities are?"

"Why, your companion might join our Nest, if she and our Eldest are willing. But we cannot consider it while she is under Silence." He looked pleased, as if he had hoped she would ask that precise question.

It was a ray of hope. "So if the Silence is lifted, she might be able to stay here?"

The dragon inclined his head. "It is a possibility."

She would find a way to make it happen. "I understand you cannot allow her to remain here indefinitely, but could you give us some time to see if I could convince her Nest to lift the Silence? It might take a little while, since letters are slow to reach Wales. Could you tolerate her presence for half a year?" By then, Darcy's mission might have happened, and she could travel to Wales with Cerridwen.

The dragon's inner eyelids drooped, and he paused, as if listening to something. "That is a fair request, but longer than is possible. The Eldest says you may have one cycle of the moon."

She swallowed. A month was not much time, but it was better than nothing, and at least this dragon seemed to wish for a solution. "I thank you."

"I am sorry for your distress, and I wish you a happier conclusion for this issue." The dragon clasped his forelegs. "This is why our Nest does not permit bonding of children. The companion bond is a matter of utmost seriousness, and should be undertaken only when a human is old enough to understand the ramifications. It also prevents situations like this where dragon and companion are lost to the Nest."

She could feel the weight of his words on her, the implicit criticism of Granny and the Welsh Nest. Was this a test of sorts? "I can see the practicality of that, although I should have been sorry to miss those early years with Cerridwen." That should be safe enough. "I have another request. Would it be possible to permit me to speak to my husband about the situation with your Nest? I cannot at present explain to him why I need to travel to Wales."

Rowan's chest rumbled with amusement. "I forget how little you know. You are a dragon companion; you may speak of us to anyone you wish, as long as you do it in the presence of your dragon. The onus is on her to stop you if she feels it appropriate."

"I thank you for that information. It is a good solution." And she would not have to keep secrets from Darcy. It was a huge relief.

Roderick stepped forward then. "Friend Rowan, I have a favor to ask and then a matter of great import to share. First, would you be willing to put this letter to Companion Amelia through the Gate to the Nest in Gwynedd? I have left it unsealed, so that you may see there is nothing in it besides what I am about to reveal to you, and it contains urgent news." He held out a thick envelope.

"I would be happy to do so." The dragon plucked the letter from his hand, and then it vanished.

"The other problem before us is one revealed to me by Companion Elizabeth's husband, and confirmed by Cerridwen, who had a vision of it. I fear it will cause you distress, as it has done for me."

"A vision? Truly? I would like to learn more of this." The dragon seemed interested, but not worried.

"It is complex and difficult to credit. If it please you, I offer myself to show it to you."

The dragon's nictitating membrane blinked slowly. "Your trust is an honor to me. Come, then." He held out his forelegs.

The Welshman pulled off his gloves and stuck them in his belt, and then placed his palms on the dragon's foreleg, where a human's wrist would be. He tilted his head back to meet the dragon's eyes.

They gazed silently at each other, and then an immense wave of anguish overtook her, bitter agony and bottomless, endless grief, a howling wail from the soul.

It seemed to echo on and on. As it finally faded, Elizabeth found herself on her knees, her fingers scrabbling in the dirt. The slow pulse of earth magic steadied her, bringing her back to herself.

Then Rowan's aura shifted abruptly to disbelief. Was it distrust, too? He pushed Roderick away, breaking their contact. "I cannot believe it. No dragon could do such a thing," he said.

"So I would have said, too, but it would explain the Silent Nests," Roderick said evenly. "And Cerridwen says she has seen it."

Elizabeth pushed herself to her feet. "I wish it were not true, but it is. My husband has met with the survivors."

The dragon turned to her, his aura still muddled with pain and uncertainty. "I must go. Companion Elizabeth and Friend Roderick, I beg your forgiveness for my hasty departure, but I must share this with the Eldest immediately."

The dragon spread his wings. Just as he was about to take flight, he paused and held out a golden chain with a pendant towards Roderick. Like the flask before it, it had appeared from nowhere.

The Welshman, with a stunned look, tilted his head and allowed the dragon to place it around his neck.

"Until we meet again, Friend Roderick, Companion Elizabeth," he said. And with a powerful beat of his wings, he took to the air.

Chapter 29

To think it had not even been a week since Elizabeth had begged Darcy to return quickly from his journey and given him a saucy smile as she promised him to make it worth his while. Now there was not even the slightest glimmer of warmth in her eyes.

She turned up her palms in frustration. "Do you not understand me? This information could make a difference in your mission, not to mention to me personally."

"If it is so important, then tell it to me!" How many times did he have to say it?

Her breath hissed out through her teeth. "If you will permit me to ask Cerridwen to join us here, I will do so. Without her, I am bound not to speak of it."

"Binding is an old wives' tale, Elizabeth, even if that beast has convinced you otherwise. Cerridwen is desperate to get me close enough to her that she can steal my secrets or alter my thinking. I have read the old stories, too, and I know they can do it. For the last time, I will not jeopardize my mission by allowing that damned dragon near me!" His mission was likely already hopelessly compromised, but he would not make it worse.

She lowered her hands to her sides, where they turned into fists. "You are your own worst enemy! Very well, if you insist on disbelieving me, call in one of the servants and try telling them that there is a dragon in the drawing room. Then you will learn what it is like to be unable to speak!"

He snorted. "There is nothing stopping me apart from wishing to avoid a panic."

"And I say there *is* something stopping you. Or you can prove it by doing so now, in front of me. I dare you!"

"That dragon has made you moon-mad! This is ridiculous."

Her shoulders went back. "You will not do even this one small thing for me." Her voice was low and dangerous.

He glared at her. So she wished for him to cause problems with the servants? Fine! He wrenched open the door and stepped outside. Two footmen – and wait, was that not Mrs. Reynolds disappearing down the stairs? She would not panic, nor would she repeat it. He called after the housekeeper.

She turned immediately. "Yes, sir?"

Too angry to speak rationally, he simply held open the door for the elderly housekeeper, and then closed it behind her.

Mrs. Reynolds curtsied. "How may I be of service, sir?"

He tried to temper his voice. "I will thank you not to panic when I tell you this. Mrs. Darcy's falcon is in fact a dragon."

She tipped her head to one side, but seemed otherwise unperturbed. "Yes, sir."

He whirled on Elizabeth. "There. You see?"

Her mouth was hanging open. "I do not understand. You are supposed to be bound against speaking of dragons."

"Which is nonsense, as I told you! Mrs. Reynolds, that is all, and I will thank you not to repeat what I told you to anyone."

"Oh, I could not, sir. I am bound, too. No doubt that is why you could speak of them to me. I can only talk about dragons to other people who are bound."

He took an involuntary step back. "You? You know about dragons? You are *bound* by them?" Mrs. Reynolds, who had practically raised him?

"Yes, sir. Many of us who lived through the Great Flood of '45 saw them then. Your own father, sir."

Fury rose in him. "And you never told me?"

The housekeeper cast a helpless glance at Elizabeth. "I am bound, sir. I could not."

Then he made the connection. "Elizabeth, are you saying that your dragon went into my mind already and changed me so I could not speak of her?" Each word was like poison in his mouth.

She nodded slowly. "It is how they keep themselves safe. She did nothing else. And if you will come and talk to her, I can explain."

"And give her the chance to meddle with me even more? Never!" He strode out of the room, seeking out the only sanctuary he had from that damned mind-altering dragon.

Elizabeth's legs were heavy as lead as she climbed the staircase. What a failure! Instead of convincing Darcy to work with the dragons, she had made him even angrier. She ought to be asking Mrs. Reynolds more questions about her experience with dragons, but after Darcy had stormed from the house, she wanted nothing more than to hide in her room and lick her wounds.

The aroma of sandalwood greeted her before she even reached the closed door. Were the servants using it to cover some unpleasant odor? It was not a scent she or Darcy used. But she had no energy to ponder the mystery, so she slipped inside the door and closed it behind her.

The odor was even stronger here, and more importantly, she was not alone. Cerridwen sprawled by the hearth in her true form. Chandrika knelt beside her, a small scrub brush in her hand, rubbing Cerridwen's flank as if there were nothing unusual about dealing with a dragon.

The Indian woman rose and curtsied. "Pray forgive me, Mrs. Darcy. I have yet to prepare your dress for dinner."

Cerridwen purred, "Oh, do not stop! There is still something under that scale, and it itches mightily."

"Yes, Wise One." Chandrika went down on her knees again, completely ignoring Elizabeth, and took up a small metal pick. She touched the dragon's side lightly. "Under this scale?"

"No, the one below it. Yes, that." Cerridwen looked back over her wing.

Chandrika bent close, moving the pick carefully around the scale until a tiny pebble popped out. "Is that it?"

"Ah! That is better!" Cerridwen stretched like a pleased cat.

First Mrs. Reynolds, now this! Elizabeth found her voice. "Chandrika, you seem remarkably comfortable with dragons," she said slowly. "Is there something you have not been telling me?"

The maid glanced up at her, but said nothing and quickly returned to scrubbing Cerridwen's side.

On a less stressful day, Elizabeth might have met this insolence with more patience, but she had exhausted her reserves. "Nothing to say for yourself?" she snapped.

"She is bound against speaking of it, of course," fluted Cerridwen.

Another one under a binding? Did half the world know all about dragons? It was ridiculous! But this was beyond even knowing that dragons existed – Chandrika clearly knew how to groom them and showed no discomfort at all.

It could not be mere coincidence. Now she had a good idea of why the Indian woman had followed her to Pemberley. "Have you known Cerridwen was a dragon all along?" she asked sharply.

After a moment of silence, Chandrika said, "In my homeland, anyone would have guessed it."

"How?" Elizabeth demanded.

The Indian woman sighed. "Birds never become familiars to humans, but falcons and hawks are the preferred form taken by Wise Ones who go out into the human world."

"Did your mistress, Rana Akshaya, know as well?" Was that why she had taken such an interest in Elizabeth?

"I cannot speak for the great Rana." Chandrika redoubled her efforts, tracing each scale with the pick, followed by a burnishing with the scrub brush. The reflection of firelight gleamed in the area she had cleaned.

That was not an answer. "But you also know something about how to care for dragons."

A longer pause this time. Was she trying to determine what she could say without breaking the bindings? "My mother worked in a Nest. Occasionally she would allow me to assist her. Enough that I can tell this Wise One has not had a proper cleaning in a very long time."

Cerridwen lowered her head onto her forelegs and closed her eyes. "This is much nicer than the cleanings at my Nest," she said drowsily.

Chandrika looked pleased. The aroma of sandalwood rose again as she poured a few drops of oil on a cloth and rubbed it onto the dragon's scales.

Elizabeth's natural curiosity overtook her annoyance that she, Cerridwen's companion, knew so little compared to her own maid. "Will you show me how you do that?" And she needed to remember to ask Cerridwen to be out of sight before Darcy arrived for his nightly visit.

If he returned at all.

The next morning Elizabeth set off for the Dower House. Normally she enjoyed the walk, but today her spirits dragged. Darcy had not visited her bed last night, nor had he been at the breakfast table when Elizabeth arrived. She was left making stilted conversation with Roderick, unable to speak freely with servants in the room.

Not only that, but the staff had been almost hostile. The parlor maids were nowhere to be found when she needed them. They had never warmed to her, but this felt like something more. They must be picking up on Darcy's displeasure with her.

If it continued, she would have to speak to the housekeeper, but right now she had no energy for problems with the servants. Not when she had to find a way to satisfy both the dragons and her husband.

She could not even look forward to her lesson with Frederica, not when she would have to spend the entire time avoiding the topics most on her mind. If only she could tell Frederica about the dragons and Cerridwen! She would be excited, Elizabeth was certain of it, unlike Darcy who could see only the worst in everything. And she might have valuable insights into Elizabeth's problems. She hated keeping a secret from her friend.

At least she would be able to apologize for her sudden disappearance during Frederica's last call at Pemberley, when the dragons had called her to the clearing. Frederica had not appeared upset about it at the time, but it must have looked odd at best.

When she arrived at the Dower House, Frederica seemed subdued, too, or least she did not jump up to greet Elizabeth with her usual enthusiasm. Instead, her curtsy was barely present before she said tartly, "Not off with Roderick, then?" Apparently she had been offended, after all, and that was fair enough.

"He is practicing with my husband. As usual. But I must apologize for rushing away when I saw you last. It was terribly rude of me." If only she could explain why she had done it!

Frederica looked away, her lips tight. "If you truly wished to be alone, that would have been understandable. But I understand that you were actually meeting Roderick."

"What? I did encounter him, but it was completely unexpected."

"I never thought I would be the one to say this, but you should take better care of your reputation." Her words dripped disapproval.

A chill ran down Elizabeth's spine. "My reputation? What are you talking about?"

"Did you think no one would notice you and Roderick returning alone together, soaked to the skin? Or that Darcy came home unexpectedly, found the two of you together, and was furious enough to want to leave

Pemberley?" Frederica threw up her hands. "You care for Darcy, I know that, but you must admit it looks very bad."

Elizabeth swallowed hard. "We fought, that is true, but not about Roderick! Good heavens, you cannot think he has romantic feelings for me?"

"Not that it would help him if he did, since you only have eyes for Darcy, but Roderick is always watching you." Then she added wistfully. "I do wish he did not dislike me so much. I am so many things he hates – a Fitzwilliam, English, and apprentice to the King's Mage."

Is that what she believed? Elizabeth was fairly certain Roderick found Frederica all too appealing. "At first, certainly, but now he seems to enjoy your company."

Frederica bit her lip, then smoothed her expression to a distant neutrality. "Well, it does not matter. He will return to the mysterious town in Wales neither of you will talk about, and I will never see him again."

Could confident, lively, aristocratic Lady Frederica possibly feel excluded? "I am sorry. We have been keeping secrets, it is true, but only for the safety of those we love. I truly wish I could tell you everything." And Frederica would know that she meant it.

The color returned to Frederica's cheeks, and she rocked back on her heels. "I suppose you must be telling the truth, but then why, in the midst of a fight with Darcy, did you sneak off the next morning alone with Roderick?"

It must look damning; no wonder she was so suspicious. Perhaps she should at least try to tell her about Cerridwen. But the moment she opened her mouth, her throat closed so tightly she could not breathe. She gasped for air, as if a steel band had anchored itself around her neck. Her chest heaved, and black spots began to dance before her eyes.

Was she going to faint? She reached blindly behind her for a chair and sank down into it. Then, suddenly, she could breathe again. She sucked in a desperate mouthful of air.

The binding had never hit her so hard before. It had just been a little tightening that eased as soon as she avoided the topic. Was it worse now because she wanted to badly to tell Frederica? It stung, that Frederica would think her so careless of Darcy's good name. "There was a reason. I cannot explain what it was, but there was a very important reason. Darcy would say the same."

"What could possibly be such a great secret? I already know about Darcy's mission." Frederica stared off in the distance for a moment, and then snapped her fingers. "I know. This must have something to do with your mysterious great-grandmother."

How dare Frederica interrogate her in this manner? "I cannot tell you. And how do you know so much about my comings and goings, anyway? Are you spying on me?"

"Of course not! All the servants are talking of nothing but how you have humiliated Darcy by carrying on with another man under his very nose!"

Elizabeth buried her face in her hands. No wonder they had been so cold to her. "Servants may see everything, but this time they have drawn the wrong conclusion." Did Darcy know what the staff were saying? He would have yet another reason to be angry at her.

Frederica hesitated. "I am sorry I accused you falsely. But you need to be more careful about appearances."

It was too much. Darcy, and now Frederica, who had never before cared what anyone thought, both angry with her. Dragons demanding that she leave Pemberley, which would truly feed that gossip. The fate of all Europe and England hanging on whether she could conceive.

She stood, her hands shaking with fury. "Enough of this. I did not come here to be lectured. I am going home."

"Wait!" Frederica grabbed her arm. "It must be something about Cerridwen. Roderick knows something about her. Those strange abilities of hers."

What a terrible time for Frederica to have one of her insights! The band of steel was back, already pressing on her throat, but she managed to squeak out, "It is no business of yours."

"I am right, though! I can tell." Frederica sounded triumphant.

Elizabeth opened her mouth to refute it, but could not. That damned truth-casting!

"See! It is true! You cannot deny it."

The steel band tightened inexorably. Elizabeth's chest heaved as she struggled for breath in vain. The blackness grew in her vision again.

With her last ounce of consciousness, Elizabeth sent a desperate plea to Cerridwen. Then the darkness swallowed her up.

A beringed hand was waving in front of Elizabeth's face as she blinked her way back to wakefulness.

It was Frederica, trying to stir the air. "Fetch the smelling salts," she cried to a maid.

"No need." Elizabeth sat up on the fine Aubusson rug she had apparently landed on. "I am not at all dizzy." Now that she could breathe again.

"You just swooned!" Frederica cried. "How many times have I warned you about falling ill again?" A calculating look came over her face. "Or are you increasing? Is that what made you faint?"

Elizabeth's least favorite subject in the world, and even though it was completely unconnected to dragons, her throat tightened. She clapped her hands over her ears. "No more questions! I beg you, no questions!"

Frederica stopped short, staring at her as if she were moon-mad. "No questions?"

"That was a question!" she snapped, her voice echoing in her covered ears. But at least she could breathe again. Could that be the solution – to avoid any questions?

"But... oh, that is another question." Frederica looked frustrated. "Well, then, I will sit here and be silent as a mouse until you decide to say something." Clearly it went gravely against the grain.

Elizabeth cautiously lowered her hands. "I am sorry I frightened you. Truly, I am not ill."

She could almost see Frederica's curiosity fighting to break forth, but before it could, a welcome tapping sound came from one of the windows.

Elizabeth hurried to open the latch, sending a confused blur of thoughts to the kestrel outside. Aloud, she added, "I am glad you are here, Cerridwen. I swooned when Lady Frederica was asking me questions, but I am quite recovered now."

The bird perched on the sill, cocking her head at Frederica. Then she stiffened, her wings still half-furled, and Elizabeth caught an echo of pain through their bond. She sent a silent question, but Cerridwen ignored it, now exuding a determined resolve.

And then Cerridwen transformed.

Chapter 30

IT HAD NOT BEEN a successful practice, even with Roderick's advice. Memories of his quarrel with Elizabeth kept intruding on Darcy, and his illusions flickered and faded in the field like those of a rank beginner. Not to mention the damned horse legs still bending the wrong way. It was inexcusable, when so many lives would depend on his casting.

What was the point in continuing when he was failing so abysmally? Even his lynx, prowling the edge of the clearing, looked disgusted. Darcy blew out a breath to dismiss his latest hopeless effort.

He would give it one more attempt before heading back to the house. The light would be gone soon, and he wanted time to make peace with Elizabeth. Or at least to make the attempt. Somehow they had to resolve this dragon-shaped chasm between them. England, not to mention his sanity, depended on it.

As if his thoughts had conjured her, he sensed her presence moving over the land just outside the clearing. Was it a good sign that she was seeking him out? Or was she angry again? If only his Talent could help him understand her!

"Try again," Roderick urged him, clearly unaware of his inner turmoil. "Close your eyes and picture the horses running, but focus only the impression of them, not the details. Imagine them feeling the wind in their manes. Empty your mind of everything else."

Darcy shook his head, gesturing to the path. "My wife is here." And then she appeared, drawing his entire attention. How could he be expected to focus on anything else when she was present?

"How goes your practice?" she asked. Her bonnet hid her expression, but she did not sound displeased.

He stepped off the iron plate he stood on for casting, and the power of the land came rushing up to meet him. "It has not been my best day. But I keep trying."

"He is learning to trust his instincts more," said the Welshman diplomatically.

She untied her bonnet strings and let it fall back from her face. "I am glad of it. Mr. Roderick, pray forgive me for being so direct, but I wish to speak to Mr. Darcy alone."

Roderick raised an eyebrow. "Of course, Mrs. Darcy. I will return to the house until there is further need for my presence."

Elizabeth gave him a rueful look. "You might wish to consider stopping by the Dower House instead. Cerridwen just revealed herself to Lady Frederica, who is fairly bursting with questions I could not answer."

His jaw dropped. "Cerridwen did what? At your request?"

"Not at all. I have no idea why she chose to tell Frederica out of the blue after keeping it a secret from me all these years." Elizabeth said it lightly, but there was an undercurrent of displeasure beneath her words.

Darcy grimaced. Was Frederica also going to be bewitched by that damned dragon?

Roderick huffed, an unusual display of irritation from the ordinarily composed Welshman. "Life would be simpler if Cerridwen could occasionally find her way to following the rules." He bowed. "Very well, I will speak to Lady Frederica."

"By the by, it turns out our housekeeper and my lady's maid both have met dragons in the past."

Chandrika, too? Was he the only one who had been left in the dark so long?

The Welshman said, "That will make it easier in the household, I suppose." He strode from the clearing, leaving Darcy alone with Elizabeth.

What should he say? So often he had blurted out things that hurt or angered her, even when he meant well. He could not afford that now.

If only he could show his love with kisses and caresses! But he could not mend things between them as easily as that. "Would you like to walk together? Or, if you prefer to sit, there is a bench on the other side of the Dragon Stones."

She tilted her head with sudden interest, more like her usual vibrant self. "The Dragon Stones? Is that what they are called?" She gestured to the large boulders.

"They say that long ago, dragons would come to this clearing to meet with the local people. In summer, one often finds an offering of flowers at the base of the stones. The folk here have long memories." He said it calmly, as if this very thought of dragons did not make his stomach churn.

Not to mention his memories of Jack. They had played together on those rocks as boys. That was why he practiced his illusions there, where the Dragon Stones made sure he never forgot what he had lost.

"This was—" She stopped abruptly, and then shook her head. "It does not matter. Yes, let us sit." And she held out her hand to him.

The ice inside him melted a little at her gesture. He grasped her fingers firmly, letting the power of the land flow through him and into her, doubling their connection. Anything to remind her of their bond.

But she dropped his hand after he led her to the rustic bench in the shadow of the Dragon Stones. It was foolish to feel bereft over such a tiny thing. "Will this suit?"

"Admirably." Her eyes flickered from side to side. "I did not notice it the last time I was here, but I was distracted then."

Oh, yes. She had come once before to speak to him while he was practicing.

As she sat, the lynx padded up beside her, butting his head against her leg. "Hello, Fire Eyes," she said, sinking her fingers into his ruff. Then she looked up at Darcy and patted the bench beside her. It might be a wordless invitation, but it was nonetheless welcome. He swept back his coattails and joined her, a few inches separating his body from hers.

And then he waited.

She gazed out over the valley, where the sun was beginning to disappear behind Mam Tor. Finally she asked, almost shyly, "Do you still carry your brother's ring?"

Her unexpected question sent pain slamming into his chest. Jack was gone, gone forever. Why was his grief still so fresh? "Always."

Her eyebrows drew together. "May I see it?"

Numbly he pulled out his watch fob, Jack's signet ring dangling from the chain. Someday he would touch it without memories lancing him, but not today.

Elizabeth studied the ring, taking it between her fingers and turning it this way and that. What was she looking for?

He could not keep the words back. "I hope you are not questioning whether dragons killed him."

She shook her head, her eyes downcast, her fingers tracing the melted edge of the ring. "I wish I could. I know it is true, that those dragons killed him and countless others." She paused to take a deep breath. "If I had lost a sister to them, I do not know how I could ever trust a dragon."

He caught his breath. This was not what he had expected to hear.

Then she raised her fine eyes to his. "Yet I also know Cerridwen would never do such a thing. She is horrified by it. That is just as true as those dragons who killed your brother."

Could it be an olive branch? Did she feel their division as much as he did?

He tucked the watch and ring away, taking her hand in both of his. "Roderick lectured me today about how his ancestors were killed by English invaders who stole his inheritance, and how his people are still impoverished by English taxes and mistreated by English overlords. He asked me if that gave him the right to think all Englishmen are murderous, thieving monsters."

Was that hope in her eyes? "It is a valid question. And this situation is even more complex. No matter how terribly you have suffered because of the attack in Spain, Cerridwen and the other English dragons could be your best allies to stop it from happening again."

She was right. He could not afford to turn down any help. But how could he trust a dragon, when they had killed Jack?

Not that Darcy was innocent in his death, either. If he had never bought the commission Jack had begged for, his brother would be alive today.

That fault was his alone.

"There is more," she said in a low voice. "I do not know if I will be able to say this, but... Cerridwen is what the dragons call a far-seer, one who can foresee certain consequences. In her case, a future attack. She is risking her own life to keep that vision from coming to pass."

His stomach knotted. "Another attack? Where? When?" If there was even a possibility...

"It does not work that way. She gets only a glimpse of it, and then only when she faces a choice. That is why she refused to leave me, and why she helped me bond to Pemberley, because the other options were worse. Think what you could do, if you knew which choices might avoid another massacre."

If he could trust Cerridwen not to lead them into Napoleon's hands. If it was even true that dragons could have foresight. If, if, if.

The lynx left Elizabeth's side to curl up on Darcy's feet. Was he trying to offer comfort? Or did he sense the division between his two favorite people and seek to mend it?

Elizabeth had made friends with his lynx when they first met, but Darcy had never liked Cerridwen, not since she had flown at him and raked his face with her talons. He had been jealous of her closeness to Elizabeth – jealous of a bird! – and he had distrusted her inexplicable powers. Well, now he knew the explanation.

And his lynx trusted Elizabeth – and Cerridwen.

Elizabeth gently withdrew her hand from his. Quietly, almost tenderly, she said, "I know you are grieving, but would your brother have wanted you to throw away this opportunity?"

His fingers clenched around Jack's ring, the ridges of it cutting into his skin. Jack had never been the cautious one. He would leap into any cause and he never bore a grudge. If he had seen a tiny chance to save his fellow soldiers from another dragon attack, he would have seized it. Even if it meant trusting an enemy.

But Cerridwen was not his enemy. He could not permit his jealousy and dislike of the unknown to stand in the way of an alliance that could put an end to Napoleon.

Once, when they were young, Jack had clambered to the top of the tallest Dragon Stone, proclaiming himself King of Derbyshire. He had scraped his arm in the scramble, enough that blood dripped from it, but that did not stop him from making a daring leap to the next boulder. It had not even occurred to Darcy that his brother could easily have broken his neck if he had fallen, because Jack was fearless and did that sort of thing all the time.

Now the giant stones before him cast long shadows in the fading light, just as the dragons they were named for cast shadows into his life, but this time he was the one who had to find a way to jump out over the abyss. With a deep breath, he took the first step. "I will try. I will speak to Cerridwen and try to find common ground." For Jack. For England. For Elizabeth.

"You will?" Elizabeth exclaimed, her face suddenly alight. "Oh, I know you can do it!" She threw her arms around his neck.

Then her warm lips were pressed against his. A chaotic mixture of relief and gratitude washed over him. As he tasted her mouth, the heat of desire made him oblivious to everything except her touch and her beloved form.

It had been too long, and now he lost himself in her. Or perhaps he was finding himself in her.

When he finally remembered where they were, the sky had been painted with broad strokes of red and orange as the sun disappeared behind the hills, as if reflecting the fire burning between the two of them.

Elizabeth breathed a sigh of relief when she reached her room. Only one servant had seen her sneak in the conservatory door with Darcy.

Their fight had been terrible, but making it up had been so sweet! After Darcy's fervent kisses in the clearing, neither of them could bear to wait to get back to the house. Instead they had raced to the cottage in the oak grove, where Darcy had all but torn off her clothing in his eagerness.

She gazed ruefully in the mirror. At the cottage, she had done her best to restore her hair and dress to some sort of order, but with very limited success. She looked like a woman who had just made love.

Swollen lips and flushed cheeks told the story, but even that only hinted at what was inside her. Darcy's lovemaking had always been ardent and deeply satisfying, but this had been even more. Was it because they had been apart, or had their ability to entwine their magic grown? Something had been different. Magic had echoed and re-echoed between them, with his deep land Talent meeting her dragon-enhanced abilities, flowing back and forth until she could feel his desire and pleasure nearly as vividly as her own.

It had shaken her, how much she had felt a part of him as they joined together. If only she could talk to Granny, who might know something of the ways of a man and a woman with Talent! But that was impossible, and it was hardly the sort of thing she could ask about in a letter.

A knock at the door announced the arrival of the tea tray, carried by the housekeeper herself. Odd, as usually an upstairs maid rendered the service.

And she had not requested a tea tray.

Was Mrs. Reynolds checking up on her, hoping to find evidence of her supposed affair with Roderick? Perhaps Elizabeth should have insisted on marching in the front door with Darcy in all their disheveled glory, making it quite obvious that she and her husband had a passionate interlude. How tiresome it was having staff who disliked her!

But her stomach rumbled at the aroma of fresh-baked breads and cakes, and she preferred to be gracious. "I thank you. Hot tea will be most welcome."

Mrs. Reynolds put down the tea tray. Instead of leaving, though, she hesitated, her hands folding in her apron, as if she had something more to say.

Elizabeth's high spirits evaporated. Apparently there was a problem she must deal with, even if she would rather luxuriate in the relief of her reconciliation with Darcy.

Only then did she realize the housekeeper's eyes were red. "Is something wrong?"

"Wrong? Oh, no, madam. I wanted to tell you that the cook is working on creating a sweet that will be similar to marzipan, using our local nuts and honey. He says it will not taste just the same, but he hopes you will like it." Her voice lacked its usual steadiness.

"Marzipan?" Oh, yes, she had mentioned to the housekeeper at their first meeting that she missed having the sweet. "How very kind. I am certain it will be delightful."

"If there is anything else that you would like, anything at all, I hope you will do me the great honor of telling me. I would be happy, most happy, to be of service." The words came out all in a rush, unlike her normally careful manner. "I would wish to help you in all matters." Now her voice was definitely shaking.

Elizabeth studied her. Why would the old housekeeper suddenly be afraid of displeasing her? There was only one person she had ever spoken to about her problems with the staff. "Oh, dear. Has Lady Frederica been complaining to you?" She had thought Frederica knew better than to pass along her problems. She would have words with her later.

"Oh, no, madam, never complaining! Not at all! She simply mentioned to me why you worked so hard to bond to the land. I had not realized that... that Mr. Darcy's life might depend upon it." She pulled out a lace-edged handkerchief and dabbed at her eyes. "I had no idea. When he was a boy, with his mother away so much, he was almost like a son to me. I would do anything for him. Anything!"

This was a side of the housekeeper she had never seen before. "We are on the same side in this battle, then," Elizabeth said carefully. "It is not a simple task, and I feel as if I am neglecting Pemberley House while I work with the land, so I am grateful to have your support."

"Is there nothing else I can do to help you?" Mrs. Reynolds' eyes pleaded with her.

How deep did this change of heart go? "There is one thing, though it may strike you as an odd request," she said. "If I could have a spinning wheel, preferably one that has been on the estate for some time, and some wool from Pemberley sheep, I can spin some of the estate's power into the wool. When Mr. Darcy carries cloth made from it, he will be able to draw on the magic I spin into it."

The housekeeper nodded. "I will arrange for that straight away."

Elizabeth blinked. "I expected you to be more surprised by that request, I admit."

"It is not the first time I have heard of such a thing," the older woman said. "Mrs. Sanford, who came when you were so ill, might be able to provide what you are looking for."

The mysterious midwife that no one would talk about! How odd. "With so many sheep about, I imagine many people could," said Elizabeth.

"There is local wool aplenty, but Mrs. Sanford uses her traces of Talent to make her own cloth. Many of our tenant farmers will not go out into their fields without a scrap of Mrs. Sanford's fabric in their pocket. They say it helps the harvest."

Superstition or some true ability on the midwife's part? It was worth checking. If it worked for Darcy, even a little, it could be an advantage. "I would like to see some of her wool, if that is possible."

"I will fetch it for you right away, madam." She paused, glancing quickly over her shoulder through the open door. "Is there anything I can do for your companion's comfort? Are there particular foods she likes? Or some sort of bedding? I know nothing about how to provide for her."

Elizabeth hesitated. What did Cerridwen eat, apart from plum cake? She had always hunted her own food as a kestrel, but was that enough for a dragon? "I will ask her."

The housekeeper leaned forward and spoke in a low voice. "When I was a girl, I was swept away in the flood waters. I would have died if a dragon had not plucked me out and saved me. I can never repay that debt." Then she straightened. "It is a great honor to Pemberley to have both of you here."

A genuine smile warmed Elizabeth's face. "I am glad to know Cerridwen is welcome."

After dinner, Elizabeth was left on her own as Darcy closeted himself with Cerridwen in the parlor. He had insisted on meeting alone with the dragon, saying the encounter would be harder if he had to worry about her reactions. She had stayed downstairs briefly, just long enough to be certain he had not stormed out immediately, which would not have surprised her. Tact was not Cerridwen's strongest point.

She was too agitated to chat with Roderick, so she retired to her private sitting room, where she tried to distract herself with her Arabic books. The hands of the clock moved slowly. What could they possibly be discussing that would take an hour? Cerridwen had never spoken to her for that length of time. Why did she have so much to say to Darcy?

She jumped to her feet when a knock sounded, but it was only Mrs. Reynolds bringing her a basket with samples of carded wool, homespun yarn, and a small swatch of hand-woven fabric. "Mrs. Sanford says she can supply you with more of these if you wish. It is from the sheep she raises herself, spun and woven in her cottage." She must have gone straight out to get it after their earlier discussion.

Elizabeth placed the basket on her lap, running her fingers over a strand of the yarn, the tightly wound fibers tickling her fingertips. Yes, there was some power there. It did not have the same tingle as thread she had spun herself, but it was similar. Beyond the musky aroma of lanolin, she could almost taste the magical flavor of Pemberley in it, the moorlands and the fertile valley. Not the oak grove in summer that she associated with Darcy, though; this was different. "I would like to speak to her, if she is willing. I am curious how she comes to have this Talent."

Color rose in the housekeeper's cheeks. "She prefers not to interact with the Darcy family."

"But why? Surely no one has mistreated her—" Elizabeth halted in midsentence as the obvious struck her. "Never mind. I suppose traces of the Darcy Talent must show up unexpectedly from time to time." Darcy's father or grandfather must have sowed his wild oats and then told their offspring to stay away from his true-born children.

"A man who cannot live with his wife becomes very lonely, Madam. Old Mr. Darcy barely saw Lady Anne. It is not natural."

So the mysterious Mrs. Sanford was Darcy's half-sister! "Does Mr. Darcy know?"

The old housekeeper wrung her hands. "I cannot say, but I do not think so. It would not be like him to ignore the situation if he did."

"And you have not told him?"

She lowered her head. "Old Mr. Darcy gave me his orders, Madam." Yet she had taken the opportunity to skirt them with Elizabeth.

It was a relief that the housekeeper no longer seemed to resent her. "Would it be possible to find a few needles for netting?" She had left all of hers at Longbourn.

The housekeeper nodded. "I can have new ones delivered in a day or two, or if you do not mind, I can see if any of the staff have some."

"I would be happy with whatever you have available."

"Very well, madam."

As the housekeeper left, Elizabeth examined the yarn again. It was well-spun, but not fine enough to use with her embroidery needles, so there was nothing she could do with it now. Reluctantly she set it aside and went back to her book.

Darcy quietly let himself into Elizabeth's sitting room. How had it come to be past midnight? The time had passed quickly while he was talking to the dragon. To Cerridwen. He needed to start referring to her by her name.

Elizabeth was asleep over her book, her head resting on her arm. She was wearing the crimson silk dressing gown he had given her, her dark curls hanging loose over the edge of the table. Her shoulders rose and lowered with each breath, and the trace of a smile curved her lips. How he loved seeing her like this, in the intimacy of their rooms! She had captured his heart so entirely.

Despite his eagerness to tell her about his meeting with Cerridwen, he did not wish to disturb her, not after the recent stressful days that had left her with dark circles under her beautiful eyes. And their passionate interlude in the cottage at the heart of Pemberley – that was a moment he would never forget, not if he lived to be a hundred.

Tenderly he scooped her up in his arms. Even asleep, she nuzzled into his shoulder, and he thought he might melt from happiness. He carried her into the next room and gently lowered her onto the turned-down bed.

Her eyes flickered open when her head touched the pillow. "William?" she asked drowsily.

"Yes, but you should sleep." He pressed a light kiss against her forehead.

She raised herself on her elbow. "What happened?"

He sat on the edge of the bed. "It went well. We talked about Jack."

She rubbed her eyes. "About Jack?"

"Cerridwen said that since he had been killed by a dragon, he needed to be remembered by dragons. She asked me to tell her about him, so that she could know him, too." He had told her stories about his brother for hours, while she asked insightful questions. It had helped, too. He had been avoiding the subject since Jack's death, and it was a relief to remember happier times with him.

"And the Nests? Did you speak about them?" She blinked hard, as if forcing her eyes to stay open.

"We left it for tomorrow. She wants you there for that. But first you must rest."

Raising her hand to cup his cheek, she said, "Not alone, I hope."

A smile bloomed on his face. "Never alone, my love."

Chapter 31

WHAT A DIFFERENCE A day could make! The sun shone bright over the clearing, gilding the wild daffodils that were starting to show their yellow heads. Anything seemed possible, after a night in Elizabeth's arms. So when Roderick asked Darcy if he was willing to try something a little different, something that might seem illogical, he agreed with good humor. After his abysmal performance the previous day, he doubted anything could make his casting worse.

"Then cover your eyes, and imagine someone looking at you with approval. Perhaps Mrs. Darcy, when she is pleased with something you have done."j

He placed his palm over his eyes. This was easy, if seemingly irrelevant. The shining light in Elizabeth's eyes when he had agreed to speak to Cerridwen, when they were sitting on the bench by the Dragon Stones. Warmth stirred in his chest. Imagining making Elizabeth happy was much more pleasant than thinking of his mission.

"How would she feel if she saw you cast an amazing illusion of running horses? Do not think about the horses, just about how she would look at you. Do you have that in your head?"

Elizabeth would be ecstatic, because it would make it more likely that he would survive to return to her. She had more faith in him than he deserved.

But now his mind was wandering, so he focused back in on her beaming face. "Yes, for what that is worth."

"Now keep your eyes closed and hold that image there, no matter what. Hold it. Keep seeing her. Now, without letting your mind wander from her, cast those horses."

Darcy flicked his wrist and cast, though only to placate Roderick. And perhaps to have a good laugh at whatever hopelessly mangled illusion he might manage to produce.

"Now look." Roderick's voice had gone up a notch.

Darcy lowered his hand.

Horses galloped across the clearing, their manes flowing in the wind. Horses of all colors and sizes, with their legs moving in rhythm. And all bending the correct direction. Perfectly convincing, down to the dust rising from their hooves.

They did not look like his horses. "You made those," Darcy said, annoyed.

Roderick shook his head. "I did nothing. Those are yours. And well done."

Ridiculous, the idea that he could cast without picturing the effect! But when he pursed his lips and blew, the horses disappeared. Could they truly have been his work? "How?" he demanded.

"I cannot say. That technique does not work for me, but I have heard of someone who used it."

It still felt impossible. What if he tried again, casting something different without telling the Welshman what he had in mind? He closed his eyes and imagined Elizabeth's approval, twisted his wrist, and cast.

The time he opened his eyes to a clearing full of hedgehogs. Including one on top of Roderick's head. Just as he had intended. Roderick could not possibly have guessed that.

Triumph surged through him. Finally, the breakthrough he had been seeking so desperately! "Will this keep working?"

"I am no expert on this method. Mrs. Morgan might know more. Her first husband was the one who used this method."

It always seemed to come down to that. The legendary Mrs. Morgan, née Lady Amelia Fitzwilliam, was the only one with answers to far too many questions. Perhaps it would be worth the risk of taking Elizabeth to Wales. But nothing could douse his spirits now, not when he had finally cast those damned horses!

Then Roderick frowned and threw up his hand, as if to stop Darcy from speaking. His eyes lost their focus. A moment later, he seemed to return to himself. "Interesting. That was a sending from the Nest. They have a package from Wales and want me to collect it. Perhaps it has a letter from Mrs. Morgan; I did not hope to hear from her so quickly."

Darcy counted days backwards in his mind. "It could not possibly have reached her yet, not even sent express."

The Welshman grinned. "Oh, dragons have their own ways of making quick deliveries. I should go right away, though. May I borrow a carriage? Rowan was not clear how large this package is."

"Of course." No point in bothering to ask more about the dragons' mysterious methods; it was doubtless under a binding. Perhaps Cerridwen would tell him later. "I will stay here and practice." He wanted to perfect this new technique for casting so that he could show Elizabeth his progress later.

"Thank you for speaking to Mrs. Reynolds, even though I told you not to," Elizabeth said to Frederica. "She is proving to be a useful ally."

Her friend flushed to the roots of her golden hair. "It would not do, letting the staff spread false rumors about you. And I wanted to do something to help, after making those ridiculous accusations. I feel so foolish about that. Not that I could ever have guessed what you truly were hiding!"

Elizabeth nodded. "I am glad you know now. How I hated keeping it secret from you!" It was a deep relief to be on better terms again. "I will come by tomorrow for another lesson, then."

"And perhaps I shall actually try to teach you then, rather than nag you with questions about dragons!"

She doubted it would be that simple, but she was eager to return to the house. If Darcy came back early from his practice, she wanted to be there. But she detoured through the orchards to enjoy the first blossoms, their heavy scent hanging on the air, and let some of her Talent trickle down into the roots of the trees. How grateful she was to have that ability again!

As she approached the house from the side, an elderly woman's voice, one with high-bred diction and an overlay of Welsh melody, drifted towards her from the front door. "They were still constructing the courtyard when I saw this place last. Brought in a fancy architect from Venice to make certain the style would be just so. Turned out well, though." The tones were deeply familiar, resonating in Elizabeth's bones.

Elizabeth froze. It could not be.

"Madam has visited before?" The butler sounded unusually supercilious.

A sharp, well-known bark of laughter. "Before you drew your first breath. I came with my father Matlock. The second Earl. Now, where is Mrs. Darcy?"

It was true. Her hands shaking, Elizabeth picked up her skirts and ran.

There she was, in the open doorway to the entry Hall, a tiny ancient woman bundled up as if for the coldest weather. Roderick stood just behind her, supporting her arm.

"Granny!" Elizabeth cried as she skidded to a stop only a few feet away from her. Her great-grandmother had always been slight, but still taller than an eight-year-old Elizabeth. Now she came barely to her shoulder. Elbowing her way past the butler, Elizabeth reached out to embrace her. "You are here!" Her voice shook.

The old woman's gnarled hands patted her back, that metal and cinnamon scent even stronger than in her memory. Then Granny stepped back to look up at her with a nod of satisfaction.

"How you have grown, child! And what a fine mess you have made of everything!" But she said it kindly, as if she were proud of her. "Never fear; I am here to sort everything out. Or at least as much as humanly possible."

In the drawing room, Elizabeth led Granny to the most comfortable seat. "Will you be warm enough? I can fetch you a shawl."

The old lady lowered herself slowly into the chair. "Hardly necessary. I am wearing half my wardrobe, after all." It was true; her shape was barely visible under all the layers. "I could only bring through the Gate whatever I could carry, and heaven alone knows how long it will take for my trunks to reach me over those barbarous roads. But I am here, and that is the important thing."

The Gate. Elizabeth's memory presented her with a vague concept of a way the dragons could communicate between Nests.

Roderick said, "I am surprised the Nest permitted it."

"They could not push me through fast enough when they heard this news from Spain. Yes, I know I can only use the Gate once in a lifetime, but at my age, there is unlikely to be a more urgent need."

The Welshman said, "I am grateful for it. You are much needed here. But I will leave you to your reunion now." He bowed and left the room, closing the door behind him.

Tears prickled Elizabeth's eyes. "I have missed you so much. I wish you did not have to undergo the rigors of travel when you should be resting by your own hearth."

"Needs must," Granny shrugged. "It has always been a possibility that I might have to intervene if our dragons were discovered, though I did not predict a crisis of this magnitude. As soon as Roderick's letter arrived, I knew this was the time. We must discover how Napoleon compelled those poor dragons to fight."

Elizabeth bit her lip. "Do they believe us, then? The dragons in Wales, that is. The one I met with here had doubts."

Granny grimaced. "They are quarreling over whether it is true. Dragons are no different from humans. They prefer to reject a horrifying idea."

"But you do not doubt it?"

"At first I wondered, but I took it seriously because you had convinced Roderick, who is the last person in the world who would ever think ill of a dragon. I had the entire family hunt through the newspapers, and what they found – and did not find – fits your explanation. Besides, I might disagree with War Office decisions, but I respect their intelligence gathering abilities."

"I am relieved you listened to our letters." Elizabeth tried to keep her voice from shaking.

Granny leaned her head back and closed her eyes, a gesture familiar from Elizabeth's childhood. "Dragons pay little attention to the outside world. I do," she said wearily.

A loud tapping sounded, accompanied by a sending from Cerridwen demanding admittance. Elizabeth opened the window. "Do you know who is here?" she asked the kestrel as she flew past.

Cerridwen fluttered to the ground and transformed. "Of course I do. Greetings, Companion Amelia."

Granny looked the dragon up and down. "You are a sight for sore eyes, nestling. It has been too long."

A puff of smoke came from Cerridwen's nostrils. "Indeed, but whose fault is that? I refuse to apologize for remaining loyal to my companion."

"Nor should you. I never agreed with the Nest about exiling you," Granny said. "So, I am told you are a Far-seer. I did not expect to meet one in my time, but you are descended from the last one, so I suppose it should not be a complete shock. Still, you might have told us."

Cerridwen raised the scales on the back of her neck. "You might have warned me it was a possibility, so I could have understood what was happening," she snapped. "How was I to know other dragons did not see these things?"

Granny shook her head. "We should never have permitted you to go so far from the Nest at such a young age. Well, water under the bridge. What is this vision of yours?"

Elizabeth held her breath. Would the dragon actually answer this time? She had refused to tell Elizabeth or Darcy.

Cerridwen sank back on her haunches, her inner eyelids coming down. She turned her head toward the wall, and then very briefly looked directly at Granny, her gold-ringed eyes blazing.

A sending? Elizabeth could sense it, but could not see it.

All the color vanished from Granny's wrinkled face. Her trembling, gnarled hands gripped the armrests. Finally she said in a strangled voice, "We will certainly want to prevent that."

"I have tried!" cried Cerridwen. "When the vision comes, I do whatever leads away from it. Staying with Elizabeth when you ordered me to return. Bonding her to Pemberley, despite the risk. Revealing myself to Lady Frederica. And more, all because any other road led to that." Her voice rose into a wordless keening.

"Choosing the other path is what dragons have always done," Granny said briskly. "The Great Concealment, when the Nests went into hiding, was done to avoid your grandsire's vision coming to fruition."

Cerridwen's grandsire? But the Nests had gone into hiding in the time of Richard the Lion-hearted! How long did dragons live?

"Well, it is past time for your fellow dragons to know about your visions," Granny said.

Cerridwen tossed her head. "You will have to tell them, since they will not speak to me!"

"That, at least, I can fix. The Eldest of the Nest sent something for you." Granny fumbled with a small pouch attached to her waist. "Curse these fingers! Lizzy, will you open this for me?"

Elizabeth bent and removed an inlaid silver ball from the small pocket. It was barely an inch across, but unexpectedly heavy, and it made her fingers tingle.

"Go on, give it to your dragon, girl!"

Cerridwen held out her taloned foreleg expectantly. Mystified, Elizabeth offered it to her.

As soon as the dragon touched it, a fine mist emerged from the ball. Cerridwen raised it to her nostrils and breathed it in. Her eyes drifted closed, her chest swelling.

Then the mist faded. Cerridwen spread her wings, shaking them out vigorously and stamping in place, like an over-sized wet dog shaking itself. When she settled, something was different, but Elizabeth could not tell what. A lessening of tension? Or a shift in her aura?

"Ah, that is better," said Cerridwen with deep satisfaction.

Granny nodded. "The Silence has been lifted."

Elizabeth clasped her hands together in joy. Perhaps now Cerridwen could become part of the Dark Peak Nest – and maintain their bond.

"Now off with you." Granny waved her hand towards the window. "Go speak to your cousins at the Nest."

A sense of delight rebounded through the room. "They will receive me now?"

"They are expecting you." Granny smiled indulgently.

Elizabeth did not wait for Cerridwen's cue to open the window. Within a minute, a kestrel was winging away towards Mam Tor. She closed the latch before turning back to Granny. "Will they allow her to join the Nest?"

"I hope so. The dragon I spoke to there seemed favorably impressed with you, so that will help."

A wave of warmth filled Elizabeth. "Thank you for coming." The words came out in a rush. "I have many questions for you, but more than anything, it is so, so good to see you again."

Granny cracked a smile. "You are a dear child, and I have missed you. Now, what about this husband of yours? Roderick says he hates dragons." Clearly she found the sentiment ridiculous.

Elizabeth's excitement faded. "At first, yes, but he has made his peace with Cerridwen. The dragons in Spain killed his brother." And now there was another dragon companion at Pemberley. Darcy might not be pleased.

Granny studied her shrewdly. "Roderick thinks you have fallen in love with him."

Elizabeth raised her chin. "He is a good man, even if he can be stubborn and proud."

"And you have lost your own family and home," Granny said, her voice laden with sympathy.

Tears sprang to Elizabeth's eyes. "It is not only that, but I do miss them so much! Jane writes when she can, but she is busy with her own life, and I have hardly heard from the others."

Knobby fingers clutched her own. "Well, I am here now, and you are no longer alone."

Chapter 32

D ARCY RETURNED TO THE house just as the sun was setting. He had stayed longer than usual in the clearing, testing out his new casting technique, triumphant at his success despite his confusion over it. Why did it only work when he imagined Elizabeth's pleasure in his casting? He had tried visualizing Georgiana, old school friends, his father, even his lynx, and ended up with a shapeless mess of illusion.

The butler was waiting for him at the door with a letter on a silver salver. "An express for you, sir."

His satisfaction vanished. An express was never good news. Darcy tugged off his gloves, handed them to the butler, and took the letter.

It was the scrawling handwriting of Cattermole from the War Office. Acid rose in his throat as he snapped open the heavy seal.

He ignored the first two paragraphs, jumping straight to the third, since the beginning was always designed to mislead anyone who happened upon the letter. There it was.

> *My uncle has decided he can complete his business in Scotland within a fortnight, although everyone else swears it would be impossible, that the work will take many months more. And I would agree with them, if only Uncle had not proven himself right before with his impossible expectations! Sometimes I won-*

der if he has a devil whispering in his ear. Still, I have learned
the hard way not to bet against him, so I am, as ordered,
planning a celebratory dinner for him next month, when he
intends to return to London. The things one tolerates in hopes
of a rich inheritance! I hope you can find your way to join us so
that I may have the pleasure of seeing you give him one of your
cutting set-downs.

A heavy weight settled on Darcy's chest. Swallowing hard, he read the words again, hoping against hope to find something different. But it was clear as day, since their code was that Cattermole's uncle was the French Emperor, Scotland was Austria, and London was Paris. Napoleon had something up his sleeve and believed he could wind up the Austrian war quickly, even though the War Office had expected it to take longer. But Cattermole was right; every time Napoleon had pronounced something like this to his staff, he had made good on it, with dragons in Spain or sea serpents sinking half the Navy or a powerful fog descending on the Italian army. What horror did Napoleon have in mind this time that could make the mighty Austrian army collapse almost overnight?

Only a month. That was when Napoleon would return to Paris, and Darcy would have to follow him there to cast his illusions. Quite possibly at the cost of his own life.

The muscles of his shoulders knotted.

Only a month until he would leave Elizabeth, perhaps forever.

Should he tell her? There was nothing she could do. The knowledge would simply hang over their last few weeks together, and God alone knew how Cerridwen would react. And the timing still might change – Napoleon could be wrong for once, and the mission delayed. Darcy folded the letter with numb fingers.

Just then Elizabeth came out of the drawing room, headed straight for him. "I thought I heard your voice!" she exclaimed. Her glad expression, so like the one he had been picturing for his casting, cracked the ice that had just formed around his heart.

He stuffed the letter in his pocket. It must be kept secret for now, until he had time to think through the implications. Fortunately, he had a subject at hand to distract her. "I had some success today. A new method for my illusions, one that was very effective."

For a moment she looked confused, but then her fine eyes lit up. "Your horses?"

"Yes. Completely convincing this time. Roderick had me try a new way of casting. It makes no sense, but it worked."

She gripped his hands, her flesh and Talent sending tingling warmth through him. "How wonderful! This is indeed a day of marvels. We have a most unexpected visitor, too – my great-grandmother, come all the way from Wales."

"She is here? That is good news indeed!" Especially now that his time for obtaining answers would be so much shorter.

She hesitated. "Yes, I think she will be able to help us. Her dragon will be here, too, in a day or two, but she says he will not come to the house."

Another dragon? It was one thing to trust Cerridwen, who had been part of Elizabeth's life for years, but a new, unknown one? Well, he would find a way to work with this one, too. Somehow.

Then it struck him. "I thought she was practically on her deathbed. How did she manage to travel all this way?"

"It seems an amazing recovery, but I am happy for it. We can learn so much from her. Will you be kind to her?"

"Of course I will be kind! You love her, and she is a distant connection of mine, too."

She seemed to relax. "She can also be opinionated and demanding."

He released her hands, but only so he could touch her cheek. "You have met my mother and Frederica. Opinionated, demanding women are nothing new to me."

"Then come, and I shall introduce you. Pray recall she is a truth-caster, like Frederica."

"A good reminder." He would have to refuse to answer some questions, then. His skin burned as they approached the drawing room. So Elizabeth's great-grandmother was not immune to repulsion and did not have an Artifact. That was reassuring. She was like any other mage.

At least now he had a solution for dealing with that problem. He reached out for Elizabeth's hand again, and the burning vanished.

"I hope you have given our visitor a room far from ours, since apparently she and I repel each other," he said.

"Actually, you are most likely reacting to Frederica. Roderick just brought her here from the Dower House so she could meet Granny. She seems to have no repulsion to her, so I doubt you will either."

Did all dragon-associated mages have special abilities? That was hardly fair. But he set aside his annoyance for Elizabeth's sake. "Given everything you have told me about your great-grandmother's dislike for the Fitzwilliam family, I am surprised there is no bloodshed happening."

"True! But Roderick has persuaded her that Frederica is also a rebel, so she is giving her a chance. Come." She tugged him toward the drawing room.

Frederica's voice floated through the door. "... foolish, but I feel as if you ought to know me already, since I spent my entire childhood whispering all my dark secrets to your portrait at Matlock. Well, mostly to the falcon in it, but I always assumed your ghost must be listening in."

A tiny elderly lady was ensconced by the fire. "I see what you mean, Roderick." Her creaky voice sounded amused. It wavered a little, but was stronger than he expected from a woman of her age. "A typical Fitzwilliam would never admit to having dark secrets, much less talking to a painting."

Then Elizabeth led him before her. "Granny, may I present my husband? Darcy, you have often heard me mention Mrs. Morgan."

The old woman looked him up and down and then nodded with apparent satisfaction. "I am glad you are here. I have a great many questions for you, young man."

Darcy bowed. "Lady Amelia, I am at your service."

She grimaced. "I suppose I shall have to accustom myself to that nonsense again. No one has called me that since long before you were born, yet your servants have already started it."

Darcy allowed himself a tiny smile. "You will have to forgive my old-fashioned ways, then."

Frederica said airily, "If you prefer to be called Mrs. Morgan, *I* will be happy to do so."

Lady Amelia tilted her head. "You might as well call me Granny, girl. Everyone else does."

"Literally true," said Roderick with a laugh. "Even those who are not related to her. She is Granny Morgan to everyone in Wales."

Lady Amelia narrowed her eyes at Darcy. "I can see you have too much stiff-necked Fitzwilliam pride to ever be so informal." But her tone was friendly, and her impertinence reminded him of Elizabeth. It made him like her a little better.

"That would be correct, Lady Amelia. And you will find that my staff are equally stiff-necked."

She waved her fingers in his direction. "We have more pressing matters. Mr. Darcy, Roderick and Lizzy have told me what they know about these dragon attacks in Spain, but I would like to hear it directly from you. All of it, if you please, from the beginning. With my greater understanding of dragons, I may see something others could not." Then she added in a gentler tone, "I understand it is a painful topic for you. I would not ask it, were it not of such great importance."

Her kind words released some of the tension from his body. Yes, he hated talking about it, but any insights Lady Amelia might have could be useful. So he told her everything, leaving out only the military plans for protecting the Army in Spain. And his mission, but that had nothing to do with dragons, anyway.

The old lady asked sharp, insightful questions. She seemed untroubled by discussing gory details of injuries as she tried to determine how the dragons had fought, and tested the limits of his knowledge of the battle. "I understand this attack led to you being given a particular mission. What is it?"

Darcy met her gaze steadily. "I cannot tell you." The letter burned in his pocket.

Roderick said tiredly, "He is to cast illusions to cover an attempt to assassinate Napoleon."

Darcy swung to face Elizabeth, betrayal burning in his throat. "You told him. Even knowing how important secrecy is."

She looked stricken. "I did nothing of the sort!"

"She did not need to," said the Welshman irritably. "You asked me to help you create illusions to distract the guards in a palace, and you are spending hours every day improving your French. Did you expect me to think it was so you could invite Napoleon to tea?"

Darcy stiffened. Was it so obvious? And worse, had he accused Elizabeth falsely? They had only just resolved their differences, and this would not help. He squeezed her hand. "My apologies," he said, low enough that only she could hear. "I should not have jumped to conclusions."

She responded with a teasing smile that melted his heart. "It is, after all, a favored habit of yours."

How had he ever lived without her? And how could he possibly leave her for his mission?

Lady Amelia tapped her foot impatiently. "And you say that Napoleon somehow controls these Spanish dragons?"

"That is what our source tells us, and he has been accurate in the past," Darcy said.

Lady Amelia nodded. "If that is true, then ridding ourselves of Napoleon would seem the best solution. No human force can stand against a dragon who is willing to kill."

"You cannot mean it!" cried Roderick. "What would the dragons say?"

"The dragons are accustomed to my disagreements with them. Just because they feel killing is never acceptable does not mean I have to concur. Had I the opportunity, I would slit Boney's throat myself." Lady Amelia folded her hands in her lap as if there were nothing extraordinary about this statement. "I cannot imagine the dragons would be heartbroken to hear of his death."

Darcy leaned forward. "Is there a chance, any chance at all, that they will help with my mission?"

"Highly unlikely," said Lady Amelia. "Dragons do not kill, nor will they help others to do so. It is anathema to them. Yes, yes, I know you have seen evidence to the contrary from Spain, but that is how we know something is terribly wrong."

Again, this romantic notion of dragons! "Most people hate the thought of killing, but our soldiers learn to live with it."

She shook her finger at him. "It is an error to assume dragons are like humans. A dragon who kills, even by accident, rarely lives long afterwards. It weakens them – and makes them extremely dangerous. No sane dragon would take that risk."

It sounded like a fairy story to Darcy, and he opened his mouth to say so. But there was no point in it; nothing would shake these dragon-lovers' fixed beliefs, not even hundreds of thousands of massacred soldiers. Instead, he said, "It is past time to tell the government that we have dragons here in England. They need to know, especially if Napoleon has the ability to turn dragons against their nature." Except the damned binding would not permit him to tell them.

Lady Amelia nodded. "Much as I dislike admitting it, you have a point. But if we reveal that information without consulting the dragons, they might refuse to work with us. We must at least make an effort to convince them. And that is why we must make plans, right now, while Cerridwen is away and before Sycamore, my dragon, arrives." From her clear satisfaction in this announcement, this must have been her plan all long.

Could this old lady possibly be his ally? "What do you suggest?"

"First, we must convince them the attack actually happened. Their instinct is to disbelieve a human reporting such an unnatural thing, much as you would refuse to listen if a dragon told you your neighbor was killing infants and eating them for breakfast. Once they accept the truth, we can present the case for an alliance."

He studied her. "It would be useful if they would share information, I suppose, but if they will not fight or help with my mission, what do they have to offer?"

She smirked. "Men! Always assuming that fighting is the only answer. Dragons are the masters of magical defense. Massive illusions to trick soldiers. Confusion spells to make them lose their way. Rockslides and walls of fire to block their advance. They can stop an invasion without shedding blood."

He leaned forward, stunned. An invasion was everyone's worst fear. "They can truly do this?"

"If they so desire. They have done as much for our part of Wales, through their alliance with Roderick's family. The question is whether we can convince them to do so for England."

A force like that could change everything. Suddenly it was not just a matter of informing the War Office. His first goal had to be to pursue an alliance with the dragons.

"What if Napoleon brings his own dragons to our shores? Could they overcome the defenses you speak of?"

Lady Amelia closed her eyes, her animated face suddenly showing every one of her years. "If that comes to pass, we will not be concerned with protecting Britain, but hoping there will be some survivors. Pray that it never comes to pass."

It was a dash of icy water over a moment of hope, but it stiffened his resolve. All the more reason Napoleon must die.

"Mr. Roderick," Frederica interrupted, her voice sharp. "How did you come to be allied with dragons?"

"I?" Roderick said. "Ask rather how my ancestors arranged it centuries ago. That has been lost in time. I was born to the alliance, and raised as much among dragons as humans."

Frederica's eyes narrowed. "I do not believe you have ever told me who your family is."

His mouth twisted. "It does not matter. I am no one in particular."

Lady Amelia snorted. "Is that what you have been claiming? He is the heir to the last Prince of Gwynedd."

Roderick glared at her. "Which makes me no one, since Edward I put a violent end to that title over five hundred years ago."

"Except in the mountains of Gwynedd, where everyone still considers your father their leader, and you to follow in his footsteps. With dragons by your side."

Frederica's mouth had fallen open, but now she snapped it shut, her face white, and the Welshman looked cross. But Darcy did not care about Roderick's forebears, though it did explain some of his extraordinary illusion-casting. The ancient Welsh nobility had been powerful mages.

Darcy leaned forward. "Back to the dragons. How can I convince them to help us, to defend our people?"

Lady Amelia eyed him shrewdly. "You cannot. They may listen to me, and to Roderick to a degree, but we must get Lizzy and Cerridwen into their councils. Cerridwen's visions will do more to persuade them than anything else. Lizzy must take her final vows, which will make her part of the Nest as well. That is when the negotiations can begin."

He looked down at where his fingers entwined with Elizabeth's, offering both love and protection from repulsion. "It seems we each have a mission now," he said softly. "Mine to stop Napoleon, and yours to rally the dragons in England's defense."

Darcy lay back in bed, running his fingers through Elizabeth's silken curls. How he loved it when she curled up beside him afterwards, her head resting on his shoulder, the warmth of her arm across his chest. While she was always a passionate partner, tonight had been... something beyond that. Something joyous. Something that could even make him forget for a few moments the letter he had received.

She raised her head to look up at him, smiling. "What do you think of Granny?"

He kissed her forehead. "I like her. She is a redoubtable lady, no question about that. I am glad she is on our side, as I suspect she would make a formidable enemy."

"That is the truth!" Then her expression sobered, and she bit her lip.

"Is something troubling you?"

She shook her head. "Just thinking of something she told me. I cannot be certain of it, though."

Something about the dragons, no doubt, when he only wanted to enjoy Elizabeth's companionship. But he had learned the hard way to listen, even when he did not wish to, so he said, "What is that?"

She blurted out, "I asked her about some changes I had noticed, and.... And she thinks I may be increasing."

Increasing? She was carrying his child?

"Elizabeth," he whispered, his heart pounding loudly enough to provide a counterpoint to his words, as a fountain of joy erupted inside him. A baby. Their child!

It was not as if he had never considered the possibility – he had been frantically obsessed with it, praying for it each and every day. But this was different. Now it was real. A child made of the two of them. Would the baby have Elizabeth's fine eyes and laughing expression? Or the Darcy cheekbones? Yet their child would also be entirely itself, a new part of their family.

And it was already growing inside his dearest, loveliest Elizabeth!

Tentatively he reached his hand down to hover over her abdomen. "Will it hurt if I touch you there?"

A laugh shook her shoulders. "Not at all, though there is nothing to feel as yet. Perhaps a tiny swelling."

With the utmost gentleness, as if he were touching a fragile holy relic, he let his hand rest lightly on her smooth skin. Even if there was no external change or blood bond yet, it was intoxicating.

He gathered her precious, beloved form to him, treasuring her closeness, a wash of love for her pouring through him. And their future child was in his embrace, too.

It was the finest moment of his life. No matter the looming problems they faced, he had Elizabeth, and they were a family. Together, they could do anything.

"Granny says it may be too early yet for you to draw on my power through the shared blood, but she can advise us on how to forge that connection. It was the same for her, since her magic entwined with her first husband. Is it not wonderful to have someone who knows what to expect?"

"A marvel indeed." But he was not thinking of Lady Amelia, but of the marvel in his arms and the miracle growing inside her.

She punched his shoulder affectionately. "I am serious. I want to work hard at it, so I can help bring you home safely."

It took a moment to understand what she meant. In his joy at her news, he had not thought once about the effect of her pregnancy on his mission – the very reason he had married her.

How little he had known then of all she would bring to his life!

He would not let anything take this away from him. It had sounded like an excellent plan back in Hertfordshire. Marry Elizabeth, get her with child, and go off to his death. As if it would not matter to leave her behind and never meet their baby. Now he knew better. Somehow he would find a way back to them.

This would not be the end, but a new beginning for them.

The adventure continues in
The Magic of Pemberley, Book 2 of Fitzwilliam Darcy, Mage
Read on for an excerpt from *The Magic of Pemberley*!

Excerpt from The Magic of Pemberley

THE LAKE PRESENTED A perfect reflection of Pemberley's manor house. It was a serene sight, at least until a dozen riderless horses came racing around it, headed directly towards their small party.

Elizabeth Darcy caught her breath. What a vast improvement this illusion was from her husband's early attempts at horses! Roderick was right; something had fundamentally changed in Darcy's ability to cast. And just in time, since all too soon everything would depend upon his illusions –including his life.

Granny eyed the horses critically. "Not bad," she said. "Still, they could be better. Come here, young man."

Darcy pursed his lips to dismiss the illusion, and the horses vanished. His clenched jaw hinted at his displeasure over Granny's reaction, but he approached her chair. "As you wish, Lady Amelia."

"Someday I will convince you to call me Granny," the old lady grumbled, which elicited a small smile from Darcy. "But not today. Lean down, so I can speak in your ear." When he obeyed, she cupped her hand so Elizabeth could not even see her lips move.

What was she telling Darcy that was such a secret?

Darcy straightened abruptly, his cheeks staining with red. "Madam!" His exclamation was a reproach.

Now Elizabeth's curiosity was racing faster than the horses. Her husband almost never blushed.

"Oh, hush," Granny said irritably. "Half a million English soldiers dead in Europe, and you are worried about your fine manners? This will help you stop Napoleon. And for some reason, my great-granddaughter wants you to come back to her alive afterwards, so pray do as I say."

His color still high, Darcy glared at her, but then he closed his eyes in an obvious attempt to master himself. "Kindly give me a moment," he said in a clipped voice.

"Take as much time as you need," said Granny expansively, her lips twitching.

What in the world was going on? But then Darcy turned to her, his expression unreadable. No, not unreadable – she would know perfectly well how to interpret it if they were alone in a bedroom, but what did it mean here when his eyes turned smoky and his gaze burrowed deep within her? Now it was her cheeks that were growing hot.

Then he flicked his wrist, the way he always did when casting an illusion, but without looking away from her. And she was just as caught as he was, desire rising in a hot current and prickling at her skin.

"Much better!" crowed Granny. "Look at that!"

Her words broke into the odd tension between them, and then Elizabeth gasped. The horses were back, but this time they were charging uncontrollably, not merely running. One tossed its head as if maddened, and steam rose from the nostrils of another. The very sight of them made her heart pound.

Darcy's mouth hung open, as if stunned by the illusion he had created. He moved his hand again, and the rampaging herd veered off to circle the lake. "Roderick never mentioned that technique." His voice was half-strangled, half-accusatory.

Granny sniffed. "It is useless to anyone who cannot entwine their magic with a dragon companion, which means almost everyone. My late husband chose not to share with others that small detail of how he re-learned to use his Talent after marrying me. At least Roderick knew to teach you the basic method."

It was a good reminder for Elizabeth. Darcy would be the one facing the desperate dangers in France, but her abilities as a dragon companion could help him succeed. And perhaps even survive.

He frowned. "This is not a good time for me to start my training anew, but I cannot deny it is effective." He looked at Elizabeth, his eyes drifting down her body in a way that hardly seemed appropriate in public, and then he cast again.

There were no horses this time. He must have created some sort of illusion, though. Elizabeth searched the scene before her. A kestrel circled above them, but that had to be real, since she could feel Cerridwen's unmistakable presence in the back of her mind. Had those two swans on the lake been there before? Elizabeth could make out their wake rippling through the water, and an illusion of moving water was far beyond Darcy's abilities – or so she had thought.

"Surely those swans are not yours?" she asked hesitantly.

Darcy rubbed his hand over his mouth. "I thought it would not work."

Whatever this new technique was, Elizabeth wanted to learn it. But then Cerridwen stole her attention away, plummeting towards her in a steep dive. A moment later the bird landed in front of her and transformed into her beloved dragon.

It still hardly seemed possible, that her magical falcon had turned out to be a dragon! It was good to see her, too. Since Granny had lifted the years-long Silence that barred Cerridwen from the company of other dragons, Cerridwen had spent every waking moment among her fellows at the nearby Nest.

Elizabeth laid her hand on Cerridwen's chest, letting the heat and powerful magic in the lustrous blue and bronze scales warm her, and spoke to her silently. *I had not expected to see you so early, dearest.*

Cerridwen's aura spilled grumpiness. *All the dragons are upset about something, and they will not tell me what. They say I am not one of them yet.*

Poor Cerridwen! She had been so glad to finally be with dragons again, after giving them up to stay with Elizabeth, and now this. Had she done something to upset them?

Although Elizabeth had not meant to send that, Cerridwen often picked up on her unspoken thoughts. *No, they say it has nothing to do with me. But I do not like secrets.* If Cerridwen had been human, she would have been pouting.

Elizabeth put her arm over the dragon's shoulders affectionately. *Neither do I, and I am glad you came here instead. I will always tell you anything you ask.*

Darcy studied the swans in shock. How could they possibly have turned out so well? It was a powerful tool that Lady Amelia had taught him, as shockingly improper as it might be. The question was how best to use it.

His thoughts were interrupted by the sound of hoofbeats and wheels on gravel. Real ones, not illusory this time. He shaded his eyes with his hand to see a carriage was coming up the drive, the top loaded with trunks and packages, as if the occupant planned on an extended stay. Could Elizabeth have invited someone without telling him? Then the answer struck him.

How could he have forgotten? It had not even been a fortnight since he had called on his sister in London and insisted she visit Pemberley. But then he had come home to the discovery that there were dragons in England, like the murderous ones who had killed his brother Jack in Spain. And one of them was in his own drawing room, bonded to his wife. Everything else, including Georgiana's arrival, had flown completely out of his head.

Now she was here, and he had not even warned Elizabeth, much less the staff.

The driver of her coach was staring at him in absolute horror. Or, more specifically, at the dragon just a few feet away.

With a quick excuse to Lady Amelia, he set off for the coach at a run. He had to get there before Georgiana spotted Cerridwen.

His sister was already stepping down from the carriage by the time he arrived, her face wreathed in smiles as he came into view. She threw her arms around him, burying her face in his chest, as if she still feared she might never see him again. Just as she did after every separation, no matter how short.

Darcy hugged her. "I hope your journey was easy." Especially as the situation was about to get complicated. She would not take it well that he had forgotten about her arrival.

"There were no problems," she said softly. "It is good to see you."

"I am glad you are here," he said, a slight prevarication, but well meant. "I have a great deal to tell you about."

She stepped back, straightening her bonnet. Her gaze drifted past him to the figures by the lake. "I am sorry. I did not mean to take you from your company." Then her eyes widened, and she gave a little shriek. She must have seen the dragon. Why had he not spoken faster? He caught her arm. "All is well," he said soothingly. "I know it is a shock, but I can explain."

She pulled away from him. "I want to go back to London. This instant!" And before he could stop her, she pushed past her companion and hurried back into her carriage.

Damnation. This was worse than he had thought. He clambered in after her. "Georgiana, listen to me. There is nothing to fear. Cerridwen – that dragon – is kind-hearted and gentle. She will not hurt you."

"But what if she can *tell*?" his sister whispered.

Not this again! "No one has ever been able to do so before. Why should this be any different?"

She curled herself into a ball on the bench, her knuckles white. "Because they are..." She took a deep breath. "In the old stories, dragons could always discover people's secrets."

This was difficult. "I am not an expert on dragons." To say the very least! But he could hardly reassure her that Cerridwen would not touch her mind, when he knew full well that Georgiana would be bound against revealing the presence of the dragons. Lady Amelia's dragon, who was to arrive the next day, might not prove as trustworthy as Cerridwen. "But I think it perfectly safe."

"I do not want that dragon to see me," she begged. "May I not simply return to Town?"

"But you just arrived. Would you not like a little time together first? And I would dearly love for you to meet my wife." How would he explain it to Elizabeth if Georgiana left without a word to her?

"I would not have come at all if I had known!" she cried."Of course I want to see you, but not like this. And you have *guests*." She said it as if he had invited horrific monsters.

"Only Elizabeth's great-grandmother from Wales, and her friend Roderick, who is training me in illusion-casting." This was not the moment to bring up that Lady Amelia was a Fitzwilliam by birth. "And Cousin Frederica, who is staying at the Dower House, since her Talent does not allow her to be close to me. You need not spend time with any of them if you do not wish it." It might in fact be easier if Georgiana kept to herself, away from the constant discussions of dragons, Nests, and defenses against Napoleon.

"Can I remain in my room? And would you ask the dragon to keep away from me?" Tears began to run down her cheeks.

He could not bear it when Georgiana cried. Perhaps if he gave her a little time, she might realize the dragons would have no interest in her. "I will ask Cerridwen to keep her distance from you. She is hardly ever here these days, in any case."

"Thank you," she whispered. "I am sorry to be such trouble."

He took her hand and held it, wishing he could soothe her anxieties. But that seemed like a hopeless task.

Elizabeth watched with amusement as Lady Frederica Fitzwilliam, followed by Roderick, made a beeline for them as soon as Darcy had turned his back. Frederica could never resist an opportunity to deluge Granny with questions about dragons and magic. How long had she been hovering about, hoping Darcy would step away so that she could come closer without suffering the usual mage repulsion?

"What was it you told Darcy to do?" Frederica demanded of Granny.

The elderly lady snorted. "Nothing you could use, young lady! That technique will only work for Darcy."

"It would still be interesting to know," she coaxed.

Granny shook her head. "Not this one, child. Some things should remain private." Then her wrinkled face dissolved into a smile, taking any sting from her words. "Those swans look quite well on the lake, do they not? The last time I came to Pemberley, nearly eighty years ago, it was a muddy stream with dozens of workmen digging. Now you would never know it is not natural. I would think the lake an illusion, too, if I did not know better."

"Perhaps *you* could cast an illusion like that, but any image of water is far beyond me," Frederica said ruefully. "Roderick told me you can cast a waterfall, but I can hardly credit that."

Granny's face was wreathed with smiles. "I cannot resist a challenge." Across the lake, the field of daffodils was suddenly replaced by a rock face, with a narrow stream of water tumbling down into the water below.

Elizabeth studied the illusion. Every detail was there, from the sunlight glinting on the falling drops to the arc of ripples crossing the lake from where the water cascaded into it. It was completely believable, except where the ripples passed straight through Darcy's illusory swans.

"Astonishing," Frederica breathed.

With a sly look, Granny said, "You have magical Talent enough, yet you are unable to cast an illusion of water. Is it your lack of ability – or a lack of proper training?"

Elizabeth winced. Even though Granny was speaking about Frederica, Elizabeth's ability with illusions had proved to be disappointing. It was hard, after years of priding herself on her mastery of other magical skills. Of course, her training had been non-existent until recently.

Frederica flushed. "You will have to blame me, since the King's Mage taught me herself."

Granny sat back in her chair with a pleased expression. "The very same who gave Darcy his first lessons, and yet Roderick tells me he went about illusions completely backwards, using his head and not his heart."

Frederica leaned forward eagerly. "What does that mean, casting with your heart? Can you teach me how? Or will this only work for Darcy, too?"

Cerridwen bumped against Elizabeth's shoulder, no doubt bored with this conversation about human mage Talents. "Who is in that carriage? I have already put a binding on the two men outside it so they can tell no one of my existence."

"I was not expecting anyone, but I should go see who it is." Elizabeth shaded her eyes to study the new arrivals, but she could make out no details. "Roderick, I will hold you personally responsible if Frederica exhausts Granny with her questions."

The Welshman laughed. "As if I could stop her! Fortunately, Granny does not need me to defend her."

But Granny was looking at Frederica with approval. "Come, girl, sit down with me, and we will see what you can learn."

Frederica did not need to be asked twice.

Elizabeth left her to it, but halfway to Darcy, she stopped in her tracks at the sight of the woman taking his hand to descend from the carriage. What was Lady Anne Darcy doing at Pemberley? Darcy's mother, the distant, powerful King's Mage, who seemed to care for nothing except finding and breeding new mages. And to suddenly appear without any warning? Did she think everyday manners did not apply to her?

Then a chill crawled up her spine. Could Lady Anne have discovered what was happening at Pemberley? Had someone managed to get word to her about Cerridwen, or worse, about Granny? Frederica was bound against mentioning dragons, but she could have sent a letter telling her former teacher that she must pay an urgent visit here. Surely Frederica would not have betrayed her that way! The very thought made her stomach churn.

Then Darcy put his arm around Lady Anne, who leaned against his shoulder. No, it could not be! The woman might look just like Lady Anne, but the King's Mage would never appear in public in a simple dress and her bonnet askew, with wisps of golden hair escaping in every direction. Nor would Darcy have that protective look towards his mother, who needed no one's protection. And the King's Mage would never, ever have a tear-stained face.

Still, the resemblance was remarkable. Not merely the same hair color and height, but identical features, as if they had been cast from the same mold. This one was just a girl, though. She had to be Darcy's sister – and she was clearly distressed.

A crying girl appearing unexpectedly was a different story than the King's Mage coming to discover their secrets. Elizabeth's fear and anger evaporated as she continued forward with a welcoming smile, even though the timing for this visit was unfortunate. She had wanted to meet her new sister, but now they would have to spend their evenings speaking of trivialities instead of dragons and the war. There was nothing to be done for it, though.

As she approached, Darcy caught her eye with a slight grimace, and his voice spoke in her head. *I am sorry. I found out she was coming when I was away. I meant to tell you when I returned, but it slipped my mind when everything happened.*

Everything, no doubt, meaning his discovery that Cerridwen was a dragon, and their subsequent fight over her. At least that was behind them now, thank heavens! Making up had been sweet indeed.

Darcy said, "Georgiana, dearest, may I introduce you to my wife?"

The girl released Darcy with apparent reluctance. She turned to Elizabeth and curtsied, the tearstains even more apparent now.

"Welcome," Elizabeth said. "I am so pleased you could join us here. Your brother has spoken of you with great affection."

Miss Darcy glanced at her brother nervously. "I am happy to make your acquaintance." At least her voice was completely unlike her mother's, quiet and hesitant instead of self-assured.

Darcy cleared his throat apologetically. "We have encountered a slight difficulty. My sister, as it turns out, has a deep fear of dragons. Would it be too much to ask Cerridwen to keep her distance from Georgiana during her visit?"

"I will speak to Cerridwen," she said. Did the girl know her other brother had been killed by a dragon? It was a well-kept secret that dragons had caused the massacre of English troops at Salamanca, but both Darcy and Lady Anne knew the truth. Perhaps one of them had told her, or she might simply be afraid of all strange creatures.

"That would be helpful," Darcy said. He nodded to a dark-haired young woman who was now descending from the carriage. "May I present Miss Lowrie, Georgiana's companion?"

Elizabeth exchanged a curtsy with the newcomer. Miss Lowrie appeared only a few years older than Miss Darcy, certainly younger and more attractive than Elizabeth would have expected for a hired companion. She glanced at Darcy, surprised that he had not insisted on the traditional widowed lady in her later years. It was unlike him to defy convention that way, especially when it came to his younger sister.

"Oh, yes, brother," Miss Darcy said. "I told Belinda that she could pay a visit to her family while I was here, but she insisted she must speak to you first."

"Rightly so," Darcy said. "I have no objection to your plans, Miss Lowrie, but I am pleased you consulted me."

"I thank you. If it is no trouble, I will stay here tonight and set out tomorrow." A flush of color in her cheeks accompanied her words. Clearly the prospect excited her.

Miss Darcy tossed her head. "Which will give you time to tell my brother everything I have done since you reported to him last." Despite her words, the girl seemed more amused than disturbed by the prospect.

Miss Lowrie's dark eyes twinkled. "That is what companions do."

"You must be longing to refresh yourselves," Elizabeth said. "Would you care to come inside?"

After the two ladies were led upstairs, Elizabeth asked Darcy, "Will she be offended to discover I have limited time to provide her with companionship?"

"Georgiana? Not at all. She prefers to keep to herself. She spends most of her days practicing her music. Miss Lowrie's family is one of our neighbors, so I expect they will still call on each other."

Elizabeth took care with her words. "Miss Lowrie seems very young to be a companion."

He shrugged. "True, but she has known Georgiana all her life, and is one of the very few people my sister trusts. That is more important to me than her age."

She debated asking him more, but she had already learned that he did not like to talk about his sister. Instead she said, "What was it that Granny told you to do? It made such a difference in your casting."

Once again, he flushed, raising her curiosity to a feverish level. "Perhaps you should ask her." But he must have seen her outraged look, for he added, "Ask me tonight, when we are alone." And that smoky look was back in his eyes.

"Promises, promises," she teased.

He raised her hand and, turning it over, pressed a lingering kiss to the inside of her wrist that sent a spiral of desire down her arm. "I always keep my promises."

Buy The Magic of Pemberley now!

Acknowledgements

It always takes a village to raise a book, and this one took more than most. I'm fortunate enough to have two fantastic critique groups who have done amazing work in making my scenes flow, so my thanks to the Sippewissett Scribblers and the Bluestockings without Borders. Laura George, Susan Meyers, Shannon Rohane, Melissa Sawyer, and Sarah Shepherd deserve medals for all their efforts on this book.

My fabulous team of beta readers caught far too many typos and helped identify inconsistencies for me to fix, and I'd like to thank Al Bradley, Arlene Brown, Angela Dale, Christie Devine, Wendy Buck Erichsen, Monica Fairview, Debbie Fortin, Michela Furia, Nicola Geiger, Melanie Gylling, Wendy Luther Moreira, Susan M. Parker, Suzanne Sakaluk, David Young, and Rebecca Young for their efforts. Any remaining errors are purely my fault!

I've also had companionship on this journey from my fellow writers at the Magical Austen website, where you can find many other fantasy variations on Pride & Prejudice. Thanks to Monica Fairview for creating a place where Darcy's magic is always real!

As always, I couldn't have done this without the support of my family. My husband kept the house running while I wrote, while Pfeffernusse, Pip, Snickerdoodle, and Bastet provided snarky feline commentary and soothing purrs.

About the Author

Abigail Reynolds may be a nationally bestselling author and a physician, but she can't follow a straight line with a ruler. Originally from upstate New York, she studied Russian and theater at Bryn Mawr College and marine biology at the Marine Biological Laboratory in Woods Hole. After a stint in performing arts administration, she decided to attend medical school, and took up writing as a hobby during her years as a physician in private practice.

A life-long lover of Jane Austen's novels, Abigail began writing variations on *Pride & Prejudice* in 2001, then expanded her repertoire to include a series of novels set on her beloved Cape Cod. Her books have won multiple awards and several have been national bestsellers. Her most recent releases are *The Price of Pride*, *A Matter of Honor*, *Mr. Darcy's Enchantment*, and *Conceit & Concealment*. You can find her other books listed on her Author Page at Amazon. Her books have been translated into seven languages. She lives on Cape Cod with her husband and a menagerie of animals. Her hobbies do not include sleeping or cleaning her house.

Visit Abigail's website at Pemberley Variations

Also by Abigail Reynolds

The Magic of Pemberley
Spellbound at Pemberley
The Price of Pride
A Matter of Honor
Mr. Darcy's Enchantment
Conceit & Concealment
Mr. Darcy's Journey
Alone with Mr. Darcy
The Darcys of Derbyshire
Mr. Darcy's Noble Connections
Mr. Darcy's Refuge
Mr. Darcy's Obsession
Mr. Fitzwilliam Darcy: The Last Man in the World
The Man Who Loved Pride & Prejudice
To Conquer Mr. Darcy
What Would Mr. Darcy Do?
By Force of Instinct
Mr. Darcy's Undoing
Morning Light
A Pemberley Medley

Mr. Darcy's Letter
The Darcy Brothers (co-author)
Mr. Darcy and the Enchanted Library (co-author)

www.ingramcontent.com/pod-product-compliance
Lightning Source LLC
Chambersburg PA
CBHW031331020726
47499CB00005B/1220